FORTUNATE HARBOR

EMILIE RICHARDS

THORNDIKE PRESS

A part of Gale, Cengage Learning

GALE
CENGAGE Learning·

Detroit • New York • San Francisco • New Haven, Conn • Waterville, Maine • London

GALE
CENGAGE Learning

LIBRARY OF CONGRESS CATALOGING-IN-PUBLICATION DATA

Richards, Emilie, 1948–
    Fortunate harbor / by Emilie Richards.
        p. cm. — (A Happiness Key novel)
    ISBN-13: 978-1-4104-3056-4 (hardcover)
    ISBN-10: 1-4104-3056-1 (hardcover)
    1. Friendship—Fiction. 2. Florida—Fiction. 3. Large type books. I. Title.
PS3568.I31526F67 2010
813'.54—dc22   2010025308

Published in 2010 by arrangement with Harlequin Books S.A.

Printed in the United States of America
1 2 3 4 5 6 7 14 13 12 11 10·

Thanks to John Fetner at www.kellycodetectors.com who patiently explained the mechanics of metal detectors. And thanks to the readers who contacted me to ask what happened to the women of Happiness Key.
This one's for you.

PROLOGUE

She wondered how everything had come to this. This wrenching decision, this wild, forsaken place, this final moment.

But the question was silly. Dana Turner knew, deep inside, what had brought her here — and what had brought *him*.

Every decision they had ever made.

Truth was always that simple, *and* that complicated. Every decision in a life filled with decisions had brought them back to Florida, back to this very place, where they had once laughed and romped together. The good decisions. The bad ones. The ones that God must be mulling over even now. Because knowing what to do was never as easy as the self-righteous believed, and from time to time, even God must scratch His head and wonder.

She, of course, wondered unceasingly. These days she often traced the path of her life, the twists and turns, as if a map was spread out in front of her. At the beginning she had not been aware that each step she took closed off one route, even as it opened another. She had believed she was walking her path with courage and resolve, even the most difficult detours. Doubt had only come with age, when the simplest decisions had suddenly ceased to make sense. When right and wrong seemed precariously balanced, but the scales could not be tipped. When everything she had done, despite all her doubts, had led her here, to the edge of the water where now she stood.

"You never worried the way I did," she said quietly. "Life wasn't simple *or* complicated for you, was it? Life just *was*. You knew what you wanted, and you always went after it. You didn't care who got in the way. You didn't care who you hurt. I doubt you even gave that much thought."

These were not the things one was supposed to say at the end of a life. She knew better. Now accusations were pointless. So were pleas. It was much too late for either. The road had ended, and there was no bridge in view here, only a wide stretch of bay glistening gold and orange in the rays of the sun setting somewhere behind her.

She watched in silence as the sky grew darker. Around her the night noises began. Alligators hid along this shore. She remembered that from other, better, days here. Poisonous snakes. Venomous insects. She was

8

cautious, and right to be so, but she was more afraid of the memories, the good ones, and the grief that would follow if she allowed them to come.

"Things could have been so different." Her eyes filled with tears. "Did you ever know that? Did you ever *feel* it?" She touched her chest with a clenched fist, and her voice faltered. "Is that why you wrote me that letter?"

There was no answer, nor had she expected one, of course. She was not a religious woman, but for a moment she imagined a reunion after death. Would he seek her out to remark on this evening and the things she had said? Would he ask for her forgiveness? Would he tell her that yes, he had loved her, despite all the things he had done and the pain he had caused?

Just feet from shore a long-necked bird sailed past, calling shrilly for a mate, or perhaps simply proving it was still alive after another day of evading predators and foraging for food. She felt a tug of connection.

At last Dana lifted the day pack off her shoulders. She unzipped the pouch and removed a plastic canister. Unscrewing the top, and without looking closely at the contents, she stepped forward and sprinkled the ashes it contained onto the narrow strip of wet sand leading to the bay. Not satisfied, she leaned forward and finished sprinkling those that remained directly in the water, where the others would follow later as the tide rose.

"Peace be with you . . ." She tried, but she couldn't speak his name out loud. No one was listening, yet even now, she could not bring herself to admit the connection between herself and the man whose remains were gradually dissolving into Little Palmetto Bay.

A prayer was needed; she wanted to say one for her own sake, but none occurred to her. The man, who now was nothing more than a memory, deserved better than the gentle lapping of waves, the flapping of wings, the whine of mosquitoes.

She did her best. "May the joy we once felt in this place accompany you wherever you've gone."

She straightened. It was as much of a prayer as she could manage. She wished Lizzie could have been here to say something, but Lizzie wouldn't have understood. Lizzie would have asked a million questions her mother could never answer. And Lizzie, who was just a little girl, might mention this night to somebody else, who would then ask even more.

Theirs was a life of secrets, and this was simply one too many to expect her daughter to keep.

"I wish you could have known Lizzie, that it had been safe to let you know her," Dana said softly. "I think she might have touched your heart."

The sky darkened quickly into the purple-black of twilight, and the lights of the town across the bay twinkled in response. Dana turned and saw that the path she had trampled, the web-draped branches she had snapped and twisted to get here, were growing dim. For a moment she imagined a better time, and perhaps those memories were a final gift to her. She felt the heaviness in her heart lift a little, and the air that filled her lungs seemed the lighter, sweeter air they had breathed together, all those years ago.

"I love you," she whispered. "No matter what you did, I hope you know that never changed."

When she finally realized that soon she might not be able to find her way back along dry ground, she left him to the bay he had loved and the little harbor where they had once believed the world was theirs to conquer.

CHAPTER ONE

So much time had passed since Tracy Deloche had gotten it on with a man that last night she'd actually made a list of things she needed to do, just so she wouldn't make an embarrassing mistake.

"Shave everything that needs it." Now she paused beside her dresser to check that one off. An hour ago she had taken a long scented bath and made sure that not one hair, one patch of stubble, remained where it shouldn't.

"Insert diaphragm." She wasn't fond of number two. She'd been on the pill most of her adult life, but at her last checkup, the doctor had asked a series of questions, then recommended she take a break for at least a year. The woman, who was even younger than Tracy's thirty-five, had fitted her for a diaphragm, explained how to use it, then given her the prescription to fill.

Sadly, Tracy hadn't needed it until now. She'd taken care of those preparations, too. So what if thinking about sex this far ahead of time lacked a certain spontaneity? She was sure Marsh knew what she had in mind for their rendezvous. He was the one who'd called to say that Bay, his nine-year-old son, was staying overnight with a friend, so he could come to her house as soon as he dropped Bay off.

Most likely her chicken Caesar salad, even if she *had* learned to make a wicked delicious dressing last week, was not the lure. In fact, she doubted they would actually get to the salad.

"Change sheets. Uh-huh. Buy new underwear." Too late for that, but she had a zebra-stripe push-up bra and thong that would serve, although these days, most likely due to frequent laundering, both were snugger than they should be.

"Sexier that way." The minute the words passed her lips, she realized the excuse sounded like something Wanda, her fifty-something neighbor, would say. The thought that Florida Cracker Wanda might be rubbing off on her was sobering.

She crumpled the list and tossed it in the wastebasket. She had cleaned her house, bought wine for herself and a six pack of Dos Equis for Marsh. She'd selected the most seductive music in her collection and loaded it to an iPod playlist titled Seduction. She had turned on just the right number of lamps to enhance the deepening twilight. A wheel

14

of Brie was baking in the oven, and hummus and chips sat on the kitchen table under plastic to protect them from the inevitable Florida bugs and humidity. Her skimpiest sundress clung to her hips and thighs, and bared a significant portion of her back, even though it was April and evenings could still be cool.

She was threading a sandal strap through a buckle when the telephone rang. Not her cell phone, the number Marsh and most of her friends used, but the landline in her kitchen. She considered abandoning the shoe, but she waited for her new answering machine to pick up first. When it did, a woman began to whine, then picked up steam and whined a little faster.

"Good ol' Mom." Tracy went back to the sandal and tried not to listen. Her mother's phone calls were rare, and one that didn't center on the past, most notably Tracy's failed marriage to one CJ Craimer, was as priceless as an invitation to a Brad Pitt wedding. Unfortunately, Tracy could tell from her mother's tone that nobody was going to pay good money for this.

"Mom, Mom," she said, shaking her head as her mother's volume increased. She tried to drown out the phone sermon with her own version. " 'How are you, Tracy? How's life in Florida? Are you still enjoying your job? This place you're living sounds charming, if primi-

15

tive. But I can tell you've found good friends and a purpose to your life.' "

She paused, her imagination having run its course, since she had never experienced that kind of real-life conversation with her mother.

In the kitchen, her mother's voice rose to hog-caller levels. "You know, this is all your fault," Denise Deloche screeched. "If you hadn't married CJ, everything he's done, everything he *is*, wouldn't matter to *any* of us!"

She must have been building to that, because the message ended. Tracy heard a dial tone, then the machine stopped recording.

After savoring the silence for a moment, Tracy filled it. "And how are you, Mom? Are you finding a smaller house easier to take care of, even if it's not in Bel-Air? Have you thought about starting a book club or buying a bike? Maybe saving to come and visit me?"

Even if her mother had been listening, Tracy had no qualms about asking the last question. Denise Deloche was as likely to come to Florida as she was to start a soup kitchen on her sidewalk.

Since CJ had metamorphosed from the duke of developers to the king of convicts — taking Tracy's parents' substantial investments with him — Tracy had borne the brunt of their fury. Her father, who billed himself as "orthodontist to the stars," claimed that because of her, he would be straightening teeth until he was eighty. His second wife insisted Tracy was no longer welcome in their home. Tracy's mother was the friendliest of the three. At least she still spoke to her daughter, although mostly to berate her. The fact that Tracy had been clueless about CJ's business dealings and lost almost everything herself, including her husband, mattered not at all.

She rose, sandals buckled in place, and smoothed her skirt over her thighs. Tonight nobody was going to bring her down. In the past year she had faced and accepted her own stupidity and unwitting culpability. She'd been young when she married CJ Craimer, blinded by the diamonds he tossed in her direction, trained to find character in the cut of a man's suit and the country clubs he frequented. Besides, if CJ hadn't chosen real estate investment to make his mark, he could have been a successful televangelist. Her ex was charismatic and persuasive. CJ could make a killing selling banana plantations in Antarctica, and probably had. Sometimes, when she looked back on the years of their marriage and all the things she knew about his profound abilities and limitless charm, the only thing that really surprised her was that he had gotten caught.

Caught, tried, convicted, incarcerated.

"Great!" Now, thanks to good old Mom, instead of thinking about Marsh Egan, the man she might be falling in love with, the man she might be falling into *bed* with in a few minutes, Tracy was thinking about her ex.

"Bloodsucking leech," she said. She waited a moment to see if the description sent CJ's image fleeing. "Washed-up thug."

She shrugged and marched into the living room to fluff the sofa pillows and turn on one more lamp. As she fluffed, she gave herself a pep talk. "Now I'm thinking about Marsh. Goodbye old, hello new."

She ran out of pillows and chitchat. In the kitchen, she opened the wine and checked on the Brie, which wasn't quite finished, so she added a few minutes to the timer. The wine hadn't been in the cheapest bin at Publix, but it was a far cry from anything CJ would have ordered from one of his favorite Napa Valley vineyards.

CJ!

She thumped the heel of her hand against her forehead, hoping to dislodge him. "Goodbye and good riddance, CJ. Hope the beans and weenies are yummy at Victorville. Maybe if you folded enough laundry today, they'll let you have seconds."

Why did she care if the wine had been on sale? Hadn't she learned anything in the year since her life in Bel-Air had been dismembered, buck by buck? Besides, she hoped the wine, like the salad, was going to be an afterthought later in the evening.

Much, much later.

She heard a vehicle slowing, and she leaned forward to see if it was Marsh's pickup. Darkness was falling, but she could see he had parked at the beginning of the short drive that led up to her cottage, effectively blocking her in. If she wanted to run, she was too late.

She sprinted to the bedroom mirror to make sure her hair was still okay. She'd left it down, where it slid straight and sleek past her shoulders, and she pushed one dark lock behind an ear, studying the effect. As she turned to view the side, she realized the pearl buttons that marched from waist to neckline were gaping just the tiniest bit. She shouldn't have washed the dress, despite what the label claimed. She shouldn't have tried to save a few bucks.

She heard rapping on her front door, and she adjusted the bodice and hoped it would stay. Then she crossed the living room and flung the door open.

Marsh's gaze traveled up and down before it came back up to rest on her face. "If I say you look like a million dollars in that dress, you aren't going to keep it on all night just to impress me, are you?"

She gave him the same smile she had practiced in front of a mirror at sixteen, the one that had snagged CJ years later.

CJ!

She tossed her head and tried to toss her mother's phone call with it. "What makes you think I'd consider taking it off?"

He leaned over and kissed her. Casually. No tongue, but warm and sweet anyway. "Well, you might say I'm forever hopeful. Those papers are all signed. Now we've got nothing between us except whatever that dress is made of, and a shirt and jeans I can be out of in ten seconds flat. And my son is safely playing video games for the night."

She hooked the opening of his polo shirt with her index finger and tugged him close for another kiss, far less casual. He smelled faintly like lime and something deliciously masculine. She didn't want to let him go.

"Ah, the papers," she said, when she'd finished but hadn't released him. "Effective libido dampeners, weren't they?"

He pulled her closer and trailed a chain of kisses to her earlobe. "You think so? My libido's been straining at the leash since pretty much the first time I saw you."

The papers were an agreement between Wild Florida, the environmental organization for which Marsh was director, and Tracy. She had agreed to put the land she owned here on Palmetto Grove Key into a conservation easement. She and Marsh had wrangled over terms for months, but in the end, she thought they were both happy with the result.

They had put the physical side of their relationship on hold for the duration. Now maybe they could find some happiness on that score, too.

Reluctantly she stepped back, and he held out a bottle. Tracy leaned over to check the label. "Wow, that's a really good Zinfandel. Too bad I just opened another bottle."

"Save this for another time, then."

"Let's not stand in the doorway all night. We have better places to be." She moved aside to let him in. She thought he looked yummy. The most casual man she knew, Marsh had still dressed up for her. The jeans were clean and appropriately faded, the dark green polo shirt looked new. He wore his sandy brown hair in its usual ponytail, but pulled back neatly. His perpetual Florida tan set off eyes the golden brown of his hair and a smile she could feel all over her body.

She smiled, too, and against all possible odds, her smile suddenly wobbled. She was nervous. *She,* Tracy Deloche, who, from the day she purchased her first training bra had been schooled in the fine art of leading men around by their noses. By the time she was sixteen, braces gone and ears flattened against her scalp, she'd graduated at the head of her class. Since then, she'd been fully confident she had a good shot at any heterosexual man in the universe.

And now Marsh Egan, Florida good ol'

boy, self-confessed Cracker, tree hugger and environmental gadfly, was making her nervous.

She tried to remember if she'd felt this way when she set out to get CJ in bed.

CJ!

Marsh crossed the room to put the wine on the counter between her kitchen and living room. "Do you know you have a message?" He reached up, and before she could stop him, pushed the play button on her answering machine.

Tracy made a flying leap, but it was too late. Her mother's high-pitched whine filled the little cottage again.

"Great, nothing like unleashing the demons of hell." Tracy heard her ex-husband's name four times before she managed to get to the phone. She hit Delete between another *C* and a *J*. She was sorry she hadn't thought to do it before Marsh showed up.

"I gather that was your mother?" Marsh lifted a brow.

"Let's not talk about my mother."

"She sounded upset."

"She's been upset for a while now. She's stuck in upset."

"About your ex, I take it?"

"CJ would be the cause. But let's not —"

"Isn't he in jail? What's he done now?"

"CJ doesn't have to *do* anything. If they'd hung him instead —"

"They don't hang people in California." Marsh sounded like the lawyer he was. "New Hampshire and Washington, maybe. I can check and get back to you."

"CJ probably had business dealings there, but hanging wouldn't do any good. My mother's life changed, and, in her view, not for the better. Even if he was six feet under, she'd still be living in a two-bedroom bungalow on the west side of LA. She can't get to CJ to rant and rave, but she has *my* number."

"She's not the only one who's upset. . . ." He laid a hand against her cheek and lifted her chin with his thumb. "You get a lot of these calls?"

"I've learned to ignore them."

"Maybe not as much as you think."

"I have some chips and hummus." She pulled away. "And a nice cold six-pack."

He took the cue. The haze of desire was fading. They needed space and some time away from talk of Tracy's ex to let it build again.

He poured a beer — she figured this must be a special night, since he wasn't drinking straight from the bottle — and she unwrapped the hummus and checked the timer for the Brie. She added three plump strawberries to each small plate and handed him one. Then she poured herself a glass of wine.

"Is it too hot to sit outside?" she asked as he dished up.

"It's okay out there, but it *was* heating up even nicer inside."

"I vote we cuddle on my sofa and see what happens."

She turned on the music as she passed the counter. Vanessa Williams began to sing "Save the Best for Last."

She settled beside him, and he put his arm around her shoulders. She took a sip of wine, then another.

"So, okay," he said, "is the wine helping? Chug it down, and I'll pour you another glass."

She rested her head against his arm and turned so she could see him. "I was trying really hard not to let my mother hook me. But it's kind of tough when I get the instant replay."

"I was just making sure that message wasn't some hunky piece of beach trash you picked up on the shuffleboard court at the rec center."

She jabbed him with her fist, but she was smiling. "Would you be jealous?"

He leaned over and nuzzled her nose. "In . . . sanely."

Maybe it was the wine or Vanessa's crooning. More likely it was simply Marsh. She felt the desire seeping back, liquid honey sliding through her veins. "Do you know that next to love, jealousy is the emotion a woman most wants to inspire in a man?"

"More than lust?"

"On an equal par."

"I've got lust down already."

"Oh, I can tell."

He brushed her hair back from her face. "You've grown on me, Tracy Deloche."

"Like a barnacle?"

"Maybe at first. Something different now." He leaned closer. "Definitely better."

Just as their kiss deepened the timer went off.

"Ignore it," he whispered against her lips.

She pulled away. "We'll have Brie running out the oven door and all over the floor. Then I'd have to get Wanda's dog to come over and clean it up, and Wanda would show up, too."

"Hurry back."

She planned to, and she thought maybe she would unbutton her dress when she did. Then she would stand in front of the sofa and hold out her hand for him. When he got to his feet, she would slip out of the dress and let it bloom like an exotic orchid on the floor. How they got to the bedroom — or *if* they did — would be up to him.

In the kitchen she turned off the oven and cracked the door. The Brie looked perfect.

She didn't care.

She was just stepping out of the kitchen, hand on her top button, when she saw somebody walking down the road in front of her cottage. During the day she often saw fishermen passing in pickups on their way to the point, where they could launch boats or find a spot on shore to settle in for the day. People on foot were rare, and by this time of evening, the only people who passed were neighbors from the four other cottages in her "development." Happiness Key, as it was called, had few attractions after dark.

This man was no neighbor.

"What are you looking at?" Marsh turned and gazed out the window behind the sofa.

Tracy's heart sped up. She couldn't answer. Her tongue felt as if it were glued to the roof of her mouth. She crossed the room slowly and peered through the glass. This was not possible. She had *not* seen the man she thought she'd seen. She pressed her nose against the window and stared into the deepening purple twilight.

"If there was anything out there, it's gone and forgotten," Marsh said.

The figure, if there had been one, had vanished into the deepest shadows. Tracy listened intently for the sound of a car starting somewhere out of sight. Unfortunately, on the counter behind her, Guns N' Roses were introducing "November Rain" with thunderclaps that drowned out anything else.

Surely she was wrong. Surely she was imagining things.

Surely she hadn't seen *CJ* strolling down the road as if he owned it. Which indeed he had, once upon a time.

"Tracy?"

She whirled. "Wow, sorry. I guess I was wrong. I don't see anything, either."

Marsh cocked his head. "I don't want to put too fine a point on this, but you look like you're going to jump out of your skin."

"Oh, I'm not. It's just . . ." Right. Was she really about to tell her soon-to-be lover that she'd just seen her ex-husband walking down the road, even though they both knew perfectly well that CJ was doing time, lots and lots of time, in a medium-security prison on the other coast?

She wondered how many seconds it would take Marsh to clear out forever.

"Well, you can't be too careful," she finished lamely. "Ken's always telling us to keep our eyes open at night. We're so far from, you know, everything out here." She turned up her hands. Not for the first time, she was glad Wanda was married to a cop, although she couldn't recall using Ken in a lie before.

"That music supposed to be romantic?"

"Not so much, huh?" Tracy was thrilled to have an excuse to move away from the window. At the counter, she skipped to the next selection on her playlist, something country, performed by a cute guy in a cowboy hat. She was too addled to remember what or whom, but she knew Marsh would like this song better. "I'll get the Brie."

"Right. Exactly what I was thinking. Let's eat some fancy-ass cheese. The night is young."

She took the Brie out of the oven and set it on the platter she'd prepared. "Didn't anybody tell you patience is a requirement for successful foreplay?" she called.

She was surprised when Marsh spoke from behind her, as he rested his hands on her shoulders.

"Don't you think I've already been the grand master of patience? If patience is what you need, I guess I'm your man."

"Well, you know, I'm not exactly used to it," she babbled. "I never thought I could ask for anything like that when I was married to C—" She stopped, horrified.

His fingers began a slow massage. "That name just keeps coming up and coming up tonight."

"Well, you were the one who played back the message."

He turned her to face him. "Is that what's going on here? It is, isn't it? Your mother's phone call got to you. She dragged up all that garbage from the past."

"I don't know what she did. I didn't listen to the message. I was thinking about you."

"Past tense. I heard that."

"No! Present. Really. But I'm jumpy tonight. I don't know why," she lied.

"Maybe because you decided this isn't such

28

a good idea after all."

"That's not it! I promise. Let's just relax and talk a little. I'll calm down."

Outside, just beyond her house, a car door slammed. Tracy jumped. In fact, she thought if Marsh hadn't been holding her shoulders, he would be peeling her off the ceiling right now.

"You know, I think this is going to take more than a wheel of Brie and a bottle of wine." He smiled a little. "It's going to take some rethinking. Like you alone in the house reconsidering whether you want to go to bed with me here. Or anywhere, anytime. Maybe I was pushing too fast."

"No, no, Marsh, that's really not it. I guess my mother's call did have some kind of weird effect. I'm sorry, but I'll get over —"

"I think you will," he agreed. "And faster if I'm not here. So we're going to do this another time. Some night when you've had the phone unplugged all day. Some night when your ex-husband's out of your head and back behind bars where he belongs, and you're all mine."

Short of tackling him and dragging him into the bedroom, she didn't know what to do. There was an instant's hesitation, as if Marsh was hoping she would find some way to convince him he was wrong. And in that moment, she heard a car start.

Her eyes widened, and she drew a sharp

breath. It was all Marsh needed.

"You call me," he said. "Bay's friend will invite him over again. You come to my house next time. Not so many distractions."

She didn't know what to say. She was a mess. All she could do was nod.

"Didn't anybody ever teach you how to say no?" he asked. "Because, you know, all you ever have to do when you're with me is say it, and I'll be listening."

"I wasn't thinking about no. I was thinking about yes. *I* invited *you*."

"So you did." He leaned over and kissed her lightly on the lips. "You lock up, in case somebody really was out there, but I don't think you have to worry. I didn't even see a palm frond rustling."

He cleared out so fast, in a minute there was no sign he'd been there except for an excellent bottle of wine sitting on her counter and the tail end of a country love song.

Tracy turned off the iPod and listened intently. And when she heard Marsh's pickup pull away, she headed straight for the door.

CJ Craimer had once held considerable real estate in her heart, but she had foreclosed more than a year ago. If she had to scour the island one grain of sand at a time to serve the final eviction notice, she would. But afterwards, she never wanted to think about CJ Craimer again.

CHAPTER TWO

"You have not yet produced a child for your husband."

Janya Kapur lowered herself to the chair beside her telephone. Then she pulled the receiver away from her ear and gazed at it in amazement for a moment before she slipped it back in place.

"*Aai,*" she said softly to her mother. "It is good to hear your voice."

"You have heard it many times before, and you know very well what it sounds like."

Janya controlled a sigh. Her mother was calling from India, where Janya herself had lived until last year, when she'd moved to Florida and the little group of beach cottages called Happiness Key.

Following a serious disagreement, she and her mother had not spoken in . . . Janya counted the months on her fingers . . . seven months. Janya had left the door open for her mother to call when she was ready, but she had never really expected this day to come.

Inika Desai was opinionated from her toe rings to the silk *dupatta* that covered her head. In her eyes, her only daughter had disgraced her with a failed betrothal, even though the fault had not been Janya's. Janya's subsequent hastily arranged marriage to Rishi Kapur, a brilliant Indian-American software designer, had not lessened her mother's humiliation.

"It is good to hear your voice anyway," Janya said, "although your choice of subject surprises me. Rishi and I have only been married a little more than a year."

"This is plenty of time to have a baby. Your father and I are not young. We expect to see grandchildren before we die."

"And Yash is not cooperating?" Yash was Janya's younger brother, who had resisted all attempts to be matched to a woman of his parents' choosing.

"Your brother is, if such a thing can be possible, more stubborn, more difficult, than you. I know he telephones. Do not deny it. And I suppose he has told you he will soon come to your country to study history. I am aware you planted this idea in his head."

At great cost, Janya had learned to stand up to her mother, but it was a lesson she had taken to heart. "No, I didn't plant it, but I helped it grow. He has a right to be happy. We all do — including you, *Aai*. And he would not be happy as an accountant, even though he wanted very much to please you and *Baba*."

"For people of our generation, making our parents happy was enough."

"I think, perhaps, you raised us differently. We would like you to be happy, but we know that sometimes we cannot make that wish come true."

Her mother was silent. For a moment Janya wondered if the line had gone dead — not that uncommon — or her mother had ended the call. As she waited, she gazed out the window and saw a slender shape disappearing down the road in the deepening twilight.

Finally her mother spoke.

"I am sending something."

From experience, Janya knew her mother liked to put bad news in writing, so she would not have to face the repercussions. Her mother's tolerance for the emotions of others was limited. "If it is a letter, I hope the news is good."

"It is not a letter. It is a gift."

"Then I will look forward to it."

There was another silence. Janya waited.

"You are well?" her mother asked at last. "Your husband is well?"

"We are."

Before Janya could ask about her family in India, her mother added, "And happy? You speak of happiness for your brother. What of your own?"

For a moment Janya was not certain she had heard her correctly. This was not only a question her mother never asked, it was one she never considered.

She searched for the right words. "I am happy. Rishi is a good husband. Kind, funny, thoughtful. I am painting again, murals on the sides of buildings and in homes. People like my work, and Rishi is proud."

"I have seen the newspaper article about you. Your brother made certain I could not avoid it."

Janya waited to be chastised. The local newspaper had done a flattering piece on the mural she had painted at the main branch of the Palmetto Grove library. Allowing public attention to be drawn to herself, instead of her husband, was something her mother would not understand.

"If Rishi is proud, this is good," her mother said. "If he is proud of you, then you are indeed lucky to be married to him."

"I think I *am* lucky," Janya agreed.

"You will remember that, then, when you receive my gift."

"Of course, I wi—"

But the phone was dead. Her mother had stretched as far as she could across the miles to bridge the gap between them. Clearly she had reached her limit.

Janya put the telephone back in the cradle and smiled. She wondered what Rishi would

34

say that night when she told him about the phone call. Because he would be interested. He was always interested. He was her defender, her admirer, and the man who would father her children.

If she could just get pregnant.

The smile died. She thought about the things she had not shared with her mother, and some of the joy in their odd telephone reunion died.

Wanda Gray had blisters over calluses that were most likely the result of earlier blisters. She sat in the living room of her little cottage and wiggled her toes in a pan of warm water, just to be sure she could still move them.

A person could never be too casual about blisters, what with blood poisoning and all. People lost their feet on account of a lack of cleanliness and inattention to pain. She wasn't going to be one of them. She'd been standing on these feet more years than she wanted to count, slapping platters of hush puppies and shrimp on tables. She figured if she lined up all the tables she'd slapped something onto in her fifty-six years, they'd stretch to the moon and back.

"You look comfortable." Her husband, Ken, passed on his way to the kitchen. "Need anything while I'm in there?"

"You're going to eat that last piece of my strawberry pie, aren't you?"

"Thinking about it."

"We could split it."

Ken didn't say anything, but in a few minutes he came back and handed her a saucer with precisely half of that final slice of pie. She wasn't sure which looked better, her husband, with his salt-and-pepper hair and trim build, or the pie, mounded with fresh whipped cream.

"You should have been a surgeon instead of a cop. I bet if we weighed these plates, they'd be exactly the same."

"We had two children. I know how to split things right down the middle."

"This is nice, being waited on and all. I get tired of being the one bringing people pie, not that anything at the Dancing Shrimp is this good."

He sat across from her, the bright floral cushion of the rattan chair rippling under a backside that was still taut and shapely. She figured she was going to love Ken anyway when everything started to sag, but for now, she wasn't sorry deterioration hadn't gotten a head start.

"Those feet of yours have seen some hard times," he said.

"It's those pointy-toed shoes. Can't figure out why the new owners are so determined to make everything twice as hard on us. Tight dresses, tight shoes, all so we can plop French fries and shrimp on wooden picnic tables out

36

on the deck. Who do they think comes to the Dancing Shrimp, anyway? Today I had to lug high chairs to almost every single table. You think those little kids care if my shoes have *any* kind of toes?"

"They giving you any other trouble?"

"Oh, they don't understand a thing. They keep fancying up the menu. Everything's either *en brochette* or *étouffée* or *en croute.* People ask me what that means, and half the time I just have to make it up. And if they order something new, when it comes out of the kitchen, it's just plain old shish kebabs or fish stew or some kind of silly-looking sandwich."

"You know you don't need to work anymore. We made good money when we sold the house in Miami, and we're not spending much renting this one. You could quit. Stay home and rest those feet."

She was touched. She and Ken had experienced their share of problems. For a while it had looked as if they weren't going to survive them *together,* but somehow they had. And Ken, who had retreated into himself for so long she'd been afraid he would never find his way out again, was beginning to sound like the man she had married.

"I do appreciate that," she said. "I really do, Kenny. But you want the truth? I don't know what I'd do with all that time. Working kind of puts my day in order, you know? And

37

even if we don't need the money that bad, it's nice to make some and know I'm contributing. You work awful hard yourself."

"About work . . ." He took a bite of his pie. Fresh strawberry was one of her real masterpieces — she added toasted pecans to a shortbread crust — and she watched the pleasure spread over his face.

"Damn, this is good." He looked up and grinned. "You'd be worth keeping just for your pies, Wanda."

"Course, you got lots of other reasons, don't you?"

"That's like asking a man to count all the stars in the sky."

She smiled despite herself. "I'm not going to snatch the plate away from you, you say the wrong thing. You don't have to go on and on."

"Found out today they're sending me up to Georgia to do some training with Homeland Security. I'm going to be gone a lot in the next couple of months, on and off. You'll be okay out here by yourself?"

Truth was that at one time, she wouldn't have been. She would have been fearsome, lonely and probably gotten herself into some kind of trouble. But not anymore. The women who lived in the other cottages were as different from her as they could possibly be, but somehow, they'd all learned to get along.

"I'll be fine," she told him. "I get too lonely,

I'll go visit Junior and the grandkids."

"I'll come back between sessions. I won't be gone too many days at a time. But the training's good, and it looks like they want to promote me after it's done. So I had to say yes."

"You want to be promoted? You still okay with not being on the streets?"

"I like having a say in things. And let's face it, I'm getting up there. Can't be running through alleys and crashing through buildings too much longer. I don't like paperwork, but I do like seeing things come together."

"Whatever you do, Palmetto Grove's lucky to have you."

"I guess they think so, too." He finished his pie, got up to take her plate and kissed her on top of her lacquered copper curls. "Gotta go in for a while tonight. Just to finish off some stuff, but I'll be back in time to watch a movie. I can stop and pick up a DVD."

"I want to see that Chihuahua movie, you know, the talking kind of Chihuahuas. Chase does, too."

Chase, their rescued greyhound, came wandering in at the sound of his name. He proceeded to Wanda's feet and lapped water out of the pan. She shooed him away, but not vigorously. She'd been a lot harder on their kids.

"I'll see what I can find," Ken promised.

She knew he preferred to come home with

a movie of the *Lethal Weapon* variety, but she was hoping he'd compromise on something in between. That had been her aim, and she'd given it her best shot.

After he left, she dried and bandaged her feet and slipped into flip-flops. She and Dr. Scholl's would have some date tomorrow. She might just go into work in sandals and let the chips fall where they may. Right now, though, she was more interested in going somewhere else.

Outside.

Through the window, in the beams of Ken's headlights, she'd seen her landlady, Tracy Deloche, prowling around on the road beyond the house. She didn't know what Tracy was doing. The houses in Happiness Key were set fairly far apart, on account of the ones in between having been bulldozed some time in the past. Tracy had no good reason to be over here poking around.

Wanda's instincts for gossip were finely tuned.

She decided the soak and the soft rubber flip-flop soles were helping. She could make it outside, if Tracy didn't disappear before she got there.

"You just hold on now, Ms. Deloche," she said. "You just hold on, and don't you go running off." She hoped the real entertainment of the evening was right outside and waiting for her to join in.

Okay, she was imagining things. Tracy had walked up and down the road twice after Marsh's departure. No car had passed — although possibly she hadn't gotten outside in time — and there were no signs anybody had been recently parked along the road beyond her house, no tire tracks, no crushed vegetation.

Of course, she lived on sand, and they hadn't had rain in the past few days. And, admittedly, she was not a detective by trade. Stalking up and down the road looking for CJ, who was probably in California trying to dig his way out of Victorville with a plastic spoon, was the act of a madwoman.

So what was up with that?

"Hey, you!"

Tracy jumped and slapped a hand over her chest. A word she rarely uttered slipped out at high volume.

"Well, cover my ears. I'm just *so* happy to see you, too," Wanda said.

"I'm sorry! You scared me to death."

"A little jumpy, are we? What do you think you're doing strutting back and forth in the dark? You lose something? See something that frightened you? Ken's gone, but I can get him back." Wanda whipped out her cell phone.

Tracy tried to imagine how she would

explain this particular vision to Ken Gray, one of the most logical men she'd ever met. "No. No! I just thought I saw somebody prowling around, that's all."

"I see. And so, unarmed and unprotected, in stiletto heels, you came outside and started prowling around on your own?"

"Okay, it makes no sense. I get that."

"Want me to help you look?"

"No, whoever it was, they've gone."

Another voice came out of the darkness as Janya joined them. "If there is a party, somebody forgot to invite me."

Sometimes Tracy forgot that nothing was private in Happiness Key. She rolled her eyes as Wanda explained.

"Tracy's just losing her mind, that's all. Looking for somebody who was never here, and doing it alone in the dark, just in case she was right and he wants to snatch her and throw her in the trunk of his car."

"There *was* somebody," Janya said. "I saw them, too."

Tracy was filled with relief. "You did?"

"Yes, just a little while ago." Janya paused. "I was on the telephone. With my mother."

"Your mother?" the other women asked in unison. For a moment that bit of news eclipsed the prowling stranger.

"She telephoned me. To tell me she is sending a gift. And she asked if I was happy."

Tracy wanted clarification. "As in, 'Well,

are you happy now, you miserable loser?' or 'Janya dear, are you happy, because, you know, I want you to be, more than anything.' "

"I think it was somewhere between those extremes. But as our conversations have gone, this one was pleasant."

"Well, there's something to celebrate," Wanda said.

"My mother called this evening, too," Tracy said. "She ranted and raved about CJ. I heard bits and pieces of her particular thunderstorm from the other room."

"I'm sorry." Janya put her hand on Tracy's arm. "She is still chained to the past?"

"Yeah, knowing Mom, she swallowed the key. I don't think she's going to recover any time soon. But I'm glad your mother saw the light."

"I would not go that far, but perhaps it's a start."

"So who was out here?" Wanda said. "Who'd you see, Janya?"

"I don't know. Someone. Thin, tall. Somebody walking quickly. I cannot even say whether it was a man or a woman. I only caught a glimpse."

"Match your description?" Wanda asked Tracy.

Tracy tried to think. She'd immediately thought of CJ, although why, she couldn't say, now that her memory of the stranger was fading. But CJ was tall, and most likely thinner than he had been during the years of their marriage. She doubted the wardens at Victorville were serving osso bucco or roasted quail.

"I don't know." She considered whether to tell her friends who she thought she'd seen, but rejected the idea. "I thought it was a man," she added. "But maybe not. It was almost dark, and I just got a glimpse."

"The person I saw had a backpack, I think," Janya said. "I noticed a little bulge."

"I didn't see that."

Wanda twisted the strap on Tracy's dress. "You know, Ms. Deloche, you are surely dressed to kill. Were you hoping this mysterious stranger might ask you on a date?"

"I *had* a date. *My* date left."

"Marsh?" Janya asked.

Wanda twisted harder. "He left when you were wearing this dress? It's one step from a slip. All he had to do was reach out and tug, and you'd have been stark naked."

Tracy brushed away Wanda's hand. "The whole evening went south. I don't know what happened, exactly. He punched the button on my answering machine and heard my mother ranting about CJ. After that, CJ just kept coming up, and I was distracted, and Marsh . . ." Tracy paused, then let out a long breath. "Gone home now."

"Well, that's pitiful."

44

"I thought so, too. Let's not dwell on it, okay?"

Apparently Wanda wasn't feeling merciful. "Then I won't say another word. Although a person does have to wonder if you just got spooked."

"Spooked?"

"About going to bed with Marsh. I mean, the two of you have diddled around so long, making eyes at each other, getting close, dancing back. You ever see an egret mating dance? That's what it looks like."

"Please!"

Wanda turned up her hands. "I think now that you're finally getting down to it, it's been so long, you both forgot how it goes."

"Wanda!" Janya took the older woman's arm. "Why not tell Tracy what you told me earlier today? About the server who works with you?"

Janya, who was only in her early twenties, had the ability to pour soothing words into any conversation. In fact, there was little the Indian woman didn't have in abundance. Gorgeous black hair, perfect features, a trim, well-rounded body, and intelligence. Tracy liked her too well to be jealous, although the feeling *had* erupted from time to time. Tracy had to work to be beautiful. Janya just *was*.

Wanda took Janya's hint, which was not always the case. "You remember me telling you about all the changes at the Dancing

45

Shrimp?"

Tracy did. All the women of Happiness Key thought it was a shame. The family that had started the town's most popular beach hangout forty years ago had sold it to a young couple from Manhattan who wanted to put their particular stamp on it. Gone were the jitterbugging shrimp T-shirts, automatic refills on hush puppies, most of the funky Florida decor. Gone, too, were a lot of the staff. And Wanda was being asked to take extra shifts to cover for them.

"I miss the old place," Tracy said.

"Don't we all? A bunch of regulars aren't coming anymore. Anyway, the owners hired a new server, a woman named Dana Turner. She's new around town, and she and her little girl are staying in that seedy old motel near the industrial park. You know, the Driftwood Something or Other? She's looking for someplace to rent. She asked if I knew of anything out here. She likes the water, but she can't afford anything fancy. I thought maybe you'd like to show her Herb's cottage."

"Herb's cottage" was the fifth house in the development CJ had named Happiness Key.

CJ!

Tracy plowed on. "She's willing to live all the way out here? With a child?"

"She seemed interested. I told her it's no great shakes."

The original plan for Happiness Key had

included a cutting-edge marina and, of course, razing all the existing tumbledown rental cottages to make way for deluxe condos. After her divorce and CJ's incarceration, Tracy had moved to Florida to manage the cottages — the only thing she'd taken away from the marriage — while she tried to interest another developer in the property. One renter, a man named Herb Krause, had died soon afterward. Since that time Tracy had rented his house twice, but only short term. Now it was empty again.

"I could use the money," she admitted. "But last time I spent almost as much as I made just to fix the damage the renters did. I have to get somebody who will take care of the place."

"I don't know how long she's planning to be here. She told me she's looking to settle down, though. She thinks this climate is healthy for her kid. Lizzie's her name. Cute girl, looks to be Olivia's age. Sometimes she does her homework outside or in the coatroom while her mother's working, though the owners aren't too wild about it."

Eleven-year-old Olivia lived in the fourth house in Happiness Key with her grandmother Alice. In her own way, each of the women looked out for her. Sometimes Tracy thought Happiness Key was the proverbial village that was raising a child.

"It would be nice for Olivia to have a friend

right here," Janya said. "We are good for her, as far as we can go, but a girl needs someone to confide in who will understand."

Tracy was still wondering who had been walking down the road and why. A man? A woman? A ghost? When she realized the others had fallen silent, she tossed out the first answer that occurred to her. "I'd like to meet her."

"It is my turn to have all of you for dinner Sunday night," Janya said. "Wanda, would your friend like to come and bring her daughter to meet us and see the house? I will make extra."

Tracy pulled herself back to the conversation. Normally the women got together on Thursdays, but this week they'd postponed. "That's a great idea. You're sure you feel like it?"

"I will be happy to help. Maybe she will be a new friend."

Wanda peered over her shoulder at her house, where Chase was barking for attention. "I'll make pies, if you'd like. It's the least I can do, since I suggested her."

"Any day with one of Wanda's wonderful pies is a happy day," Janya said.

Tracy thought of Marsh's bottle of wine, but that was earmarked for another, better, night with him. "Settled, then. I'll bring a nice wheel of Brie."

They said their goodbyes. Wanda bustled

off to quiet her dog. She was a raw-boned woman fast approaching her senior years. Tracy had never been able to guess what color Wanda's hair really was, but the coppery red suited her somehow, as did the fashion faux pas blue eye shadow she loved so well. Wanda was Wanda. One of a kind.

Janya stopped Tracy before she could start home. "If you will be uncomfortable alone tonight, because of this stranger, you would be welcome to sleep at our house."

"I wasn't really worried about anyone breaking in or anything." Tracy hesitated. "I just thought . . . I mean, I thought he looked like . . ." She shook her head. "It's crazy."

"Like someone you know?"

"Someone I used to, but it doesn't matter. It couldn't have been him. You're not even sure you saw a man."

"It is possible we saw different people."

"And why would *anybody* be out here? Maybe driving out to the point, but not walking around."

"Perhaps a flat tire? Somebody saw something on the roadside and stopped to check? There are many good reasons."

Tracy knew Janya was right. And if she hadn't thought the stranger looked like her ex-husband, she wouldn't have given his presence much thought. Not with Marsh waiting with open arms.

"You sleep well," Tracy said. "And if I have

49

any problems, I'll call."

She walked slowly home, making certain to peer behind every tree and bush along the oyster shell road. But whoever she had seen was gone.

As she unlocked the front door, she wondered if Wanda had actually hit this particular nail right on the head. Tracy had made elaborate preparations to be with Marsh tonight. She'd cooked and primped and cleaned. She'd been uncommonly concerned about every detail.

She was certainly no virgin. Before CJ there had been other men. She was a woman of her generation, but a picky one. She had shown considerable discretion, but she *had* used her head and occasionally her body to get her heart's desires, a man who could take care of her, a man who could give her whatever she wanted.

Now, she was a different woman entirely. She wanted to sleep with Marsh just because she wanted to. And maybe that's what all the anxiety was about. She wanted Marsh just because he was Marsh. It could be that made all the difference.

Inside she sat to unbuckle her sandals. The telephone rang, and again she ignored it. But she stopped fiddling with the strap and listened as the message began, hoping it was Marsh, with something reassuring to say about the evening.

Instead a woman's voice began to record after Tracy's message.

"Tracy? It's Sherrie. I imagine you're frantic, but I had to call. CJ's all over the news here. I'm not sure the media's going to bother to find you for your opinion, but just in case —"

Tracy flung an unbuckled sandal across the room and limped at a rapid pace to the telephone. Sherrie, her old college roommate, was one of the few people who had stuck by her after the divorce. But she'd never had news like this to share. Tracy grabbed the receiver.

"Sherrie?"

"You *are* home. Well, no surprise you're not answering your telephone."

"What do you mean about CJ?"

"You mean you don't know? Nobody called to tell you?"

"What are you talking about?"

"CJ was released from prison, but it didn't hit the news until this afternoon. It's a big deal in California —"

"No, it's not possible. He was in Victorville for life. For a couple of lives!"

"I guess not. His attorneys got him out, at least until they can have a new trial. I don't understand it all, but they're talking about prosecutorial misconduct. Altered records and testimony. The Feds wanted him so badly it looks like maybe they messed with the

51

evidence. At least that's what the papers are saying. Everyone says they'll try him again, but in the meantime, he's out as of yesterday. I don't know how they kept it quiet as long as they did."

Now Tracy understood her mother's telephone call. If only she had listened. If only she hadn't just assumed the call was another baseless rant.

CJ!

"Listen to me, Sherrie. Do you know where he went? Where he is now?"

"No idea. He's not giving interviews. I'd guess he's holed up with his attorneys, figuring out what he should do next. Didn't he say all along he was innocent, that he just trusted the wrong people? They're probably preparing his defense for the next go-round. He hasn't contacted you, has he?"

Tracy stared out the window.

"Tracy?"

"If he did, what do you suppose he would want from me?" she asked.

"*Has* he?"

"No. No. At least, I don't think so."

"You know, you don't sound so good. Do you need me? I could fly down next week. Hold your hand, or fend off CJ, if he shows up."

The road outside Tracy's house was as empty now as her bed. She had *not* seen her ex-husband. Even if CJ was out of jail, he had to be in California. He probably wasn't even allowed to leave the state.

"I'll let you know if I need you," she told Sherrie, "but CJ must realize I don't want anything to do with him. He's an old hand at ex-wives. I was just the last bimbo who made him look good. If he wants companionship, he'll find somebody younger and thinner."

She wasn't sure where that last adjective had come from. She really *was* a mess.

"If you're wrong, stay away from him, okay? I mean, prosecutorial misconduct is not the same as not guilty. It doesn't mean CJ is innocent."

They talked for another minute, then Tracy hung up.

She couldn't help herself. Still wearing one high heel, she turned off the lights, then limped to the window.

She stood absolutely still for half an hour, gazing into the darkness, but only tree limbs moved in the lazy Florida breeze.

CHAPTER THREE

Rishi rarely slept past dawn, but this morning Janya had already been up for an hour when she finally heard the shower. She suspected her husband's long hours at work had finally caught up with him. By the time he arrived at the table, an omelet, coffee and fresh fruit were ready in the kitchen.

"I did not mean to sleep so late." Rishi took his seat and rested his head in his hands, as if he wasn't yet ready to hold it erect.

She thought many men would phrase the sentiment differently. "You should not have let me sleep so late," they would say, and she, as a woman, would be expected to accept this as just. But Rishi was not such a man. He took responsibility for his own actions. Raised by a resentful aunt and uncle after the death of his parents, no one had cared enough to be responsible for him. Everything Rishi had become was due to his own hard work.

She poured cream into his coffee and brought it to him. "I am glad you slept. You are tired. It's no wonder you stayed in bed a bit on your day off."

"You are good to me."

He was easy to be good to, but she didn't say so. Theirs was not that kind of marriage.

"I made your favorite." She returned with the omelet, prepared the way they were made in Mumbai, where she had grown up. The eggs had been whipped with finely chopped red onion, tomatoes, chilies and herbs, cooked on one side, then flipped. The fruit was fanned out at the bottom of the plate like a happy smile.

"Ah, Janya, I have no idea what I did to deserve you."

"You arrived in India at precisely the right moment." She smiled to let him see that even if this was true, the truth was now a joke. She was sure Rishi knew he was more to her than simply the man who had rescued her from a bad situation in her home country.

"Lord Vishnu must have guided my footsteps."

"I am glad he was not too busy to guide them to me." Janya returned with her own plate and settled herself across from him.

"I am particularly sorry I overslept," he said. "I had hoped to spend some of the morning with you, but now I must get ready and go to work."

"Again?" Janya was surprised, and surprise was quickly followed by worry. Rishi was a wiry, athletic man in excellent health. But lately he had been distant, a fact she blamed on exhaustion. He was working later and later each evening, and this was not the first Saturday that he had gone into the office. In fact, working through the weekend was becoming normal. She missed her husband and the intimacy they had slowly begun to develop, the give-and-take of a marriage built on more than convenience and tradition.

When she didn't speak, he cocked his head. "And now you are angry with me?"

"How can I be angry? My mother telephoned last night." Janya shook off her concerns and proceeded to tell Rishi what had transpired.

He finished the last bite of his fruit before he spoke. "And you have no idea what she is sending?"

"Perhaps a photograph album of all the grandchildren of her friends. To shame me."

Rishi looked uncomfortable. "You told her that we have decided to have children?"

"There was no time and no inclination. We do not need my mother keeping track of our progress."

"That we do not."

Janya lifted one shoulder. "Besides there was nothing to tell her. No good news, anyway."

He looked uncomfortable, as men often seemed to when anything personal was dis-

56

cussed. He glanced past her to the clock in the kitchen, then he stood. "Do you have plans for the day?"

She wanted to say her plans had included him, and now they would have to be remade. Instead she shook her head.

"Will you be home for supper?"

"I will try." He picked up his plate and took it into the kitchen.

Janya wished she could remind her husband that leaving her alone for so many hours was not the best way to start their family. But that, like so many things, was too direct, too emotional. They might be living far away from the country of their births, but they were still products of its culture, a culture they respected. She told herself she would see Rishi through this difficult time at work. And everything else would take care of itself.

Saturday's lunch shift at the Dancing Shrimp was always jammed and tips were good, but despite that, it was Dana's least favorite shift. During the week, when Lizzie was in school, Dana didn't have to worry about child care. Tips weren't as good, but at least Lizzie could walk to the restaurant after school. Usually by then Dana was ready to take her back to the Driftwood Inn, the run-down motel that nowadays passed for home.

Unfortunately, on Saturdays Lizzie had nowhere to go. She was the only child who lived in the two-story building, so there was no hope of a friend's mother watching her. Dana thought of the Driftwood as the *Drifter* Inn, since the residents — mostly male — seemed to drift here and there while they tried to find a reason or place to set down roots. Before she and Lizzie had moved in, she'd insisted that the manager install a sturdier chain lock and tighten the dead bolt, but still, she would never leave her daughter in the room alone. Dana even took her along when she paid the rent.

"So, you doing okay?" Dana asked Lizzie, after an afternoon of delivering the luncheon special, a blue crab salad with shredded jicama, raw sweet potato and cold rice noodles. If she had ten dollars for every time she'd had to explain what jicama was, or why the sweet potato wasn't cooked, she and Lizzie could leave right now. A hundred for each time she'd removed a salad that was only half eaten and they wouldn't need to be in Palmetto Grove at all.

They could spread their wings and fly far, far away.

"I'm tired of sitting out here." Lizzie wasn't a whiner, but this time Dana couldn't blame her. The afternoon was beautiful, and Lizzie was spending it in a beat-up beach chair just outside the service entrance. Dana had brought all kinds of things for her daughter to do, but it was no surprise that even adaptable Lizzie was more than ready to leave. The little courtyard where the staff took breaks — courtyard being the kindest possible term — was clean and safe, but the smell of seafood was strong, and sometimes the kitchen crew came out to smoke a quick cigarette and curse the new owners. It was not the kind of place where Lizzie should be spending her day.

"I know you're tired." She ruffled Lizzie's pale honey-colored curls. Dana had streaks of the same honey in her dark blond hair, but while her hair was spiky short with just a hint of wave, Lizzie's curls spiraled past her shoulders.

"It's time to go," Lizzie said. "It's past four already."

Dana had saved the unfortunate news so Lizzie wouldn't spend the whole afternoon steaming about it, but now she had to tell her. "I hate to say this, but there's a staff meeting in a few minutes, sweetie. I have to be there, but you can come inside and sit with me. I got permission."

"I want to go somewhere fun. You promised! The beach, or McDonald's, or even the stupid library."

"I really am sorry, and we will, just as soon as this is over. You can choose. McDonald's *and* the beach, if you want. We can stay until the sun sets."

"You'll make me get a salad."

"Uh-huh. But you can have a hamburger with it." Dana saw that hadn't done the trick. "And fries, just this once."

"And a milk shake."

"Nice try. Fries or shake, you choose."

"How long is this going to take?"

"I'm not sure." Dana lowered her voice. "They probably called the meeting to tell us they've changed something else. Maybe I'll have to wear a bikini and serve in my bare feet. How'll I look?"

Despite her annoyance, Lizzie giggled. "Silly!"

Dana ruffled Lizzie's hair once more. "Okay, come on, and please be on your good behavior, okay? As much as you don't like being here, it's nice of them to let you hang out while I work. Let's not spoil a good thing."

"I'd like to spoil it. Then I could hang out at the mall."

"Too young. Sorry. But not for long. You're growing up so fast."

"Not fast enough." Lizzie tried to pout, but when she stood, she let Dana give her a quick hug.

Dana led the way through the kitchen to the dining room. The waitstaff had set the tables for the dinner shift. Dana's feet throbbed, and she was grateful to take a seat in the circle that had been set up for the meeting.

Rena and Gaylord Stutz, the couple who owned the Dancing Shrimp, were, in Dana's opinion, most notable for the way they resembled each other. Late thirties, dark slicked-back hair, hips so narrow that from behind, it was impossible to tell who was whom.

Staff who hadn't been on the lunch shift began to trickle through the front door. Dana saw Wanda limp in. This was a job for athletic shoes, not for pointy-toed pumps. She caught Wanda's eye and gestured to the seat beside her. Wanda joined them, pulling out a plastic bag of chocolate chip cookies and passing them to Lizzie.

"For when your mom says you can have them."

Treats like homemade cookies were such a luxury that for a moment Dana didn't know what to say. In the past few years she couldn't remember an oven reliable enough to produce such a thing. She couldn't remember having the money to splurge on real butter or walnuts, either.

"Yum," Lizzie said. "Thank you, Mrs. Gray."

"You know what? You're in the South now, Lizzie, though some folks don't think Florida qualifies. Anyway, you can call me Miss Wanda, if that's okay with your mother."

"Miss Wanda." Lizzie giggled.

"The little girl down the road just calls me

Wanda, but she knows me real well. Maybe you'll know me that well pretty soon, too."

"What's her name?"

"Olivia. Olivia Symington."

"I know her! She's in my class. We're friends!"

"Well, if that don't beat all."

Dana smiled her thanks. "She'll really enjoy those. Store-bought's nothing like the real thing."

"I bake when I'm upset, and I bake when I'm happy. It's good to have somebody to give my cookies, too, although mostly I bake pies."

People were still straggling in, and the Stutzes were now at the front, conferring. Dana wished they would get moving, but they were the kind who seemed to feel larger when they made other people feel insignificant. She was afraid the meeting would drag on and drag on as they postured, and she hated to think how Lizzie might handle that. Lizzie took matters in her own hands, at least for the moment, and went to the restroom.

Wanda leaned closer and lowered her voice. "I talked to my landlady. There's an empty house in our little development. More of a cottage, really. Concrete block, little rooms. Nothing fancy, that's for sure, but the setting's pretty, and Tracy — she's the landlady — has had some work done on it, so it's tight and sound enough. There's just one bedroom, but there's another room one of the renters used as an office. Used to be a laundry room. Might be it's big enough for a single bed for Lizzie. A lot bigger and nicer than anything at the Driftwood Inn, anyway. Best of all, it's not far from the water, and, well, there's Olivia. Lizzie would already have a friend."

Dana wondered if prayers really could be answered. When she'd asked Wanda about houses on Palmetto Grove Key, she had not expected a hit. And not right there. Not just down the road from Wanda herself. For a moment she pondered this news, afraid to speak. Then reality intruded.

"I . . . we don't have much money. And we don't travel with much in the way of furniture. I'm . . . I'm not sure we could swing this."

"There's furniture there. Nothing to crow about, but sturdy enough. And I can tell you the rent's probably cheaper than your motel. You're paying, what? Three, maybe four hundred dollars a week? Tracy'd charge you less, I'm certain. And the last long-term renter, old man name of Herb, did a little handyman stuff to offset some of *his* rent. Maybe you could, too."

"I can paint, but I can't repair much." Dana glanced at Wanda. "I love to garden. I'm a whiz with a shovel. I could do some landscaping."

"I doubt Tracy would care whether anything

was growing or the place was all gravel and sand, but you could ask."

"She really said we could look at it?"

"Better than that. One of our neighbors, Janya Kapur, is having the whole gang over to dinner tomorrow night, and you and Lizzie are invited."

Lizzie arrived back at that moment and heard the invitation. "We're going to somebody's house for dinner?"

"One of my neighbors," Wanda told her. "And your friend Olivia will be there, too."

"Oh, wow! Can we go, Mommy?"

"But this Janya doesn't know us," Dana said. "I mean, it seems awfully presumptuous."

"Not so much. See, we all got to be friends. I'm still not sure how it happened, but I think they'd all expect to meet you. Tracy and Janya and Alice — she's Olivia's grandmother. We're what they call a community, and the last couple of renters didn't fit in. Now that won't stop Tracy, push comes to shove. She's got to keep body and soul together, after all, and that rent helps. But she's like the rest of us. Somebody who fits in would be best. I think you'd fit nicely."

Dana heard the subtext. If she passed this test, she would be allowed to rent the house, but she would also be expected to be part of their little circle.

Dana made certain never to be part of

anything. Yet how could she refuse? This gift was heaven-sent. And Lizzie? With a friend already in place? Her beloved daughter who had put up with so much, more than she would ever even remember?

"You can come see the house and figure out if you like it enough to rent it. Then, either way, you can have dinner with us. I'm making pie."

Dana was trapped between logic and yearning. This was the kind of situation she stringently avoided, yet how could she say no? She didn't believe in omens, but she suspected every blade of grass in Palmetto Grove was pointing toward the key.

Palmetto Grove Key, where by now the ashes she had sprinkled in an overgrown cove at dusk last night had probably washed deeper into Little Palmetto Bay with the first high tide. Palmetto Grove Key, where once she had been happy.

Gaylord clapped his hands to get everybody's attention. Dana was surprised to see that the entire kitchen staff was there, as well. All shifts, all positions.

"We have handouts," Gaylord said, without preamble. "Rena will pass them out. I'll explain as she does, so not to keep you later than we must."

Dana was watching Rena slouch along the front row, handing out sheets of paper, and she missed the next sentence.

"What?" Wanda demanded. "You're closing the Dancing Shrimp?"

Dana put her hand on Wanda's arm. "Is that what he said?"

"Darn straight he did."

Gaylord looked bored, an expression Dana thought he'd probably cultivated since childhood. "Hear me out. Rena and I are not interested in running a typical Florida seafood joint." He said "joint" as if he was talking about something distasteful.

"We've decided to renovate, then reopen as a tapas and wine bar. Palmetto Grove has nothing like it. We feel we'll be successful and *challenged*."

"The Dancing Shrimp was plenty successful until you started making all these changes," Wanda said.

"Let him finish," Dana whispered.

"Our contractor predicts the renovations will take perhaps two months. Since business drifts off in the summer, we plan to close in July and August, and reopen in September. We'll call the new place Gaylord's, and we're bringing in a chef from one of the finer restaurants in New York to help us execute our menu."

"I'd like to do some executing myself," Wanda said, but this time not loud enough for anybody but Dana to hear.

"It will be a very different kind of place," Gaylord went on. "Sophisticated. Tasteful.

66

We will be striving for a different look, a different feel, a different taste, of course. Because of this, after a great deal of discussion, we've made a list of staff we'd like to have with us for this next round. Of course the rest of you have not failed in any way. It's just that we need a special sort of look and attitude in every aspect of Gaylord's, and you won't be happy here once we've transformed."

"Let me see that." Wanda snatched a paper away from Rena, who had finally made it to their row. People were beginning to murmur in front of them. Some were giggling.

"So is this the list of the ones you're kicking out or the ones you're keeping?" Wanda demanded.

Dana took her own copy and saw her name there, but not Wanda's.

"I hope you won't think of it as kicking anybody out. We feel it's only fair to be straightforward about our needs. Those are the people we hope to keep."

"Every single one of these names is wrinklefree." Wanda glared at him.

"I told you we have a special look in mind. It's certainly not personal."

"Not personal?" Wanda jumped to her feet. "I've worked here — done good work, too — ever since I got to Palmetto Grove. Customers ask for me by name. Some of them tip the hostess just to be at one of my tables.

Just because I'm over fifty —"

"Yes, you have been an exemplary employee, and we'll be sure to tell your next employer that very thing."

"Seems to me we could sue you for age discrimination."

"Our attorney says you can't, but you can always try. It is, however, an expensive and time-consuming affair, I'm told. And despite our best intentions, it might have an impact on your remaining months with us. After all, we're letting you know well in advance about these changes."

"I'm not remaining here even a minute, much less months!" Wanda turned and started toward the back.

Gaylord seemed to realize he'd been given the cue to end the meeting. "We'll be happy to talk to anybody individually who needs help with planning for the future," he said. "In the meantime, that's all we needed to tell you today. Go home and think about this, then get back to us about your plans. Meantime, our routine will be business as usual here until the Dancing Shrimp becomes Gaylord's."

Dana grabbed Lizzie's hand and pulled her to her feet, then started after Wanda.

They reached her just as she was opening the door.

"You're quitting?" Dana asked. "Before you have to?"

Wanda held the door for them, and the three stepped into a late-afternoon haze. The sunny sky had darkened, and Dana knew immediately that plans for visiting the beach had ended.

"I'm the best server they have." Wanda glanced at Dana. "Present company excepted, of course."

"No, you're the best, and they're nuts. A tapas bar? Why didn't those two stay in Manhattan? Heck, even in Manhattan, a tapas bar has to be old news."

"Funny thing. Last night Ken told me I ought to quit. And I just did."

Dana put her hand on Wanda's arm. "I'd quit in protest, only I need this job. But I'll be looking for something else. I can't take July and August off. Especially not if I'm living out on the beach with you."

Wanda smiled a little. "Well, at least something good came out of today. You're still coming to dinner? Even though I'm officially blacklisted?"

"Of course I am. *We* are." She put her arm around Lizzie's shoulders.

"Just bring yourselves, then. No need to fuss with anything. Come about six, and Tracy can show you the cottage afterward. You have a favorite pie?" she asked Lizzie.

"Chocolate!"

"French silk, then. Or German walnut. Maybe one of each. Something tells me I'm going to be baking and baking and baking to get over this." She lifted a hand in farewell and started out to the parking lot.

"I like Miss Wanda," Lizzie said. "And we're going to be living at the beach? Really? With Olivia?"

Dana could feel the trap closing. The only question was who had forged the steel jaws, and she was afraid she had to take the blame.

CHAPTER FOUR

By Sunday evening Tracy was convinced she had imagined her CJ sighting. Scouring the Internet until the wee hours of Saturday morning, she'd found news of his release. With one of his attorneys at his side, he had stated that he was thrilled to be out of prison and planned to spend every minute working toward full exoneration.

"Good luck with that," she'd said, before she finally fell into bed.

Tracy knew she was a lot of things, not all of them desirable. But once she had been forced to examine her life, she had tried to do so without flinching. She hadn't deluded herself that CJ had simply caught a bad break. He *had,* of course — unlike other white-collar criminals, who were still jetting off to Papeete and Santorini on their clients' dollars — but Tracy was pretty sure CJ really had deserved prison. She remembered a steady stream of mystery guests sporting heavy gold chains and shoulder holsters, snatches of suspicious telephone calls, unexplained bundles of cash in ice-cream cartons, unsavory "assistants" who'd stood out among the country club crowd like orangutans in Ralph Lauren polos.

So while CJ might hope for a not-guilty verdict down the road, she wasn't going to take bets on it. If he got one, it would simply be due to his uncanny ability to cover his butt.

By Saturday afternoon the reports had dwindled. CJ was said to be holed up with his attorneys, working on strategy. Once a new trial geared up, he might be newsworthy again, but for now, the papers seemed to have more important crooks to cover.

This morning Tracy had finally broken down and called her mother, but good old Mom had only snarled recriminations. Still, there was no reason whatsoever to believe CJ was anywhere except Southern California, staying with a friend or associate who was probably afraid to say no. Considering the number of people who had lost money under his care, she hoped he moved in the dead of night — and often.

The only unanswered question was why Tracy had imagined him. Residue from her mother's phone message? Or something far more insidious, like fear of getting naked with Marsh.

She had decided to tell her friends the story at dinner tonight and ask their opinions. She could almost hear Wanda's interpretation. Even thinking about *that* made her ears itch. Janya's response would be mature beyond her years. Alice, who could sometimes be a bit foggy, could also, in turn, say exactly the right thing. Of course, children would be present, so Tracy would need to edit carefully or wait until they left the table, which, being kids, they would do at the first opportunity.

Now she slipped on Target jeans and topped them with a frilly Vera Wang blouse, left over from her last life. She caught her long hair in an artfully messy ponytail high on her head with a Dollar Tree scrunchie and chose Tiffany earrings with tiny diamonds that the Feds had passed over.

She was standing at her bedroom window, fastening the second earring, when she saw movement at the edge of what she considered her yard. Janya said that the leggy border shrubs, badly in need of trimming, were oleander, which had bloomed sporadically in bursts of pink and white last summer, although they were unadorned now.

Tracy was less interested in the shrubs than what had just gone behind them. She was sure she had glimpsed a man dressed in earth tones, fading into her scenery as if garbed expressly for that purpose.

CJ!

No, she wasn't going there again. She ticked off the possibilities, starting with her unoccupied thumb. Ken Gray, the lone male resident of Happiness Key, although she'd never seen Ken walk his greyhound in her yard. She held up her index finger and stared at it. A fisherman? Somebody hunting alligators? There'd better not be any alligators within a mile of her house!

She held up her middle finger and realized exactly what that one connoted.

"Great." She balled all her fingers into a fist. Somebody was in her yard again. It was time to put a stop to this. Just as soon as she found something to protect herself.

The utilitarian cottage had no fireplace, and consequently no poker. She ate very little meat, so she was minus a carving knife. She only played baseball at the rec center; she was not an archer, and she'd tried target shooting in college and found it a bore. She did have one mean golf umbrella, though. She grabbed it on her way out the door, brandishing it over her head like a club.

Death by umbrella.

She looked ridiculous, but she didn't care.

Halfway around the house she faced the fact that this burst of derring-do was not about scaring away a stranger. No, she had to convince herself once and for all that CJ was not tormenting her. Then she could laugh at herself, a skill she still needed work on.

Someone was definitely crunching through the palmetto underbrush ahead, and she followed as quietly as she could. To her untrained ear, it sounded as if the man was attempting to be as quiet as possible. She had only rarely walked in this direction herself, because it was overgrown with clinging vines and led to the marshy side of the island facing the bay. Still, she wasn't afraid of getting lost. She was just glad she could still see where she was stepping. This was, after all, the state that bragged about harboring every variety of poisonous snake in North America. Unfortunately, she was wearing skimpy little flats.

The noise stopped suddenly, and so did she, flattening herself against the trunk of a Sabal palm. She'd never been a fan of slasher movies, but they'd taught her how *not* to handle this sort of situation. Of course, if the man was CJ, she would have a few things to say to him.

The noise began again, a whisper of feet, the faintest brush of clothing against tree trunks. Her senses tingled. The stranger was making a serious attempt not to be heard. And now he'd moved west, as if making for the swampy cove just up the road. The fact that he was approaching it from this angle was suspicious. He could have parked and walked in. The place was normally deserted. She couldn't imagine why he was hiding his approach.

He moved, and so did she. She'd left her

house far behind before she began to seriously question her actions. She was distant enough from the other cottages that if she screamed for help, nobody would hear her. She hadn't grabbed her cell phone. No, she'd grabbed . . . an umbrella. At least if a thunderstorm began — unlikely, since there wasn't a cloud in the sky — she was ready.

The noise stopped. She stopped, too. Then she heard crunching to her right. Was earthtone man circling back? Had he spotted her? She squatted behind a stand of coastal willows and waited.

Frozen in place, she thought she heard a noise to her left. She might be in view from that direction. She was more than concerned, a bit less than panicked. She inched forward at a crouch. The bay was somewhere up ahead, after a stretch of what passed for marsh. If she cut right just before she reached that point and remained at the edge of the woods, she might outsmart him. She knew the best way back. She would be safe.

She had an athlete's balance and coordination, but now the sun was sinking toward the horizon, and shadows hid sticks and briars, as well as dips in the sandy earth. Droopy Spanish moss brushed her arm; she barely avoided a spiderweb with a resident as large and colorful as a rhinestone brooch. The trees were thinning out, and soon she wouldn't be able to remain hidden from any direction.

She picked up speed, making for the marsh so she could orient herself and head toward home. So what if the man was CJ? With luck he would sink into quicksand, never to be seen again. Besides, she no longer heard anyone moving. Maybe he had spotted her and gone back to his car, wherever it was. Maybe he was more afraid of meeting up with her than she was of him.

Maybe —

"Eeeee!" Just before she reached what she hoped was the marsh, Tracy slid around a tree and collided face-to-face with a man dressed in dark khakis and a forest green parka. She couldn't help herself. She screamed, then screamed again for good measure. As she did she raised her umbrella, as if she was planning to hit a home run.

"Stay away from me!"

People materialized out of nowhere. A regular band of men and women, but this wasn't Sherwood Forest, and this band wasn't one bit merry.

"Shh . . ." The earth-tone man backed away, hands over his head to show he had no intention of harming her. "Shh . . . Please. Be quiet," he whispered.

But it was too late for silence. Ahead of her, she heard the sudden beating of wings. Hundreds of wings, she realized, maybe more, but she was too confused to watch the flock of birds rising from the marsh beyond her. Her eyes were fixed on a group of old men moving in her direction, men she knew only too well.

"Tracy Deloche," one of the men said, eyes narrowed. His pencil-thin mustache was trembling over indignantly pursed lips. "Who else would ruin a birding expedition we've been planning for weeks!"

"Birding?" She croaked the word. "You're looking for *birds?*"

"Well, girlie," he sneered. "We sure weren't looking for *you!*"

Wanda could not believe Tracy's explanation of why she'd been late.

Tracy, who looked as though she'd been dragged through the woods by her topknot, glanced up at her friends seated around Janya's dinner table and finished the tale. "So, to make a long story shorter, the birding club was there because somebody reported sighting a masked booby."

Wanda shook her head vigorously. "The whole story was ridiculous enough. Now you're joking, right?"

"I am *not.* The masked booby is a seabird, white, black tail, wingspan like so. . . ." Tracy stretched out her arms and nearly hit Dana and Alice, who were sitting on either side of her. "Of course, I didn't even glimpse one. Every bird for two miles took wing when I screamed."

Wanda snorted. "I've lived in Florida all my life, and the only boobies I ever did see were the ones in my bedroom mirror."

"Which could not be avoided," Tracy said, with an edge to her voice. "Considering the expanse of that particular real estate."

Wanda preened. "One of my finer features."

"Look, this is humiliating enough, okay? I know what happened. And now, so do about fifteen men and women, including the shuffle board from the rec center."

Tracy was a supervisor at the county recreational center, and well thought of, although she'd certainly had detractors along the way. The shuffle board — the official board who controlled the center's extensive shuffleboard program — had been at the head of that list.

"You're talking about those old men you nearly took down in the park last summer?"

Tracy sent her a dirty look. "Those would be the ones. Mr. Moustache, the hoverer . . ." She shook her head. "Who knew they crawled around on their bellies in the swamp? They said I ruined their life lists. We were becoming friends. Now they'll never speak to me again."

"They were crawling in the swamp? With gators and stuff?" Olivia looked fascinated.

Tracy smiled at the girl, but she still felt glum. "Just an expression. But they were tiptoeing around and peeking out from behind trees. They were being quiet, trying not to scare away the birds. I thought there was just one person after me, but I was more or less surrounded."

"Well, dear, you had quite a shock." Alice held up a bowl. "Finish this off. You need to eat to keep up your strength." Alice was a grandmotherly vision, silver hair, silver-rimmed glasses, deep lines in her smiling cheeks. She hadn't been young when her beloved daughter gave birth to Olivia, but some gifts were worth waiting for, even though now that her daughter was dead, Olivia was her sole responsibility.

Tracy took the bowl and began to spoon a generous second helping of spicy lentils on her plate. "I must be completely wacked out, you know? Up close, the guy I was trailing doesn't look anything like CJ. Ten years older, darker hair, three or four inches shorter, and I can guarantee CJ would never wear a nylon parka. Just not possible."

"So was this the same man you saw that first time?" Wanda passed the dish of eggplant and tomatoes to go with the lentils. Tracy emptied it, and Janya got up to clear the serving dishes, waving Alice back to her seat.

Olivia set down her fork. "Grandma, can I show Lizzie around? We're done, aren't we, Lizzie?"

Wanda was pleased the two girls were so enthusiastic about going off together. She saw Dana frown as her daughter pushed back her

80

chair, and intervened before Dana could refuse.

"Perfectly safe," she promised. "Olivia's up and down that road a hundred times a day. Nobody much comes out this way."

"Except a flock of tiptoeing bird-watchers," Tracy mumbled.

"Well, I guess it's okay." Dana still looked worried.

Wanda supposed Dana's caution was the result of having only one child. Wanda knew the downside of human nature. A cop's wife got an earful every day of her life. But when her own children were as young as Olivia and Lizzie, she'd felt wrenched in two, one kid needing one thing, one needing the other. She hadn't had time to worry about every little moment they were away from her.

"They'll be fine, dear," Alice promised, as she nodded to her granddaughter. "You two be back for pie in a little while, though."

"And watch out for old men with binoculars," Wanda called after them.

"Very funny." Tracy reached for half a chapati to scoop up her eggplant, while the others, who had finished before her, began to send their empty plates around the table to Wanda, who stacked them neatly.

"So. Back to CJ," Wanda said, once the girls were gone. "You think that bird-watcher was the man you saw Friday night?"

Tracy shook her head morosely. "I asked

him if he'd been out there on Friday, and he said no. I don't know what I saw." She paused between bites. "I wonder . . . Maybe I was just nervous about Marsh being at my house. It was supposed to be a romantic evening. No kids. No papers we hadn't signed. Just us. For the *night.*"

Janya came back to remove the dirty dishes. In a moment she brought in Wanda's pies, then returned with dessert plates and cutlery, and set everything on a side table. "You did not want Marsh there? Perhaps he's not the man you want to be with, now that you can?"

"No. No, that's not it. I . . . well, I think he's kind of special, actually. And maybe . . ."

Wanda waited. When Tracy didn't go on, she gave up. "Well, if nobody else is going to speak up, I will. I just read a whole article on this in some women's magazine when I was having my hair fixed. It was all about the excuses women on the verge of menopause make to avoid having sex."

Tracy fumbled and dropped her fork. "I am not on the verge of menopause!"

"No? Didn't you tell me a couple weeks ago, your periods are all screwed up? Maybe you wouldn't be cruising toward the change in normal times, but could be your body's forgotten what it's supposed to be doing. You're sure not using it the way God intended. No sex, no children —"

"Wanda!" Janya cleared her throat. "You

are, perhaps, premature in your diagnosis. Tracy is much too young."

"And you are much too opinionated," Tracy said, narrowing her eyes at Wanda. "My periods would be as regular as clockwork, thanks, except I went off the pill, and now they're confused."

"Unfortunately, so are mine," Janya said.

The table fell silent.

"What does that mean?" Wanda asked at last. "You're trying to have a baby?"

Janya looked embarrassed. She gave the slightest of nods.

"Without telling us?" Wanda asked.

"Is that a prerequisite? Is that why it's yet to happen?" Janya disappeared into the kitchen again.

Dana, who had been taking in the entire conversation, leaned forward. "Do you always talk to each other like this?"

Wanda sized her up for a moment, wondering how the other women saw their guest. Dana was in her forties, nice to look at, if not actually pretty. She was tall and willowy, with messy Meg Ryan hair, long face and large teeth that made for a spectacular smile on the rare occasions she attempted one. When it came to dress, the women of Happiness Key were an eclectic bunch. No matter what she wore, Tracy was designer chic. Janya preferred the flowing fabrics of her native country, deep rich colors and lots of gold bangles. Alice was fifties homemaker. Wanda herself liked bright prints and spandex — a woman couldn't have too much spandex. She classified Dana as somewhere between sporty and classic. She would look equally at home hiking in the Adirondacks or processing a mortgage application at the local bank.

Wanda liked Dana, although her new friend was a shade too reticent. Most of the time Dana kept to herself, but Wanda could see their table conversation had shaken that right out of her. They had tried to catch her up on who was whom and what was what. Dana still looked bewildered.

"Sometimes we're even worse," Wanda answered, "but I'll admit we don't always have this much to talk about. Tonight's a real surprise, what with Tracy heading for hot flashes, and Janya trying to get pregnant and all."

Tracy pointed at Wanda with her fork. "I am not heading for anything except a catfight on Janya's floor!"

Wanda liked to see Tracy all riled up. Color was flowing back into her cheeks. She'd been pale as an ice cube when she arrived.

"You might think on it," Wanda said. "First those unpredictable periods. Then you lost your appetite for men. You're gaining weight —"

"What?" Tracy shrieked.

Wanda was just as glad she wasn't sitting

next to her landlady. "Don't pretend you haven't. I was at Target with you when you bought those jeans, lady. Your other jeans shrunk? After what you spent on them back in California?"

"I think Tracy looks wonderful," Alice said. "She is . . . blossoming."

"I never said she didn't look wonderful. She needed a little weight. Round her out a tad."

"The power of suggestion can be strong." Janya was clearly trying to reestablish decorum. "I think your former husband was on your mind, Tracy, and you saw movement on the road where none was to be expected. The man reminded you of him somehow. That is all that happened."

Wanda figured they'd gone as far with Tracy as they could go, so she turned to Janya. "So, you're trying to have a baby? It doesn't always happen the first time or two you try." She frowned. "And twenty-five is awful young."

"You'll be a wonderful mother," Alice said. "You will have such . . ." As she sometimes still did, she had to search for the right word. "Energy."

Tracy was still glaring at Wanda, but she addressed Janya. "You're really ready? I mean, you're doing so well with your murals. Everybody wants one."

"Rishi has waited so long for a real family. I can give him this."

They were all silent for a moment. Wanda

didn't know how to respond to that. She had no qualms about going after Tracy, but Janya was sensitive, and questioning her didn't seem proper.

"I was fired," Wanda said, to change the subject once more.

"What?" Tracy's annoyance visibly vanished. "Are you making that up?"

"Nope. They're changing the Dancing Shrimp into a tapas bar and calling it Gaylord's. Like in this economy people have the money and appetite for teensy little plates of food. People want lots to eat, and a bargain to boot. So it won't stay open more than a month. Remember I said so."

There was a round of indignation, then another of sympathy. Wanda enjoyed both.

Janya looked relieved to be off the hot seat. "Will they not need servers?"

"None my age. Dana's been asked to continue. I was put out to pasture."

"The new owners haven't one bit of talent or sense, but they're rich in opinions." Dana patted Wanda's hand. "She's the best server in the place. I don't know what the Dancing Shrimp will do without her."

"Too bad," Wanda said. "I'm gone for good. Left yesterday, and I don't regret it."

Everybody got up to get a slice of one of the pies, and Janya took orders for coffee or tea.

In a few minutes they were all seated in

Janya's small living room. On a rainy winter day in January, Janya, who liked to experiment with color, had painted the walls a deep sage green. The wall behind the low platform sofa was now a mural of the Taj Mahal, but painted as if Monet had joined her for the experiment. Prints in brass frames adorned the other walls, and plants sat anywhere they received even a ray of light.

Wanda noticed that talk of weight gain hadn't deterred Tracy from a slice of French silk pie.

"Should we call the girls?" Dana still sounded worried.

"We'll save them some," Wanda assured her.

Alice rolled her eyes in pleasure. "This German chocolate tastes like pie must taste in heaven. I think you should sell these, Wanda. We can't buy good pies. Those expensive ones at the Sunshine Bakery? They aren't even as good as the frozen pies . . . you know, at the grocery store. I bet you could make them for the owner to sell."

Wanda was flattered. Talking to Alice was a little like playing the lottery. Sometimes you struck out, and sometimes you won big. Tonight, Alice was on a winning streak.

"As much as I hate to be nice to you right now, Wanda," Tracy said, a smudge of chocolate on her lovely chin, "Alice is right. There's no good place in this town to buy a pie. Everything at that bakery is just okay at best, but her pies aren't even *that* good. Of course, you've spoiled us all."

"You really think anybody would buy them?"

"I think anybody who ever had a slice would be lined up at her door."

"Well, it would give me something to do while Kenny's in and out."

Dana interrupted. "Kenny's your husband?"

"Right. A cop. Officially he's Sergeant Gray, but he's Ken to everybody else." She glanced at Dana, who looked surprised. "Didn't I tell you about him?"

"I don't think so."

"He's the best kind of cop, too."

"What kind is that?"

"The kind that does his job real well."

Dana looked vaguely uncomfortable. Wanda knew cops did that to people, and she was used to it. Some poor woman who was driving the speed limit suddenly started crawling ten miles below it when she saw a cop, sure she was going to be arrested just for sitting behind the steering wheel.

"So Ken's sort of a bonus out here? Your own watchdog?" Dana asked.

"Don't worry about Kenny clocking your car with his radar gun, or checking to be sure your county sticker's up to date. He's not like that. He just makes sure nothing's going on around here that shouldn't be. Only he's not going to be around much for a while. He's going to be training up in Georgia."

The others asked about Ken's training, and Wanda told them what she knew.

"Don't let any of this sway you from renting the cottage," Tracy told Dana. "We don't have problems out here. I probably just saw a fisherman or something. We watch out for each other. Even without Ken around all the time, you'll be safe, and I hope happy."

The girls came charging back inside, and there was a flurry as they chose which pie they wanted and got milk to go with it. The talk turned to lighter things; then it was time to clean up and leave. The women thanked Janya for the wonderful meal, and divided the leftover pie to take home.

Wanda figured that even for Happiness Key, this had been a pretty exciting night. Tracy'd had an adventure. Janya had dropped a bombshell about her personal life. She herself had gotten some well-deserved sympathy and maybe even an idea for the future. And Dana had gotten the introduction of a lifetime.

Nobody could say the woman didn't know what she was in for if she moved out here.

"Ready to see the cottage?" Tracy asked Dana and Lizzie, when everybody was ready to go.

"I want to live here. I don't care what the house looks like!" Lizzie and Olivia had clearly plotted strategy while they were outside together.

Dana didn't look as convinced, but Wanda figured once she finally went inside the house, she would say yes. Even a one-room hut with outdoor plumbing was better than the Driftwood Inn, and the cottage topped that by a mile. Best of all, Lizzie would be safe and happy on Happiness Key. And if she knew anything about Dana, Wanda knew Lizzie's happiness was right at the top of her list.

CHAPTER FIVE

Just to be certain Wanda didn't have a point, Tracy went home Sunday night, turned on her computer and read everything she could find on menopause. At thirty-five, she was sure she was too young to be going through it, but Wanda had gotten under her skin.

Afterward she felt better. Her periods were irregular but not greatly so. She only had hot flashes when she stepped from air-conditioning into Florida's violent sunshine. She might occasionally have mood swings, sure, but those were always due to PMS. She slept like a rock at night, still craved sex, and wasn't losing hair or growing more in places she didn't want it. Nope, there was nothing physical happening to her, nothing prematature. Wanda had been trying to get a response, and she had succeeded.

Still, she lay awake too long thinking about Friday. She had half expected Marsh to call over the weekend, but her phone had been silent. She was pretty sure she had hurt his feelings. And why wouldn't they be hurt? She'd been as jumpy as a virgin. He had come for a good meal — okay, the meal had been the least of it. He had come to spend the night, and instead, she had been thinking about CJ, a man who, without remorse, had dropped her into the worst mess of her life.

Tracy had made a mistake by not telling Marsh what she thought she had seen. At least then they could have talked. She could have admitted she was spooked by her past. Marsh was divorced. He would have understood. Comfort would have turned to something far more interesting.

On Monday morning she woke even earlier than usual and dressed casually for a day at the rec center. Spring vacation was over. Marsh would be busy getting himself to work and his son to school, but she thought he might spare her a few minutes. She would stop by to explain and ask his forgiveness. She would tell him that any time he could get away again, he had a standing invitation to come to her place. She gave herself an extra half hour to get to work and took off.

Marsh lived on the other end of Palmetto Grove Key, near the bridge to the mainland, in a house his family had owned for four generations. She passed both the island's Indian mound and an abandoned fish camp; then she wound her way through forest scrub that reminded her of her unfortunate search and destroy mission yesterday.

Someday soon she would have to find her way back to that spot and look for her golf umbrella, which she had abandoned after nearly clubbing earth-tone man over the head.

Marsh called his rambling home a Cracker house. It sat on brick pilings, high enough that when storms blew through and flooding ensued, the house usually withstood both. The tin roof jutted over screened porches for shade, and windows had been placed for maximum ventilation. Once in the fall, she, Marsh and Bay had camped out in mosquito-net-draped hammocks on one of the porches, listening to insects and the remnants of a faraway thunderstorm. She had fallen asleep, drugged by the fragrance of citrus blossoms and the faint sulfur of distant mangroves. The unlikely combination had been intoxicating.

Gratified when she saw that Marsh had not yet left, she pulled her vintage BMW convertible to a halt beside his pickup. A Chevrolet sedan with Florida plates sat on the other side. She remembered that Marsh's cleaning lady came on Mondays.

She climbed the steps and opened the screen door to the porch where they had camped that night. She crossed and rapped on the front door. About to pound a little harder and call through the open windows, she was surprised when the door opened.

Tracy took a step back. The woman in the doorway was about her own age. She had pale blond hair and a porcelain complexion that proclaimed the hair color — or at least some version of it — was natural. Her features were narrow and perfectly aligned, and her eyes were almost violet. Tracy examined her quickly, hoping for something that wasn't perfect, to pump up her diminishing confidence, and decided the lovely eyes were spaced too close together.

That did not, of course, offset the fact that she was dressed in a bathrobe the same shade of violet.

"May I help you?" she asked sleepily, tying the belt of her robe around a Scarlett O'Hara waist.

Tracy was at a complete loss for words. Obviously this woman, whoever she was, had spent the night here.

In whose bed?

She was expected to say something. She settled for the perfunctory. "I was looking for Marsh."

"Well, he's a popular guy. I'm sure you aren't the first woman who's come looking for him."

The woman did not have a voice that went with her general appearance. Tracy had expected a Southern drawl, something soft and purring, like melting butter on moist corn bread. Instead she clipped her speech,

94

as if each word knew it was allowed only so much time to hang in the air. Tracy pictured a spreadsheet. She pictured graphs.

"Is he home?" Tracy asked at last, although she wasn't sure why. Confronting Marsh here and now was one of the worst ideas she'd had in a few days filled with them.

"I'm sorry, but Marsh is getting our son ready for school. I would call him, but I know he doesn't want to be interrupted. We both take Bay's education very seriously."

Sylvia Egan. Now Tracy had a name to put with the face. Marsh had told her all about his ex-wife, Sylvia, or at least she'd thought so. He had just neglected to mention that Sylvia could have been Miss America.

Or maybe she had been. Maybe Sylvia had put herself through law school on all those scholarships. Because Tracy knew that when she wasn't standing around in a bathrobe, Sylvia was a hotshot criminal attorney in Manhattan. Marsh *had* told her that Sylvia was a phenomenon, a woman who sent prosecutors running to jobs in private law firms, just to avoid facing her.

What he hadn't told her was that Sylvia the shark was also Sylvia the temptress.

"So, you're Bay's mother," Tracy said. "I'm Tracy Deloche. I know Bay from the recreation center."

Sylvia looked blank, as if she couldn't

imagine how that had anything to do with her.

"I was in charge of his program last summer," Tracy elaborated. "We got to be good friends."

"Oh, right. His little youth camp. I think he told me about it."

Tracy felt a flash of anger on behalf of the little boy. Bay had been enrolled for the entire summer. Of course he had told Sylvia about it. What else did a nine-year-old talk about except the things he did every day?

"Are you here to talk to Marsh about Bay?" Sylvia asked. "Because I can certainly relay the message. We share *everything* and always have."

Tracy schooled her jaw not to drop. Sylvia had just declared war, woman to woman. Tracy might not understand everything about the world, but she'd learned *those* dynamics in preschool.

"No, it was more personal than that." She sent Sylvia her most enigmatic smile. "And not something he'd want me to share with you."

Sylvia was well armed, but she wasn't impervious. Tracy's salvo hit home. Tracy could see it in the narrowing of the other woman's pupils. "I'm sorry your little tête-à-tête will have to wait, Daisy, but I'll be sure to tell Marsh you stopped by."

Tracy didn't correct the name. This was

probably a trick Sylvia had learned in court, a guaranteed route to make a witness feel inconsequential.

"Oh, don't bother," she said, as if she really didn't want to disturb the other woman. "I have his private line at work. I'll just give him a buzz. I know he'll be interested we finally met."

"Finally?"

"Yes. More or less historic, wouldn't you say? The woman from his past and the woman from his future."

"You toss beanbags with nine-year-olds and tell fortunes, too?"

"Lawyers aren't the only people who can put facts together and draw conclusions." Tracy glanced at her watch. "As fascinating as this has been, gotta go. Give Bay a hug for me."

She told herself not to say it. She told herself to bite her tongue, but unfortunately, she didn't listen. "If you've finally learned how to hug him, that is."

Then, angry at herself for stooping so low that she'd use a little boy as ammunition, she took the fastest route to the screen door, took the steps two at a time and started toward her car.

She was heading down the driveway when Marsh emerged from the house. He was alone. Maybe Sylvia was inside hugging Bay. Maybe by the time Marsh went back inside,

Sylvia would have hugged him so hard the kid would need CPR. Tracy considered sailing right past, but she'd already chalked up one immature act for the day, and it wasn't even 8:00 a.m.

She stopped beside him and rolled down her window, leaning over the empty seat. "Lovely morning," she said sweetly. "I hope Sylvia made you a big pot of coffee."

"Turn off the engine and get out, okay?"

She considered. Maybe, just this once, she could allow herself two immature acts before breakfast. Everybody needed a break from routine. In the end, though, she got out and walked around the car, leaning against the passenger door with her arms folded.

"You never told me how stunning she is," she said.

"I know how this looks."

"Good. Because finding the words might take me most of the day."

"She showed up yesterday morning. Just like that. Seems she lost a big case, something she and her firm were sure she was going to win. She's devastated."

"So you gave her solace and a place to stay."

"I wouldn't have given her *anything,* but we share a kid, remember? And you know how much Bay misses her. Could you see me explaining that I don't want his mother anywhere near us? If this was summer, she could take him on a vacation somewhere far,

far away. But he's in school. This is the only way she's going to be able to spend any time with him."

She considered that. It made sense.

"We aren't sleeping together," he said, when she didn't respond.

"Neither are *we*."

"I'm aware of that."

"That's why I came over."

"To sleep with me?" Just the faintest hint of a smile touched his lips.

"No! Well, not right now, anyway. I, well, I just needed to explain what happened the other night. At least as well as I understand it."

"Give it to me in a nutshell."

She considered. "Okay. Friday night when I was crossing the room to the sofa to sit with you, I thought I saw CJ on the road in front of my cottage."

"There's that name again."

"Marsh! At least CJ's not sleeping in my house."

"Touché."

"It was my mother's phone call, I guess. Stirring up all kinds of stuff. And you being there, and me being kind of . . ." No sane woman told a man she was nervous about getting into his bed, because that gave him all kinds of power. "Kind of wanting to make things perfect," she said lamely.

"You really thought you saw him?"

"You want to hear something stranger? He actually *is* out of jail, holed up somewhere in California, working with his attorneys to make sure he stays that way. If I'd actually listened to my mother's phone call, I would have known. I guess she thought I was aware of it and she wanted to harass me."

"And that's why you went all squirrelly?" He rested his palms on the car, one on each side of her head, and leaned toward her.

" 'Squirrelly' is an exaggeration."

"Could it have been him?"

"Not likely. I thought I saw him again yesterday but I tracked that man down. Not CJ." She declined to tell him the rest of the story, since admitting to visions of her ex-husband was embarrassing enough. "I guess all this just brought up a bunch of memories. But they don't have anything to do with the way I feel about you."

"And how *do* you feel, Miss Tracy?"

She smiled a little. He was smiling exactly the same amount. Both of them waiting, she thought, for the other to make the first move.

"Like we missed an opportunity," she said softly, her gaze dropping to his lips. "And there are so few opportunities in this life, we should never let that happen."

"You know, now that Sylvia's here, I have a built-in babysitter."

"We should take advantage of that."

In the end, he was the one who covered the

slight distance and kissed her.

When the kiss ended, she opened her eyes and looked beyond him. Sylvia was standing on the porch watching, her expression a complete blank.

"We have an audience," Tracy said.

He straightened and turned.

"Marsh?" Sylvia called. "Hate to bother you, but I don't know where you keep your bread, and I need to make Bay a sandwich for lunch."

"You go," Tracy told him. "We'll make plans later."

"I'll hold you to that."

She watched Marsh walk back to the house. Now Sylvia was smiling sweetly. She lifted a hand and gave Tracy a half wave.

Tracy's elation vanished. Silhouetted in the doorway, Sylvia was the woman every man dreamed of coming home to.

Marsh might think Sylvia was here to lick her wounds and visit her neglected son, but Tracy had grown up with too many women just like her. She was sure war had been declared, and Marsh was the prize.

Wanda spent Monday morning baking. She wasn't one to sit around and think about things until she was so confused she didn't know where to turn. She liked the idea of baking pies for the Sunshine Bakery. Of course, she figured getting hired to do it was a long shot. The owner probably thought her own pies were just fine, but baking took her mind off the Dancing Shrimp, and besides, she needed to contribute.

There were only so many books a person could take in. To be considerate she'd let Alice teach her to crochet, but how many granny square afghans could she foist off on her kids and grandkids? Sure, she couldn't survive without *All My Children,* but that was why God had invented TiVo, and Ken had surprised her with one for their anniversary.

No, baking was the thing, though she could foresee a serious problem if she didn't find a way to sell all the pies she was planning. Ken could only take so many to work, even when he was home. Her neighbors were game, but not enough to double their weight — although Tracy was trying. No, selling the pies was the answer, and Sunshine was the place to start.

She settled on a traditional double-crusted apple pie, since that was the favorite of people with no imagination. Of course, she added her secret touches. A pastry recipe she had perfected. A careful mixture of spices. A generous sprinkle of whiskey, her own secret ingredient that made all the difference. She was proud enough of the pie, even if it wasn't her favorite.

She baked her famous Key lime, as well, the one they'd served instead of cake at her son's wedding. And to show that she was an innovator and not just somebody who perfected the ordinary, she made a green tomato pie, with green tomatoes from a farm stand in Palmetto Grove. Her mama had made green tomato pies every fall and spring, a woman who used what she had and never complained. But Wanda knew that most people had never had one, and certainly not one as good as her very own version.

At noon she put the pies in two carriers, one double, one single, that she used for church suppers, and set them carefully in her car. There was nothing she could do to make herself look as wholesome as Betty Crocker, but she wore her simplest dress and flats, and played down her jewelry. Then she made the trip into town.

Sunshine Bakery was on State Street, in an ideal location near restaurants and a small grocery store in the central shopping district. The place had changed hands in the fall, and she hadn't heard much about it one way or the other since.

There was a park on the next block, where parents gathered to watch children's soccer matches or Little League games, and couples played tennis on half a dozen courts. Wanda imagined children and parents alike stopped by for brownies or cookies, or something to bring home for dessert.

State Street itself needed sprucing up. She

noted a couple of empty storefronts, although one looked as if it were in the midst of renovation. The city had torn up the sidewalks across the road from Sunshine, but new sidewalks would be an advantage. It looked as if they might be putting in some landscaping, too. All in all, the spot was good.

She found a parking space at the end of the block, and gathered her pies and the sheet she'd printed with her information and what she expected to charge per pie. The last had been the hardest. She had no idea what people might really pay. She'd made a run to Publix that morning to see what their pies went for, then figured how much hers would be worth per slice. By the time she subtracted the cost of ingredients, there hadn't been that much left over to pay for her time. But pies were a labor of love. And if she started making them in bulk, she could buy in bulk, too, and that would save her some money.

From the outside, Sunshine Bakery was no great shakes. The plate glass window needed cleaning, and the displays of fake wedding cakes looked as if they'd been bought at a garage sale. Wanda knew that most people in town bought their wedding cakes from a woman one town over who specialized in nothing but and was more or less famous in South Florida. Apparently the Sunshine Bakery wasn't trying hard to compete.

Inside, the bakery was narrow, with a

counter on the right over a glass display case. While the room should have smelled like something baking in the oven, the smell was more like a house that had been closed up too long. The woman minding the counter was on the telephone, and she signaled to Wanda that she would be with her in a moment.

Wanda used the time to examine the baked goods. She was surprised there was so little to see other than bread. Shiny, seeded loaves sat on a shelf behind the counter, long tapering loaves Wanda might buy if she wanted to pitch baseballs to one of her grandsons. Then there were round loaves of differing colors and textures. Sandwich loaves that ached to be slathered with peanut butter or layered with cheese.

She spotted three cakes, all covered with fluffy commercial icing that probably tasted like paste, and four platters of perfectly symmetrical cookies that looked like cardboard. One shelf was devoted to éclairs that were sadly dripping chocolate on parchment paper. The final item was a lemon meringue pie missing two slices. Due to the dissection Wanda observed an anemic graham cracker crust, an egg-yolk-colored filling that was much too shallow and meringue that was much too deep. If a person wanted nothing for dessert but meringue oozing sticky little droplets, Sunshine was the place to come.

The woman hung up and sighed. "I'm sorry. Problems with a supplier. Prices going up, up, up, or so he says. I'll be darned if I'm going to pay college tuition for his children."

Wanda thought the woman sounded like maybe she was happiest trying to get people to give her more for less. There was nothing wrong with getting a bargain; Wanda shopped on sale when she could, but she also knew times were tough. Likely the man just wanted to put food on his table, not send his children to Yale or Harvard.

The woman gestured to the case. "So, what can I help you with? We have some nice éclairs on sale. That first cake's chocolate, with raspberry filling. If you want it for a special occasion, my daughter can write on it in a jiffy."

The woman was pushing sixty, round as a doughnut, with frowsy brown hair and a little smile that seemed to be engraved on her face. Wanda thought the smile was as fake as the frosting on the cakes.

"As a matter of fact, I thought maybe I could help you." Wanda set the two carriers on the counter. "I'm a pie baker. It's what I love to do most in the world." She was glad Ken wasn't there to hear the insult to his charms. "I decided it's time to start selling them, and I wanted to give you first crack. I brought three for you to try, but I make about a hundred different kinds. I'm just wondering if we could work out some kind of partnership."

The little smile widened just a bit. "Did you make them in a *professional* kitchen?"

"No, I make them in my own kitchen, but I can turn out a lot if I need to."

The woman looked pleased, as if educating Wanda was the best part of her day. "You haven't looked into this very much, have you? You can't sell *anything* you make at home, not in Florida. A kitchen and living quarters have to be completely separated. And you have to have permits. My, the permits you have to have." She shook her head and looked even more pleased.

"Well, do *you* have a professional kitchen?"

"Of course. My daughter and I make most of what you see here."

"Then I suppose I could come in and bake here for you, if you were interested, that is. It's not my preference, but it sounds like the way to go."

"I *have* pies."

"Not like these, you don't." Wanda began to take off the covers. "I can tell you that nobody who eats one of my pies ever forgets it. Your customers won't, either. By the way, I'm Wanda Gray."

"I'm Frieda Mertz." Frieda walked over to examine the pies. "What did you bring?"

Wanda told her. "But like I said, I have about a hundred carefully tested recipes. I could make just about anything you wanted. Why don't you give one a try?"

"Well, I am partial to apple."

This didn't surprise Wanda, although it would surprise her if Frieda could turn out a tasty one herself. Frieda left, and returned with a knife and a plastic fork and a paper plate. She didn't offer to share. She just cut right into the pie and slapped a small slice on the plate, then dug in.

Wanda, who hadn't eaten lunch herself, felt her stomach rumble.

"Good," Frieda said, when she had finished. "A little unusual. You've added something different to the traditional recipe."

"I have."

"I don't think I can have a pie on my shelves without knowing what's in it."

Wanda thought a discussion of ingredients was premature, but she shrugged. "Whiskey. Just a splash."

"Is that so. And the spices?"

Wanda told her. At least she told her *some* of them. She could always plead a memory lapse later, but for now, she wasn't ready to share every little secret.

"And what else did you bring?"

They followed the same routine with the other two pies. Frieda tasted, and questioned her. By the third pie, Wanda was getting suspicious. At one point Frieda excused herself and went into the back. She returned a few minutes later.

"The pies are fine," Frieda said. "But I think I need to taste a few more before I commit. And I'd like to take these and pass them around my family, just to see if they think hiring you to bake for us would be a good idea. What else can you bring me?"

Wanda wasn't about to let Frieda have her pies. Not until they had an understanding. She didn't like the woman well enough, and worse, with every passing second she was growing more suspicious something was wrong.

She put the lid back on the carriers and removed them from the counter before Frieda could run off with them.

"I'm sorry, but I planned to take these over to the police station. My pies are a big hit with my husband's buddies over there. What other kinds would you like to sample?"

A young woman with Frieda's frizzy hair came out from the back, holding a sheet of paper in front of her. "Mom, is this supposed to be some kind of recipe for me to follow? Apple pie with real whiskey? We don't have any whiskey on our shelves, that's for sure, and you're really going to spring for some?"

For the first time Frieda's smile wobbled. She didn't take her eyes from Wanda. "No, of course it's not a recipe, you idiot. I just made a few notes to jog my memory when I talk to this lady again."

"Sure looks like a recipe. Names of spices. Whiskey. How many apples. Sounds good. Sounds better than ours." The young woman wandered back into the other room.

"I thought you asked too many questions," Wanda said, gathering the pies up higher and closer to her chest.

"I told you I just need to know what you put in them if I'm going to sell —"

Wanda was getting angrier and angrier. "You're not planning to sell my pies. You're planning to steal my recipes! You even tried to steal these samples. Family my eyebrow! Bet when I walked out the door you'd have put them on those shelves of yours, professional kitchen or not! Well, guess again! I wouldn't bake a pie for you if I was starving. Bet you wouldn't pay me even a fraction of what they're worth, either. And you know what? I figured out what you were up to, and I only told you a little and some of that was a lie. You won't be able to duplicate my recipes no matter what you do, 'cause you're a no-talent hack!"

"I didn't ask you to come in here. I can make my own pies. My customers seem to like them just fine."

"What customers? There hasn't been a soul since I came in, and it's lunchtime. People ought to be streaming in, buying something to go with their sandwiches, or picking up a treat for supper." Wanda headed for the door.

"Somebody ought to give you a run for your money. Palmetto Grove deserves real dessert for a change."

The door tinkled loudly when she slammed it behind her.

The air outside smelled fresher and sweeter than the air in the bakery. She took a deep breath before she started back to her car, but she was steaming, and not because she was in the sun.

Under the anger, disappointment was blooming. She did two things really well. One was taking care of people and making them feel special. The other was baking pies. First she'd been fired as a server, just because she was past fifty. Now an overblown apple dumpling was trying to steal her pies. It seemed like there was some sort of eternal vendetta going on, but Wanda couldn't figure out why. Nothing had changed on her end. She'd done her job well. She'd baked pies and been willing to offer them for sale at very little profit.

As if the Fates were conspiring to make a point, she stumbled over an uneven piece of sidewalk and nearly fell to her knees. She managed to stay her fall by bouncing against the wall of the store just in front of her. Shaken, but pies intact, she rested a moment, breathing hard.

The store was one of the empty ones she'd noticed on her walk down the block, but not the one that was being renovated. As she gathered herself, she peeked inside the window and saw this hadn't been a store at all, but some kind of restaurant. She pressed her face against the glass and saw a short counter with several stools, the old-fashioned kind she remembered from the soda fountains of her youth, chrome, with red plastic seats that twirled round and round. She could see where tables had probably clustered. Swinging doors led into the back.

She heard somebody walk by, then turn and approach her. She looked up and saw an old man with a halo of fluffy white hair.

"Luncheonette," he explained, as if she had asked out loud. "It was here almost forever, but it's been closed most of a year. Never could figure why the space hasn't been rented or sold. It's a good location."

"Well, it's tiny," Wanda said. "Any decent-size restaurant would have to knock out walls and expand into the place next door."

"Yeah, and they'll never sell. Mom-and-pop establishment, and so's the one on the other side of the alley." He pointed to what was really just a walkway that ran beside the shop. "Been here for years. This place used to buzz, though. I guess egg salad sandwiches and a bottomless cup of coffee can't make any man rich enough today."

After he left, Wanda stood there for fifteen minutes wondering what the little luncheonette could do for a woman who didn't care if she got rich, a woman who only cared if she could bake pies and make people happy.

CHAPTER SIX

Janya stared at the open box in front of her. "*Aai* has sent me not one gift, but two. At least her generosity cannot be questioned."

Something about the way Janya said the last made Tracy take notice. "Your mother?" She continued after Janya's nod. "So what did she send?"

When the other woman didn't answer, Tracy peeked over a cardboard flap to see for herself. She had lugged the surprisingly heavy package to Janya's door after it had been left by "mistake" in Tracy's own generously sized mailbox. This mistake was one the carrier made frequently. Tracy's box was the largest in the little development, and leaving packages inside it saved him a trip to the true recipient's front door.

Janya grimaced; then she pried out a red stone statue that was wedged tightly inside. "It is Nandi, the bull." She held it up for Tracy to see, using both hands.

"Well, that's . . . something else."

"It is well-done." Janya didn't sound happy.

Tracy viewed the bull, who was lying on his stomach, an elaborately carved saddle adorning his back. It was well-done, yes, but it was also heavy.

"I guess I don't understand," Tracy said. "If my mother was in the mood to give gifts, which she's certainly not, she'd send me a blouse or a scarf. You get a bull? And one that must have cost a fortune to ship?"

"Nandi is the bull Shiva rides. He . . ." Janya seemed to search for the right word. "Symbolizes? He *represents* sexual energy." She looked up. "And fertility."

"Ah, I get it. Grandchildren."

"So it would seem."

Tracy tried to think of something to say. "Well, that's a really interesting way to get them. What will you do with him, or shouldn't I ask?"

Janya lifted an eyebrow, but she was reading the letter that had been enclosed in the box and didn't answer. Even when Tracy peered over her shoulder, she wasn't able to decipher the characters, which were entirely different from anything she'd seen. She wasn't even sure which direction they were to be read.

Finally Janya looked up. "She suggests that I display him in our bedroom."

"Right. Very . . . exotic."

Janya sighed and put the letter down. "*Aai*

115

has outdone herself."

"What's the second thing?" Tracy nodded toward a white jar that looked as if it had contained a drugstore cleansing cream, although there was no label.

"It will be harder to explain."

If Janya thought that would lessen Tracy's interest, she was mistaken. "I've still got almost an hour to finish Dana's cottage before she arrives with all her stuff."

This sigh was louder. "It seems there is a temple in Tamil Nadu devoted to the goddess Garbharakshambigai." The long name rolled off her tongue. "She blesses couples who long for a child. Many make pilgrimages there, my mother says. They offer ghee to put at her feet."

"Ghee?"

"You have eaten it at my table. Similar to your clarified butter. It does not spoil in our heat the way ordinary butter might."

"So they pour it on the feet of the goddess?"

"Something like that, yes. And when they have said the *shlokas* — prayers — they are told to say, and performed other rituals, they are given the ghee to take home. Then they are to eat a little of it for forty-eight days, both man and woman, and a child will come."

"Hum . . . yummy." Tracy made a face. "Still, to my Western ears, that sounds a lot saner than taking your temperature ten times

116

a day to figure out when you're ovulating, or making love with your knees over your ears. Give it a try."

"Can a woman truly make love with her knees over her ears?"

"Your people wrote the Kama Sutra. Look it up."

"Rishi will wonder what I have told my mother that she would send these to us."

"I bet you didn't have to tell her anything. I bet she's been counting on her fingers since your wedding night."

"Did your mother do the same when you were married?"

"My mother would have had a cow." Tracy grimaced. "I'm sorry, nothing like this one," she said, gesturing to the statue. "My mother has had at least two face-lifts, breast enhancements, liposuction, tummy tucks, you name it. A grandchild would just point out how old she actually is. So the advice I got went more like, 'You and CJ have no need for children, and I hope you don't plan any.' "

"Someday we will lock our mothers in a room together and see which emerges the victor."

"I didn't want a baby anyway." Tracy paused. "Not with CJ. I didn't know how to be a mother. Now it's a moot point. But for you it's a different story, huh?"

"Rishi has missed having a real family. He is ready."

Tracy rested her hand on Janya's shoulder. "Are you ready, too? I mean, it's a big job. I see all kinds of parents at the center, and some of them are pretty resentful because they never get a break."

"I hope I would be different."

"Of course you would be. I just want you to be happy."

Janya smiled sadly. "You want me to be happy. I want Rishi to be happy. Who does Rishi want to be happy?"

"Well, you, I hope."

"My husband will make an excellent father. He is a good man."

"So he is." Tracy glanced at her watch. "I guess I ought to get over to Herb's — make that Dana's — cottage. It's in pretty good shape, but I want to do a little more sprucing up."

"Do you need help?"

"Need? Nope. Want? You bet."

After Janya put her gifts away, she and Tracy walked over to the soon-to-be-occupied cottage. Tracy had been in that morning to air it out and hadn't locked up. She threw the door open, and Janya went in first.

"Go see what I did to the old study this week," she told Janya. "Lizzie's new bedroom."

"Come and show me."

They went together. The former laundry room adjoined the only bathroom, a pink-

and-gray affair that had been all the rage in the 1950s. Unfortunately, Lizzie would have to squeeze through a doorway beside the shower whenever she entered or exited, unless she crawled through the window. The room was so tiny Tracy had been afraid she couldn't fit a bed along the longest wall, but she had found a daybed and new mattress that fit exactly, both on sale at a discount store going out of business.

She'd been under no obligation to provide the little girl with a bed, but something had told her weeks might pass before Dana found the money to buy one. Besides, brightening Dana's and Lizzie's lives was good karma. And working on the room had given her something to do other than think about Marsh at home, cooking one of his fabulous dinners.

For Sylvia.

"Oh, you painted it." Janya sent Tracy a big smile. The room was now flooded with sunshine, the pale buttery kind that comes from a paint can.

"Olivia told me Lizzie's favorite color is yellow. And the walls were so shabby, the room needed a new coat of paint anyway. I had some extra time one evening." Tracy had also clipped coupons and bought sunflower sheets and a matching comforter. The entire renovation had cost very little.

"She will love it."

"Well, it's not an ideal situation. She's going to have to develop some patience coming and going, that's for sure. But I'm pretty sure it's a big step up from that awful motel."

"And I have just the right print for that wall," said another voice.

The two women turned to find Wanda behind them in the bathroom doorway.

Wanda flapped her fingers in a wave. "It's a big old shaggy sheepdog rolling around in a flower-filled meadow — with some sunflowers, even. Goes with the theme. I bought the frame for something else and the print was already in it. Do you want it?"

Wanda's taste was questionable, but Tracy figured this might be enough of an exception to put on the wall. "Let's give it a try."

"Got some sheer green curtains to put over the window, too. Used to hang in our guest bedroom back in Miami."

"And I have a carved table we can put beside the bed," Janya said. "Very lightweight. I will bring it. And a little pink lamp I bought at a garage sale and have no place for."

By the time they finished moving everything in, the room looked surprisingly inviting. Tracy was sure Lizzie would be pleased.

"It seems odd, don't you think, that they have no furniture of their own?" she said. "I mean, even I had a few little things with me when I came from California. In a sports car, no less."

"You want the truth?" Wanda lowered her voice. "I think maybe they've been homeless, or just about, a time or two. Dana hasn't said so, exactly, but we all know what the economy's like, and how hard it is to find a job. From what I can tell, they've moved a lot, and they don't seem to have much in the way of savings. I'm betting they've left a lot of stuff along the way."

Tracy knew how many people were suffering. In fact, she had worried she might not find renters at all. So once she'd seen that Dana liked the cottage, she had waived the security deposit. She had wanted Dana and Lizzie to have the house. Olivia was so excited about having her friend just down the road. And Dana? Well, Dana just seemed to need it.

They were interrupted by somebody knocking on the front door. The women went into the living room, and Tracy found Alice and Olivia waiting outside.

"She'll need groceries," Alice said. "I have . . ." She was carrying two brown bags, and she held them out to finish her sentence without words.

Olivia held out a plate wrapped in aluminum foil. "And I made brownies."

"Well, if this isn't a party," Wanda said, taking a grocery bag from Alice's arms, as Tracy took the brownies. "Come on inside, ladies."

Tracy put her arm around Olivia's shoulders. She was more than fond of the girl. Olivia had gone through difficult times, first losing her mother, who had drowned, then her father, who was now in jail. But Olivia was still a sweet, thoughtful kid who worried about others. She was growing taller by the moment, and her brown hair was growing out after a short cut she'd hated. Now, due to some careful trimming under Tracy's expert supervision, it fell silky and smooth to her collar. Olivia showed all the signs of being a beautiful young woman someday. Tracy just hoped she would get through adolescence trouble free — or close enough.

"You're excited about having Lizzie here?" Tracy asked.

"It's gonna be great."

"I don't know. . . . Didn't I hear something about you having a whole lot of homework, with the year winding down?"

"We'll do it together." Olivia poked Tracy in the side. "You know it'll get done."

Tracy hugged her, then let her go. "Go see what we did to Lizzie's new room and tell me you approve."

While Olivia inspected, Tracy joined the other women, who were checking out the kitchen. "Everything's pretty much finished," Tracy said. "I just thought I'd give the cabinet shelves another quick wipe and some shelf paper." She brandished a roll lying on the kitchen counter. She was not a shelf paper kind of woman, but the old shelves needed something bright.

"You clean the fridge out good?" Wanda asked.

"I tossed out everything the last tenants left there. You want to wipe it down for me?"

"Not a problem."

Alice had already busied herself sweeping the floor. Alice could find enough dirt in a sterile operating room to fill a dustpan. A good mopping would come next. Tracy knew the way the older woman worked.

Olivia ran in and told the women she was going home to go through her books and games so she could give some to Lizzie for her new room. The announcement was quickly followed by the slam of the front door.

Without being asked, Janya began removing the few dishes in the cabinets. "I think Herb would be glad Dana and Lizzie were moving in. I will ask Dana if she wants some of his plants to put near the windows. I have many."

Herb, who had died the past summer, had nurtured a full-fledged garden in pots. After his death, Janya had appointed herself to watch over them. She had been certain his heirs would claim them, but in the end, she'd inherited them for herself. Now she spread them around when she could. Tracy thought the generosity was an unconscious memorial to the old man, a way of keeping something he had enjoyed alive.

Wanda finished filling the sink with soapy water and found a sponge. "I know she'll want plants. Dana told me she likes to dig in the dirt. I think she was hoping she'd get a discount on the rent for doing some gardening around here."

"I gave her the best break I could." Tracy dipped a cloth in the soapy water and hoisted herself to the counter to begin wiping shelves. "But she knows she's welcome to do any gardening she wants." She didn't add that Dana had made it clear she would do some landscaping just as a thank-you. For Tracy, getting a reputation as a do-gooder was too strange to contemplate.

"So," Wanda said, head now in the refrigerator, "tell us about getting pregnant, Janya."

Janya sounded disgruntled. "I should not have said anything."

"Sure you should have. Who else would you talk to about this? You've been to the doctor to see what's what?"

Janya looked as if she was contemplating a change of subject, although she had to know that would be like heading off a hurricane with a paper fan.

Finally she shrugged. "The doctor says it is too soon to worry, that we will talk again when a year has passed."

"I've been reading up on this," Wanda said.

"Along with my mother. Do you, perhaps,

have a fertility statue to give me?"

Wanda came out of the refrigerator at that. "A fertility statue?"

"A really cool red stone bull that anyone would be proud to have," Tracy said. "And aren't you being a little bit nosy?"

"It's my job to make Janya happy." Wanda pulled out the vegetable bin and brought it to the sink. "If she wants a baby, it's my job to help."

"No, I think that's Rishi's job," Tracy said. "He's better equipped for it."

Wanda narrowed her eyes. "I did some reading, as I started to say. And there are ways to help things along."

"This is a personal matter," Janya said.

"Not since the moment you brought it up to the whole crew, it's not. So I went to Wal-Mart, and I got you something." Wanda abandoned the bin on the counter and left, returning with her purse. She removed a small bag and thrust it in Janya's direction. "For you."

"I think it is the second time today I am afraid to look."

Tracy was curious now. "Janya, after the bull and the butter, how can that hurt?"

Janya carefully spread the bag wide and took out a CD. " 'Country Love Songs,' " she read out loud. " 'Your Favorite Songs by your Favorite Stars.' " She looked up. "This is very kind, Wanda, but —"

"See, the thing is, you're more likely to get pregnant if —" Wanda lowered her voice, although Olivia was at home sorting through her belongings "— you have an orgasm," she finished, hissing the s. "And we all know that's a lot easier if there's some romancing going on first. So you just put that on in the evening and sit close to Rishi on the sofa, or better yet, get him to dance with you —"

Janya covered her ears. "Stop."

"Oh, please, if you're *that* shy, maybe there's your problem," Wanda said.

Tracy couldn't help herself. She giggled.

She glanced at Alice to see how the older woman was taking this, and saw that Alice's eyes glistened mischievously behind her glasses.

"Janya could dance for Rishi," Alice said. "Like she did . . . for us. He would like that."

Now Tracy hooted. With Janya's brown skin, it was hard to tell if she was blushing, but Tracy thought if she wasn't, she should be.

"Good idea," Wanda said. "Some sexy Bollywood dancing. Just the thing. After a little country snuggling."

Despite herself, Janya was smiling. "Now you are finished? We can talk of other things?"

"You'll try my CD?" Wanda said.

"I will be sure to."

"You can name the baby after me." Wanda went back to scrubbing the vegetable bin.

126

"And I *will* change the subject. I have an announcement."

"*You're* pregnant?" Tracy asked, fluttering her eyelashes innocently.

"I said an announcement, not a medical miracle."

Tracy realized Wanda wanted to be prodded. "We're all ears. Tell us before we're interrupted."

Wanda smiled, and the smile took ten years off her face. "Well, I went and bought me a store, only it's more than just a store, it's a restaurant, too. So I got a lot for my money."

"What are you talking about?" Tracy hopped down off the counter to get a dry towel.

"I got me a little place all my own to sell my pies."

The room was silent; then as if they'd waited for a cue, all the women yelped together. They grabbed Wanda for a group hug.

"If I'd known you were going to do that, I'd have waited until poor Alice was done sweeping. Look what we did to her dirt pile!" Wanda extricated herself, but she looked pleased at the show of support.

"I can sweep again." Alice lifted the broom off the floor and began to do just that.

"So tell us!" Tracy demanded. She listened as Wanda explained about going to the Sunshine Bakery with her pies.

Wanda sped up. "So there I was, walking back to my car, and I nearly fell flat on my face. While I recovered, I peeked in the window and saw this place. On a whim, I called a Realtor I know from the Dancing Shrimp and asked her to see what was up with the place, and she checked for me. Seems the owners thought they had it rented, which is why there was no sign in the window, but the deal fell through. She said they were so tired of the mess, they were about to give it away. So I made an offer to buy it, and they grabbed it. And the deal's been sealed. Ken and me, well, we had the money in the bank, and he was all for it. Said the world needs my pies, but I think he just needs me to be busy." She took a deep breath, having told most of the story in a rush.

"You did all that without telling us?" Tracy asked indignantly.

"I didn't want to tell you if it fell through, and it almost did a time or two this week. But now it's a fact. We close next week, since it's a cash-and-carry deal."

"Wanda, you are in business," Janya said. "A businesswoman."

"Well, I'm hoping you'll all help me." Wanda looked radiant. "I want Janya to paint a mural all over the front. Pies, of course. Apple trees, bakers, you know. I'll leave it to you, Janya, to work your magic. And I'm hoping you'll come in, Tracy, and tell me what

128

you think about fixing it up, doing a little decorating inside. I want to get this moving fast after we close. Got inspectors lined up for a license. Nobody much is opening anything, so they're mostly standing around wondering why the city's paying them, I guess. I'll have to update a little, but it was a luncheonette not that long ago, so most everything's up to code. I need new tables, more stools. See, we'll serve pie there, and sell pies to take home. I don't know what I'm going to call it yet."

"Wanda's Wonderful Pies," Alice said, as if she couldn't imagine why Wanda hadn't thought of it herself.

Everyone was quiet; then Tracy found herself nodding. "She's right. It's perfect. 'Wanda's Wonderful Pies' says everything. Maybe it's long, but everybody will just call it Wanda's when they talk about it."

"I like it, too," Janya said. "I think it will be easy to remember and impossible to forget what kind of place it is. And I think Wanda's should be very homey inside, a little old-fashioned."

"It has a counter," Wanda said. "Like an old-time soda fountain, with twirly chrome stools. I thought I'd keep that idea alive."

Tracy was beginning to imagine it. "Checked curtains in the windows. Maybe window boxes outside on the sidewalk, and glass vases with flowers on the tables. Paper place mats, like they have at the Dancing Shrimp, only printed with your own logo and a special recipe you don't mind sharing. That way they'll take the place mat home, and every time they look at the recipe, they'll want to go buy one of your pies instead. Everything light and bright and happy, like a grandmother's kitchen — if grandmothers still cooked. Anyway, a reminder of pies baking and families sitting around a dinner table together."

Wanda sobered. "Momentum just carried me along. I was so mad at that Frieda So-and-So, I got the idea and just kept going forward. But I'm in for a lot of work. What if nobody comes?"

"They'll come once they find out how good . . ." Alice smiled.

Tracy finished the thought. "And they *will* find out how good they are. But you're right, it's going to be a lot of work. You can't do this alone."

"I'm thinking about asking Dana if she wants to work for me. I have to have somebody help me manage it, and the hours'll be more regular than the Dancing Shrimp. Besides, they'll be closing down to renovate in the summer, and she'll need another job."

"She insisted we stay with a month-to-month rental on this place," Tracy warned. "I don't think she's ready to commit to long-term anything."

"Maybe she will if she has a job she can count on during Lizzie's school hours. I'm thinking I'll close up about six, so people still have time to buy a pie to take home on their way back from work. But I can get a high school student to work after classes."

There was noise from the front of the house, and the giggles of young girls. Tracy heard the front door whack the wall as it was thrown open. Tracy was glad concrete block was impervious to almost everything.

"They're here!" The shout was Olivia's.

Dana came into the kitchen, wearing denim capris and a white shirt with the sleeves rolled up and the tails tied around her waist. "I'm sorry. They're just so excited."

Tracy heard squeals from the other room, and she smiled. She would bet Olivia had taken Lizzie right in to see her new room.

"Welcome! We're just doing a little extra cleaning," Tracy explained. "Alice and Olivia brought you brownies and some groceries to get you started."

"That's so nice of you."

"We'll have the shelf paper up in a minute, then we can help you carry your things inside."

"No, we have very little. Lizzie and I can get it. Please don't worry." Dana seemed to need to explain. "We . . . travel light. Especially now that jobs are so hard to find and harder to keep."

131

"The house already has furniture, pots and pans and such, and you have clothes. I've seen you wear them, so you can't deny it. Seems to me, then, that you're all set," Wanda said. "And not having a lot of stuff just frees you up not to work so hard."

Dana seemed to relax. Tracy thought hers was a face that needed a smile to be attractive, and with it, she far exceeded that goal.

"I like the way you think," Dana said.

"Well, maybe you'll like this, too." Wanda launched into the story of Wanda's Wonderful Pies, but a condensed version. "And I'll need a manager," she finished. "I thought about you."

"I'll be happy to have Lizzie after school," Alice said, without even a pause to regroup.

Dana looked unsure. "That's a lot to ask."

"I like to play bingo at my church. I like . . . to go to needlecraft guild. I sometimes . . . need someone to keep an eye on Olivia at night. Your help would be appreciated then."

"So you could trade," Wanda said. "And we'll be closed on Sundays and Mondays, so you'll have a weekend day with Lizzie. Open on Saturdays, I'm afraid, but Lizzie can come in and help if she wants."

"Or stay . . . with Olivia," Alice said.

Dana didn't answer. Tracy was watching her closely. Dana was an enigma, someone who kept her thoughts and feelings to herself. But Tracy thought the woman was torn. She wondered if money was the problem. Working for Wanda would be a steady job, but on a good day at the Dancing Shrimp, she probably made more. Of course, there were also bad days, when tips were few and far between, especially now. And soon enough it would be closing for renovations.

"You . . ." Dana clamped her lips shut, then shook her head. "You are all so kind. I'm, well, I'm just not used to it."

"I'm not being one bit kind," Wanda said. "I'm being selfish. I need somebody good to help me. I've watched you work. You'll do nicely."

"We'll talk," Dana said, and followed it with one of her transforming smiles.

"You bet we will." Wanda, who had been drying the vegetable bin, shoved it back into the refrigerator. "Now, let's get you all moved in."

"Mommy! Come here! Right away!"

Tracy watched Dana revert from relaxed — at least a little — to cautious. She drew herself up as if ready to spring, a lioness preparing to rescue her cub.

"I think she just wants you to see her new room," Tracy explained quickly. "We fixed it up since you saw it last time."

As if to prove Tracy right, Lizzie ran into the kitchen, her wide freckled face wreathed in smiles. "They painted my room yellow. And there's a bed with sunflower sheets, and

133

a comforter and a pink lamp on a pretty table. Just for me!"

If Tracy had been forced to name what she saw in Dana's eyes, she would have said the woman looked as if she'd been shut into a jail cell. Dana recovered quickly, but just for that moment, Tracy thought she'd looked sorry they had been so nice, sorry that Lizzie was so pleased with her new room.

"Thank you," Dana said. She sounded as if she meant it.

Tracy was not convinced.

CHAPTER SEVEN

Janya knew better than to take her neighbors' suggestions. She might be the youngest woman in Happiness Key, but she was an excellent judge of what worked best with her unique cultural roots. So with that in mind, it was a source of great mystification that on Friday night, she found herself following Wanda's advice.

Of course, all signs pointed toward this being a "special" night, which explained a bit of it. With a little calculation involving a calendar and a pregnancy manual from the library, she knew that tonight, she might be at her most fertile. Then, right after she had done her calculations, Rishi had called to say he would be home earlier than usual. He'd invited her out to dinner, an unusual treat, since he was usually exhausted by the time he left work, but instead she had told him she preferred to spend the evening at home.

At home — in their bedroom.

Signs. All of them good.

Janya knew Rishi's favorite foods. She was a strict vegetarian, and he was less so, but he loved her potato *bhaaji,* a dish served in many homes in Western India. The recipe was simple, potatoes with chilies, chopped coriander leaves, and other herbs and spices, fried together until crisp. Rishi said the result was similar to American hash browns, but to her, *bhaaji* was a beloved childhood comfort food. Tonight she prepared it to serve with dal and rice. In the end, choosing something she knew Rishi liked instead of something to impress him made the most sense. Particularly since she intended to spend more time than usual dressing.

She prepared dinner, then went to shower. Afterward she scented her hair with jasmine oil, and carefully lined and shadowed her eyes. She had polished her nails a bright red that morning, and now she slipped rings on her fingers and toes to accent them. After thinking carefully about her wardrobe, she had settled on a black sleeveless top beautifully embroidered in gold, worn over a loose, pajamalike *salwar,* although these pants were cut to ride low on her hips — which Rishi would discover when he undressed her tonight. She wore gold sandals, spiraling gold earrings and the two bracelets Rishi had given her for her last birthday. She was a little dressed up for a night at home, but she didn't intend to stay that way.

When she heard Rishi parking his car in their driveway, she started Wanda's love song CD. After he had removed his shoes, she greeted him with mango juice and a plate of *paneer pakora,* cubes of breaded fried cheese with mint chutney on the side, setting the food on the table near the sofa.

"Coming home to a house that smells this good is a gift." Rishi put his arms around her and pulled her close. "Coming home to you is a bigger one."

She put her arms around his waist and her cheek against his shoulder. "I am so happy we have a whole evening together. You work so hard."

"I was not being productive today. I was too tired, and missing you too much."

She liked the sound of that, although she could hear the fatigue in his voice. Rishi was rarely subdued, but tonight that was the best word to describe him. She pulled away reluctantly. "We need to spend more time together. I've looked forward to this since you phoned."

"And what is this music?"

She smiled. "A present from Wanda. Do you like it?"

He listened a moment. "Love can be very sad. Here, as well as in India." He turned away. "Let's say our prayers, then we have the night all to ourselves."

Janya had prepared a *puja* room in what

was meant to be a coat closet in the living room. Hindu homes usually had a special room set aside for worship, and this, even though modest, was theirs. She opened the doors and together they went through the familiar rituals with a statue of Krishna watching over them. She ended by placing several pink hibiscus flowers at Krishna's feet. Later she would use one to snuff out the flame she had kindled in the oil lamp on the *puja* tray.

"Someday we will do this with our children beside us," she said when they had finished.

Rishi looked uncomfortable. "Someday, yes."

She ushered him to the sofa, turned on the music, which she had paused while they worshipped, and joined him for a glass of juice.

"Tell me about your day," she said after a sip. "Did you have a good one?"

He still seemed tense, even after prayers, but he relaxed as they chatted. By the time she told him to take a seat at the dinner table, he seemed more like himself. He ate the dinner with relish, took seconds of everything and complimented her lavishly. She had heard stories of ungrateful, critical husbands from friends she had grown up with, and Janya knew how lucky she was.

"What would you like to do this evening?" he asked, after he had helped her clear away the dishes.

She wondered how she could have signaled her intentions any more clearly. Her lovely blouse was cut low between her breasts and bared her shoulders. Her scented hair was down, the way Rishi liked it best. As they cleaned the kitchen she'd stood close to him, resting her hip intimately against his, turning when she could to lightly brush his arm with her breasts. From their CD player a man with a gravelly voice was explaining that a woman decorated his life. She hoped her husband was listening.

Still, she had prepared for this, just in case. "I thought we might watch a DVD." She smiled softly, her gaze lingering on his lips. "Unless you have something else you'd prefer?"

"No, that sounds perfect. I'm too tired even to take a walk."

She hoped the movie would energize him for what she had in mind.

"What DVD is it?" he asked.

"Kama Sutra: A Tale of Love," she said innocently. "Have you perhaps seen it already?"

Rishi looked uncomfortable. "No, I don't think so."

"I believe you would remember. The director is famous, and the story is supposed to be quite touching. I have heard wonderful things about this film." She didn't add that she had also heard *Kama Sutra* was one of the most beautifully sensuous films ever made in India. She turned off Wanda's CD, which had played and replayed several times by now. Then she turned down the lights, turned on the DVD player and settled beside him on the sofa, her hand resting lightly on his thigh.

She was not surprised when half an hour later, Rishi had his arm gripped convulsively around her. Her own fingers were locked into place, digging deeper in his flesh. Half an hour after that, she was afraid Rishi might hyperventilate. The film *was* gorgeous, the most sensuous tale she had ever encountered. She had almost forgotten her real reason for putting it on. Now she was less concerned about making a baby and more concerned about simply getting her husband into the bedroom. She had bought the movie online. The rest of the story would keep for another night, hopefully when, once again, she was fertile.

She put one arm around Rishi, cupping his cheek. Then she kissed him with the practiced fervor of the major character, courtesan to a king.

"We could finish this movie another time," she whispered. "We could practice what we have seen so far." She couldn't remember ever being this bold with Rishi, but they had been married more than a year. Surely this was allowed.

He stood and gathered her in his arms.

They kissed hungrily. Somehow she found the remote and stopped the DVD. Somehow they ended up in the bedroom on their bed together, their clothes in wrinkled piles along the way.

She moaned when he fell on top of her and kissed her, bringing her knee between his legs and moving it slowly up and down. She wrapped her arms around him, moving her hips in a slow rotation, pressing her naked breasts against him.

Rishi was whispering in a Hindi dialect, the language he had learned as a child. He was not a man who frequently gave in to emotion, but when he did, the dialect emerged. She could understand some of the words, but what she understood most of all was that Rishi was entranced with her, that he wanted her in the same way that she wanted him. That at this moment, when they might create a child, they were together in every way.

He opened his eyes and stopped moving. He stopped kissing her. He was still warm against her, but now his body seemed inflexible, rigid. Worse, much worse, as he lay there, he lost all desire to be with her. One moment they had been one entity. Now they were two, and one was strongly resisting the other.

"What's wrong?" she asked softly. "Did I do something wrong?" Such a thing had never happened before. Normally she was the one who had to be coaxed.

He didn't pretend. He rolled to his side, then to his back. She had been so warm, so caught up in their lovemaking. Now the soft breeze of their ceiling fan rippled unpleasantly against her heated skin. She wanted to cover herself with the sheet, but she was afraid to move, afraid she would completely destroy the spell that had brought them here — if any part of it was left.

"It's looking at me. It's staring at me."

She propped herself up on one elbow and stared at *him.* "Rishi, what are you talking about?"

"The bull."

She had set Nandi near the head of their bed, on a table near the window. She had thought little about it, laughing when she told him her mother's intention. She had teased him and said they should be grateful for all help.

"Nandi?" She sat up and looked at the bull. "Rishi, it's a statue made of stone. I do not think it can really be staring at you."

He didn't reply.

"I will remove it. Don't concern yourself." She got up and went to the table, lifting the statue with both hands to carry it around the bed. In the living room she looked for a place to set it. Nothing seemed quite right. In the end she opened the door into their *puja* room and set the statue next to Krishna. She closed

142

the door again and went back into the bedroom, picking up their clothes as she went
and draping them carefully over her arm.

"It's gone," she said softly as she moved
around the bed, lay down and eased herself
against him. "Rishi, I didn't know having
Nandi beside the bed would upset you. I
won't put it in here again."

There was no answer.

"Rishi?"

Again, no answer.

She didn't know if her husband was really
asleep or just pretending to be. She considered shaking him awake, but wasn't that more
pressure than a statue?

In the end she got up, brushed her teeth,
washed her face and slipped into a nightgown. When she came back to bed, Rishi
hadn't moved, but his breathing sounded
shallow. It was not the breathing of a man so
fatigued he had not been able to remain
awake long enough to make love to his wife.

She told herself she was wrong. But the
hour was too early, and her thoughts too
heavy. She knew she would lie awake for
hours staring out her window at the moon
drifting across the night sky.

She was considering therapy. In the week
after Dana moved in, Tracy thought she saw
CJ twice more.

The first time happened when a strange

man walked jauntily up her driveway wearing a meter reader's uniform. On closer view, of course, nothing but the walk was the least bit familiar. The hair color was wrong. The height was wrong. And the man was a good ten years younger than her former husband. But for a moment . . . for one whole moment, she had expected the real CJ to knock on her front door.

The second time, she spied CJ from a distance, disappearing down the road toward the point on foot. This sighting was more disconcerting. She knew if she jogged in that direction, she might lose him. So she actually, *actually,* got in her car and sped toward the point herself. But in that brief time span, the man disappeared, most likely off to some favorite fishing cove on the bay. And having chased one impostor through palmetto scrub, she was not anxious to chase another. She still hadn't found her umbrella.

Now, on Friday night, she tried to put this growing insanity out of her mind. She and Marsh had negotiated a date, and negotiated was the only word for it. Things probably went faster and smoother when Hillary Clinton visited the Mideast. Marsh's place was now off-limits since, more than a week after her arrival, Sylvia was still in residence. Tracy's place was off-limits because she didn't want to chance another CJ sighting. Besides, her instincts told her that she and

Marsh needed a night together with no pressure. A chance to reconnect.

They had finally agreed to a late dinner at a restaurant he loved and she tolerated. Skeeter's was the kind of dive where it was best not to wear sandals in case something scuttled under the table. But the shrimp was fresh and the beer icy cold. Best of all, Tracy would be there with Marsh. If they got food poisoning, they could comfort each other over the telephone.

To avoid another confrontation with Sylvia, they'd agreed to meet at the restaurant, which sat on the bay in Palmetto Grove proper. Lights were just coming on in the other cottages when Tracy got into her car. On the way out she saw the flicker of a television from Janya's, and the kitchen light at Wanda's, where she was probably elbow-deep in piecrust, obsessing about what to make and sell.

She arrived at Skeeter's just in time to meet Marsh in the parking lot. He was dressed for the occasion. Ragged shorts, a Wild Florida T-shirt, canvas shoes without socks. Definitely no sex on the horizon tonight or he would have made *some* attempt to impress her. She was encouraged and disappointed simultaneously.

"You just can't *not* dress up, can you?" His tone said he didn't mind one bit.

"You think this is me dressed up?" She

145

kissed him hello, then again for good measure. "These are cleaning rags."

He let her go with obvious reluctance. "For who? Billionaires?"

She wore capris and a flirty Betsey Johnson charmeuse blouse, along with faux snakeskin flats she hoped would scare away the vermin.

"Not a thing I'm wearing is new," she pointed out.

"Tell me no snakes died for those shoes."

"They did not." She didn't add that she had other shoes she couldn't say the same about. She had lost so much when the Feds cleaned out her closet and left so much behind when she moved to Florida. But she did have an obscene number of shoes left over from her former life, and now she was determined to wear them out.

"I'm starving." He put his arm around her waist and hauled her toward the door, his fingertips searching for and finding bare skin. Over the unmistakable twang of Willie Nelson, she could hear raucous laughter through the open windows. Half a dozen couples lounged against the porch railing, waiting for tables, but she wasn't sorry to be among them. She was enjoying the feel of his fingers slipping under the waistband of her capris.

"Looks like it's going to take some time to get seated, even at this hour," she said, snuggling closer.

"Sorry about the timing. Sylvia had a

bunch of things to take care of, so I was minus a babysitter earlier."

"You could have brought Bay. He loves Skeeter's."

"Bay doesn't want to miss a chance to be with his mom. It was better not to fight him on that."

Tracy told herself not to feel hurt. So, okay, Bay had grown on her. For a kid with a bunch of problems, he could be fun to have around. And he liked her; she knew he did. In fact, she'd kind of thought she was special. But Sylvia was his mother, the mother whose attention he'd worked so hard to gain, probably since birth. His preference tonight was perfectly normal.

"You would know best about Bay," she said, after Marsh reluctantly stepped away and asked the gum-cracking hostess to put their names on the wait list. "And I'm assuming Sylvia's going to be on her way home before long?"

Marsh steered them to a corner on the far end of the porch where the noise wasn't as bad. She perched on the railing and rested against a post. He stayed on his feet and leaned against it, his chest snug against her hip, one hand resting on her knee.

"I don't know what her plans are," he said. "I thought she'd be gone by now, but Bay's so thrilled to have her, I'm afraid to rock the boat and ask."

"Marsh, does Bay think she might stay? Does he know this is just temporary?"

"Kids know things on a variety of levels."

"Meaning he's holding out hope."

"I've talked to him. I've explained that relationships change, and one day some people realize that they just can't live together. I told him that's what happened with his mom and me."

Tracy knew what was coming. "And so then Bay said, if relationships change, maybe yours will change back, and you'll want to be a family again."

"How did you know that?"

She shrugged. "Maybe because I was a kid so long myself, I just know the way they think. I grew up kind of late. Like maybe last year."

She realized she had said just the right thing to break the ice. He grinned, and she felt the warmth of it moving across her body.

"Bay's crazy about you."

"And I guess I'm —"

Marsh's pocket began to play "Wild Thing."

"I'd better get that." He pulled his phone out of his pocket and held it to his ear, stepping away from her as he did. She didn't pretend she wasn't eavesdropping.

"Uh-huh." He listened a few moments. "Right. So far so good." Listened some more. "The chocolate sauce is in the door of the refrigerator, and the strawberries are in the freezer. Yes, he can eat strawberries. He's not two anymore." And listened some more. "I don't know when I'll get home, Sylvia. We're waiting for a table."

He closed the phone and put it back in his pocket, but he didn't resume the position he'd abandoned.

"Ice-cream sundaes?" Tracy asked, as pleasantly as she could.

"She's out-of-date on what he can do."

Tracy struggled to be charitable. Some struggles were hopeless. "Bay is her son, and that's pretty basic stuff."

"Tell me about it. At least she's making a stab at being his mother. Maybe she's even serious. It remains to be seen."

She was encouraged that Marsh hadn't fallen for Sylvia's story hook, line and sinker. "I kind of get the impression she's interested in being a wife again, too."

"Nah, you're way off base."

"She seemed pretty territorial when I was there."

"She's territorial by nature. She's used to going after anything that moves. That's who she is and why she's so good at her job."

"Her job . . ." Tracy smiled tightly. "I always thought attorneys had trouble taking time off. And she's been here, what, almost two weeks?"

"She brought work. Bay's still coming to my office after school when he's not at the rec center, so she can make phone calls."

Tracy tried to imagine that. Sylvia was in Palmetto Grove to see her son, but she didn't want to see him in the afternoons when he was actually free? She saved work to do then? Why? So she could be finished in the evenings when Marsh came home?

"Enough about my ex," he said, as if he was reading her mind. "How about yours? Any more mysterious CJ visitations?"

She was still thinking about Sylvia and growing more annoyed that the woman was still in Marsh's house. "Just a couple." Then she realized what she'd said. "Umm . . . not really."

He was not smiling now, and he didn't look as if he intended to in the near future. "Which is it? Not really? Or my personal favorite, just a couple?"

"Okay, there seem to be a lot of men in the world who resemble CJ, and now that he's, you know, out of jail, I seem to see them everywhere. But it's no big deal."

"Maybe you're conjuring him."

"Like creating him, you mean? I don't think so, thanks. If I did, he'd be materializing on a mountaintop in Nepal. Or maybe an active volcano. Do they have volcanoes in Nepal?"

"Maybe it's good we cooled things down."

For a moment the words seemed to hang in the air between them; then she slid off the railing so they were face-to-face. "Exactly what do you mean by that?"

"Wild Thing" began to play again.

"Maybe you ought to just keep the phone in your hand," she said. "Saves you rooting around in your pants. Although if this conversation doesn't change direction, you're certainly the only one who's going to be tonight."

He held up the hand under discussion and spoke into the phone. "What, Sylvia?"

Tracy cocked her head and lifted an eyebrow.

"Of course he doesn't want to go to bed," Marsh said. "It just got dark a little while ago. Sure he can watch television. Tomorrow is Saturday. Just make sure it's something appropriate." He listened. "You have a law degree, Sylvia. You should be able to figure this out." He closed the phone with a hard snap, then shoved it back into his pocket.

"What did you mean, 'it's good we cooled things down'?" she demanded.

Whatever he was feeling didn't show in his face. He was looking at her the way he probably looked at developers under indictment, right before he pulled out a damning piece of evidence. "Issues. Lots and lots of them, apparently."

"Whose? Mine or yours?"

He expelled a long breath. "We're blowing this, Tracy. I don't want to blow it tonight, okay? I want to eat a pound of boiled shrimp and drink just enough beer to keep my blood

151

alcohol level under the limit. I want to look at you over the table and think about how lucky I am that you and I somehow managed to overcome our differences and get this far together. Okay?"

"Marsh, I want our relationship to heat up, not cool down. I've told you I want it to go further. CJ doesn't have anything to do with you."

"And Sylvia doesn't —"

"Wild Thing" started all over again.

"I am beginning to hate that song," she said too loudly. "Please, please! Change your freaking ringtone!"

He was rarely profane, but he made up for it while he dug the phone out again and snapped it open. "Listen, Sylvia, I am trying to —"

He fell silent. Even though the phone was pressed hard against his ear, Tracy could hear Sylvia's voice, like a coloratura practicing scales before a concert. Up and down, up and down. Marsh didn't say a word.

Tracy turned up her hands in question. "Bay?"

He shook his head, still listening.

"Okay, I'll be there shortly," he said at last. He put the phone back in his pocket.

Tracy waited. The silence — if you could call LeAnn Rimes wailing over the speakers silence — extended. Finally he sighed.

"Sylvia was fired. She's a mess."

152

"Now? She was fired *now?*" She looked at her watch. "At eight o'clock on a Friday night? Isn't that a new low, even for a law firm?"

"I guess she's known it might be coming, but she just got the word. Of course they're saying it's the economy, that they just can't afford to keep her anymore, but it's really that case she lost. You don't lose a high-profile case and live to tell about it."

Tracy really didn't care. This was the woman who, from the moment of Bay's birth, had always put her job first and her baby son on hold. This was the same woman who had been mooching off Marsh for almost two weeks but still didn't know whether Bay could have strawberries on his ice cream.

This was the woman who'd made it perfectly clear to Tracy that she would fight to the bitter end for her ex-husband, even if she didn't really want him.

She struggled to sound logical and calm. "I'm sorry, Marsh, but what exactly does she expect you to do about this on an empty stomach?"

"I don't think she expects me to do anything except listen. But I'm worried about Bay. She's a mess. He shouldn't have to deal with his mother when she's like this."

Bay. Not Sylvia's beloved son, Bay. Sylvia's secret weapon, Bay. Sylvia knew Marsh, and she knew that nothing would stop him from shielding their little boy from emotional distress.

"Do you think she really just found out?" she asked.

"What do you mean?"

"I mean maybe she's known all along. Maybe she chose this moment to tell you because you're out with me."

"That's paranoid and clueless."

She bristled, and all caution fled. "And you're clueless if you think she's not capable of something like that. Look, she's been here almost two weeks. How many phone calls has she gotten from her law firm while you've been there? How much work was she actually doing? I bet she was fired before she —"

"Look, leave my ex-wife to me, okay?" He was angry now. She could see it in his eyes and the hunch of his shoulders. "You've got enough on your hands with your imagination and your fantasies."

"Imagination?"

"Right. All these CJ appearances. I know where I stand with Sylvia, and I know I wouldn't take her back for anything, no matter what she says or does. But maybe the same's not true for you. Maybe that's why you keep seeing your ex everywhere. Maybe you're hoping he really will come back and hand you that silver platter life you lost."

She stared at him. For a moment she thought maybe she saw the beginning of remorse creeping across his features, but even if she was right, it was too late. She took a deep breath, but the voice that emerged did not sound like hers.

"Don't forget to tell the hostess we won't need that table. Or hey, maybe I ought to grab it anyway. Maybe the phantom CJ will sit across from me and keep me company. Of course, this kind of place isn't really CJ's thing. He'd probably like the yacht club a lot better."

She gave one short nod in goodbye, then she wound her way through the porch crowd and the parking lot and unlocked her car door. Marsh didn't follow, but she hadn't expected him to. The last thing she heard from Skeeter's was a woman she didn't recognize singing the unfortunate choice, "How Can I Help You Say Goodbye?"

"I don't need a bit of help, thanks," she said, as she revved her engine and took off for home.

CHAPTER EIGHT

Tracy had calmed down just a fraction by the time she passed the sign that announced she was now in Happiness Key. Happiness Key was the last piece of private property on the north end of Palmetto Grove Key — a prime piece, however, that stretched from bay to gulf and nearly out to the point, which was protected public land. To this day Tracy wasn't certain why CJ had put the land in her name without explanation, and how he had managed, somehow, to protect it sufficiently so that this shabby old collection of shabby old cottages had not been seized after his arrest, along with everything else that belonged to them.

Once upon a time the property had been called Happiness Haven, a quasi resort with ten cottages, a rental office, and plans for a modest-sized motel and miniature golf course. Even though development plans had stalled, and nobody had been as happy as they should have been, the complex had stayed in the same family until it became so run-down, there was no hope of expansion. One by one, five cottages and the office had fallen to the wrecking ball.

When the last family member finally gave up and left Florida, CJ snapped up the property. He spent a small fortune securing permits, having plans drawn up, finding ways to circumvent myriad statutes so that the ecologically sensitive land could be developed. Then history and infamy collided. Florida real estate went from gold mine to black hole, and the Feds swooped in to part CJ and all his investments forever.

Or at least Tracy had thought it would be forever.

Now CJ was out of prison. If he stayed out, she wondered what he would do with the rest of his life. She was fairly sure whatever it was wouldn't involve her. When she looked back on it, she realized her life with CJ Craimer had been built on lies. She had loved his power and status. At most he had loved her nubile young body and pliability. And could he be faulted? There'd been nothing much else worth loving. Tracy's moral compass had pointed toward the Bel-Air Country Club and Rodeo Drive. Until CJ's arrest, she had never questioned it.

Still contemplating her life, she parked in her driveway and stayed behind the wheel. She was furious at Marsh and his double

157

standard. From negotiations over the Happiness Key conservation easement, she knew he could be intractable, even arrogant. But the man under the cocksure cynicism was a sensitive guy with a big heart, a man willing to give up a partnership in a top Manhattan firm to earn a fraction of that income managing a grassroots environmental organization. His consummate skill and bulldog tenacity had turned Wild Florida into a force to be reckoned with. And his devotion to his son told her everything else she needed to know about him.

So why was Marsh falling into Sylvia's trap? No matter what he claimed, did he, like his son, harbor hope of reconciliation?

Darkness had fallen, and Tracy saw she'd forgotten to leave a light on inside. Not surprisingly, Happiness Key had no streetlamps. The bulb on her porch light needed to be replaced, and tonight even the stars were blanketed by clouds. She felt completely alone and insignificant in a way she had never experienced until she moved out to the key. Marsh had taught her to appreciate the wilderness beyond her house, but tonight she wasn't that fond of it.

She opened her door to the cacophony of a Florida evening. In one direction she heard the squawk of seagulls, and from the other the whirring of insects and croaking of marsh dwellers. She contemplated the remainder of her night, and decided she would slide into bed and pull the covers over her head.

Halfway up the walkway to her house, she heard movement behind her. Not directly, but something that sounded like footsteps on the road. She debated between whirling to see what or who was there, and making a run for the door. With a lock between her and whatever was out there, she could peek through the window to her heart's content.

Peek and never see a darned thing worth seeing.

She whirled, ready to cut loose with a scream if she needed to. She thrust her keys in front of her, ready to strike out with them.

"I wouldn't want to face *you* in a dark alley," said a familiar voice.

Tracy was more surprised that the man had already gotten so close than she was at the man himself. For a moment she couldn't speak. Her heart seemed to be rooted in her larynx.

Finally she gathered herself enough to answer. "Seems like you would have picked up some pretty good self-defense skills where you've been, CJ."

He smiled ruefully but looked perfectly relaxed. "If you're not careful, that's not the only thing you can pick up in a place like Victorville."

Tracy studied her ex-husband until the pounding in her throat had dropped back to

159

her chest. Then she regained control with a shrug. "Would you like a glass of wine? That is, if you'd like a break from skulking around in the dark. I hate to get in the way of a steady job."

"Florida's been good for your sense of humor."

"I had to develop one or curl up and die."

"It sits well on you."

She turned around and started toward her door. "I have to make a phone call. But come in and make yourself at home. Just don't plan to make it a habit."

"Just to let you know, Marsh," she said into the kitchen telephone a few minutes later. "CJ is sitting in my living room right now. I haven't been imagining him. Maybe I'll follow your example and invite him to live with me. It seems to be working so well for you."

Then she slammed the receiver back into its cradle.

"If I'd thought I might be invited back into your bed, I wouldn't have moved into Edward Statler's guest house," CJ said, from behind her.

Tracy took her time turning around.

"A sense of humor isn't the only thing I've developed," she said. "My bullshit meter is so finely tuned I can't even watch the news, in case they interview a politician."

"That's a good thing to have. It can save

your life."

"For starters, it would have saved me from marrying you."

He held up his hands. "I didn't come all this way to dig up the past."

Tracy examined the man she'd been married to. A little more than a year in prison hadn't exactly agreed with CJ, but the lines imprisonment had engraved on his face sat well enough there.

CJ was a man women always looked twice at, then tried for a third if he happened to notice them. With a head of thick, curly silvering hair, expressive dark eyes and an assertive nose, along with olive skin that tanned at the slightest provocation, CJ looked more Italian than German or Dutch, as the Craimer name suggested. But while sorting family papers after his arrest, Tracy had learned that until age twenty-two and a brief court appearance, CJ's surname had been the Lebanese "Karam," a name that ironically meant "kind and generous."

Of course he *had* been generous enough with her. For no apparent reason, he had deeded her Happiness Key.

"So why have you been skittering around the edges of my life instead of just coming right to my front door?" she asked.

"Didn't you mention wine?"

"It's not a vintage you'd appreciate, but considering where you've been, I guess you won't spit it out." She opened a cupboard and considered the bottle of wine Marsh had brought the night of her first CJ sighting, then nixed it. This occasion was nothing to celebrate.

Instead she found the corkscrew and opened a bottle of grocery store red, a sale wine she'd actually developed a fondness for, and set it on the counter to let it breathe.

CJ lounged, looking for all the world like somebody posing for a GQ photo shoot. Her ex-husband wore clothes as if he never gave a thought to what he put on his body, looking relaxed and elegant simultaneously. For all she knew, he'd rooted through a Dumpster to clothe himself in these twill pants and subtly printed shirt, but he looked as if he'd just walked out of Neiman Marcus or Saks.

"I held off approaching you because I didn't know how I would be received," he said.

"Apparently you finally decided to find out. After making me think I was losing my mind every time I caught sight of you."

"The male ego's funny. It was one thing when you divorced me the moment the Feds closed in, but the possibility you might slam the door in my face now that I'm out was too much."

"I could jump up and down on your ego in my spikiest Manolo Blahnik heels and never do the slightest damage." Tracy reached for two wineglasses, then opened the refrigerator and rummaged for food. Right this minute she was sorrier that she and Marsh had never shelled a single shrimp at Skeeter's than she was about the fight. CJ on an empty stomach was twice as upsetting.

He changed the subject. "I can't believe you moved into this place."

"Where else was I going to go?" She spotted a wedge of low-fat cheddar, and emerged a moment later with the cheese, a carton of fresh strawberries and four oatmeal cookies Olivia had baked last weekend. Olivia had given her a dozen. She was afraid to think where the other eight had gone.

By now CJ was rummaging through her utensil drawer. "I thought you'd sell this quick, move to some resort area and find yourself a brand-new husband."

"Somebody I could live off after I went through all the millions I was supposed to get for Happiness Key?" Tracy didn't even pretend to be angry. She was too hungry, and too off-kilter. "Didn't sound good to me. I went the rich husband route once, without great results. I've sworn off rich men and sociopaths."

"I hope that last doesn't refer to me."

"Not while you're holding that knife, it doesn't." Tracy took the cheese knife away from him, then got a plate for the food and held it out to him. "Let's eat at the table. I'll pour the wine."

They were seated, and she was opening crackers she'd found in the cabinet, before it occurred to her how charmingly domestic this looked. CJ home from the wars, fed and pampered by the little wifey. She almost snorted.

"I don't remember the house being this nice," he said.

"You mean you actually came inside? Why? You were planning to bulldoze everything in sight."

"We were renting the cottages, remember? Until we could start? I was just making sure they were habitable until we were ready to demolish them."

"Apparently you didn't look very hard. I've spent a small fortune making repairs. I did the ones in here myself. I even put down the floor."

He smiled, disbelieving. The man had a fabulous smile, made more fabulous against his olive skin. Tracy had always thought that without it, he would have been so ordinary, nobody would have taken his get-rich schemes seriously. With an overbite CJ would have been an accountant or a mortgage broker, cheating high school English teachers and veterinarians. Instead, his grin had catapulted him to a position where he'd been able to cheat supermodels, discount store tycoons and trust-fund babies.

"I did almost everything," she said. "You'd be amazed at what I can do. I found a job running the recreation program in town. I'm everybody's favorite landlady. Even little kids adore me. The brand-new Tracy Deloche."

"I thought you were pretty good the way you were."

Okay. So she was feeling low as a lizard. Marsh was shacked up with his ex-wife and refused to see Sylvia for the schemer she was. His son was so thrilled to have Mommy in the house that he had probably forgotten Tracy's name. She knew she was ripe for flattery. So why did she let his words make her feel just a tiny bit better?

She didn't let on, of course. That would be like feeding the local alligators and not expecting them to grab an arm or a leg for dessert. Instead she asked the obvious question.

"What are you doing in Florida? More accurately, what are you doing in my house?"

"Where else was I going to go?"

He had purposely echoed her words, but she wondered if they were true. "What made you think you were wanted *here?*"

"If by *here* you mean *your life,* I didn't. But as soon as the news broke that I was out, Edward Statler got in touch and suggested I stay with him as long as I wanted to. Since I'm only big news on the West Coast, I figured this would be a good place to hang

165

for now."

She pondered that. CJ had never lacked for friends. He gave gifts lavishly, bailed out the down-and-outers when he could, befriended other people's castoffs. Of course, through the years, she'd noted he frequently called in favors, too. How could anybody say no to the man who had stood up for him in a pinch? A man who had generously held out a hand when it was most needed? She wondered if this Edward Statler had owed CJ something, and if he'd been forced to offer help. She was certain there were other places her ex could have gone, other friends who couldn't avoid paying him back.

"You have friends all over the world." Tracy picked up a strawberry by the stem and bit into it to give herself time to think. "You want me to believe that this Statler, whoever he is, was the only one who offered you refuge?"

"How many people extended their hands to *you?*"

She nearly winced. CJ's aim was excellent. "But I was just the eye candy, CJ. *You* were the one they owed."

"You forget, I was the one who took their money and never gave it back."

"Good point. It's hard to love somebody who steals everything you have."

"Something I never did."

"So you said."

"So I *say.* I trusted the wrong people, but I

could have cleaned up that mess. Only then I was targeted by a prosecutor trying to make a name for himself. They tied things up so tight I couldn't get back in to fix the problems. I'm fairly confident that's what a better investigation will show, and I'll be completely vindicated, even get back some of my assets or at least some portion of their value. Edward believes it, too. He stood by me then, and he's opened his home now to prove he still believes. He's even trying to find something I can do here to put my talents to good use."

CJ's situation was so complicated that Tracy had never understood every nuance. But she did know there had been more to the charges than what he was claiming now, real evidence that things had been amiss in her husband's multitude of businesses. She found it hard to believe all that evidence had been concocted.

"Well, we've covered why you're in Florida. Let's move on to why you're sitting at my table."

"Because I turned down a dinner party at Edward's so I could come out here."

"We're getting closer to the truth." She plunked cheese on a cracker and ate it in one big bite.

"I don't remember you eating with such relish," he said.

"The cooks around here are less interested in presentation than flavor. The food's too

167

good not to eat."

"Well, the extra weight agrees with you."

"What?"

"Ten pounds? Don't worry about it. What's ten or fifteen pounds?"

She shoved her plate away and ignored her wine. "I haven't gained an ounce. I run after kids all day. I jog, I swim, I play tennis whenever I can."

"You did all those things at home, except for the kids, but you ate like a sparrow. I never thought you liked kids. What's that about?"

"I'm unaccountably good with them. And I mean it. I haven't gained weight."

"It would be hard not to, if you've learned to enjoy eating. I might gain some myself. Have you been to the yacht club? The chef is talented."

"I see prison didn't interfere with your ability to ignore questions you don't want to answer."

"I don't remember you ever asking any before. I admired that in you."

"Admire no more. I'm a get-to-the-bottom-of-it kind of gal these days. And I want to know why you're sitting here."

He fiddled with the cheese. She figured an untrained monkey could have managed to plop cheddar on a cracker in half the time. Finally he met her eyes.

"I owe you something."

"What? A slap in the face for my so-called desertion? At the time, you said I *ought* to divorce you."

"Did you need my approval?"

Tracy knew better than to attempt to read CJ's expression. His dark eyes could convey almost anything, an asset nearly as powerful as his smile. Still, the man looked hurt, maybe even genuinely so, as if the speed with which she had divorced him still throbbed.

"Did we have the kind of relationship where loyalty meant something?" she countered. "I was a trophy wife. Maybe I hoped the third time was going to be a charm for you, but I grew up watching marriages fall apart. I really wasn't expecting ours to last forever."

"I was hoping it would."

She sat back. "Well, you didn't factor prison into that equation, I guess."

"I'm sorry."

For a moment she wasn't sure she'd heard him correctly. "You're sorry?"

"That I couldn't make the charges go away. That I thought I could fix everything. That I waited so long to tell you I couldn't."

"I remember that afternoon in the sun-room. You probably showed the same amount of emotion when you told your janitorial staff to dust off their résumés after they finished the baseboards."

"Somebody else told *them*. I didn't know any other way to tell you except to lay out the facts. I was dying inside. I wanted to preserve something. I wanted to look strong in the face of disaster."

She thought about that. "I don't think a good marriage is about looking strong, CJ. But ours wasn't a good marriage, and there's no way you can fix that now. I don't want anything from you, except maybe an explanation of why you put Happiness Key in my name. That's a mystery I'd love to solve."

He didn't hesitate. "Wasn't that obvious? To protect you. In case things got completely out of control."

"Because my happiness was such a high priority?"

"If worse came to worst, I wanted you to have something left."

"You must have known I really *couldn't* sell it, not with all the problems inherent in developing such an environmentally fragile property."

"I took care of that."

"Sure," she scoffed. "You got permits, but you had to know they'd be challenged in court. And you're too smart not to have realized land in Florida was going to plummet in value when the economy faltered. So why this, instead of something more easily converted to cash? Like our art collection? Or the house in Bel-Air?"

Again he had an answer handy. "Happiness Key was farther away and easier to bury in

170

paperwork than our house or anything else. And *I* could have worked around those obstacles you cited. I was sure you'd find a developer who was willing to buy the property and work around them, too. Instead you pissed it away and handed it over to your boyfriend at Wild Florida."

She crossed her arms. "I see you've been doing more than skulking in the shadows. You know about the conservation easement?"

"Edward's in land development. In fact, we were going to develop Happiness Key together. When I arrived, he told me what you'd done."

"Funny, I don't remember Edward's name on any documents, and I don't remember him offering to take the property off my hands when I was trying to sell it. I've never met the man."

"A friend doesn't get rich off another friend's misery. Edward hoped I'd get out in time to help you develop it myself."

"Now it can't be developed. Which brings us back to what you think you owe me."

This time he hesitated, as if he had to piece the words together. Finally he looked away. "They may retry me. I may go back to prison, although I think it's unlikely. But after one rigged trial, I could be a candidate for a second. If that happens, I want to know for sure you're okay, even if it's my last act as a free man."

171

"Brutal," she said sarcastically. "Do we need to call for the violins?"

He looked back at her. "I'm serious. You've been on my mind every single day. The mess I left you was my only real regret. I don't want that on my conscience anymore. I want you to be financially secure."

"Don't trouble yourself. I'll be okay. Not rich, but okay. And there's nothing you can do here. The easement's very specific."

"There are things *you* can do. The easement's public record, and I've seen it. You can build cottages on the foundations of the buildings that were demolished. Six more, counting the site where the rental office stood. And you can fix up the ones that are here, add wings, garages or carports, any number of serious improvements, so they're worth at least twice what they are now."

He turned up his hands. "There's a lot you can do, Tracy. None of it begins to compare with what we *could* have done, if you hadn't gotten all misty-eyed about the environment, but it'll bring you a strong, steady income. Plus, when you're ready to sell, improvements will make the property that much more appealing, even with an easement."

"And what do you get? Peace of mind?"

He got to his feet and went to the sink, and filled a glass from the tap. He stayed there, leaning against the counter, watching her.

"Do you think you're the only one who's

gone through a transformation? You talk about my ego? Is change your personal territory? I've been in prison. Do you have any idea what that's like? And it's worse when you know you shouldn't be there. The only good thing? I had time to reflect, and I didn't like what I found. I don't know how long I'll be free. For that matter, I don't know how long I'll be alive. I'd like to do this so I can feel good about something in my life before I lose it again, one way or the other."

Tracy was surprised at her rush of emotion. She wasn't falling for everything CJ said. She was no fool. But she couldn't discount it all, either. Victorville was not Club Fed, and she was sure her ex-husband's sojourn there had been traumatic. Maybe it *had* been enlightening, as well. Who was she to determine whether he was telling at least some of the truth?

Score one for CJ, then. But how about Marsh? What would he say if he discovered CJ was looking into developing Happiness Key in accordance with the conservation easement? She could just imagine the fireworks.

She had one man, her ex-husband, who swore he wanted to take care of her and one who was busy taking care of his own ex-wife. The irony wasn't lost on her.

"So you've been checking out possibilities?"

173

she said. "That's what you've been doing out here?"

"I wanted to have something on paper to show you. I've got enough information now to draw that up. Do you want me to?" He set his glass on the counter. "I am a developer, or was. And I know this property as well as I knew my childhood backyard. I'm your man for this."

"You won't be my man for anything else," she cautioned. "I'm not interested in a reunion. We weren't good for each other when we were married. We wouldn't be good for each other now. And there's another man in my life. . . ." Or had been until tonight.

"Not one worthy of you." He held up his hand when she started to protest. "You're a class act, Tracy, and always were. Sure, you were young when we got married, immature and maybe a little spoiled. But you were special, too special to waste yourself on a man who's running a nothing little environmental organization because he can't make the grade anywhere else."

Despite herself, she rose to Marsh's defense. "If that's the way things are going to go here, please don't come back. My personal life is off-limits."

"I just don't want you to make another mistake."

"Meaning I made one the first time?"

"Undoubtedly. And I made one when I lost

you." He held up his hand again. "But I did lose you. I know that. Just let me see what I can do for you. It'll help us both, and give me something to do while I wait and see what's happening in California."

"Nobody's going to believe this."

"Does that mean you'll let me put something together?"

She tried but failed to see how that could hurt. Besides, CJ's involvement would annoy Marsh no end, and right now, that seemed a plus — even though it also proved she was not as mature as she'd hoped.

She rose. "We'll see how it goes."

"I'd like to poke around in the daylight a bit, if that's okay. You'll let the renters know they don't have to worry if they see me around?"

"They aren't just renters. They're my friends. All of them."

He seemed amused. "I'll remember that."

"We take care of each other. I'm warning you."

He gave a mock half salute. "I've been warned."

Tracy walked him to the door. The wine was untouched on the table, but as far as she was concerned, they were finished for the night.

He paused. "It really is good to see you again." Then, before she could stop him, he leaned down and kissed her cheek.

He was on his way out to the road before she tried to summon a response. Even then, she wasn't sure anything could adequately explain the way she felt. She finally just closed the door.

CHAPTER NINE

On Monday morning CJ arrived just in time for coffee. Tracy was sleepily fumbling to fill her new single shot coffeemaker when he tapped on her front door, then poked his head inside before she could answer.

"You really ought to keep this locked," he told her.

From the kitchen doorway she blinked in her ex's direction, remembering any number of mornings when he had started her day with advice. CJ was a born advisor, always certain he was right, and unfortunately, far too often right about that, as well.

"No duh." She turned back to the counter and pushed the requisite buttons before she faced him again. "If I'd locked the door, you'd still be on the other side."

"You always were cutest in the morning."

She was wearing knit boxers and a tank top, and CJ had seen her in less, of course. Still, she wished she'd pulled on a robe. CJ was too smart to actually stare, but his eyes were definitely not riveted on her face. Something stirred inside her, and she felt herself flush.

"So you noticed I was cute when?" she asked. "Between phone calls to the office? Or maybe between telling me what I ought to wear and whose friendship I should cultivate?"

"You were a work in progress. I couldn't resist."

"I wasn't *progressing* one bit. It took our divorce to jump-start that." She leaned against the counter, arms folded protectively across her breasts. "So why are you up so early. I'm assuming not just to stare at my legs."

"I was hoping for a cup of coffee."

"I have regular and decaf." She gestured to the coffeemaker. "I bet you can figure this out. Make your own while I change."

She grabbed her cup and took it into the bathroom with her. Unfortunately, with the cup came an image of a morning early in their marriage when CJ had followed her into a much more luxurious bathroom, and they'd taken a shower that had tested even the state-of-the-art water heater in their Bel-Air home.

After one cool shower, a minimal amount of primping and a silent reminder that old intimacies were best forgotten, she came back into the kitchen wearing jeans and a blue Palmetto Grove Rec Center polo shirt with her name and Staff embroidered on the pocket. CJ had not only made himself coffee, he'd produced toast with butter and jam for both of them.

He held up her plate. "When do you leave?"

"In a little while. I usually run first, but apparently not today. You still haven't said why you're here."

"To make sure you eat breakfast."

"One minute you tell me I've gained weight, the next you're fattening me up." She took the toast and bit into it without sitting down. "I was married to you, remember? What I eat and when never concerned you one bit."

"Food becomes important when you lose the freedom to choose *what* you're eating and *when*."

She wasn't sure it was the words or the way he said them that momentarily pushed past her defenses. "I guess prison wasn't much fun."

"It was a year-long root canal. Without Novocaine."

"Why did you let it get to that point? You're a smart guy. You must have known the good guys were closing in. Why didn't you just get out of town?"

"I was positive I was going to beat the whole thing. I underestimated how badly they wanted to take me down."

She was starting to feel sympathy, a bad sign. She set her plate and half-eaten toast on the counter. "Is the chitchat over? I really need to get moving."

"I'm actually here to give you a list of the problems I found."

"Did you talk to any of my neighbors while you were sneaking around their houses?"

"You mean did I blacken your name with your friends? No, I was discreet. I waited until people were gone."

She said a silent thank-you. She had announced CJ's return to her incredulous friends, who had for the most part been startled into silence. She had taken that rare occurrence as a sign and fled, and avoided them since. She had little stomach for what they might say. She would have to introduce him sooner or later, but later sounded better.

CJ took a small pad from the inside pocket of his sport coat. "You've got issues with the cottages that are still standing —"

"Tell me about it. I was on a first name basis with Handy Hubby until they moved out of the area last month. Unfortunately for them, people are walking away from their houses, not fixing them up."

CJ pulled several sheets of paper off the pad and handed them to her. "Well, that's lucky for you. There'll be a bunch of unemployed guys dying to do the work. At cheaper rates, too, without a referral service."

She scanned the pages. Problems with the foundation on Janya's cottage. Possible roof repair or replacement at Wanda's. She looked up. "I had a leak patched over Wanda's bathroom right after I moved in."

"Stopgap measure. How many buckets does she have?"

She was reading again. "Outside wiring at Alice's? And you really think there's a problem with the well and the pump?"

"One of these days you'll wake up and find it's as dry as the Mojave at Happiness Key."

"Man . . ." She shook her head. "What did you do to me, CJ?"

"What was the point of making long-term repairs when the whole place was going to be smashed flat and hauled away?"

The list was too depressing to contemplate. "I'm assuming you're not volunteering to take on these projects yourself."

He smiled, and she had to admit that the way the smile creased his cheeks and warmed his eyes was charm itself. "I don't get my hands dirty, TK. You know that."

CJ had called her TK from the moment he'd discovered her middle name was Katherine. They'd been a matched set. If they'd had kids, they could have used up the alphabet. She had never liked the nickname, but for a moment it made her feel like the old Tracy, the one with the sexy, generous husband other women envied. The one whose life had been simpler.

She pulled herself back to reality. Life was *never* simple.

"I bet you got your hands dirty at Victorville," she said, folding the pages in half. "Or did you wheedle your way into an office job?"

"There were better wheedlers, so I started out washing pots and pans. Eventually they moved me to record keeping."

"Because you promised somebody something."

"What could I promise? I didn't have anything left."

She stuffed the pages in her pocket. "I've got to get going. Thanks. I suppose now I'll have to look into all these repairs."

"I put them in order of importance. Some can wait a good long time. I can supervise and make sure you're not getting cheated. Edward has a slew of guys who work for him. I'll get names."

"No way. I'll find somebody on my own. The only thing I know about Edward Statler is that you two were going into business together. I'd like to keep him far, far away from Happiness Key."

He looked amused. "I'll keep poking around, unless you don't want me here. I owe you."

"So you do. But, I'll warn you, I don't think that's all there is to this."

"I need something to do while I contemplate my navel, okay? You know how much I hate to sit still. So I'm killing two birds with one stone. I'm paying a debt to you, and I'm rethinking my life."

That she didn't buy. "You know what? I *do* know you. The moment you had all your limbs and a beating heart, you decided you were going to take over the world. I can't believe you have anything to rethink, CJ, unless you're planning how to make good use of this little mess you got yourself into."

"If I could take over the world, TK, I'd lay it at your feet."

She snatched the empty coffee cup out of his hand and plopped it on the counter. "You are such a con artist." But even to her own ears, she sounded half-hearted.

"You don't mind having me around? I'd like to work on house plans using the footprint of those old cottages. I can work up a development plan for you. Nobody else is going to bother. There's nothing in it for them."

She didn't buy any of this. Still, while CJ was feeling philanthropic and even, possibly, sentimental, he might actually be of some use to her.

She gave a slight nod. "But you do anything even halfway bogus and you're out of here."

"You're welcome." He smiled. "Those boxers made my morning."

She steeled herself. "Don't count on ogling me again. From now on I'm sleeping in a flannel nightgown."

"Not in this heat." Smiling, he left the way he'd come.

■ ■ ■

Half bait shop, half gourmet grocery, Randall's was as much a statement about the changing character of Palmetto Grove Key as a local hangout. Tracy liked to stop on the way into work, so she could rub shoulders with bare-chested good old boys snacking on pork rinds, or businessmen with Lincolns idling while they slipped in for a latte from Randall's brand-new cappuccino machine. The lattes were out of her price range, and the pork rinds were loaded with sodium, but splurging on a glass of freshly squeezed orange juice was a treat she allowed herself twice a week.

Today she bypassed the juice and looked for a paperback thriller. Since she seemed doomed to spend her nights alone, she needed the excitement.

Before checking out, she wandered over to the community bulletin board to see if any handymen were advertising. There was a similar board at the rec center, which she planned to check, as well. She jotted down two possibilities, then tore off a sheet of paper and scrawled her own ad.

Jack-of-all-trades needed for a variety of house repairs on Palmetto Grove Key.

She added her home and cell numbers, and

tacked the ad at eye level between a circular for a local Baptist church and photos of a new litter of water spaniels.

As she stepped back, a tall man with broad shoulders came up beside her and gazed at her contribution. "Jack-of-all-trades?"

She took her time examining him. She liked what she saw, but apparently she had a fondness for sociopaths. Take CJ, for instance.

The guy was in his middle forties. Nice enough to look at, but not handsome. Rugged was a better word, more like somebody who sloshed through the Everglades in waders, hunting ducks or alligators. He had short dark hair, a cleft chin and five o'clock shadow at eight o'clock in the morning.

"I own five houses up the road toward the point, and they all need repairs," she said. "I'm hoping I can find one person to do the work. Simpler that way."

"You need permits?"

She shrugged. "Maybe. I don't know. I won't be looking over anybody's shoulder." CJ might be looking, but she suspected her ex was a no-permit kind of guy.

"How about licenses?"

"I don't know what Florida requires." She paused. "Maybe I don't want to know."

"I'm from out west, but I'm staying around for at least a couple of months, and I'm looking for something to do when I'm not fishing." He grinned, a white splash against tanned skin. "Fishing comes first."

"How first?"

"I could probably give you twenty hours a week. More to start, if it's an emergency, especially if there's someplace to fish near your property."

"No emergency, and I bet there are places to fish *on* my property. You're welcome to them. Can you do anything in twenty hours?"

"If I work hard and fast, which I do."

"You have experience?"

"I built a couple of hunting cabins, just for fun. Wired them, did the plumbing, you name it. The sale of the first one helped me retire sooner than I expected."

"Retired?"

"Military. I'm taking a sabbatical, if you want to call it that. Traveling around, trying to decide where I'll hang out in the winter. I like it here, so I'm going to stay awhile to see if I still like it when the new wears off."

She held out her hand. "I'm Tracy Deloche."

Without crushing her fingers, he gripped them hard enough to let her know he meant business. "Pete Knight."

"I was going to check around to figure out what to pay."

"Fifteen bucks an hour to start, in cash, no paperwork. If we're happy together, you'll raise it to keep me. You'll be happy."

"There's a water pump, a leaky roof, some

wiring. . . ."

"If I can't handle something alone, I'll find the right person to back me up."

She didn't know what else she could ask for. Fifteen dollars an hour sounded like a steal. Of course, if Pete Knight worked at turtle speed, she would be wasting her money, but then she could fire him.

"I'll think about it," she said, "but I'm interested. Do you have a number?"

He jotted it on a scrap of paper, and she thanked him. In the checkout line, she looked back to make one more assessment, but Pete Knight was already gone.

Ten minutes later she parked in front of the Henrietta Claiborne Recreation Center and gathered her things for the day ahead. Almost a year ago, against her better judgment, she had taken the job as recreational supervisor. She had a degree in recreation and leisure studies, though only limited experience, but the director had been desperate.

In college the degree had seemed a perfect choice. She was an expert on leisure time, plus she'd always been good at athletics. With a little more effort and a lot more interest, she might even have excelled at some sport and gone professional. But Tracy had been content to spend her hours on golf courses and tennis courts trolling for a husband.

Now she was grateful that laziness had led her in this direction. She had no idea why she was good at managing a complicated agenda, instilling order in the ranks of the young and old, and creating programs to entice people through the rec center doors, but she liked her job, liked the kids — who were her first priority — the seniors, the facility, the rest of the staff.

She was particularly surprised she got along so well with the kids, never having given more than a passing thought to having children someday. Sometimes she thought detachment was the reason she excelled. She had nothing invested in rejection or messes or rebellion. The kids knew she wasn't easily impressed by misbehavior, so they gave up quickly. Since she was genuinely pleased when they made her life simpler, they complied.

This morning, as early as she was, people were already streaming in and out of the building. Two weeks before, the center had initiated sunrise exercise classes for residents on their way to work. Plus the indoor pool now opened at seven. Tracy greeted the regulars and smiled at the rest. By the time she made it through the glass doors leading down the dusky rose hallway to the reception desk, she had already made a mental note to see if Woody, the director, might agree to set up a coffee urn. She just had to work out the details first, so she wasn't the one in charge of keeping it filled.

Gladys Woodley, Woody's wife and the

receptionist, was already in place behind her desk. Gladys was a middle-aged woman completely comfortable in her own skin, which was now stretched to capacity. Always overweight, in the past year she had added another fifteen pounds and vaulted up a dress size. At least once a week she threatened to diet, but so far she hadn't chosen a plan.

"It looks like the sunrise classes are paying off," Tracy said in greeting. "And I bet they'll be better attended as the weather gets hotter and outdoor exercise loses its appeal."

"We just had our biggest class. And the swimmers were waiting at the door when Miriam arrived to let them in." Miriam was the swim instructor and lifeguard who ran the morning programs.

Gladys handed Tracy a stack of mail, including several professional journals. "We have news. Do you have time?"

"Always, if it's good."

Gladys leaned forward, which was getting harder. "It's excellent. Henrietta Claiborne is coming to town."

The recreation center was named for Mrs. Claiborne, the benefactor who had presented a check to the mayor after her Jaguar broke down in Palmetto Grove on her way from her Palm Beach home to her home in Newport, Rhode Island. Mrs. Claiborne had been so impressed with the courtesy and honesty of Palmetto Grove's citizens that she had written a check on the spot. The mayor, who fully expected the check to bounce, had waited a week to deposit it so the eccentric old woman had a head start. No one was more surprised than he when the check went through and suddenly Palmetto Grove had the funds it needed to build a state-of-the-art recreation complex.

"She's coming to visit?" Like most people at the center, Tracy had never met Henrietta Claiborne.

"She's coming for a banquet in her honor. The mayor and council arranged it. We'll have it here, of course. It's going to be a very big deal."

"When?"

"A lot sooner than we'd like. She's a little hard to pin down — the mayor's been trying for months. She's got a very full social calendar, but she finally agreed to May 23. The invitations are being printed this afternoon, and we hope to have them in the mail no later than tomorrow."

"Wow. I guess this will be a big deal."

Gladys lowered her voice. "The biggest. It's very important that *everybody* pays attention to Henrietta and treats her like the benefactor she is. She's everybody's darling, and any word that she hasn't been treated like a queen will get back to the mayor, even if Henrietta doesn't tell them."

Tracy smiled brightly. "You're talking to

the wrong woman. I'm nice to everybody."

"Really? I heard a rumor you had another run in with the shuffle board."

"I had no idea there was a flock of old men sneaking up on the marsh, much less the shuffle board!"

"They're still talking about it."

"You make one mistake around here . . ."

"Find a way to get back in their good graces."

"Maybe I can trap that bird they were looking for and have it stuffed. Would that still count for their life lists?"

Gladys glared at her.

"I'm kidding." Tracy shook her head. "I'll think of something."

"And you'll put your best effort into making Henrietta Claiborne feel welcome?"

"Of course. She may never want to leave."

"You'll be expected to attend and show her what you've been doing. Displays would be nice. But you'll need to get right on it. You don't have a lot of time." The telephone rang, and Gladys lifted her hand in farewell.

As the day progressed, Tracy thought about ways she could impress Mrs. Claiborne. She had supervised the placement of a large bulletin board in the corridor leading to the pool and locker rooms, and she decided to ask Janya to help her plan a splashy collage using photos from the past summer's youth camp. She had trophies and ribbons that various rec center teams had won, and photos to go with them.

By the end of the day, though, she had added something punchier. She would select children she could count on and ask each to memorize a paragraph about rec center activities. Then she would station them, in uniform, along Henrietta Claiborne's route. Who wouldn't be impressed by cute, well-mannered kids in soccer uniforms and swim team garb, rattling on about how much they loved being here?

By five she was preparing to head home when the door to her office flew open and Bay Egan sprinted in. He had his swim team bag clutched under one arm and two untied shoelaces. Tracy jumped up to catch him and Bay fell straight into her arms.

"Don't let them get me!"

"Who's after you this time?" She set him away from her but kept her hands on his shoulders, just in case.

"I'm s'posed to be waiting for my mom on the front bench, only she's late, so I sneaked in here."

"I see. You know, we make those rules about where you're supposed to wait to keep you safe. Besides, how's she going to know where you are?"

"She'll be a while. She gets busy."

Tracy didn't know what to say to that. Now that she'd been fired, what was Sylvia so busy doing that she couldn't pick up her son?

Bay had sandy-brown hair and matching brown eyes, along with his father's smile. Maybe he had his mother's nose, Tracy wasn't sure, but if so, it was the only sign Sylvia had been involved in his creation. Of course, Sylvia hadn't been particularly involved in his infancy or early childhood, either, and now she seemed determined not to be involved all over again.

"How was swim practice?" Tracy asked. "You can tell me on the way back to the bench."

"Do I have to wait out there?"

"Tie your shoes first, okay?"

"You'll come, too?"

"It's on my way to the car."

"Swim practice was great! I did my best butterfly yet."

She socked him on the shoulder. "Good going, kid. Are you going to win us a trophy this summer?"

Bay crouched in place and tied his shoes. "I want Mom to see me swim. I want to show her I can win."

Tracy was all for winning, but she didn't like the sound of that. She tried to be generous. "She'll be proud of you no matter what."

"She doesn't like swim meets, but she said she'd come to my next one anyway. With my dad." He looked up. "I'll be like everybody else."

This was not the best conversation of Tracy's day, rating lower, if possible, than her encounter with CJ. The vision of the three Egans in a little family huddle was more than she wanted to deal with, but she liked Bay too much to shut him up. He was brimming over and had to tell somebody.

"That's great." Her tone was hollow, but he didn't notice.

"And she promised to take me to Disney World if she can find the time." He looked up. "She's real busy."

"I'm sure she is." She couldn't help herself. "Cleaning the house, cooking meals, mom stuff."

"No, lawyer stuff. She says when I grow up, I'll understand."

Tracy hoped he never did. She tried to be kind as well as generous. "I know you like having her here, even if she's not always available."

"We went on a picnic. Her, me and Dad. She got sunburned, though, so I guess she didn't like it so much."

Sylvia with a sunburn made Tracy feel a little better.

"Tonight we're going to the movies," Bay said. "Like a real family. And before we do, we're going to shop for new shoes 'cause these are crummy. On the way home!"

Now Tracy wasn't sure whether she wanted to cry or scream. The little boy was so thrilled about buying shoes with his mom, and all Sylvia had ever done to deserve his adoration was forget a birth control pill, or whatever similar lapse had caused her pregnancy.

Bay leaped to his feet. "She said I could have popcorn and a candy bar."

"Well, you're a little piggy, aren't you?" Tracy put her arm around his shoulder to guide him out the door. She couldn't take much more of this. "I bet your dad's going to make you eat a good dinner first, huh?"

"We're having catfish. Me and him caught some on Sunday while Mom was taking a nap."

Tracy played that imaginary film footage in her head. Marsh sweeping Bay out of the house so that beleaguered Sylvia could sleep in peace. The more Tracy heard, the less she liked any of it.

She wondered if Marsh was growing as enthused as his son about a long-term family reunion.

As they headed out front they chatted about the swim team. In the reception area, Tracy ran interference when Gladys nailed Bay for disappearing from the bench without telling anybody.

"I know, I already gave him the lecture," Tracy promised.

"I just had to tell Tracy stuff," Bay said. "Sorry."

Tracy and Gladys exchanged looks. Gladys

knew about Sylvia's return. Although she'd never commented, Tracy suspected Gladys had her doubts about Sylvia's intentions, too.

Tracy was gearing up to make Bay promise he would wait on the bench and not make any new field trips when she realized that Marsh had just parked and was crossing the lot toward them. He wore a suit and tie, although the latter was undone, and she suspected he'd just come from the court-house.

She really couldn't abandon Bay without looking as if she was running away. She took a deep breath.

"Hey, there's your dad," she told the little boy. "Looks like he and your mom switched places today."

She hoped Bay would run to his father, but he waited beside her for Marsh to approach.

"Where's Mom?" Bay demanded, when Marsh got close enough.

"She got caught up in some business stuff. She asked me to pick you up."

"You're late."

Marsh didn't say anything. Tracy almost felt sorry for him. Clearly Sylvia had forgotten Bay, then called Marsh at the last minute. If Marsh told his son the truth, Sylvia looked bad. If he didn't, *he* looked bad.

Tracy looked down at Bay so that she wouldn't have to look at his father. She realized the boy was empty-handed. "Did you forget your swim bag, kid?"

"Man!" Without another word, Bay took off back the way they had just come.

Marsh wasn't having any problem figuring out where to look. His eyes were riveted on her face. "Sylvia got a phone call from a firm in Fort Myers as she was leaving to get Bay. She managed to call me."

"You don't owe me an explanation."

"I thought I did. You seemed to be babysitting him."

"Funny, I don't think of it that way. We were having a conversation. I happen to like him."

"She's looking for a job in Florida, so she can be closer to Bay."

"That will be a comedown from Manhattan."

"Maybe she's tired of the rat race."

Or maybe Sylvia just wanted to keep Marsh on a shorter tether. Tracy dug for her car keys. "Well, I'm on my way home."

He put a hand on her arm to stop her and stroked the inside of her wrist with his index finger. Back and forth, slowly, with just enough pressure that Tracy felt the flutter all the way to her toes.

"Look, I'm sorry about the other night. Things got out of hand. All those interruptions . . ." He smiled a little. "I changed my ringtone."

She didn't smile back, but neither did she

pull away. She had never realized how sensuous one little finger on one narrow wrist could be.

"A cricket chirping," he elaborated. "It's not nearly as annoying."

"The ringtone was the least of it."

"And, as it turns out, you really weren't imagining your ex, were you? So I was wrong about that, too."

She melted just a fraction more. "I didn't know men could admit to imperfection. I thought it went against your basic nature. Like asking directions and reading maps."

"And were you the least bit snarky?"

She considered and finally found the strength to remove her wrist from his grasp. "No."

"I'm not falling for Sylvia's line, and you as much as said I was."

"I think what I said was that she was trying to reel you in, Marsh. I have no way of knowing if you're just nibbling at the bait or dangerously close to being filleted."

"For somebody who practically grew up on Rodeo Drive, you manage a passable fishing metaphor."

"I'm a quick study."

"So CJ is really here in Palmetto Grove?"

"He was at my house this morning."

He frowned. "You're spending time with him?"

Did she like this jealous streak? Did it make

her feel loved? She wasn't sure. At least he was paying attention.

"We've had two brief conversations," she said. "Does that qualify?"

"About what?"

"He's at loose ends. He's been making a survey of Happiness Key to see what needs to be done. And he's volunteered to draw up some plans for the old cottage sites."

"He knows about the easement?"

"He thinks I'm crazy."

"Do you really want to hang out with this guy? Remember how much trouble he caused you?"

She slapped her palm against the side of her head. "Gosh, no. Thanks. I'd completely forgotten."

"I just don't see how anything good can come of it."

"Isn't there some old expression about the pot calling the kettle black?"

"As reconciliations go, this isn't going to win any awards."

"CJ and I —"

"No, stop! I meant you and me, not you and him. I apologized, and it seems to be spinning around the stratosphere somewhere. Where's the incentive for groveling?"

"You call this groveling?"

Bay screeched to a halt beside his dad, this time with swim bag in hand. "I want Mom to help me pick out shoes, not you."

"I figured," Marsh said.

"Are we still going to the movies? All of us?"

"I haven't heard otherwise."

"Then let's go!"

"You boys run along," Tracy said. "Bay, eat some popcorn for me."

Bay wrapped his arms around Tracy's waist for a spontaneous hug, then took off for the car.

"I hate to be jealous of my own son," Marsh said. "It's not seemly."

"This is too complicated, Marsh. *We're* too complicated."

He held her gaze, and his expression was serious. "I'd like to think we can move beyond a few minor roadblocks."

"These are walking, talking, troublemaking *major* roadblocks, complete with historical markers."

"So you want to just table *us* for a while?"

She didn't. She wanted to drive home with Marsh and Bay, pack Sylvia's bags and dump the woman at the Greyhound station. But things really were more complicated than that. For now, Tracy didn't see any way she and Marsh could move forward until the road ahead was cleared of ex-spouses and the painful yearnings of one little boy.

She nodded. "I'll clean up my mess. You clean up yours. Then we'll see where we stand."

If he disagreed, he didn't say so. "That timeline is pretty indeterminate."

She melted just a little more. "Let's aim for the short side."

"At least we agree on something." Before she realized his intention, he put his hand on her cheek, but when he leaned forward to kiss her, she backed away.

His gaze never left hers, but he nodded slightly, as if the terms of their treaty were being acknowledged.

"See you around," he said.

"I'm sure you will." She watched him follow his son to the car. She was still staring at their parking spot when Marsh was on the road leading home.

CHAPTER TEN

Dana had never seen her daughter happier. In the two weeks since she and Lizzie had moved into the house on Palmetto Grove Key, Lizzie hadn't been bored for one moment. Everything was new; everything was special.

Years ago Dana had lived next door to Buddy, a floppy-eared hound, chained night and day to a post beside his doghouse. When the neighbors fenced their yard and ditched the chain, the dog suddenly had half an acre to explore. From the frolicking Dana had witnessed, the grateful hound had felt the world was his again.

Lizzie reminded Dana of Buddy, thrilled beyond measure at her good fortune and determined to make use of every moment. Olivia had loaned her an old bike, and when Lizzie wasn't pedaling along the oyster shell road, she was running from one end of the key to the other with her friend, exploring every twig and leaf, shell and piece of driftwood. She ate better, slept better. And the smiles? The smiles nearly tore Dana's heart in two.

This afternoon was no exception.

"You mean it's mine?" Lizzie looked at the metal detector in the box beside their kitchen table, then back up at her mother. "Really?"

Dana drew her daughter closer for a hug. "I told you I was going to get you a better birthday present once we settled down. New jeans and tops aren't very exciting. What's better than a metal detector for somebody who collects coins?"

"You mean I can find coins with this? Real coins?"

"Lots of stuff. Jewelry, pirate treasure, you name it."

"How'd you think of it?"

Dana stroked her daughter's curls. "A little bird told me you'd like it." Or, more honestly, a vendor at the beach flea market that morning had seen Dana eyeing the metal detector and offered a decent price. The detector was gently used and, best of all, light enough for a girl Lizzie's age. Dana had not been able to believe her luck.

"Wait until Olivia sees this!"

"You two won't dig anywhere you're not supposed to? You'll check with me before you dig too deep?"

"I might find a 1943 penny."

"Stranger things have happened."

"I need one! And a 1916 double-dated buffalo nickel."

Dana tried not to smile. "If nothing else, that will give you a great reason to examine every smidgen of dirt. I might even use it myself."

"Does this mean we're going to stay here? I don't want to move again. I really, really really like it here."

Dana tried to be both supportive and noncommittal. "I don't blame you for not wanting to move." She lifted the metal detector out of the box and held it out. "Why don't you read the directions, then you can take it over to Olivia's?"

"Why don't you come, too? Everybody will probably be there."

Dana had accepted the offer of a job at Wanda's Wonderful Pies, and she'd already given notice at the Dancing Shrimp. Because of all they'd done for her, she felt obligated to join the other women when they socialized. But a part of her worried about all the togetherness. The others seemed completely comfortable with each other, able to say whatever they pleased. She was a stranger, and there was a lot about her life she had no intention of sharing. The better she knew them, the harder that was going to be.

"I want to do some landscaping," she said, which was not untrue. "Remember? I promised Tracy that I'd do a little for her."

"Don't you like Wanda and everybody?" Lizzie asked.

"It's not that. I just want to do a little gardening, that's all."

"Sometimes I think you're scared to have friends."

Dana was surprised. "What do you mean, honey?"

"When I went to school in Alabama, some people were really mean to me. After that I didn't want to be nice to anybody, 'cause I was scared everybody would be the same way. Was somebody mean to you? Is that why you don't want to be real friends with people?"

"You never told me anything like that was going on at school."

Lizzie grimaced. "It didn't matter. We weren't there very long anyway."

"It *does* matter. You can always tell me when you're having a problem."

"Can *you* tell *me?*"

Dana could almost see her daughter growing up in front of her eyes. Sometimes Lizzie's new maturity stunned her, and sometimes it frightened her. How long would Dana be able to placate her with tiny portions of the truth?

"I guess I just haven't had time for friends," Dana said. "Maybe I've forgotten how. Maybe I'd better learn, huh?"

"Can I take the metal detector to the beach? Once I read the directions?"

Dana was glad to see the child reemerge.

"You can if you're very careful. I'll be down the road if you need me. Be home at five."

By the time Dana gathered her gardening supplies, slathered sunscreen on all skin bared by her shorts and tank top and drove up the road to the entrance to Happiness Key, Lizzie was already at Olivia's.

The beds around Dana and Lizzie's cottage hadn't looked like much before Dana started to dig, but luckily they'd been in good condition, and she'd only had to weed and turn over the sandy soil to ready them for assorted annuals she had found on clearance. Time would turn the seedlings into mounds of bloom, but even now, the effort made the cottage seem more like home.

While planting her beds, as well as a narrow strip of dirt in front of Wanda's shop and two massive pots by the shop door, she'd used up one and a half flats of annuals. Now she still had as many to plant. Since hot weather had arrived, she was running out of time.

The entrance to Happiness Key was marked by a sign that no one had bothered to remove, although now it lay on its back staring at the sky. Faded lettering announced a brand-new deluxe condominium community where happiness was guaranteed. Of course the sign was seriously outdated, but once upon a time, when this property was still called Happiness Haven, an office had stood on this site, and the foundation was still visible to anyone who searched hard enough. Right where Dana intended to plant the rest of the annuals, there had been a garden, a perfect oval carved out of the sand between the road and the driveway up to the office, with a small "wishing pond," a flourishing palm tree, coral and scarlet hibiscus, and clusters of zinnias and marigolds rimming the edges.

Although she had no intention of sharing her memories, Dana remembered exactly what the oval had looked like. She also remembered the pastel-painted houses, the playground, the cool depths of the stuccoed, red-roofed office with its soda machine and pamphlet rack detailing wondrous destinations like Cypress Gardens, Weeki Wachee Springs and Gatorland.

No traces of the palm tree or pond remained, and the driveway to the office was barely visible. A few scraggly shrubs hung on, despite weeds that were taller and in better condition.

Dana had wondered if she had the physical strength to clear the whole bed without a chain saw, but once she began, she was pleasantly surprised to find it wasn't as hard as she'd expected.

Half an hour later she stood to stretch. She was making headway, but slowly. Another half hour and she would have cleared enough room to plant, but she needed a break. She strolled to the office site and examined the debris. A few broken cinder blocks lay beside chunks of concrete. The demolition team had removed almost everything else, which Dana was glad to see. If Lizzie arrived with her metal detector — and she certainly would — she wouldn't have to contend with broken glass or roofing nails. Dana circled the perimeter, just visible because of the gravel base that had once cradled the concrete foundation and deeper pockets of concrete that had surrounded the borders.

The site looked untouched, as if once the office was demolished no one had given it another thought. Perhaps, until she had come with tools in hand today, no one had. Perhaps her memories of this welcoming place, where guests had come to buy Grape Nehi and chat, were the only memories that survived. She wished she knew.

She had just completed her examination when a dark SUV passed on the road leading to the cottages and, eventually, to the point at the end of the key. As she watched, the car slowed, then stopped at Alice's house. She frowned and shaded her eyes. A tall figure unfolded from the driver's seat, clearly a man by his height and the breadth of his shoulders. He stood without closing the door and spoke to a woman who had intercepted him. She thought it was Tracy, although at this distance, with most of her body shielded, Dana couldn't be sure. As she watched, the man shut the door, and the two started up the path to Alice's.

For a moment the world went dark. Lizzie might be in that house, and a strange man was on his way inside. This could be perfectly innocent. The man could be a friend of Alice's; he might be there to read a meter or take a survey. Maybe he was just asking for directions and needed Alice's advice.

Or maybe her worst fears had finally come true.

Dana started up the road to see, leaving her tools in a heap behind her.

Once upon a time, Tracy had routinely apologized for CJ. If he forgot a name, an appointment, a charity banquet, she apologized. If he didn't want to attend her mother's cocktail parties or a childhood friend's wedding, she invented reasons. If he refused social engagements because no one he needed to shmooze was on the guest list, she went into action.

Today, she made no excuses. In fact, she skewered her ex with enthusiasm.

"I'm sorry," she told Pete Knight, as they started up the path to Alice's door. "He was supposed to be here half an hour ago, but CJ's as reliable as a tornado. You never know where he's going to touch down or how much damage he'll do."

Pete didn't look annoyed. He was dressed like a laid-back guy, in khaki shorts and a navy T-shirt. He shrugged and didn't even glance at his watch. "You've got his list. I can look around on my own."

"First we'd better introduce you to the other women. Otherwise they'll be freaked when you start scratching in their yards and peeking in their windows."

"If you don't mind me saying so, this is kind of an odd little development."

"You'll think it's odder when you've met all of us. But as long as the houses are still standing, I'll keep renting them. Which is where you come in."

"Glad to do my part."

Tracy knocked on Alice's door. Earlier she had seen Janya walking in this direction, so she hoped to do a two-for-one introduction. Wanda opened the door, and Tracy realized she'd hit the jackpot.

"It's a party and I wasn't invited?" she asked.

"Keep your shirt on, woman. Janya came over to help Alice with something, and when I saw there was a gathering, I brought a pie for everybody to taste. I'm thinking it might be good for opening day."

"What pie?"

"Elvis Surprise. Elvis's favorite sandwich was peanut butter, bacon and banana."

Tracy made a face. "Bacon? That's bogus."

"Crushed peanut brittle, mashed bananas and chocolate chips." Wanda looked up at Pete. "You look like a man might appreciate a slice of pie."

Tracy made the introduction, and Wanda stepped back to let them inside. Janya, Lizzie and Olivia were clustered around the dining room table, with Janya pouring iced tea from a cobalt glass pitcher. Alice was just coming out of the kitchen with matching plates.

Everybody stopped as Tracy introduced Pete.

"Pleased to meet you," Pete said. "Is this everybody?"

"My mom's not here," Lizzie told him. "Olivia and me were playing with my new metal detector, then we came inside. It's heavy! Miss Alice made a tablecloth for Olivia. She crocheted it. It's beautiful."

"Where is it?" Tracy knew how hard Alice had worked on the pineapple pattern tablecloth, and how many obstacles she had overcome to finish it for her granddaughter. Tracy had seen the tablecloth right after Alice completed it, but Alice had insisted it had to be washed, starched and stretched out to dry before it could grace a table.

"On the floor in Nana's room," Olivia told her. "First you put down a shower curtain, then a sheet, then you mark the sheet as a pattern, then you put down the tablecloth and pin it to fit.

211

Pete smiled at the girls. "Sounds like quite a project."

"My mom's planting flowers," Lizzie told him.

"I probably saw her. Up the road?"

"Maybe. She's around."

Wanda left for the kitchen. "I'm dishing up pie. I'll just assume everybody wants a piece. Don't tell me if you don't, on account of my feelings will be hurt."

"Do you have an extra minute?" Tracy asked Pete. "Wanda's pies are spectacular."

"I never turn down pie."

The girls made room at the table, and Pete took a seat beside Lizzie, who, without a hint of shyness, began to explain how she and Olivia had made certain there wasn't a single ruffle or pleat in the tablecloth as they pinned. Pete, who clearly liked kids, asked all the right questions.

Wanda was just bringing in the pie when the front door opened and Dana appeared. She stood in the doorway a moment, as if her eyes were adjusting.

"You're just in time," Tracy told her. "Wanda's testing another pie, and we're the guinea pigs."

"We'll make room for you over here," Janya said, sliding her chair closer to Olivia's. "Come sit with us."

Dana didn't move, and she didn't smile. "Thanks, but I can't. Lizzie and I need to head home."

"I haven't had pie!" Lizzie held up her wrist, adorned by a watch and pointed to the dial. "You said I could stay until five. We were going out to the beach."

"I forgot. I need to hit the dry cleaner before it closes."

"Lizzie is welcome to stay here," Alice said.

"Thanks, but I have other errands, and I need Lizzie's help."

"That's not fair! Can't I at least have my pie first?" Lizzie asked.

Wanda held up a hand. "I'll just pack up two pieces, one for each of you, and you can eat them at home tonight. No need to fuss."

"It's still not fair," Lizzie muttered.

Tracy didn't think so, either, but she wasn't going to throw fuel on that flame. "Let me introduce you to Pete before you go." She explained who he was and made the introduction.

Dana gave a short nod. "Lizzie, come on please. Now."

Wanda returned with a plastic container and handed it to Dana. "Better stick it in your fridge before you go."

"Thanks."

Lizzie was still muttering, but she trailed her mother out the door.

"Well, that was something," Wanda said when they'd left.

With the door open, Tracy saw that CJ had

finally arrived and was getting out of a black sports car in front of her house. And not just any sports car. This one had never seen a Detroit assembly line.

How had CJ come by an Aston Martin?

"The introductions aren't over," she said. "You're about to meet my ex. Take your time and finish your pie, Pete. He can wait." She edged out to the porch and beckoned.

"This is a whole lot of drama for one afternoon," Wanda said. "Me, I think I'll eat an extra slice, just to make sure I make it through to supper."

An hour later Tracy left CJ and Pete to finish their discussion on the road and went back inside Alice's house. Janya was gone, and Olivia was in her bedroom on the telephone. On the sofa, Alice was demonstrating a new crochet stitch to Wanda. Both women studiously ignored the fact they had finally made the acquaintance of the infamous CJ Craimer. Even though she had never given them much of a chance to question her, Tracy wondered if they were leaving her to squirm on purpose.

"I'm never going to get the hang of this," Wanda complained. "My fingers don't work right."

"You will." Alice put her hand over Wanda's and guided the hook. "There. Try it again."

"She's a taskmaster," Wanda told Tracy.

Tracy played along and didn't mention CJ.

"I thought you said you'd made enough granny squares to last a lifetime."

Alice answered. "She . . . saw a pattern. A top."

"For Janya," Wanda said. "Let's just say when she wears it, Rishi won't know what hit him."

"Like you don't have enough to do?"

Wanda looked up. "Be smart here, Ms. Deloche. In a minute Alice is going to see this is beyond me, and she's going to volunteer, seeing as the pineapple tablecloth is now drying on that floor in there and well and truly done."

"This is a new low, even for you."

Wanda was unperturbed. "I'm doing my part. I bought Janya sheets. Black satin. I told her it was a thank-you for all the work she's done on that mural at the shop. Now I hope she uses them to good advantage."

Tracy spoke without thinking. "You should have bought green."

"Her walls are red. You want her bedroom to look like Christmas Land?"

Christmas Land was Palmetto Grove's annual attempt to bring holiday spirit to a town with no prayer of a white Christmas. Every shrub and palm in a downtown park was smothered with lights, carols screeched from speakers, and Santa Claus promised toys no one could afford to suspicious children who tugged his beard for proof of identity.

"According to feng shui green is the correct color." Now Tracy was embarrassed. "Green sheets enhance fertility."

"And you know this why?"

"I just happened to ask my friend Sherrie. She's up on all that New Age stuff."

"So you're meddling, too. Good thing. I can't carry the burden alone. Alice here's about to volunteer, aren't you, Alice?"

Alice looked resigned. "I'll make the top."

"You'll be glad you did when that baby comes along," Wanda said. "We need a baby out here to spoil. So what else did your friend tell you about this feng shui stuff?"

Tracy was sorry she'd spoken. "It's supposed to create positive energy flow in your life. And Sherrie mentioned a few other things."

"In for a nickel, in for a dime."

"Well, for one thing, there's not supposed to be anything under their bed, so the energy can circulate. And she's not supposed to dust or sweep under there, either. Disturbs the good vibes or something."

"I'm not sure we can do much about that." Tracy certainly hoped Wanda didn't go poking around under Janya's bed. "Elephants are good. An elephant statue in the bedroom will —"

"She already has a bull."

"Feng shui's from China, not India. Elephants are in, bulls are out. Also, nothing's

216

supposed to block the entrance to the front door, and Janya's got one of Herb's potted trees on her stoop. I noticed it last time I was there. I had to step around it."

Tracy had learned more, but even though she was from the New Age capital of the world, the whole thing sounded crazy to her. Besides this was Janya's future they were plotting.

"I'll complain about that tree," Wanda said. "She'll get Rishi to move it."

"You're not going to tell her why, are you?"

"Not unless I have to."

Tracy looked out the window and saw that Pete was walking CJ to his car. Apparently they had finished their tour.

"Am I imagining things," she asked, "or was Dana rude to Pete? Did she seem upset he was here?"

"I don't know what was eating her," Wanda said. "But something got under her skin."

"I read all his references and made a few calls. People seem to think highly of him. I don't think Dana's got any reason to worry about Pete being in our houses."

"Maybe she had a bad experience somewhere along the line and doesn't trust men."

There was no time to wonder about Dana. Not when Tracy had CJ to consider. "He's awfully dressed up to show Pete what needs to be done around here, isn't he?"

Wanda could switch topics with the best of

them. "Your ex? You mean he doesn't usually tramp through weeds in a thousand-dollar suit?"

Tracy thought maybe CJ's suit *had* cost that much. And having bought the man any number of shirts in her day, she knew the one he was wearing wasn't a designer knock-off, nor was the Italian silk tie. Several questions had occurred to her when he stepped out of his car. Who was bankrolling CJ's wardrobe? And why was he wearing it for a handyman tour?

She turned back to the two women. "Okay, you've been polite long enough. What *did* you think of CJ?"

There was a long moment of silence, then Alice, who was always kind, spoke first. "He put us right at ease."

Tracy glanced outside. The two men were standing beside CJ's car, still chatting. "He could lull the venom out of a cobra, right before he chopped off its head."

"I can see why you married him," Wanda said. "Easy enough to look at, charming and rich. Most of us settle for one of the three. But it's amusing you think something good might come from letting him hang around."

Tracy tried to explain what she didn't understand herself. "I haven't fallen for any of the lines CJ's tossing my way. But I'd kind of like to keep him in sight, so I can watch and see what he's up to. Besides, it'll annoy

Marsh no end, which is seriously okay with me right now. Maybe Marsh will think twice about rolling out the old red carpet for Sylvia."

"So . . . why is your ex-husband here?" Alice asked. "Really why."

Tracy had asked herself the same thing every waking hour. "A couple of things come to mind. One, that he couldn't live without me."

"Spoken like a true Beverly Hills princess," Wanda said.

"How could he not love you?" Alice asked.

Tracy smiled wanly. "Truthfully, CJ knew he could count on me. No matter how much stuff he threw my way, I'd stay right there and wait for more. There are a lot of women who could take my place now, and probably will. CJ can be very appealing."

"Appealing enough to convince you to go back to him?"

"I don't have any real reason to think that's what he wants, so I'm guessing it's something else."

"Is he . . . hiding from something?" Alice asked.

"Wow, a detective in our midst," Wanda said. "Could she be right?"

"If so, he's hiding in plain sight. He'd be easy to trace here."

"Then maybe he wants Happiness Key."

"That would explain his interest in fixing

219

things up," Tracy said, "but I don't think there's any way he could legally get his hands on it. Besides the conservation easement's in play now."

"Could he be reformed?" Alice looked hopeful, as if she had no desire to believe something sinister might be happening to her friend.

Wanda clucked in disapproval. "Me, I've seen too many born-again liars in my time, and heard about a whole lot more from Kenny. Somebody like Tracy's ex wouldn't even notice the light on the road to Damascus. Or wherever it was Paul was going that day."

"Paul?" Tracy asked.

"We got to get you to church. They don't have churches out in California?"

Tracy peeked out the window again. The men were still deep in conversation. "CJ acted like he was telling the truth. The thing is, CJ always acts like he's telling the truth."

"And knowing that, you're going to let him hang around?"

"I called some people, and they made some calls for me. So far, things are pretty much the way he says."

"You're keeping an . . . eye on him?" Alice asked.

"I have a life myself, more or less, and I also have a job."

"We could . . . help." Alice looked intrigued.

"We should."

Tracy managed a half smile. "If you're going to play detective, go over to Marsh's house and find out where Sylvia is sleeping."

"No, Alice is right," Wanda said. "Watching CJ's a good idea. There would be ten eyes counting Olivia, maybe more if we enlist Dana and Lizzie."

"So not a good idea!" Tracy shook her head. "Next you'll be saying I ought to put an announcement in the paper, so everybody in town can get in on the fun."

"Seems to me it's just what he does when he's around *you* that matters. That part we can take care of."

Alice was clearly determined to make CJ a pet project. "Where is he living?"

Tracy told them the little she knew. "With somebody named Edward Statler. I checked. He's the president and CEO of a business called Creative Development and Investment. Ever heard of him?"

Alice pressed her lips together, and the lines between her eyes deepened in concentration. "The name . . ." She shrugged.

"I don't exactly run in CEO circles," Wanda said. "Kenny could check them both out, only he's not around that much right now."

"I guess we should look into it, at least a little," Tracy agreed reluctantly. "CJ said Statler was going to help him develop Happiness Key, so why didn't he come to me when

I moved in and suggest I sell the land to him?"

Wanda sniffed. "Maybe he's a CEO without *C.A.S.H.*"

Tracy checked out the men once more. "So why *do* you think he's all dressed up?"

"He was late, wasn't he? Maybe he was at some event that got out later than he'd expected, and he didn't have time to change."

"On a Saturday afternoon? More likely he's on his way to something, and he realized he'd have to go from here, so he'd better dress for it. I want to know."

"You could follow him," Wanda said.

"He'd catch on right away. My car stands out."

"Mine doesn't. The key's . . ." Alice made a turning motion with her hand to demonstrate. "In the ignition."

"That's a *bad* idea," Wanda scolded. "The key in the ignition, not Tracy driving your car. That's a good one. I'll go with her."

Tracy hated that she was even considering the offer. She directed her question to Alice. "You really don't mind?"

"Just . . . tell me what you learn."

Tracy couldn't believe she was going to tail CJ. Of course, maybe if she'd tailed him a time or two in California, she would have been better prepared when the Feds lowered the boom. "I'll fill the gas tank."

"No need."

"I can keep an eye on him while you drive." Wanda got to her feet. "We'd better head out the moment he does, or we'll lose him."

Tracy looked outside once more and saw Pete walking back to his SUV. That meant CJ was leaving. She didn't have time to reconsider. "Thanks, Alice. We'll let you know."

Wanda followed her to the door, and they both paused. Pete was turning around in the road. Then CJ got in his car and did the same thing. He took off like a shot, passing Pete on the left.

"We're out of here." Tracy threw the door open and ran for the side of the house where Alice's Hyundai sat. It was as old as Olivia, but Alice had driven it so rarely that except for the inevitable Florida rust, she'd had few problems with it.

"I'd offer to drive, only I've seen you behind the wheel," Wanda said as she threw herself into the passenger seat.

"You haven't seen anything yet."

Before Wanda could even reach for her seat belt, Tracy backed the Hyundai out of the driveway.

Wanda buckled up quickly. "So, you got any guesses where he's headed?"

"I don't have a clue. And I don't have a clue about that car he's driving, either. His share of what was left when the Feds got finished went into a savings account, so he'd have spending money in prison. But it wouldn't have stretched to a daily pack of cigarettes, much less an Aston Martin."

"*That's* what he's driving?"

"The lower end of the line. Still costs a fortune."

"That's a James Bond car."

"Well, let's see if he's got a James Bond girl stashed somewhere."

"You think that's what the suit's all about? Are you jealous?"

"No! I just want to keep tabs on him." Tracy drove faster. She could see Pete's car ahead, but not CJ's.

"I'm glad I had that extra piece of pie. It settled my nerves. Now I'm just going to pray you don't burn out Alice's engine before we get to the bridge."

Pete turned off at Randall's, and without his SUV blocking most of her view, Tracy could see CJ's car far ahead. There was a stop sign before the turn to the bridge into Palmetto Grove. She hoped he observed it. Then there was a light just before the bridge. She prayed for red.

Luck was with her. By the time she got to the light it was green, but she could see CJ just ahead on the bridge. "Okay, now keep an eye out, and I'll slow down so I don't get right on top of him."

"I got my eye on the car. Just drive."

Tracy concentrated on traffic, which thickened the moment they got on the bridge. It was a beautiful Saturday, and late enough that people were heading home from the beach or going out for an early dinner. CJ was caught up in the crowd, and she was able to stay several cars behind.

As always, Palmetto Grove looked bleached, even wizened, by the sun. Waterfront houses and condos quickly gave way to cheaper developments with patchy yards, and strip mall traffic. Still, she supposed she was developing a different perspective now that she had to worry about upkeep on five houses battered by the effects of sun and salt. These days she concentrated on riotously blooming bougainvillea and powderpuff, or happy kids playing on swing sets and vacant lot baseball diamonds.

Wanda pointed. "He turned right."

"Saw him. Thanks." Tracy turned right, too.

"Back way into town," Wanda said. "We aren't far from my shop."

"I thought maybe he'd be going to Edward Statler's, but he lives on the water. I checked out his house. You ought to see it."

"He just turned again. You see?"

"I did." Tracy made the turn, as well. The street was familiar, but for a moment, she couldn't place it. Then it hit her.

"This is my Realtor's street. The office is a block ahead on the right. Sessions Realtors: Homes of Distinction. Of course, these days it's more like Homes of Foreclosure."

"Slow down. *He* is."

Tracy saw that CJ had indeed slowed and was, in fact, pulling up against the curb directly in front of Sessions Realtors.

"Park!"

She had already begun to pull into an empty space about half a block from where CJ had landed.

Wanda gave her a report. "He's getting out. He's walking around his car. He's going into —"

"Sessions Realtors." Tracy turned off the engine.

"How'd you choose this particular outfit when you were trying to sell the property?"

"They helped broker the original deal. Maribel Sessions called me Tracy Craimer until I thought I'd scream. I think she had a thing for CJ."

She stopped and turned to look at Wanda. "You don't think . . ."

Wanda was still staring out the window. "She got dandelion fluff hair and four-inch heels?"

Tracy's head snapped front and center just in time to watch CJ close the door behind Maribel, who was wearing a white cocktail dress with a plunging neckline.

"No way." She shook her head, but the vision of Maribel and CJ didn't change.

"That's got to be some party they're going to," Wanda said.

"What's CJ doing with my Realtor?"

"Maybe it has something to do with all that sneaking around at Happiness Key."

"He doesn't own even one grain of sand on that key. It's all mine."

Wanda didn't look convinced. "Are you going to follow them?"

Tracy considered, then reached for the key. "No, I'm going to stop by Gonzalo's on the way home, and buy their extra-large sausage-and-mushroom pizza. You're invited."

"Thanks, but Ken's going to be back for dinner. You're sure you need a greasy, fattening pizza?"

"Don't start on me, okay? These days, every man I know has a pretty blonde on his arm. After I eat the whole pizza, I'm going to bleach my hair."

"You sound jealous to me."

Tracy started the engine. CJ and Maribel were gone now, and no, she wasn't jealous. She was just heart-deep lonely, but that sounded too pathetic to voice.

"There's nothing wrong that pizza won't cure," she said, keeping her voice light. "Men come and men go, but pizza's always there when you need it."

"Not all that much fun cuddling up to one, though."

"Maybe I'll buy some ice cream, too. I think I have a coupon."

"It sounds like you got a long night ahead

of you. Drive slow on the way home so it starts a little later, okay?"

Tracy heard the sympathy in Wanda's voice. It was funny how a little compassion took away the worst of the sting.

A few minutes later she pulled into Gonzalo's parking lot. She sent Wanda a half smile. "I can hear you thinking. I'll skip the ice cream."

"Kenny loves Gonzalo's. Why don't we go in on a medium and eat at my place? Saves me from cooking tonight."

"You're trying to cheer me up, aren't you?"

"Don't you know me better than that?"

This time Tracy managed a full smile. "It's working."

"Well, don't mention it. And I mean what I say. Don't. Not to anybody."

"Pizza's on me," Tracy said. "Let's go see what we can dump on top of it."

CHAPTER ELEVEN

The more Wanda thought about everything she'd done, the more worried she became. Sure, buying the luncheonette hadn't been nearly as expensive as it would have been a few years back. Her agent had assured her the price was a steal, considering the prime location. With the city doing all it could to beautify the central business district, even if Wanda decided she didn't want to keep the place, she would probably sell at a profit.

The carpenter who'd built new storage shelves had been grateful for work and priced them accordingly. The plumber had done the same. Two friends of Ken's had come in after work four nights running and painted the inside a creamy white. The entire population of Happiness Key had come in on a Sunday to paint the trim and baseboards Williamsburg blue.

Wanda had decided that since pie was so all-American, she would capitalize on the theme. She and Janya had stenciled red cherries and apples on the new white wooden tables, and the chairs had red cushions to coordinate with those on the counter stools. Framed covers of old *Life* magazines were hanging in strategic spots.

The narrow storefront had been given a fresh coat of pale blue paint, and Janya, Olivia and Lizzie had painted a mural of trees with assorted pies hanging from the limbs in between the windows and door. Janya had added Wanda's Wonderful Pies over the windows in script and designed a similar logo for paper place mats. Between friends and discounts, Wanda had made out well. No, her biggest worry was that nobody would buy her pies. Nobody who didn't know her and feel obligated, anyway.

On the Monday morning of her grand opening, she squinted at the bedside clock. Five o'clock. Wanda's Wonderful Pies flung open its doors in just five hours, and she was worried there were still things she needed to do besides get all the pies finished and displayed.

Unfortunately, she wasn't sure what those things were, and that worried her more. Even in the midst of a sunrise panic attack, she knew the place looked spiffy. The health inspector had complimented her on the shop's appearance. He'd found a few problems, of course, but she had slapped a couple of coats of paint on the pegboard behind the stove, and raised the bottom shelf on a butcher-block table so it cleared the floor at the requisite height. She had gotten her permit on time.

"You get any sleep at all?" Ken turned over and flopped his hand onto her shoulder.

Wanda was sorry he was awake, since she preferred to worry alone. "Slept like a baby."

He grunted. "A baby with colic. You tossed and turned all night long."

Every morning Wanda pondered the unfairness of life. When he first woke up, Ken looked wonderful, hair mussed, eyelids drooping, beard bristling. Somehow all that made him sexier. In comparison, every single morning she was scared spitless at the sight that greeted her in the bathroom mirror. She suspected more divorces occurred over this simple difference between men and women — something no psychologist ever seemed to take into account — than any other.

"I kept checking the clock," she admitted.

"You set the alarm, didn't you?"

"I was afraid it might not go off."

"You set your cell phone, too."

"That would be just the way. Set two and have 'em both malfunction. I guess I'll feel better if everything's ready earlier than later."

"You go ahead. Better than holding yourself back."

She leaned over and kissed his cheek. Any other morning she might have tried for more, but today, sex was the last thing on her mind. She would be baking pies in her head, and as sexy as pie was, thinking about it shouldn't be anything but a prelude.

In the bathroom she avoided so much as a glance at herself and took a shower first. Still, when it was time to paint her drooping eyelids Shady Lady green, she wished she had used the money she'd spent on the shop for a face-lift. This morning she looked every one of her fifty-seven years.

Once her hair and makeup were done, she slipped quietly back into the bedroom and donned her new uniform. She and Dana had decided on navy blue shirtwaist dresses covered by voluminous red-and-white-striped bib aprons with Wanda's Wonderful Pies embroidered on them. Wanda fastened shiny earrings shaped like cherries in her earlobes. Tracy had found them, along with apples, and slices of limes and lemons. All that shopping experience from Ms. Deloche's former life in California was good for something.

Her last act before leaving the bedroom was to slip on comfortable white sneakers. She and Dana had left their Dancing Shrimp heels on the Dancing Shrimp stoop one day last week, just for fun.

By the time she got into the kitchen she was too worried to manage breakfast. She figured she was as ready as she was going to be. It was time to face the day.

She heard a noise behind her, whirled and saw that Ken had gotten up to see her off.

"Everybody at the station knows you're opening today," he said, after a yawn. "But I told them to take their time and stop in over the next week. You don't want them descending all at once, or the other businesses on State Street will think you're in trouble with the law."

"There'll always be a free cup of coffee for a PG cop. I'll alert my neighbors, so they won't think it's a raid."

"You got good advertising," he said, as if he could read her insecurities, which, of course, he could.

Wanda had put expensive ads in the local daily and weekly papers. In exchange for pie and coffee, she had bribed nearby shopkeepers to let her post the pretty flyer Janya had designed; then she had paid three high school students to stand on street corners to give away more of them, complete with a discount coupon good all week. Most important, she had told everybody who worked at her busy beauty salon to pass on the word, which was probably the best advertising she'd done.

"There's a lot more to this than I thought there'd be." Wanda didn't even try to smile. Ken knew her too well to be fooled.

"You've managed it like a pro, Wanda. Finding a good spot, fixing it up, planning your menu, getting out the word. Now just go and make some great pies. Nobody does it better."

She nodded. "Okay, then. Off I go."

"Your feet aren't moving."

"Aren't they?"

He enfolded her in his arms for just a moment; then he turned her and aimed her toward the front door. Chase, who was sleeping in his bed in the corner, lifted his head to see what the fuss was about.

"What if I made too many pies?" she wailed. "What if I didn't make enough?"

"If you didn't make enough, take orders. If you made too many, bring them to the station at the end of the day."

"Am I moving yet?"

"Looking like you're about to."

She put one foot in front of the other and made it to the car.

Dana hated to see anybody suffer. In fact, overblown empathy was probably the single most significant thing about her. As a girl she had rescued crows with broken wings, grasshoppers with the hop gone, pond fish her father and brother had cast aside as not worthy to grace the supper table. In school she had befriended the new girls, the girls with bad complexions or plus size figures. The moment she got her driver's license, she'd signed up to visit three shut-ins from church, a route she covered every week in the family pickup until she went off to college.

She hadn't really been a do-gooder. She'd been popular, and as self-centered as any teenager. She just hadn't known how to ignore other people's misery. Unfortunately, despite a lifetime of trying to armor herself and the consequences she had suffered, she felt other people's sorrows right to the marrow of her bones. Some people read minds, or had prophetic dreams or visions. Dana just felt other people's pain.

Right now she was deeply in touch with Wanda's, and it felt like a sledgehammer pounding in her chest.

"I should have known that Mertz woman would do something to spoil my opening day," Wanda said at two o'clock, as she stared at the empty sidewalk in front of Wanda's Wonderful Pies. "I should have figured that out. Any good businesswoman would have known."

"Nobody can read minds." Dana tried not to let compassion ooze through every word. "How were you to know the Sunshine Bakery would spend all that money just to keep customers from coming here?"

"Free doughnuts all morning with free orange juice. Cakes and pies for lucky winners all day long. Free cookies *and* coffee all afternoon? Tell me why *anybody* would want one of those cardboard cookies, free or not?"

Dana didn't have the heart to tell Wanda

that on her late-morning spy mission to Sunshine Bakery, the cookies had not looked like cardboard. They'd been riddled with chips, nuts and dried fruit, and she suspected the coffee had been brewed at a nearby Starbucks.

Worse, the pies had looked passably good. They weren't anything like Wanda's, which were perfect enough to serve in heaven, but they wouldn't shame anybody who set them out for dessert. The crusts had been golden-brown and flaky, and the fillings had plumped them out nicely. The decor wasn't nearly as fresh or innovative as Wanda's, but the place had been too packed to notice.

"How'd it smell in there?" Wanda demanded. "The day I went, it smelled like an old lady's attic."

"I didn't notice."

"Well, the smell is the first thing you notice when you walk in my door. Butter and fruit and spices. If anybody walked in!"

Of course they'd had customers. As soon as they opened, half a dozen people had streamed in bearing coupons, and two of them had bought entire pies, one chocolate sin, one luscious lemon. The owners of the gift shop next door — which had more flamingos per square inch than any shop in the world — had come to indulge in pie and coffee, and had insisted on paying, despite Wanda's protests. The children's bookstore across the street had sent their cashier to buy a pie for lunch and paid their way, as well.

Of course Wanda's husband had stopped by with several other enthusiastic cops. Wanda had waited on them, and Dana hoped that was going to be a trend, since it was a nice break for Wanda. Tracy had darted in and bought two pies for her rec center coworkers. Alice had driven all the way to town for a slice of Key lime and coffee. Rishi and Janya had arrived after lunch and bought a pie for Rishi's staff. Undoubtedly, as the day wore on, more customers would trickle in.

The problem was that Wanda couldn't make a go of the shop if friends, acquaintances and her husband's colleagues were her only customers. Of course the Sunshine Bakery would not be able to sustain the ads that had flooded the newspaper and local radio station, or the tasty giveaways. Plus, if they continued to outsource their baked goods, they would go broke quickly. But Frieda Mertz had scored a point by stealing Wanda's opening day thunder. When people thought about today, they wouldn't think about Wanda's Wonderful Pies. They would think about the Sunshine Bakery, where they had stuffed themselves with sugar and caffeine for free. And that was a memory they would savor for months.

"I bet she took out a loan," Wanda

grumbled.

Dana tried to sound matter-of-fact. "Well, she'll have to pay it back, and once people realize the quality's slipped again, and it's back to business as usual, she won't have any revenue to pay it with."

"But will they find their way here in time to keep *me* from going broke?"

Dana had considered this all morning. She had no doubt once people found out how fabulous the pies were, Wanda's shop would flourish. But sooner was better than later. She didn't know anything about the shop's finances, but she did know something about Wanda's state of mind. She could feel her fear of failure. She understood fear as well as she understood pain, and she didn't want Wanda to suffer either.

"Care to make a guess how many pies we'll have left by, say, four o'clock?" Dana asked.

"Since I made way too many, I'd say at least a dozen." Wanda looked dejected. "Kenny said I should bring them to the station."

"Well, here's my thought. Those cops are already your devoted audience. They'll be by a lot, especially with you giving anybody in uniform free coffee. So you don't need to recruit them. That's more than $300 worth of good publicity down the drain — or rather, the gullet — if you look at the price for a whole pie, and more if you add it up slice by slice."

Wanda still looked bedraggled. "You got a better idea?"

"What if we close up at four o'clock, put a sign on the door saying we're all sold out for the day, turn on the answering machine and leave the number, so anybody can call if they want to make a special order. We were going to close at five this week anyway."

"Just so we can say we sold out?"

"No, so we can find the tallest, most important office building in Palmetto Grove and go office by office to offer a pie for free. Take the pies right to them. The most exclusive offices, the kind that order from top restaurants for working lunches, offices with executives who'll tell their wives and give them your card after they've had a piece of pie, so you'll be contacted for the next big party."

Dana watched Wanda think this over. "You think that will do some good?"

"It sure won't hurt."

"You think it's legal?"

"I don't think there's a PG cop who would arrest you."

Wanda smiled a little at that. "I guess it's worth a try. In for a carton, in for a case."

"That means yes?"

Wanda began to untie her apron. "It does."

Wanda narrowed the choice down to two three-story buildings, both just a short drive from the shop. She wanted to stay nearby to

239

increase the likelihood her targets could easily find her. She and Dana parked between the possibilities and scouted a little more. In the end, the building without a security guard in the lobby was the logical choice.

Now they stood by the elevator and read the names of businesses on a marble plaque so shiny they could see their own reflections. Each of them had six pies in two triple-decker carriers.

"Creative Development and Investment," Wanda read out loud. "Why does that sound familiar? That where you keep your millions?"

Dana pulled out a notepad. Wanda admired how organized her new manager was. Besides helping with prep work in the kitchen, she'd already set up an easy accounting system, a procedure to keep track of inventory, a work calendar, and this morning she'd called the local high school to see if the guidance counselor had any thoughts on a responsible teen with computer skills to develop a simple Web site. Next she planned to see if Tracy had any recommendations for someone to work behind the counter.

She began to jot notes, then she glanced up. "Investment groups are a no-brainer. Attorneys, too, and accounting firms. For now we won't try doctor's offices. More patients than staff, and short on space for conference and break rooms. Realtors might not be too bad, except these days they're broke."

Wanda admired her logic. Dana finally held up her pad. "We'll start with these. I think we want to be forthright. We'll tell them that bringing pies right to them is part of our opening week strategy, and we're hoping they'll enjoy the pies and recommend us."

"I never had a problem pushing a special at the Dancing Shrimp, but this feels personal."

"You believe in your pies, right? They're delicious, and they're a bargain. Right?"

Wanda nodded. "Let's go."

Thirty minutes later, Wanda had to admit that giving away pie wasn't all that challenging or ego bruising. The receptionist at the first law firm had immediately opened the doors to the inner sanctum, and before Wanda and Dana could set two pies on the conference room table, three attorneys and a paralegal had gathered to argue over the selection. Better yet the paralegal and receptionist had promised if they liked the pies, they would stop by to purchase a selection for their next bimonthly staff meeting.

They were welcomed at the next three stops, as well, and departed with the feeling those pies might reap benefits in the future. One accounting firm had a dour receptionist who refused their offer, and another had closed early for the afternoon. But they stopped by an insurance firm that hadn't been on Dana's list when they realized it took up more than half a hallway. They left pies with an enthusiastic audience.

"Let's try Creative Investment and Development," Dana said. They had reached the top floor and were down to three pies. Creative Investment appeared to be the only tenant on the floor, and Wanda hoped she and Dana could dispense with the rest and call it a day.

"You're good at this. You ever done this kind of thing before?" she asked Dana.

"You saw my résumé. I've done just about everything else, but never door-to-door sales."

"Moving so much must have been a trial."

"It's not the best way to raise a child, but Lizzie has asthma, so we've been looking for the right climate. We're hoping the warm weather and gulf air will keep it at bay. So far she's done well here."

"We're all hoping you stay. We like having you at Happiness Key."

"You're like one big family, aren't you?"

"We get along okay. And family's a good thing when you have a child with health problems. Yours helps when they can?"

"It's just me and Lizzie. But we manage fine."

Privately Wanda thought that was a shame, but they were already at the door to Creative Investment, and besides, she sensed the conversation had reached its limit.

"You gonna talk 'em up, or shall I?" Wanda asked.

"I blow your horn better than you do."
Dana pushed the door open. She smiled at
the receptionist and gave the speech that was
now refined to perfection.

"Pies?" The woman's eyes lit up. "For
anybody here who wants them?"

"We hope you'll spread them around, so
more people can sample." Wanda held up the
two she carried. "We have peach and luscious
lemon, and Dana there has an Elvis Surprise."

"Elvis?" The woman leaned over her desk
as Wanda explained the story and listed some
of the ingredients. "Just a minute. I'm going
to find Mrs. Statler."

Now Wanda remembered why Creative
Investment and Development sounded familiar. Edward Statler was the director or president or something, and he was the man Tracy's ex-husband was staying with.

"Mrs. Statler?" she asked, as if she couldn't
figure out the connection.

"Mr. Statler is our CEO, and Mrs. Statler
just stopped by a little while ago." She
lowered her voice. "She is a *huge* Elvis fan.
You have no idea. She actually has one of his
stage costumes on display in her house in a
climate controlled case."

"Bingo," Dana said softly, as the woman
headed down the interior hallway.

"If I could sing worth a darn, you'd be
hearing all about fools rushing in, about

now," Wanda said under her breath.

Apparently Mrs. Statler wasn't hard to find. The two women returned in less than a minute. Mrs. Statler was perfectly bronzed, and blonder than she had a right to be. Wanda guessed the woman was somewhere near her own age, although she could have been surgically altered to look that way and be several decades older. Her hands were nearly smothered in diamonds; her shoes had cost more than the renovations at Wanda's Wonderful Pies.

"Did I hear this right? You have an Elvis Surprise pie?"

Wanda gave the spiel again, then held it out. "We're sharing our pies as part of our opening day promotion," she said. "This one's got your name on it, Mrs. Statler. I hope you enjoy."

The woman beamed, although nothing wrinkled in response. "And what else do I see there?"

"Luscious lemon, which is the best lemon pie you'll ever taste. And peach, which makes use of some of Georgia's finest, plus a hint of Florida oranges to go along with them."

"I am *so* intrigued. And if these pies are anywhere near as good as they look, I'll be calling tomorrow. I'm having a reception at my house, and I'm not at all satisfied with the desserts my caterer suggested. Elvis Surprise would be absolutely perfect. If I like it, can you deliver twenty, a week from this Wednesday?"

Wanda didn't even blink. "Not a problem."

"And twenty more, a mixture of flavors, I think. Will forty pies feed two hundred people, maybe a few more? It's quite a large reception. You'll send me a list to choose from?"

"I will, and if there's something you'd like that's not on it, I'll make it for you anyway. I have a hundred tried-and-true recipes."

"I like the way you do business."

All the worries of the day evaporated. Wanda smiled at Dana, who looked enormously proud of herself.

Wanda thought maybe *she* liked the way she did business, too.

Chapter Twelve

The Henrietta Claiborne banquet couldn't have been scheduled for a more inopportune time. For the past week, in addition to planning summer youth camp, Tracy had been forced to work nonstop on banquet plans, too.

At least she'd had no personal life to interfere. In fact, she had welcomed falling into bed after long days and getting up early to repeat the process. That way she hadn't had time to brood too long over CJ's new love life or the absence of messages from Marsh. She had worked herself into a stupor, medicated with fast food and Wanda's pies, and geared herself for the next round.

Now banquet day had arrived. Normally she had Saturdays off, but there was nothing normal about the rush to put together an event worthy of the rec center's benefactress. Tracy was dressed for work by seven and on the road fifteen minutes later. She picked up orange juice and *two* chocolate-covered doughnuts at Randall's, but by the time she arrived at the center her fingers were sticky and she was empty-handed.

Gladys was already in place at the reception desk.

"You could just live here," Tracy said. "We could put a cot in my office. Or you could sleep on the sofa."

"Don't think I haven't considered it." Gladys looked tired and heavier.

Tracy was glad her own job required so much running around that her admittedly poor diet hadn't settled on her hips. "You still have things to do?"

"We haven't been able to contact Henrietta. I thought if I tried all the numbers we have early this morning, I might get lucky."

"You don't think she's going to blow this off, do you?"

Gladys chewed her lip. Then she lowered her voice. "There's a word that describes a woman who's so impressed with a few people who treat a stranger nicely that she writes the town a check the size of the Grand Canyon."

"Nuts?"

"Eccentric. She's just the sweetest little thing —"

"Little?"

"Oh yes. Somewhere under five foot. Ninety pounds soaking wet. And genuine right down to her toenails. Which are probably painted passionate purple or Day-Glo orange. Anyway, she's the soul of kindness, but she's, how shall we say it? Flighty? We've reminded her and reminded her to be here. But I'm not sure she'll remember."

Tracy thought of all the work she'd done to get ready for the banquet. Using her minimal artistic skills to set up a table with youth camp journals and craft projects. Helping Janya select and add photos to a lovely bulletin board display. Drilling her best campers until they could repeat their script if a hurricane swept in and the rec center fell down around their ears.

Her eyes narrowed. "She'd *better* be here."

"Yes, well, I see where you're coming from. Now why are *you* here so early?"

"On the way out last night I checked the nursery. It's a mess, and if she shows up tonight, I'm sure she'll want to see it."

The nursery, where limited child care was provided, was the rec center's weak spot. As a whole, the facility lacked little. But the designers had underestimated the need for a suite of rooms where mothers could leave babies and preschoolers so they could participate in the programs. The planners had reasoned that mothers could afford to hire their own babysitters or use the two day cares in town.

Unfortunately, they hadn't factored a recession into their equations, a recession that had led to the closing of one day care center and severely reduced hours at the second. Now the limited spots were always booked, with long waiting lists during classes. Hard feelings often ensued.

Last night before leaving, Tracy had taken a good look at the scuffed and stained walls, the games with missing pieces, the peeling decorative decals, the battered wooden cubes where children stored their belongings. She planned to make a list this morning and sweet-talk the custodial staff into quickly sprucing up the place. If necessary, she would find a herd of preschoolers and bribe their moms to bring them in to hide the worst offenses.

"That nursery." Gladys shook her head, and her third chin wobbled. "Woody tried to tell the planners we needed to spend more there and less other places."

Tracy listed several other things she had planned for the day.

"Be sure to leave enough time to run home and change for the banquet and the tour," Gladys said. "I had to buy a new dress this week. I've gained so much weight, I couldn't fit into anything I had. This has to stop."

"Maybe we both ought to do the early-morning dance class to shape up." Tracy smiled encouragement.

"It would be nice to work on my weight problem with somebody who understands."

Tracy couldn't think of a thing to say to

that. She wasn't sure what Gladys meant, and she wasn't sure she wanted to know. She gave a brief wave and started down the appropriate hallway.

An hour later she had done what she could in the nursery. She had stored some toys and disposed of others, remade the lone crib with brighter sheets, moved two tables to cover the worn spots on the nylon carpet and tacked a package of cheerful alphabet letters on the bulletin board, which had contained nothing but printed information about the center. For the rest, she went in search of one of the weekend custodians.

Al was a middle-aged curmudgeon with a thick Russian accent who maintained a daily schedule as rigid as the chalkboard Tracy had just scrubbed clean. Today he grumbled his way through her sweet talk, but in the end he agreed to wash walls and baseboards, even slap a coat of paint on the worst stains if she promised to leave him alone so he could work in peace.

She made a quick trip to the hardware store with a piece of the baseboard, and when she returned with paint, she found him gesturing wildly to a woman Tracy had never seen.

From experience, Tracy knew Al's English was basic at best, and when it didn't suffice, he lapsed into hand gestures, and finally his native tongue. Personally, she was glad she didn't understand Russian, since she wasn't sure she wanted to know what Al was saying by the time he got to that point.

"Why don't I see if I can help you?" Tracy said, inserting herself between the woman, who looked to be in her seventies, and Al, whose eyes were flickering back and forth as if he was searching for a weapon.

"I'm afraid I've been annoying."

"Al, I'll take it from here," Tracy said. He made a gesture that was probably rude in every language and stalked off.

"I'm sorry," Tracy apologized. "He's really a good worker, but his first language is Russian, and when his English fails, he goes a little crazy. He's already frustrated because I asked him to do a few things he hadn't planned on."

"I can't imagine not being able to communicate."

"When I moved here I thought I was living on another planet. So I can sort of relate."

"Where did you move from?"

"Bel-Air. California," she added.

"Yes, I know Bel-Air. This would feel different. So tell me about this room."

Tracy had a million things to do, but she had learned the hard way that even the friendliest smile and sweetest excuse didn't offset rudeness. "It's our drop-in nursery for preschoolers. I'm afraid what you see is what you get. Don't judge the facility by this. It's the only flaw. The rest of the place is unbelievably perfect."

"It looks well used."

"Oh, it is. It's in constant use, with a long wait to get in and a lot of moms who can't take classes because there's no space for their children."

"You need a bigger space."

Tracy nodded, held out her hand. "You must be new to the center. I don't think I've seen you. I'm Tracy Deloche, supervisor."

"My friends call me Nanette. And I have been here once or twice, but I always like to see how things are going."

Tracy did a quick exam. Definitely mid-seventies. Thin white hair in a halo of corkscrew curls. Eyes that reminded Tracy of the two doughnuts she'd consumed earlier, chocolate brown with wide doughnut hole pupils. Rail thin, maybe a size subzero. The woman wore a coral polo shirt, khaki pants and no jewelry, and most likely she had shrunk to her present size. She looked like a thousand other Florida senior citizens, right down to her comfortable white sneakers.

"Have you been up front yet?" Tracy asked. "Gladys, the receptionist, will find somebody to show you around if you'd like."

"I'm in favor of sneaking around. You find out so much more."

"Well, sneak to your heart's content. We have a big banquet tonight, so the place is bustling with preparations."

"What does a supervisor do?"

Tracy heard the seconds ticking by. "A little of everything. Right now I'm organizing the summer youth camp. During the school year I oversee youth and adult programs, and supervise the leaders. I develop new programs when we need them."

"Fundraising, too?"

"Not usually. Not unless it involves a new program. That's Woody's department."

"Something tells me you'd be good at it."

The observation surprised Tracy. "Why?"

"Well, you're lovely and well-spoken, and even though you're frightfully busy, you've taken the time to be kind to an old lady this morning. Kindness is key, don't you think?"

"I don't know. Is it? I thought you had to be ruthless and calculating to make money."

"That's certainly one model. But that always comes back to bite you."

Tracy thought about CJ. "Although some people are really good at escaping consequences."

"Sounds like you've had some experience."

"More than I ever wanted."

Tracy heard a noise in the doorway and turned, hoping this wasn't Al, back to gesture, this time with scrub brushes and cans of paint.

Gladys came into the room, a smile as wide as Little Palmetto Bay on her face. "Mrs. Claiborne!" She glanced at Tracy, and her eyes said it all. Gladys was hoping, praying, that Tracy had behaved herself.

"Mrs. Claiborne?" Tracy frowned. "Nanette?"

"If you were named Henrietta, wouldn't you opt for a nickname?"

"Wow."

"I was hoping to remain undiscovered. But I did well enough. The place is in good hands. I'm delighted." Henrietta shook hands with Gladys, who was cooing like a mourning dove — or possibly gargling on anxiety.

They were still shaking — Tracy was afraid Gladys had lost muscle control of her hand and couldn't release Henrietta's — when Al stomped back in and began to gesture.

Tracy tried to wave him back. Al was glaring. Any moment the torrent of Russian would begin.

Henrietta smiled at Al, and the torrent of Russian began. *Her* torrent, both guttural and musical. In a moment Al was beaming, and the two were clustering and hissing consonants like old pals. Henrietta turned back when she and Al had finished.

"I promised him we'd move on so he can do his job. He's a very nice man, you know."

"I always thought so." Knowing a cue when she heard one, Tracy headed toward the door.

"He suggested you begin English classes here."

"The high school's got that covered, but

come fall we're going to offer a monthly night of activities for all their ESL students, along with tutors. I thought it might be a nice way to teach a recreational vocabulary and have fun at the same time."

Henrietta winked at Gladys. "She's a keeper."

Gladys was looking less like a mole in the sunlight now. "We think so."

Henrietta stopped just outside the room where Al was already scrubbing walls. "So why haven't you organized a fund-raiser to expand your nursery facilities?"

Gladys didn't mince words. "Asking people for money when there's so little to go around seems futile."

"Not if you have a benefactor who's willing to match dollar for dollar."

Tracy and Gladys looked at each other.

"Yes, me," Henrietta said. "And if you just reorganize your space, you won't need to add on to the building. Do a usage assessment. You'll need equipment, renovation, I'm sure. I suspect you need full-time personnel and some training for volunteers, too, but the cost shouldn't be too bad."

"You've already done so much," Gladys said.

"Yes, and the town needs to shoulder the rest of the burden. But a little incentive is always welcome. And I know Tracy can organize something people will want to support. I bet she already has ideas."

"*I* actually have an idea," Gladys said. "Tracy got me thinking about it."

Tracy, who had *no* ideas about anything except getting through the evening, was properly grateful. "Glad to help. Uh . . . what is it?"

"We have a Biggest Loser contest!" Gladys looked delighted with herself. "We organize teams based on how much weight needs to be lost. All the entry money goes to the center, with prizes for the winners. We have a nutrition consultant give classes and diet tips, special exercise programs, weekly weigh-ins. Anybody can be on a team."

"You mean like the TV show?" Tracy had seen commercials.

"More teams, but yes."

"I think it's charming. Delightful!" Henrietta's eyes were twinkling.

"Woody and I would both join in the fun," Gladys said. "We need it."

"It's a wonderful summer activity," Henrietta said.

"Summer? You mean, soon?" Tracy tried to imagine the work a new project was going to entail.

"Oh, don't worry. You form a committee to help make all the plans. I'll be on it myself," Henrietta said.

"Long-distance from Rhode Island?"

Henrietta shook her head. "Oh, no. I suppose none of you know, do you? My house in Newport's undergoing some serious restoration, so I've decided to stay in Florida for the summer."

Tracy was just coming to grips with the fact that the darling of Palmetto Grove wanted to work hand in hand with her. So far she had made a good impression on Henrietta, but that could change. At least Palm Beach was on the other coast.

She smiled brightly. "Well, great. Palm Beach is definitely closer."

"Oh, no, I'm going to be right *here.* I've decided to stay on my boat in your harbor. I hate the summer social whirl back home." Henrietta put her hand on Tracy's shoulder. "I just know that you and I are going to be friends. And I'll be right on the spot. You can count on me."

Wanda's Wonderful Pies did a steady business all morning, and by three o'clock Wanda shooed Dana out the door. A few slices of this and that remained, but since the shop was closed on Sunday and Monday, Wanda wasn't baking more. She told Dana to rest. The real work would come on Tuesday and Wednesday, when they prepared forty pies for the Statler reception.

Dana considered staying in town. Lizzie and Olivia were at a friend's birthday party, and since Alice was playing bridge with friends, Dana had promised she would pick them up at six and bring them home for dinner. But with nothing to do except a little shopping, she drove home instead. Outside the front door, flowers drooped from lack of water. Inside the house, laundry cascaded out of the basket. In her bedroom, the bed whispered sweetly. Bed won hands down. She set the alarm and slipped between the sheets.

At five the alarm pulled her from bad dreams. The moment she woke she forgot most of the details, something she had trained herself to do. Of course she had been running. That part wasn't new. Nor was her pursuer, a man who was larger and faster than she was. More than that she didn't need to know.

Having the house and the bathroom to herself was a luxury. She let a long shower wash away what was left of the nightmare.

When she got back in her car, she had just enough time to stop for a rotisserie chicken and salad fixings on the way back to town. Wanda had made the girls a luscious chocolate "Vesuvius" pie, and they would be thrilled with dessert.

Plans changed when she turned her key in the ignition and nothing happened. Lately the car had been harder and harder to start. Now there wasn't even a rumble in response.

Grunting words she would never say in front of her daughter, she slid out and popped the hood, although she wasn't sure what she was looking for. As she'd feared, she saw a complicated engine, and despite an auto maintenance class, she couldn't remember one thing that might help now.

She didn't hear footsteps until Pete Knight was just a few feet away. Startled, she stepped back.

He held up his hands. "Sorry. I didn't mean to scare you."

"Maybe we should tie a bell around your neck."

He nodded, casual, nonthreatening. "I was over at Tracy's house doing some work on her gutters. Saw the hood go up. It's a distress signal."

"I wasn't signaling anybody."

"Then you have the problem taken care of?"

"Not exactly." Her shoulders drooped a fraction. "I'm guessing the battery finally expired. I should have replaced it a while ago."

"Words we've all said." Pete leaned under the hood.

"You don't have to help," she said.

He backed away and straightened. "Okay. Would you like me to anyway?"

She imagined Olivia and Lizzie waiting impatiently for her arrival. She imagined the mother who would, by now, be more than ready to have her house back. She imagined trying to call a cab, or asking one of her neighbors for a ride — if any were home.

As if he had all the time and patience in the world, Pete watched her decide. She supposed if Pete Knight had followed his fortunes to Hollywood, the studios would have cast him in Gary Cooper remakes, the strong, silent cowboy putting the world back together all by himself.

"Maybe you and I ought to start over." She summoned the shadow of a smile. "I'm not always this prickly."

"Glad to hear it."

"I'm just used to doing things alone."

"I know the feeling, but nobody's expected to be good at everything. Me, I can't imagine raising a little girl."

"Me, either."

This time he smiled, which softened his face. Tracy had told her Pete was ex-military, but now she thought there might be more to the man than following orders and doing his duty. He had a dimple in one cheek that hinted at another side.

"I'm sorry I've been so . . . ." She shrugged.

He gave the hint of a nod. "Let's take a look at the battery. The car's old enough it's probably not maintenance free, so it could be low on water."

Dana had babied the Geo Metro for years, but love wasn't going to hold it together forever. She watched as he slipped on sunglasses, then leaned over again and began to unscrew battery caps.

"It's got six cells," he told her, as he unscrewed. "A couple look about empty. Make that three. There's a mark inside each, and the water should be level."

"Water will fix it?"

"You have distilled?"

"No, darn it. And I'm supposed to pick up Lizzie and Olivia in town in a few minutes."

"I have some in my truck. I'll get it."

"You're really handy to know."

He left for Tracy's, and she admired the view. He was wearing shorts, and his legs were long, tan and muscular. She imagined she wasn't the first woman who had appreciated the way his shorts fit his well-toned, masculine body.

He drove back in his SUV and pulled up alongside her before he got out. He opened the back and retrieved a gallon jug of water. "We'll have to jump it afterward, but might be the water will give you a little more life before you have to buy a new one."

"Do you rescue damsels in distress a lot?"

"Just the ones who look like they'd be good to know."

"I'm surprised I fit in that category."

"I'm not sure about you, but I do like your daughter. She just assumes I'm a good guy. I don't have to pass tests."

"Ouch."

"Wasn't meant to hurt. That's the difference between adults and kids. Lizzie doesn't know what kind of world it is out there. I figure you do, and you're careful for a reason."

"Any mother raising a daughter should be careful."

"You won't get an argument from me."

She was not quite ready to be swayed, not without a little grilling. "Where are you from, Pete?"

"I own a little place up in Alaska that feels most like home."

"Alaska?"

He looked up from the battery. "Doesn't appeal to you?"

"It appeals a lot. I've always wanted to visit Alaska."

"You went the wrong way."

She laughed. "Didn't I, though? And you, if Alaska feels like home, why are you in Florida?"

"My place is out in the country. I tried spending a winter alone and couldn't finish it. So I'm looking for someplace different to hang my hat for the worst part of the year."

She wondered if that was all he was looking for. Another place or someone to share Alaska with? Then she wondered why that had occurred to her. She lived by one ironclad rule: Don't get involved. And the moment she started trying to figure out somebody's motives, she was halfway there.

"What about you?" he asked. "What brought you here?"

"The weather, mostly. Lizzie has asthma."

"Florida's good for that? Seems like all the molds and pollens would make it worse."

"I guess every case is different. Might be that we just need to keep moving around so she doesn't have time to develop allergies to palm trees and hibiscus."

He finished filling the cells and screwed the tops back on. "We'll jump it now, and hopefully the charge will hold awhile."

Silently she changed the grocery store rotisserie chicken to something she could buy at Randall's while she left the girls in the car with the engine running. Fish sticks or frozen corn dogs.

Pete hooked up cables in record time and told her to get behind the wheel. The engine started with a reassuring roar.

She rolled down her window, and he came around. "That'll do it. Just don't turn off the engine too soon. Make sure it's had time to run."

"Will do." She leaned out. "Not sure what I'd have done without you, Pete. Can I —"

"You're not going to offer to pay me, are you?"

She was sorry the thought had zipped through her head. She supposed payment had been a way to keep him at arm's length, to lessen the impact of a neighborly act.

"Can I interest you in some pie?" she asked instead. "Dinner's not going to be much, I'm afraid, but if you're still around, we have Vesuvius pie for dessert, disgustingly decadent."

"Thanks, but one of my fishing buddies has a son playing first base for his Little League team tonight, and I promised I'd watch."

"That sounds like fun."

"You and the girls could join me. I think he's about their age."

Dana tried to imagine something that ordinary. Sitting in the stands with a bunch of other parents, cheering on somebody's son just for fun. Sitting beside Pete Knight, maybe feeling the length of his leg against hers. Lizzie and Olivia laughing and running around under the bleachers.

She opened her mouth to say no, but before she uttered the word, she saw her answer in his eyes. She closed her lips. She hated doing what was expected. Among other things, predictability was dangerous.

"Yeah." She smiled. "Believe it or not, I like baseball. I'll ask the girls. If they want to come, we'll meet you there. Can you tell me where the field is?"

He looked surprised. She thought he might even look pleased. He gave directions. Then he pulled out a handkerchief and cleaned a smear off her side mirror, something she'd intended to do for a week.

Finally he stepped back. "So, if they're willing, I'll see you there."

"Thanks again."

"My pleasure."

As she drove off, she wondered about that. Did Pete Knight just like helping people? Was he an old-fashioned guy who saw service as his duty? Or had there been more to getting her back on the road again? And if so, what?

She wondered what it would be like to have a normal life, to accept help and friendship without questioning the motive behind it.

She suspected she would never know.

Chapter Thirteen

Tracy was sorry she had to attend Henrietta's banquet alone. She'd been told to bring a guest, but when she sheepishly resorted to inviting the other women at Happiness Key, they turned her down. Wanda knew she would be exhausted; Alice was playing bridge; and Dana was babysitting. Even Janya, who rarely left home unless she was working, was going off to dinner with Rishi.

For one split second Tracy had even considered inviting CJ or Marsh. She hoped she never felt *that* desperate again.

She'd planned an hour to shower and dress, but by the time she got home she had half that. Henrietta had promised to take the "official" tour at six, but for most of the day she had shadowed Tracy, asking questions and offering suggestions. Tracy liked the woman just fine, but Henrietta's interest in every aspect of the program had doubled the time it took her to finish all the details. Now she was afraid she was going to be late.

At home she showered in less than a minute and sprinted half-naked into her bedroom to pull on the dress she'd chosen, a Nina Ricci strapless sheath with a bolero jacket. The simplicity belied the price, and anybody who knew clothes would understand that. It certainly wasn't new. She was out of the designer world now, but the dress was classic enough to remain in style. She slipped on the appropriate undergarments, then carefully stepped into the dress and even more carefully zipped it.

Right up to her waist.

She sucked in a breath, and the zipper slid to the point where she had to reach over her shoulder to finish. Except that as she reached, she realized that if she continued, she would have to wear the dress forever, because unzipping it was going to be impossible. If she wanted to eat, if she wanted to breathe, she had to find something else.

She reminded herself the sheath had always fit like a second skin, but previously, she had been too vain and foolish to let that stop her. She unzipped it with some effort and went back to her closet for another look.

She didn't have time to try on everything appropriate. She reached for a green silk dress with a bow that tied over her breasts and draped gracefully to a skirt that poufed over her hips. So, okay, this one hid more of her body, and it was cute, not sexy, something she'd been forced to buy for her role in a friend's wedding, but the dress was still a designer original, and she could breathe as often as necessary. Anyway, who was going to notice her tonight?

She did her makeup in record time, left her hair down, and fastened on dangly diamond earrings and a small pendant. Since her shoes still fit, she chose her favorite peep-toe pumps. The woman who looked back from the mirror was not elegant or provocative. She looked fresh, friendly, even pretty. Unfortunately, she still looked like somebody's maid of honor.

There was no time to do anything about that. Tracy threw the necessities into a little purse that went with the shoes and silently congratulated herself on attending the banquet alone.

At the rec center, she parked in the staff lot and gathered the scripts for the children doing presentations on the tour. If anybody got nervous, she could hand them their lines.

She started toward the front door, reaching the public lot just as a familiar rental car brushed past and screeched to a stop in a space in front of her. A rental car she'd last seen parked in front of Marsh's house.

Instead of kicking the tires, she stepped around the rental, head held high, as if she hadn't noticed that Sylvia had nearly run her over when there were dozens of empty parking spaces along the row. She hadn't expected Sylvia to show up tonight. Yes, Bay was one of the guides, but Tracy had, at most, expected to glimpse Marsh as he delivered or retrieved his son.

The driver's door opened and Sylvia stepped out. "Oh, Daisy. I'm sorry. I didn't see you until it was too late to change course."

The passenger door flew open, too, and Bay popped out. "Tracy!" He circled the car and threw his arms around her waist. Tracy could not ignore him.

"Hey, kiddo, you all prepared for the tour?" She ruffled what was left of his hair after a swim team buzz cut.

"Bay, you're going to mess up Daisy's sweet little outfit." Sylvia looked stunning. Her midthigh-length dress was the palest possible shade of blue, with tiny straps and a ruffle along her breasts. The fabric seemed to be rows of ribbon, and it fit as if it had been tattooed onto Sylvia's perfectly proportioned body. Her blond hair fell in symmetrical waves past her shoulders.

"Not a problem," Tracy said, looking back down at Bay. Silently she prayed he *would* mess it up, so she would have an excuse to go home and change. So what if she couldn't breathe or eat? At least the sheath would give Sylvia a run for her money.

"I gotta go!" He pushed away.

"I'll see you downstairs," Tracy promised.

She started to follow, hoping Sylvia would take the hint, but Sylvia kept pace beside her.

"You look *so* comfortable," Sylvia said. "It's hard to know how to dress in this heat. Too cold inside, too hot out. But I just had to wear this dress. Marsh is so fond of it."

"You may be a little chilly," Tracy said, since about 99 percent of Sylvia's skin was exposed. "And a little dressed up to watch Bay tell visitors about swim team."

"Oh, Marsh and I are going to the banquet. Didn't you know? He's agreed to be on the board next year. I suppose that will make him your boss?"

Tracy wasn't sure which was worse. Marsh and Sylvia together at the banquet, or Marsh on the rec center board. Or possibly her almost insurmountable urge to push Sylvia into the row of prickly shrubs beside the entrance.

"You know, what you do here is so admirable," Sylvia said. "Playing games with children. Camping. Hiking. Or whatever it is they pay you for. I always thought jobs like yours were done by much younger women. You know, sorority girls working their way through college."

Just a little to the right. One well-aimed shove, then a horrified apology. *My goodness, I am so sorry I stumbled, and there you are, facedown in the bushes. . . .*

Tracy glanced at Sylvia. "I have a degree in

recreation, and a *job*. How's your job search coming? It can't be easy finding one now with the economy and, well, everything. . . ."

"What do you mean, 'everything'?"

Tracy considered all possible answers, including the one in which she would push Sylvia into a metaphorical prickly shrub, which in this case was the job from which Sylvia had just been fired.

Once upon a time she might have taken pleasure in that. Okay, not that long ago. Apparently she still wasn't beyond *thinking* about it, but now she seemed to be too mature to follow through.

She supposed that was a good thing, although there was very little immediate satisfaction built into it.

"Everything," she went on, although grudgingly. "You know, trying to relocate to Florida after Manhattan. Making new contacts. I'm sure it feels like you're starting over."

"Oh, not at all. I have connections everywhere. It's a matter of time and finding just the right place."

"I wish you luck."

Sylvia stopped and took Tracy's arm — and not with a friendly grip. "Listen, don't play with me, Tracy. You want me out of Florida. Don't pretend otherwise. You want my husband, and you want my son. Don't think I don't know."

Tracy shook her off easily. "Marsh is your

ex-husband, so in case you missed that class in law school, that means you are no longer married to him. And I'm not trying to steal your son. I've just filled in for you when you were too busy to be a mother, which was, until recently, all the time."

"You don't know a thing about it."

Tracy expelled a long breath. "Listen, Sylvia, we can fight over Marsh. I'm game. But I'm *not* fighting over Bay. I would never do anything to hurt that kid. As little enthusiasm as I have for being nice to you, for his sake, let's try to get along. He adores you. I can live with that."

"You don't have to. I don't see Marsh breaking down your door, and Bay doesn't need anybody to fill in for me. I'm right here."

"Then I suggest you enjoy what he wants to show you tonight and stay out of my way, okay?"

"And you stay out of *ours.*"

Tracy knew better than to utter another word.

Inside and fuming, she made the rounds, making certain children were stationed appropriately and everything was running smoothly. Although by now Henrietta had toured every nook and cranny, Tracy was impressed with her enthusiasm when, dressed in a lovely peach silk suit, she moved along the official route escorted by Woody and Gladys and several members of the present

272

board. She listened and nodded, speaking to each child and calming their stage fright with casual questions.

No disasters ensued; no child got so nervous that he or she couldn't remember what to say. The displays looked lovely, and even the nursery, with the lights turned low, didn't look like a place from which a responsible mother would run screaming and clutching her newborn against her chest. She saw Marsh at a distance when she was finally heading upstairs from the pool area to the gym, where the banquet was being held. She steeled herself to spend an entire evening trying not to watch him sitting beside Sylvia, gauging whether Sylvia's crusade was working.

On autopilot, she nearly ran straight into another man.

She stepped back, and her eyes widened. "CJ!" She glanced around, saw they were too close to others for the rest of what she'd been about to say, and jerked him into the nearest corner.

"What are you doing here?" she demanded.

The faintest hint of a smile played on his lips. "Attending the banquet. How about you?"

"What kind of game is this? You can't be here without an invitation."

"I have an invitation." CJ's gaze flicked behind her, and the smile bloomed.

"Nanette!"

Tracy's head jerked around of its own accord. At their rear, a radiantly smiling Henrietta Claiborne was coming up fast.

"Nanette?" Tracy grabbed the jacket of CJ's suit, a very nice suit indeed.

"I've always called her Nanette. All her friends do, TK."

"Don't call me that!" But it was too late to say another thing. Henrietta was now in earshot.

"CJ! CJ!" Henrietta took both of CJ's hands and leaned forward to kiss him on his cheeks. "I am so glad the government finally came to its senses! But what a terrible ordeal they put you through."

"I'm looking ahead now. And speaking of looking, you look wonderful. You're getting younger."

She grinned. "I see you've met our Tracy. She's the darling of the rec center, aren't you, Tracy?"

CJ didn't allow Tracy to answer. "I can't believe you don't know. . . ."

"Know what?" Henrietta's eyes were sparkling. "A secret? Someone's kept a secret from me?"

"Tracy's my wife." CJ's gaze flicked to Tracy when she gasped, then back to Henrietta. "That is, she's my *ex*-wife, I'm sorry to say. I forced her to divorce me when I was afraid I was going to be in prison the rest of

274

my life. She came here to start over."

Henrietta looked shocked. "But I never met her. You," she added, looking at Tracy now. "Why not?"

"I have no idea," CJ answered smoothly. "She had a busy social life of her own, didn't you, TK? We weren't always together at the same events. Maybe that explains it."

"Tracy, why didn't you tell me you're married to my good friend CJ Craimer?" Henrietta demanded.

"But I'm not . . ." Tracy tried again. "Anymore. And I had no idea you, umm . . . even knew CJ."

"Of course I do. We have a million friends in common, and we were once on Hydra together for a lovely week-long house party." Henrietta snapped her fingers Zorba style and hummed a few bars before she leaped back in. "When I heard he was in town, I made sure he was invited tonight. How silly, though, since of course, you two are here together. *I* didn't even have to invite him." She was beaming again, this time like a satisfied matchmaker.

Tracy was afraid that next Henrietta was going to launch into a solo from *Fiddler on the Roof*. Before she did, Tracy knew she had to correct the impression that she and CJ were about to retie the marital knot, because the only knot she wanted to tie anywhere in her ex's vicinity was a noose.

"We're not together," she said bluntly. "Not here, and not at all." She thought of Gladys. She thought of the center. And on the heels of both, she thought that she really did like Henrietta and didn't want to be unkind when the woman clearly wanted to help. Tracy struggled to find an acceptable way to state her feelings. "There's been too much . . . We're both . . ."

"What TK's trying to say is that she'll need some convincing before we have a genuine reconciliation," CJ said. "But I understand. I put her through a lot."

"Oh, my dear," Henrietta told Tracy, shaking her head.

Tracy tried to imagine how tonight could get any worse. Immediately, as if all the heavenly hosts had planned for the moment, she got an answer. When she looked up, Maribel Sessions was heading toward them, her expression as predatory as Sylvia's.

"Let me guess," Tracy said softly. "Your date, CJ?"

Henrietta wisely took in the situation, then put Tracy's arm through hers as CJ went to intercept the other woman.

"I know how to fix this." And before Tracy could stop her, Henrietta proceeded, in great detail, to tell her.

CHAPTER FOURTEEN

"I'm baking pies in my sleep." Wanda stared up at a cloudless blue sky. A light breeze swept over her sunscreen-slathered skin, and, as always, she wondered how people lived anywhere other than Florida. "I used to bake pies just for fun, remember? Those were the days."

Janya, beside Wanda, stared up at the same sky. "Those days were just one week ago."

Waves rolled in just below them, and Wanda was afraid the sound and the sun might lull her to sleep right there, with her friends watching as she drooled and snuffled.

She was tired to the bone. One week into her new career, the only thing she was sure she had done right was close on Sundays and Mondays. Sure, she would have to spend Mondays making piecrust, cleaning and ordering supplies, but she'd already decided that on Sundays she wasn't going to lift a finger. She was going to lie out on the beach with Ken or her neighbors, and she wasn't going to so much as *eat* a piece of pie. Not even when fresh strawberries were in season. Not even when Georgia peaches, juice running freely like a stream of pure nectar, were sitting in crates waiting to become peaches and cream pie.

Although that might be hard to resist.

"I gotta get more help," she said to nobody in particular. Alice was lying on the other side of her, and Olivia, in a bright red bathing suit, was down near the waterline, prowling for shells. "But first I gotta get more business."

"You may not want more . . . after you make forty . . ." Alice trailed off.

Wanda was alternately thrilled and terrified that on Wednesday she and Dana would be delivering forty pies to the Statler residence, in addition to making the usual number to sell at the shop. Unfortunately, for now, more help was a dream, and she was simply going to be tired and grouchy for a while. Just not on Sundays.

Olivia came back with her shells. Janya, who had brought a guide, helped identify them.

"This one is a banded tulip." Janya held it up for the other women to admire. Frankly, Wanda didn't care what a shell was called, but she was glad to see that Olivia, who had been moping because Lizzie was off somewhere with her mother, was perking up.

"This sharp one is called an auger." Olivia

sat down at Wanda's feet. "I already have about a million. Lizzie likes to collect them."

"Lizzie's turned into a beach bunny. I never saw a kid who likes being out here as much as she does."

"She even makes me tired." Olivia held another shell high. "What's this?"

Janya researched. "A kind of clamshell, I think. Yes, look." She held out the book.

"Cal-i-co clam," Olivia read upside down, before Janya handed the book to her.

"Lizzie does a lot of running around for a girl with asthma," Wanda said. "That surprises me, since it seems like she'd have trouble catching her breath after a while." She propped herself up and turned to Alice. "You know about the asthma, right? You and Dana worked out what to do if she has an attack when she's staying at your house?"

Alice nodded. "Inhaler. But she's never . . . needed it."

Olivia looked up from the book. "Lizzie only has asthma if she spends time around cats. Last night there was a cat at the party we went to, but she didn't pet it, and we were outside a lot, anyway."

Wanda thought that was surprising. Dana had told her that they'd moved around so much because Lizzie's asthma had demanded it. But then, kids played things down so they would look just like everybody else.

"I thought her asthma was worse than

that," she said out loud. "Maybe living here on the beach just agrees with her."

"She said she used to wheeze, then she had shots, and now she's okay if she's careful. But she loves cats, so it's not fair."

"Give me a dog any day." At that reminder, Wanda shaded her eyes and saw Chase streaking up and down the beach, perfectly happy to chase seagulls the way he had once chased a fake rabbit at the greyhound tracks. He had the same chance of catching either.

"Some people are allergic to dogs," Olivia said.

"That would be worth worrying about."

"Chase is a good watchdog."

"Chase?" Wanda laughed. "He'd lick a burglar to death. He could sure outrun one, though."

"He was barking a lot at Tracy's old husband."

Janya closed the book, since shell identification had ended. "When was that?"

"When Mr. CJ was over at Wanda's poking around her yard."

Wanda snapped to attention. "When was *that?*"

"I don't know. . . ." Olivia considered. "Friday afternoon, maybe. I saw him when Lizzie and I got home from school. Chase was barking so loud I thought he was going to jump through the screen and eat Mr. CJ. Mr. CJ didn't stay around to find out, either."

Wanda had hoped the story was more interesting. "Tracy said he'd be poking around. He's helping her get things figured out here. What needs repair. What she can do to make improvements."

"Do we want improvements?" Janya asked. "Will this man, who caused her so much trouble in the past, improve us right out of our houses because we can't afford them any longer?"

"My house . . . is fine," Alice said.

Wanda wasn't sure. "I guess we'll have to wait and see what old Mr. CJ is up to. In the meantime, I'm going to get my toes wet on this pretty beach while I can. Anybody want to join me?"

Janya stretched. "I will wade. If we are going to be looking for a new place to live, we should enjoy this one now."

Wanda was surprised at such a negative sentiment. "You don't really think Tracy would let that happen, do you?"

"Mr. Craimer put this land in Tracy's name, and she has never really understood why. With his unfortunate history, would it not be possible he has *more* plans she doesn't yet understand?"

"But there's an easement. It can't be developed."

"I have not lived in this country as long as you, but can you tell me that there is no corruption? That agreements are not overturned?

281

That if there was something wrong with the title, perhaps, that Mr. Craimer might establish claim to the land again and turn over the easement so he could create his Happiness Key after all?"

"Overturn," Wanda said. "*Overturn* the easement, and I am surprised that you'd be thinking that way. *I'm* the one who thinks that way."

"Perhaps I am learning from you?"

Wanda wasn't sure that was such a great idea, but she couldn't help feeling proud anyway.

Tracy had never been much of an overachiever, not unless she counted all the hours she'd spent at spas, surgeons and salons to improve whatever beauty Mother Nature had bestowed. But since Henrietta Claiborne had materialized, Tracy's workload had increased dramatically. So on Sunday morning, with the banquet now last night's memory, she got up and headed to her office, fondly called the rec room because of its cavernous size and decor. With youth camp looming, she had very little time to pull together plans for the new fund-raiser if the participants were going to spend the summer together agonizing over every calorie. Overachieving or not, she had to get moving right away.

By the end of Sunday afternoon the program had a name: "Losing to Win." She'd written up a proposal to go over with Henrietta and some key members of her staff tomorrow. She'd written a tentative description for the next newsletter and roughed out a press release headlined Waist Time with Your Friends at the Henrietta Claiborne Recreational Center.

At five she pushed away from her desk, tired and actually sorry she was done for the day. As little as she liked overtime, working was better than facing an empty house. The neighbors had other plans for the evening, so Tracy was on her own. She considered a movie or just wandering around the Palmetto Grove mall, but she was exhausted from her long week. Instead she packed up and headed home, only to discover she was not alone after all.

These days she only knew one man who drove an Aston Martin like the one parked in front of her house. She zipped into her driveway and sat for a moment, wondering why CJ was parked there and where he had gone. They hadn't spoken since Henrietta had gushed over him at the banquet, right before Maribel stomped across the room to pull him away for the evening.

Maribel and CJ had been seated at one corner of the table where Tracy had ended up. Sylvia and Marsh had adorned the other, like diabolical bookends. Tracy had spent the evening trying not to look in either direction while she chatted with two neighboring women, one who regaled her with tales of a tennis championship she had won twenty years before, and the other with tales of her pole-vaulting grandson. When not called upon to respond, Tracy had mentally weighed that night against the one back in Bel-Air when CJ had told her that life as they knew it was over.

She hadn't been able to determine which was worse.

Now, with nothing else to do, she stayed in her car and considered her alternatives. She could head to a remote beach and watch the sun go down. She could ask Alice for refuge and brave another crochet lesson. She could rearrange the plants on Janya's porch so the laws of Feng Shui were satisfied.

Or she could find her ex-husband and see what he was up to.

Never let it be said that she had learned nothing from the days of her marriage. Keeping an eye on CJ was as vital as a regular bikini wax. Ignore either for too long, and the result was anything but pretty.

First she unlocked her front door and peeked inside, sure CJ would be perfectly capable of letting himself inside with a credit card or a set of skeleton keys. But the house looked empty, unless he was sleeping in her bedroom. And the man had to know better than to head that way uninvited.

Outside, she circled the house and wandered through what passed for a yard. CJ wasn't hiding behind the stands of oleander, and she certainly wasn't going to make her way toward the marsh, in case she scared up another gaggle of bird-watching seniors. In the weeks that had passed since that evening, she had made a campaign of sucking up to the rec center's shuffle board, who had been so furious that night. She was making progress. While not forgiving her, they no longer left anonymous photographs of the masked booby on her desk as silent reminders that she was on popularity probation once more.

When the circle took her back to her driveway, she considered which way to turn. She didn't have to think for long. She saw CJ coming from the direction of Wanda's backyard, but he didn't notice her. He stopped about halfway between Wanda's and Tracy's cottages, knelt, then took something from his pocket and fiddled with it for a moment before he began to brush the sandy soil away from the spot with his fingers.

She took her time approaching him, hoping to catch him in the act, but when her shadow fell over the ground at his feet, he didn't even look up.

"I was about to give up on you," he said.

"I gave up on you a year ago. I guess it's your turn."

He got to his feet easily, without pushing

himself upright. Apparently he'd made good use of the prison yard at Victorville, or he'd made up for it since. CJ had always kept himself in terrific shape. As much, she thought, to get a head start when necessary as for concerns about health.

"Mind telling me what you're doing?" she asked.

"An amateur survey. Figuring out approximate lot sizes with my handy-dandy little GPS."

"And why would you do that?"

"Part of trying to figure out what, if anything, you can do here to make this a thriving little community with houses worth money, instead of these wrecks you have now."

"I resent the term *wrecks*. Play nice, CJ. *Dumps. Shacks.*"

He turned his most spectacular smile on her, and darned if she didn't feel herself basking just a little.

"Do you know why I married you?" he asked.

"You needed arm candy, and I was easy."

"You always stood up to me. You were never wowed, never afraid. You were all about yourself, and nobody else, not even CJ Craimer, got in the way of that."

"A selfish little fluff ball."

"Come on, there was always a lot more to you than that. I saw it as strength, a healthy ego. Maybe you were a little shallow, but you were a lot young, too. I figured you'd age well."

She lifted a brow in question. "Did you plan to keep me around that long? You dispensed with your first two wives about the time their boobs began to sag."

"I wasn't much of a bargain. Mandy and Gina just went on to better things. By the time you came along I was more promising husband material. Besides, you weren't as needy."

"Right, that's me. Oprah calls weekly, begging for tips." The flattery was having an effect, and that worried her.

"I'd rather have been sitting with you at the banquet."

Now *that* was just like CJ. Pull down the defenses a little, then move in for the kill. Clearly he knew she'd been uncomfortable last night. Now he was using his knowledge to make her feel closer to him, and darned if it wasn't working.

"Well, if you had been, you could have helped me come up with a plan."

"For what?"

"To keep Henrietta from playing match-maker."

"You've lost me."

"It's clear Henrietta thinks you and I should get back together. She told me Maribel has no class. And for some reason beyond

287

my comprehension, Henrietta adores you."

She looked away to compose herself. "CJ, she's insisting you and I come on a sunset dinner cruise on her boat next Monday night. She asked me to invite you. You're going to say no, of course."

"Have you seen her . . . *boat?*"

"No."

"*Yacht*'s the correct term. An amazing vessel, too. We'll have a wonderful time."

"Wait! We can't play along with this."

"TK, Nanette can't make you marry me again. She's not that powerful. She's just an old woman in love with lovers. She wants happy endings for everybody, and we didn't get ours, so she's trying to fix it. What are you afraid of? If there's nothing left, she'll see that. She's as shrewd as she is rich."

"Did you ever invest money for her? Manage any property? Give her any financial advice whatsoever? Is she taking us out to the middle of the gulf so she can dump us off the side?"

"I told you, she's shrewd. We were friends, not business partners. What's the harm in going for a sail? It won't be our first time on a yacht together. You used to love sailing with me."

She felt trapped. She couldn't insist that CJ refuse the invitation. And she couldn't refuse herself, not and live to tell Gladys what she'd done. Besides — and she hated to admit this, even to herself — a beautiful evening on the gulf in Henrietta's yacht was exactly the thing to ease the funk she'd fallen into since Sylvia moved in with Marsh. Even if CJ was part of the package.

"This is probably more strategizing than we indulged in when we were husband and wife." Tracy glanced at her watch and realized that CJ had given it to her. The Rolex and the Cartier collection had gone with everything else, but this one, a quirky, clunky silver and lime-green enamel combination from some designer whose name she couldn't remember, had been far cheaper and hadn't interested the Feds, so she'd gotten to keep it. She had considered pawning it, but even poor folks had to know what time it was.

"I picked that out," CJ said, looking down at her wrist. "At some little boutique jewelry store when I was traveling. Boston, I think. Newbury Street. It reminded me of you."

She steeled herself against sentiment. "Okay, you've explained why you're here at my house. Why are you here *now?* No cocktail parties? No intimate little dinner with Maribel?"

"I tried to call earlier and see if *you* wanted to have dinner with me."

"I've been at work. Your good friend Nanette is some taskmaster."

"I know. I drove by the center and saw your car."

"The man always finds out whatever he needs to know."

"And I figured you were working, and you would end up too tired to go out afterward, even if you agreed."

"Which I would not have."

"So I brought dinner to you."

For a moment Tracy didn't know what to say. This was unexpected and, despite every instinct telling her to run the other way, welcome. "Here?"

She could tell he heard the interest, the hope. CJ smiled. "The way to a woman's heart —"

"Do not say it."

"Do you know about the new Italian place down by the pier? Something or other 'Tuscan.' Edward told me about it, and they pack up meals to go. Do you still like lobster ravioli?"

Her mouth began to water. "You found lobster ravioli?"

"I had to beg. I told them it was for a woman who needed it badly. And I got the most incredible antipasto salad you will ever lay eyes on. And tiramisu."

She started to say no. He so clearly expected her to say yes, and giving CJ anything he was angling for was dangerous. Then she saw two things in his eyes she had never seen before. Hunger, and loneliness. She wasn't sure which one stopped her.

"Did you dream about a meal like that in Victorville?" she asked at last.

"You don't want to know all the things I dreamed about. When I could sleep. The noise at night is part of the punishment."

"I really thought you'd go to some Club Fed, not a medium-security facility. You had so many friends in high places."

"It's funny how few remained."

"Apparently Edward Statler did."

"Edward has a deep appreciation for everything I've learned through the years. I'm really quite useful to know."

She wondered if CJ was going to be useful for her, or if there was more to this than she'd figured out.

"I'd like to take a shower and change," she warned.

"I could wash your back."

"You could hop in that fancy little Aston Martin and eat your lobster ravioli at Statler's house, too."

He held up his hands. "Ground rules clear. I'll warm up everything while you shower. And I'll pour the wine."

She still had the bottle Marsh had brought the night their relationship had taken its first nosedive. "I have a good Zinfandel," she said.

"I bought wine when I bought our dinner. You don't have to worry about a thing."

"Except you."

"I'll behave. Although did you know that

statistics show many divorced couples still have sex after the decree?"

She thought of Marsh and Sylvia, and her spirits took a nosedive, too. "How about you? Did you indulge with my predecessors after the prenups were satisfied?"

"You know about the praying mantis and her mating habits, don't you?"

"You thought one of them might bite off your head in the act?"

"It occurred to me."

"I'll remember that image. You remember it, too."

They walked back toward her house. "How do you like living in Florida?" he asked as he opened the door and she preceded him inside.

"Surely you can see the draw. Sun, sand, surf."

"I could see Palm Beach, Miami, even Fort Lauderdale."

"You're the one who bought this property and planned to make millions off it."

"But I never planned to live here."

She thought about that as she showered, and slipped on shorts and a comfortable T-shirt, purposely choosing clothing that was not the least bit provocative.

She went into the kitchen and revived the conversation as if there had been no break. "So where do you plan to live?"

"I guess that depends on the federal government."

"What are the chances you'll go back to prison?"

"My attorneys are hoping not good."

"And you?"

"There are some determined people on the other side. And because all my financial dealings collapsed when they sent me away, there are now a lot more people determined to get me. If I were a praying man, most of the time I'd be down on my knees."

"My mother thought prison was too good for you."

"If everything the prosecutors claimed was true, she would have been right."

For the first time Tracy really wondered about CJ's guilt. Sure, at the very beginning, she'd denied any possibility he could have done the things the prosecutors claimed. But that notion had passed in a blink.

Now, she wondered if she really had jumped to conclusions. She had been so furious at the destruction of their life together and the looming uncertainty of her future that perhaps she, like her parents and others, had believed the worst as a small measure of retaliation. They couldn't do anything about CJ's fate or their own, but they could blame him for both. By doing so, they had absolved themselves of responsibility for their reduced circumstances.

"Can you honestly say you're not guilty?" she asked.

CJ looked up from a platter where he was mounding marinated mushrooms. "Of course not."

"Then you *are* guilty?"

"I can say I made mistakes. And I didn't strictly abide by the law on every single thing I did. But I didn't do anything other businessmen, developers, financiers, weren't and aren't doing. I used money to make money, and I took chances. I cultivated a few friendships I shouldn't have, because I thought, in the long run, dealing with a few shady people to make money for a lot of good people was an okay price to pay."

He was talking in generalities, but the complexity of CJ's case had always made her dizzy. She was just as glad he wasn't giving examples.

"Where did it all go wrong?"

"I got greedy. I started to think I couldn't make a mistake. I stopped looking over my shoulder."

"To see if anybody was after you?"

He grinned. "No, to see where I'd come from so I could remember I didn't need to leave it so far behind."

She liked the image.

He placed slices of Italian cold cuts and cheese around the mushrooms, added artichoke hearts and a variety of olives. Finally he held up the plate.

"How'd I do?"

"I think it looks fabulous. Shall I pour the wine?"

"It's breathing on the counter."

"It's warm outside, but we can sit on what passes for my patio, if you'll give me a minute to put a cloth on the table."

"Then I'll pour the wine while you do."

She pulled a cloth from her linen closet and wet a sponge to clean off the old metal table that had come with the house. When she finished, she went back in to tell him everything was set.

He held up the platter. "I'll take this out if you'll get the rest."

She took her time, putting the wine on a tray with napkins, plates and silverware. When she joined him, she noted he'd lit the citronella candles to ward off mosquitoes. The table was covered by more than a cloth. He'd added sheets of paper with drawings.

"I wanted you to see what I've been up to," he told her. "Come sit beside me."

She couldn't very well refuse. CJ claimed he was doing this for her, and even if she wasn't convinced, there was always the chance he really was.

"Okay, this is a rough sketch of the property." He opened up a sheet almost as large as the table, moving the antipasto to a vacant chair to make more room. "Here's your house, here's your neighbor, the one across the street. . . ."

"Got it." She pointed to a circle between Alice and Janya's cottages. "And what's that?"

"That's where you could put one of the three environmentally friendly houses I've roughed out designs for."

"Environmentally friendly?"

"I've run these by Edward, and he's had his own attorney look over the easement. There's nothing here that would conflict. There were cottages on these sites originally, and the easement requires you to build where they were, but you're allowed to extend the footprint by about a third, since they were so small. It also requires you to consider your surroundings, use environmentally friendly materials, etc. But really, the easement's surprisingly liberal. If I'd been on the other side, I wouldn't have been so lax. I'm not sure that whoever drew it up was much of a businessman."

Marsh had designed and written up the easement, and he was a crackerjack lawyer. Though known for his fierce desire to eliminate every golf course and housing development in the state, he'd still allowed Tracy these perks. Now she recognized his generosity for what it was. Marsh had been concerned for her future. And he had been kinder than he'd probably wanted to be, most likely kinder than his job required.

For a moment she didn't know what to say.

She made herself speak. "Well, that's a great idea, but where's the money coming from? We're deep in a recession. When I agreed to the easement, I gained just enough to stay solvent. I didn't gain enough to build so much as a doghouse."

"Interest rates are at an all-time low. The land's your collateral. You'll get a loan for at least one house. Build it, sell it, and build another."

"Who's buying now? Especially out here, surrounded by funky old beach cottages?"

"You probably need to do some renovations first. That's the best way to start." He pulled out a stack of papers stapled together and set them on top of the first. "I've sketched out plans to improve all the existing houses and bring them more into line with the new ones."

She leafed through. Lanais, extra bedrooms, carports. A second story on the back of Wanda's, a whole new wing on Janya's. And hers? A master bedroom and bath with a lanai opening off it, as well as an expanded living area. She almost drooled.

Finally she turned the pages upside down, so she didn't have to see them anymore. "I can't afford this, and I doubt my renters could afford to live in them if I did all that."

"There are other renters. You're living on a gold mine."

"I'm happy with the renters I have."

"I realize fewer people are in the market for houses right now, but that means the building trades are suffering. We could probably find a crew to do the needed work for about half what we'd normally have to pay. And I think Edward might invest, or some of his friends."

That was the wake-up call she'd needed. Just what she didn't want. Edward Statler, CJ's new best buddy, with his hands on the reins of her finances. And all that talk of "we"?

She busied herself removing the papers and putting the antipasto back on the table. "I remember the night the FBI came to the door with a search warrant. I stood in our bedroom and watched strange men going through my underwear drawer, CJ. Hours later, I locked up behind them. Everything you and I owned had been pawed over and tossed here or there, and left for me to deal with. The last guy out the door told me to do myself a favor and not try to hide any assets, because they would find them anyway, and I'd be in bigger trouble than I was already."

She looked up. "That was one of the better days. Let's not even talk about the day the moving van came."

He reached over and took her hand. "I'm sorry, TK. Sorrier than I can tell you."

She looked down. Her hand in his looked and felt so familiar. She knew better than to

298

leave it there, but somehow, she couldn't find the incentive to pull away.

"I told myself it was all your fault," she said, "but now I know it wasn't. Not completely. I wanted the things we had. I was willing to look the other way whenever I had the slightest doubts everything wasn't on the up-and-up. I figured that was the price I had to pay, and it was so small in comparison to everything I got. Beautiful houses, and country club memberships, and the way people looked at me when you and I were together. Maybe knowing that, knowing how much I wanted all of that, made it easier for you to just get it for me, for us, any way you had to. I can't discount that entirely."

"I cut some corners. I took too many chances. But it was never your fault. And all the things that happened? You didn't deserve any of them."

"Didn't I?" She really wasn't sure. And she really wasn't sure she would still want what she'd once had, even if somebody set it in front of her again. No strings attached.

He lifted her hand and kissed it before she could stop him. Then he folded her fingers and let go.

"Wine. Antipasto. Let's talk about some of the good times."

"We aren't going to have any more of those," she warned. "Not together."

"I'll settle for the past right now. Okay? And

299

lobster ravioli?"

"Lobster ravioli *is* the past. And don't tell me where you got the money to buy it."

"Nothing for you to worry about, I promise."

She doubted that. She knew that her job now was to stay so far on the outside of whatever CJ was doing that she didn't have to worry. At least not about herself.

But she had a sinking feeling that she *was* going to be worried about *him*. Despite their checkered history. Despite her conviction he still wasn't telling the truth.

Because she had to face the fact that despite everything she had wanted to believe since the divorce, once upon a time, she really had been in love with CJ Craimer.

CHAPTER FIFTEEN

Dana had good ideas, and Wanda was proud of herself for hiring the woman, instead of letting her languish at The Dancing Shrimp. She was probably paying Dana too much, considering that the shop would be in the red for months to come, but she had estimated how much Dana made at the restaurant and matched it. Wanda's Wonderful Pies was never going to make Wanda a rich woman, but if eventually she and Dana could both make a living, then that was fine by her.

Today Dana was more than earning her keep. Not only was she packing up forty pies in the kitchen, Wanda was reaping the benefits of Dana's good ideas on the telephone.

"I'm glad you liked my Charleston pie," Wanda told the caterer on the other end of the line. "And we're always happy to work with you. We have a special list, just for caterers, so our regular customers won't already be tired of what you serve them. Plus, don't forget, caterers get a ten percent discount, and that's on top of our bulk pricing. So we'll take that right off today's invoice." She listened, nodding her head. "Friday night, then. And you'll come by so we don't have to charge for delivery?" She nodded again, then thanked the woman and hung up.

"Whoopie!" She did a little dance behind the counter, glad nobody was in the shop to see.

"What's up?" Dana came out to see what the fuss was about.

"You are full of good ideas!"

"What'd I do this time?" Dana looked pleased.

"That was Yummy Tummy catering."

"Can you imagine anybody coming up with Yummy Tummy for their business?"

"They can call themselves Botulism Betty's for all I care. They just made an order for six assorted fruit pies, our choice. They'll pick them up on Friday at five."

"Oh, that's great!" Dana looked even more pleased.

"And you're the reason they found us."

Last Tuesday — a particularly slow day, since Sunshine Bakery had run a two-for-one special — Dana had called a dozen caterers chosen at random from the telephone book and asked if they would like to sample a pie. She had delivered four of the day's leftovers on her way home, and promised four more for the following day. And now the giveaways were paying off. This was the first real order from a caterer, but another had called with questions, and another had dropped in to see the shop and sample another slice. That young man had promised to keep Wanda in mind when he got too busy to do dessert on his own.

"Well, tonight's going to be even better advertising," Dana said. "The pies are gorgeous, especially the Elvis Surprise. And we know they're delicious. So everybody's going to be impressed, and some of them will want to know where the pies came from. You'll get more orders."

"I hope so." Wanda checked her watch. Lizzie had a late-afternoon dentist's appointment, and though Dana had offered to postpone, Wanda had recruited Janya to help with the delivery instead. "I guess you'd better scoot on out of here."

"You're sure you and Janya can manage?"

"We're borrowing a van from her husband so we can set up everything in the back. Don't worry."

"Then I've done everything I can. The Elvis pies, and the luscious lemon and Key lime, are in the racks. The fruit pies are all in boxes."

"You drop by tonight and I'll tell you how it went."

Dana smiled her thanks, as if she might really do it, but Wanda knew she wouldn't.

Dana kept to herself. Even when she was socializing, she always seemed on guard, as if every word she spoke had been weighed and judged before it was allowed to pass her lips. She never suggested a get-together, even though she'd been living at Happiness Key for a month. She seemed to like everyone, but she seemed to like them best at arm's length.

Dana went back to the kitchen and returned with her purse. "Good luck. I know the pies will be a success."

Janya passed her in the doorway, and the two women greeted each other quickly, but Dana didn't stop to chat.

Janya was wearing one of her India getups. Wanda could never remember what she called them. A long raspberry-colored tunic over gauzy matching pants that ended inches above her ankle. She had silver bracelets on both arms, and her hair was woven in a French braid pinned under at the nape to show her lovely neck.

"You look too pretty to deliver pies. Even prettier than usual."

"Rishi and I are going to dinner afterward."

"That sounds like progress. Hasn't he been working too hard lately?"

Janya's tone was crisp. "Rishi works hard all the time."

Wanda finished closing out the register and locked all the bills in the safe Ken had

304

installed under the counter. Most days he stopped by and took her cash to the bank before closing time. She'd also put a Palmetto Grove Police Department sticker on the front door, and anybody casing the place would see that cops were her most frequent customers.

"Okay, let's roll," she said. "I got the address. You got the van. We're in business."

Fifteen minutes later, with the pies safely wedged together in the back and Wanda at the wheel, they were heading toward the most exclusive gated community in Palmetto Grove.

"I hope you're going somewhere tasty," Wanda said. "For dinner, I mean."

"There is an Indian restaurant at a motel outside of town. It has just opened. We are going with his staff."

"Have something to celebrate?" Wanda was ever hopeful.

"I am not pregnant, if that's what you mean." She glanced at Wanda. "Rishi is . . ." Her voice trailed off. She shrugged.

Wanda knew she ought to tread carefully, but that wasn't what she did best. "Rishi is what? Unhappy? Unsure if he wants children?"

"Rishi is not cooperative."

For a moment Wanda couldn't speak. Then she exploded. "What man in his right mind would not cooperate with *you?* A man and a woman decide to have a baby and suddenly she's saying yes every time he asks for sex. It's a man's dream come true."

"Not for Rishi."

Wanda was having trouble putting this together. She turned onto the private road leading to the development, and stopped at the gatehouse to tell the security guard who she was and where she was going. He checked his clipboard before he raised the bar.

"So what's his problem?" Wanda asked once she was moving again. She figured they didn't have much time for conversation before they were too busy unloading pies.

"He says nothing is wrong. But I think he is so disappointed I have yet to conceive, he does not want to try anymore. He is disappointed in *me*."

Wanda could tell this was serious and deserved her full attention. Unfortunately, she was also gawking at a long line of over-wrought minimansions. She had to be even blunter than usual.

"I don't know Rishi like the back of my hand, but that sounds like nonsense. Everybody says he's brilliant. Brilliant men know it takes time to conceive. He couldn't be expecting you to do it on command. Besides, maybe he's the one with the problem."

"Do men consider that? In a man's mind, isn't the woman always at fault?"

"More like they're so scared it *might* be

them, they don't want to even think about it."

"Perhaps this is true, but if I am wrong, why is my husband finding so many reasons not to . . ." She shrugged again, and the raspberry silk rippled.

None of the reasons that occurred to Wanda were good ones to mention. Could be Rishi was having an affair. Or maybe he had decided that men were more to his taste. Or maybe he regretted his arranged marriage and didn't want to bring a child into it.

"My bet?" she said instead. "Stress. Plain and simple. He works too hard, and he doesn't want making a baby to feel like more of the same. I bet he's just tired and cranky and needs a vacation. Why don't the two of you go somewhere for a few days? Shack up in a nice motel outside Orlando where they're real cheap and let nature take its course."

Janya sank her white teeth into her lovely bottom lip. "This is a good idea, I think. I will suggest it."

Wanda figured even if the pies were a failure, at least she'd done one thing right today.

They found the Statler house, and she thought Mrs. Statler could simply have mentioned that her home was the largest in a development of huge houses, with the biggest lot and best view, directly on the water.

The house was two-story and Mediterranean in style, with a red tile roof and honey-colored stucco exterior. Wanda guessed the size was in excess of six thousand square feet, probably somewhere closer to ten. It spread across the property like a motel, only no motel she'd ever been in was half this luxurious.

"Well, I can see why hosting a reception as large as this one is no skin off Mrs. Statler's nose," Wanda said.

"In India, many families would live inside."

"I imagine the only people living in this one are the Statlers and their household help. You know the butler, the chambermaid, the stable boys. I hope the kitchen's in the back, so we can see the view."

Wanda pulled the van into what looked like a parking spot to the right of the towering entry. "We'll leave the pies inside for now. There might be a better place to park."

"I will always be happy to deliver pies if it brings us to places like this."

The courtyard was paved in marble. Wanda rang the front doorbell and wondered as she did if she should have looked harder for a rear entrance. But Mrs. Statler herself answered, and she beamed one of her eerie unwrinkled smiles when she saw Wanda and Janya.

"You're just in time," she said. "I have to go out for a little while, the caterer's not going to be here for another hour, and my

308

housekeeper is out, too, so I was worried I might miss you."

She delivered this flood of information without any change of expression, but she sounded genuinely glad to see them.

"We'll bring the pies right in," Wanda said. "Is there a place we should park to get them to the kitchen?"

"No, you're fine. I'll prop this door for you. My housekeeper cleared space in the largest of the two refrigerators for all the pies that need refrigeration. But once you're finished unloading and putting everything away, would you mind closing this door and fastening the dead bolt, then leaving through the back? We won't worry about the security system. I'm heading out this very minute. The back door will lock behind you. You'll turn right and follow the path past the pool house. We have a guest staying there, but he's not home at the moment, so don't worry. You'll see a gate beside the bougainvillea, and you can go through that, along the side of the house and back here to your van."

Wanda followed the directions as closely as she could and nodded as Mrs. Statler spoke.

Mrs. Statler finished up. "I left your check on the counter, so you won't need to go to the trouble of billing me, and the kitchen is that way." She pointed toward the back of the house. For the first time she seemed to see Janya. "You are too pretty to believe. The world is not fair." Then she lifted her hand in a wave, gave another taut smile and moved past them to a gray Lincoln parked not far from the van.

"She's a trusting soul, isn't she?" Wanda asked, once she and Janya were alone.

"Perhaps she has so much, she isn't afraid to lose some of it."

"More likely she just knows where to find us to get it back. And even if the alarm is off, there have to be security cameras everywhere. Not that they'll see us doing anything we shouldn't."

"It's a very grand house."

"A little overdone, even for my fancy tastes. Wouldn't you feel like you had to be dressed up every minute or the house might just boot you out and lock the door behind you? Let's go find the kitchen and take care of business."

They passed through several rooms, some of which Wanda could not identify by name. Everywhere she looked, the wood was heavy, dark and highly polished. The whisper-soft Oriental carpets under their feet hadn't come from Taiwan.

"The place sure has been florified," Wanda said. "The florist must have spent the whole morning just carrying in arrangements and fondling his bankroll. I never saw such displays."

The formal dining room, which looked as if it could easily seat twenty at a Windsor

Castle–worthy table, had already been set up with crystal and small china plates, as if this was the place where guests might first be channeled. Wanda made a wrong turn into a butler's pantry, retraced her steps with Janya right behind her and found the kitchen just a short hallway from the dining room. Once there, Wanda was surprised they had missed it the first time, since it looked to be responsible for half the square footage of the house.

"Have you ever seen anything like this?" She stopped in the doorway. Stainless steel appliances worthy of Manhattan's finest restaurants adorned every wall. A massive granite island bisected the room, and over it a skylight brought in natural light and bathed a suspended glass shelf of potted herbs. The sleek cabinets were unadorned except for the grandeur of the wood itself, a rainforest exotic that was nearly black.

"I'm not leaving," Wanda said. "I'm going to stay right here and bake pies until I drop dead of exhaustion." She crossed the room to a marble counter, clearly designed for rolling pastry. She ran one finger along it reverently. "I want this. I'm going to pry it right out and take it back to the shop. You're going to help."

Janya was busy examining the eight-burner stove with a built-in grill. "Do you think that anyone ever cooks in here? Everything looks new."

Wanda sighed and, with one last swipe of

her finger against marble, joined her. "It's doubtful."

"Is that not a waste? Shouldn't this kitchen belong to a mother with many children to feed, one who spends all day on her feet cooking for them?"

"People like the Statlers are too busy making money and spending it to have a flock of children. And if they did, some poor woman with her own brood at home would be their cook. I always figure when we all get to heaven, there won't be any streets of gold. There'll just be a little rearranging of resources. People who don't need a kitchen won't get one. People who do, will get a beaut, like this. Everybody'll be happy."

"It seems as if, with a little thought and energy, that might happen now, on earth."

"No, that's *communism*, unless it's managed from on high. Until we're glorified, we just have to suck it up."

"I am always interested in the way you think."

Wanda liked the sound of that. Educating Janya was one of her missions in life.

They made a dozen trips back and forth to the van, careful not to carry more pies each time than they could safely manage. Wanda set the pies that didn't need refrigeration on the island, then carefully took the Elvis Surprise, Key lime and luscious lemon out of their carriers and set them in the refrigerator.

When they were all finished and had locked the front door, she took the check made out to Wanda's Wonderful Pies from the island and folded it in quarters, sticking it inside her ample bra, since her purse was in the car. "I guess we're done."

"They make a beautiful sight. She will be pleased, I'm sure."

"Where do you suppose she has Elvis's costume on display?"

Apparently Janya knew this was not a casual question. "Please! I don't want to be found wandering through a stranger's house."

Wanda considered. The temptation to go looking for the King's stage regalia was extreme. In the end, though, she had to admit Janya was right.

"Maybe I'll be back," she said. "And maybe next time someone will be here to show me."

"There is a better chance of that if we leave now, as we should."

"I guess." Wanda took one more look around the envy-worthy kitchen. She wanted to remember every detail for that day when the heavenly hosts started reassigning assets.

She followed Janya through a doorway leading into a long, glassed-in porch. The kitchen had no view of the water. The view had been saved for this.

"Ohmigod." Wanda stopped to stare. "Will you look at this?"

Janya was doing exactly that. Beyond them

was a pool with a grotto set off to one side and a waterfall cascading over rocks. But straight ahead the pool melted into the gulf, which melted into the sky. Wanda felt as if she had been plunged into eternity.

"They must spend their lives here," Janya said. "How could they ever be enticed to leave? They must eat all their meals here. Sleep here."

Wanda hoped that was all true, although she doubted it. People got used to their blessings, forgot they were blessed at all and went in search of more. She'd done it a time or two herself. That was just human nature.

"Where do you suppose that pool house is? That skunk CJ Craimer gets to look at this whenever he wants. You need further proof life's not fair?"

"Perhaps the pool house is over to the side so it is not in the way."

"Well, we'd better get going." She ushered Janya through the door, then with an audible sigh, she closed it behind them and heard the lock click. She expected to be hit with a wall of heat, but a soft breeze blew off the water and rippled across her skin.

"If that don't beat all. I bet they don't even have mosquitoes here."

"Will mosquitoes be split up and portioned out in this heaven of yours?" Janya asked. "Will anybody want them?"

"Mosquitoes go somewhere down below,

I'm pretty sure."

"That's good."

Wanda started toward the grotto, then around it, where Janya had guessed the pool house might be hiding. Sure enough, a perky little building in the same color stucco and with the same red tile roof sat immediately beyond the highest part of the rock formation, separated from the remaining edge of the pool by a narrow podocarpus-lined patio. Just in front of the pool house, cast-iron chairs clustered around a matching table shaded by a green-and-white-striped umbrella. Inside, curtains graced the windows. Clearly this was not a storage shed.

"So this is where CJ hangs out," Wanda said. "He could have done worse. He can take a dip in privacy anytime he wants to."

"After a year in prison, he must feel he is living in a castle."

"No, when he needs a castle, he just knocks on that door." Wanda nodded back toward the house, which was no longer visible.

"I wonder if Tracy has seen this."

Wanda faced her. "You think she's *that* friendly with him, he'd invite her?"

"She's lonely, and once she must have cared about him."

"I don't trust that man. And I'm a cop's wife. I have a sick sense."

"Do you mean sixth sense?"

"No, I mean I know when something makes

me feel sick, and CJ does. I get a queasy feeling around him, like something's just not right."

Janya looked worried. "Tracy says she's watching him, but I don't know. . . ."

"We should keep our eyes open, too. Let's have a look in his window. Eyes wide-open."

"No, watching is good, but that is an evasion of privacy."

"*In*vasion, and how can it be if the man's not home?"

"It is still not right."

Wanda knew that, in theory, Janya was correct. But even for a cop's wife, right and wrong could be slippery at moments like these. What if she and Janya saw something that saved Tracy heartache? What if they saw something that saved Happiness Key from legal shenanigans?

"Just a quick peek," she decided out loud.

"You peek. I will enjoy the sound of this waterfall."

That seemed fair. "You enjoy it from around the other side, okay? And if somebody comes this way, say 'hi' real loud, so I'll know we got a visitor. That work for you?"

Janya gave a nearly invisible nod.

Wanda looked around, just to be sure nobody was already sneaking up on them; then she hurried over to the pool house and peeked in the first window she came to. She had her nose up against the glass before she realized a dark bamboo shade was drawn. With the afternoon sun reflecting off the panes, she hadn't been able to tell. The next one proved to have the same drawn shade, but the door was next, and this time she hit pay dirt.

She hit more than pay dirt, she almost hit the floor. Leaning against the door to peer inside, she nearly fell in when it swung open to reveal that the pool house living room was as cute as a button. Cute and cluttered with papers. Papers everywhere. On the wicker coffee table. On the sofa upholstered in a tropical floral. On the woven jute rug.

She checked the doorknob. The lock was uncomplicated and in lock position, but apparently CJ hadn't quite pulled the door shut, which was the reason she was now standing inside. Wanda calculated. She had no idea how long she had before Janya insisted they leave, or, worse, somebody caught her rifling through CJ's belongings, because that was exactly what she was about to do. She'd fallen into something here, almost literally, and was she a woman to let fortune pass her by? Not likely.

Before she could listen to the voice in her brain that was screeching a warning, she stomped farther inside and went right to the sofa, adorned with pages like fallen autumn leaves.

Scooping up a bunch of papers, she perched

on the edge and flipped through them. She had no idea what she was looking for, but she planned to commit what she saw to memory, then ponder it as soon as she found time.

"Well, forget that!" she said out loud.

Suddenly she was looking at a familiar floor plan. Her own house, with its measly little kitchen and postage-stamp living room, and on the next sheet, stapled to it, an expanded version! A kitchen she could move around in, living room opened up and extended with walls of windows. That sure wouldn't be smart in a hurricane, since the windows were on the gulf side of the house, but still . . .

She squinted at the rest of it. This bathroom was double the size of hers, where, right now, she could brush her teeth in the sink, spit in the toilet and take a shower, all without shifting her feet. Two sinks. Two! And a shower stall with room to move around.

She didn't have time to wonder what it meant. Reluctantly, she sifted through the other papers on that stack. More house plans. Without looking harder, she couldn't be sure of specifics, but she was almost certain these were the other cottages on Happiness Key.

But why did CJ have these plans? Exactly what was he going to do with them?

Again, she had no time to wonder. She put the stack back where it had been and picked up the next one within reach, leaning back against the cushions to study the pages. These drawings took more time to figure out. She finally realized she was looking at the pieces of a map. She imagined if she had time to assemble them all, she might be able to figure out the whole thing. But there were notes in some sort of jargon or code on every page, and areas shaded in a variety of colors. She wasn't certain, but she thought she might be looking at some sort of topographical map of Happiness Key. But what were all the notes about? Was this left over from the days when CJ had planned to build an upscale development and marina where her own house now stood?

If so, why did he still have it? To help Tracy plan for her future? Or was he conniving to steal what had once been his?

She put that stack back, too, then sat motionless for a moment and listened to be sure she had more time to investigate. Janya would be looking for her soon. There was only so much time a woman could contemplate a waterfall, even for a good purpose.

When her ears said all was still calm outside, she dived into more piles. Notes this time, not maps and not house plans. Just notes, and she thought they might coordinate to the codes she'd noted on the maps. Again, though, she couldn't make heads or tails of what CJ had written. He'd been doing some sort of research, she could tell that much. He seemed to be ticking off things he had checked. But beyond that, she was in the dark.

Her time had run out. Janya was going to have a hissy fit when she realized Wanda was making herself comfortable in the living room, instead of playing Peeping Tom at the window. She got up to leave and did a quick check to be sure she'd put everything back the way she'd found it. That was when she noticed a file folder more than half-hidden behind a sofa cushion. She realized she had probably dislodged it when she sat. Now she was torn. She didn't have time to discover what CJ Craimer thought he should hide from view.

But she didn't have the willpower not to.

She tugged the folder from its hiding place and opened it, expecting more Happiness Key documents. Instead she realized she was reading papers on Creative Development and Investment letterhead. Copies, and not particularly well made ones, as if whoever had done the work had been in too much of a hurry to center the paper or find a setting that would have made for a cleaner copy. She held the folder closer and leafed through the pages inside. A picture emerged. Each page was documentation on the sale of a residence. Basic information at the top, like owner's names, address, square footage, name of subdivision and lot number.

Below that, the price paid and the new owner's name. So maybe these houses had been bankrolled by Creative Development. Nothing strange about that, although why CJ had bad copies in his possession, and why he had them *hidden,* was more interesting.

She looked more closely at one. Under the price paid, she noted an appraisal price that was substantially higher. So maybe somebody got a good deal. Then she saw a list of problems with the house, plus estimates for repairs and renovations, some of them substantial. The next line was most puzzling. A bank — not Creative Development — was listed as mortgage holder, then the amount of the mortgage appeared, which looked to Wanda as if it was the entire appraisal figure. That was when she noted the date. This transaction had occurred several years ago, when real estate was booming and banks were clamoring to give away money to anybody with a beating heart.

Had Creative Development bought these homes recently to rehab them? Or maybe the new owner was a contractor who worked with Statler. But how could a dilapidated house be a worthwhile investment now, at a time when every residential block in town either had a short sale or foreclosure sign in front of at least one house? Was Edward Statler simply a genius who could pick up houses cheap with no money down, renovate them, then sell them for a handsome profit? What was that called these days? Flipping? Sure, Florida was full of homes that probably needed to be flipped, but in this economy, who was going to buy the finished product?

More important, why did CJ have these pages hidden away? What did any of this have to do with him?

She didn't think twice. She removed one of the sheets, folded it, then folded it again until it, too, fit inside her bra. Then she finished looking through the file. The pages at the back were something completely different. These were simple loan applications, like the ones with which a buyer started the loan approval process. Again, she didn't think. She grabbed one — these were copies, after all, so who was she going to hurt? — and folded it quickly to stuff beside the other. She turned to hide the file where she'd found it.

That was the moment when she heard voices.

"I can't believe you want to be here while the party preparations are going on. You could have waltzed back home in time to dress."

The voice was male, and familiar. Considering where she was standing, Wanda guessed it belonged to one CJ Craimer. For a moment she froze. She was about to get caught red-handed. As far as she could tell, the house had one door, and she was facing it.

Somebody answered. "Sally's made it plain that if I'm not here to listen to her gripe and grouse while she does the last-minute stuff, she's going to divorce me."

The second voice was male, too. And since she knew from the check that Mrs. Statler's given name was Sally, Wanda was pretty sure she was listening to the voice of Edward Statler.

Not only was CJ going to catch her red-handed, but the husband of the woman who had practically bailed out Wanda's Wonderful Pies with her order was going to catch her, too.

Wanda tried to imagine hiding somewhere to emerge later, when CJ left again. But the pool house was tiny. She could try a closet or the floor under the bed, but she still had Janya to think about. Janya was unlikely to leave her here to her own devices, plus Wanda had the van key.

What would Janya do when Wanda was nowhere in sight?

She heard a rattle and a sharp scraping noise, and she figured the men were coming in through the side gate Mrs. Statler had mentioned. Her brain was spinning, but dizziness was the lone result. She realized the moment she heard voices she should have leaped for the door. She might have had time to get out, although that was iffy. She started forward and saw Janya come around the edge of the pool. Janya glanced toward the pool house, frowning; then suddenly she saw the open door and her expression turned from irritation to horror.

Janya looked right at Wanda, then at the men coming around the side of the pool house. As if she hadn't even considered what to do, she took one step to the side and gracefully toppled into the pool.

Now Wanda was horrified. Before she could do a thing, the two men came around the house, saw the woman in the pool shrieking — and who would ever have thought Janya could shriek with that kind of conviction? — and rushed forward to help her.

When the men's backs were well and truly turned, Wanda slipped out of the house and gently shut the door behind her until the lock clicked.

She waited a moment until the men were both trying to haul a sputtering, screeching Janya out of the pool, before she, too, rushed forward to help.

"Who are you?" Edward Statler, a dignified silver-haired man in an expensive suit looked both annoyed and suspicious.

"I'm so sorry!" Wanda came from behind them and helped Janya get to her feet, now that the man had gotten her out of the pool. "We were just delivering the pies for tonight's party and we were on our way out. Your wife asked us to lock up and leave by the gate. I realized I'd dropped . . . the check your wife left me. I went back to find it and Janya here was . . ."

"I was waiting," Janya said in a hoarse voice. "And when I heard voices . . . I was startled and . . ."

Wanda picked up the cue. "She must have stepped backward into the pool. Or tripped."

CJ laughed. "It's okay, Edward. Wanda and . . . Janya?"

Janya nodded, water flying emphatically in all directions.

"Wanda and Janya are friends of Tracy's," CJ went on. "Good friends. They're on the up-and-up. Sally told me she was getting her pies for the party from Wanda's shop. I'm going to get towels."

"Please . . . you don't need to," Janya said. "I'll be —"

"Don't you dare leave until we dry you off a little." CJ unlocked his door and disappeared into the pool house. Wanda waited for an angry bellow that never came. He emerged with two fluffy beach towels, and Janya took one to hurriedly dry herself.

"Well, we really made a splash, didn't we?" Wanda cleared her throat and tried to smile at her own joke. "I sure hope the pies make just as much of one. And we're so sorry. Aren't we, Janya?"

Janya narrowed her eyes. "Yes, *both* of us are sorry." She handed the towel back to CJ.

"The best thing I can do is go home and change," she said. "Thank you both for your help."

"We'll just let ourselves out," Wanda said. "You've been so kind."

CJ was smiling, and even Edward Statler seemed to find the whole thing funny. Wanda hoped that neither man's suspicions had been raised. If the pool house had security cameras, too, they would get a real thrill if they reviewed the tapes of her rifling through CJ's papers.

She wondered why that possibility hadn't occurred to her before.

Janya started toward the gate, and Wanda followed. The men had their eyes trained on them, or rather on the lovely Indian woman whose soaked clothing was clinging to her curvaceous young body. Once they were through the gate, Wanda began to breathe easier. Until she glanced at her friend.

"What would you have done if I had not thrown myself into that pool?"

Wanda didn't know. She slung her arm over Janya's shoulders and didn't care if she got wet or not.

"The real question? What would I do without Janya Kapur as my neighbor? That's the question I don't ever want to have to answer."

CHAPTER SIXTEEN

Before the advent of Henrietta Claiborne, summer at the rec center had looked busy. Now, with Losing to Win gaining momentum, Tracy had put in so much overtime she was afraid some night soon, she might not remember the route back to Happiness Key. The center had showers; there was fast food nearby. She had even stored toiletries and an extra change of clothing, just in case some morning she really did wake up on the rec room sofa.

Youth camp, which had started last Monday, had been her first priority. At least those activities felt familiar, since she'd organized and run the camp last summer, too. She had great counselors, a full schedule of activities and field trips, and, so far, no problem kids. Even Bay, last year's boy-in-the-ointment, was behaving, making friends, and struggling to be number one at everything. Last summer he'd done everything possible to get tossed out of camp, so he could go live with his mother. This summer Sylvia was living right down the hall, so he was doing everything he could to impress her.

Tracy wasn't sure which was worse.

This morning, Losing to Win was finally having its debut. The committee had decided to organize weight-loss teams from the center's activity groups, since their members already knew how to pull together. A publicity blitz, plus some not so subtle arm-twisting, had resulted in six teams. Young mothers, senior swimmers, summer softball. Plus creative cooks — they had been a natural, since weight gain came with the territory; photo pranksters — who had been made to promise they would not Photoshop their "before and after" photographs; and finally, the shuffleboard team.

Tracy still had hopes for more. Eight would be perfect, but a summer forgoing barbecued ribs, potato salad and strawberry shortcake in favor of salad with low-fat dressing was a hard sell. Plus each team member was required to ante up five dollars a week toward the new nursery, an amount to be matched by local businesses that were sponsoring teams and again by Henrietta.

There were compensations, and Tracy had played them up. At summer's end the winning team would be selected, using percentage of weight lost as the standard. Palmetto Grove's premiere hotel had agreed to donate massages and the use of their extensive spa facilities for half a day. The grand prize winner, the single participant who lost the highest percentage of their body weight, would receive an entire package of treatments, plus dinner and a night in a luxury suite.

And the others? They would have healthier, slimmer bodies to console them. If all went as planned, thousands would be raised to renovate the nursery, everyone would have fun, and the sponsors would receive plenty of publicity.

Before she headed upstairs for the opening festivities, Tracy slipped into the ladies' room to splash cold water on her face. She felt the way she might if she'd been dragged for miles behind a Jet Ski. Next year maybe the center would raise money by competing for hours slept. The team with the most would win, and that was one competition she would be happy to enter.

She was halfway out the door when a small body slammed into hers and tumbled to the ground with an "oof!" Several other boys scooted past, but Tracy corralled the familiar one and set Bay back on his feet.

"Here's the thing about doors," she said. "They open, and people come out of them, which is why it's a good idea to stay close to the middle of a hallway so you can avoid collisions."

"My group's got the softball field. We want

to practice before our big game this afternoon!"

She dropped her hands. "Then go get 'em, tiger. But watch out for other people on the way."

Despite the initial rush, now Bay seemed in no hurry. "My mom might come and watch us play."

Tracy wondered if Sylvia would show up. Marsh had been at swim team practice on Wednesday. Tracy had seen him from a distance, but not to speak to. The only time she'd ever seen Sylvia at the center was the evening of the banquet. And she was suspicious that Sylvia had come that night not to see her son deliver his lines, but to be seen herself. Palmetto Grove's finest had been in attendance, and networking was always good for job prospects.

She hoped for Bay's sake that Sylvia would come this afternoon to cheer him on, even if there was no one in the stands to impress.

"I'm going to pitch." Bay's golden-brown eyes — an uncomfortable reminder of his father's — were glowing. "And I got a real home run at our last game."

"Good for you." She held up her palm, and they high-fived.

"Mom says if I get another one today, she and Dad will take me out for pizza."

Tracy wondered why Sylvia and Marsh just didn't take Bay for pizza on general principles. Who cared if the kid made a home run? At his age, winning and losing was as much about remembering to run after a ball as it was about skill. Bay already felt he had to work hard to please his mother. He didn't need more pressure.

She wondered if she ought to talk to Marsh, then realized that these days, she was the last person who could. Anything she said would sound like a criticism of Sylvia. And although there was, in her view, a lot to criticize, she was in the unique position of not being able to say a word. Everything would sound like sour grapes.

"You know what?" She ruffled what there was of Bay's hair. "Don't worry if you don't get a home run, okay? You're a good teammate, and maybe it's somebody else's turn today. Just tell your mom and dad you played your best. That's worth pizza any time."

He grinned, and again she was reminded of his father. "I gotta win," he said, almost as if he was talking to a younger child, explaining a fact of life in words she might understand. "That's what counts."

"Playing well, having fun and being a good sport, *that's* what counts." She wondered when she had actually started to believe her own words. Nowadays when she mouthed these good sportsmanship platitudes — and mouthing them came with the territory — they actually sounded like gospel.

"I gotta go."

"Yep, you gotta." Tracy waved him off, then watched him sprint the rest of the way to the door.

The interlude with Bay meant she arrived at the kickoff a minute or two later than she'd planned. Luckily things seemed to be going well.

The event was scheduled to last all morning, and they were serving a nutritious, low-calorie lunch at the end. Judging from something that smelled suspiciously like steaming broccoli, the creative cooks were putting the finishing touches on the meal.

Chairs, a projector and a screen had been set up in the front, as had an industrial-sized digital scale. The center's new weight loss guru, a perky middle-aged cheerleader named Kitty Wallace, was setting up a PowerPoint presentation. Role model Kitty, with her washboard abs and Michelle Obama arms, would conduct a weigh-in for each team, perform voodoo rituals to determine how many pounds each person should lose, then talk about diet strategies and nutrition. Tracy had convinced both the daily and weekly newspapers to send reporters and photographers, who hadn't yet arrived. Unfortunately, Henrietta wasn't going to be here. She was preparing for tonight's intimate little gathering of about twenty on her yacht. Tracy was looking forward to it, since once she was on board, she couldn't work anymore.

Gladys was bustling about with stacks of folders Tracy had made up for the participants. When she saw Tracy, she dropped them unceremoniously on the nearest chair and came right over.

"Senior swimmers dropped out. They're doing so well in their meets, they think they'll be on the road too much to participate. Besides, they're already in great shape. If they each lost just a couple of pounds they'd cinch it. There's not a one of them whose BMI needs a tweak."

Tracy had known the senior swimmers were the iffiest of her teams. They hadn't been enthused from the get-go, and she'd had to work and work to get them to say yes.

She thought out loud. "We can do this with five, but we won't raise as much money. And the more people we include, the more excitement we generate."

"It's time to have a staff team, Tracy." Gladys held up her hand. "I know all your objections, but with senior swimmers gone, it's a natural for us to step in."

Tracy and Gladys had discussed this for the past week. Tracy worried that pitting the staff against rec center members might cause hard feelings. Gladys believed it would be a bonding experience, everyone rooting for everyone else, with renewed insight into what friends and competitors were undergoing.

"A morning at the spa," Gladys said. "Nobody's going to care that much if they win or lose. It's not half a million dollars and national television exposure. It's going to be all for one and one for all here. And I need this."

Tracy could argue with everything but that. Indeed, Gladys and Woody both needed the competition to make them pay more attention to their health. "But we need at least six people," she countered, staying away from the personal. "That's the minimum. And some of the groups have as many as nine."

"I've got six!" Gladys ticked off names. Clearly she'd been busy. In addition to herself and Woody, she had recruited two instructors, a maintenance man, and the woman in charge of the center's extensive swimming program.

Tracy knew when she'd been beaten. "I guess we're set, then."

Gladys looked pleased. "Here come the Shuffleboarders. Go make nice."

Tracy pasted on her most winning smile, although she knew with this particular group, a smile meant little. Last year their leaders, the shuffle board, had taught her a lot more than how to play a better game of shuffleboard. They'd knocked her personal disk off the shuffleboard court of real life a few times, and she could admit — with a certain amount of annoyance — that she had needed it.

Now she approached them warily, as she had ever since the unfortunate bird-watching incident.

The three old men she'd first been introduced to last year were here with a handful of others from the Palmetto Grove Shuffleboard team. Roger Goldworthy, who she always thought of as Mr. Moustache because of the razor-thin line above his top lip, approached her. She greeted him warily.

"It's nice to see you here. Are you, umm . . . one of the participants?"

He snorted. She was glad he saw the humor. He weighed maybe a hundred pounds, and his pants were gathered in folds under a tightly cinched belt. She suspected he couldn't find pants that would fit outside the boys' department.

"We had plenty without me," he said. "Or we thought we did until about an hour ago. Sally just dropped out. She's going in for surgery, and that doesn't seem like a fair way to lose weight."

"I hope it's not serious," Tracy said. Sally was a dimply octogenarian who could slam a shuffleboard disk into prime position with her eyes closed.

"Knee replacement. She'll be at our next tournament on crutches and still beat the competition."

"Bad news for her and Losing to Win."

"She won't be doing any bird-watching for

a while, but what's the need? Her life list's already as long as my arm, and somebody scared away the only masked booby for a hundred miles."

Tracy smiled sweetly. "Do you have anybody else who could replace her?"

His lips curved into something approximating a smile. "We'll just have to see."

She didn't have time to question him. Gladys was pointing toward the front, where Woody had taken his place at the microphone to welcome everybody. Tracy joined her, and they stood together.

Tracy thought that under the circumstances, the turnout of close to a hundred was great. Serving lunch helped, plus friends of team members had come to cheer on the competitors. And a lot of people were probably interested in hearing what Kitty had to say about weight loss and health, but maybe not quite ready to commit to the competition.

Woody had a droll sense of humor and used it to warm up the crowd. Nervous titters turned to gales of laughter by the time he'd finished, and his announcement that he was joining a team himself met with wild applause. Tracy realized Gladys had been right all along.

He introduced Kitty, who proved immediately she was the right person to lead the charge. She had everybody up and stretching and greeting their neighbors; then, guessing that there might be shy people in the audience who wanted to join a team, she promised that nobody would ever be embarrassed by anything that happened during Losing to Win. She suggested a new team called Losers Anonymous that would be part of the fun, only the members would never have to admit it. She promised the audience that she would be taking secret registrations and doing secret weigh-ins.

"She's good. That'll be our sixth team," Tracy whispered to Gladys.

"Don't you mean seventh?"

Tracy broke the bad news in another whisper. "The Shuffleboarders are down a member, so they won't make the minimum, but maybe somebody will step up to the scale."

Gladys made a worried noise. "Whoever joins them had better tow the line. Those folks play to win."

Tracy's attention wandered. She had a list one mile long of things she hadn't done in the two weeks she'd been working nonstop. She figured when things slowed down, she could fight off loneliness by doing laundry and grocery shopping, maybe even look over CJ's plans to see if there was any prayer she could start to renovate the cottages. And whose would she start with? That difficulty alone might make the entire idea unfeasible.

Kitty had launched into her own weight loss

story, and Tracy half listened. Kitty claimed she'd once weighed close to two hundred pounds. Her cholesterol and blood pressure had been out of control, and none of the diets worked for more than a pound or two. Finally, desperate and depressed, she got involved with a program that put her in touch with other people in the same boat. For Kitty, the camaraderie and support had made all the difference. Just the way they would make the difference in Losing to Win.

"She's absolutely perfect," Gladys whispered. "I can feel myself losing weight just listening to her."

Tracy hoped it was going to be that easy, since by summer's end, they really needed something to show for all this work.

Finally the time came for the teams to stand up and be counted. Tracy had volunteered to be Kitty's recorder, so she went up front, and the weigh-in began. First the young mothers group, who had decided to call their team Big Mamas, weighed in. Only Kitty and Tracy saw the scales, and Kitty made her calculations on paper and handed the verdict to each woman. Some of the moms were only ten to fifteen pounds overweight. In the end, the team of six needed to lose a hundred and ten pounds.

Kitty announced the total goal, and everybody applauded.

The other teams followed suit.

Summer softball had taken the name Bases Loaded, and between the eight of them, they needed to lose a hundred and eighty pounds. Creative cooks, now called Calorie Crusaders, needed a hundred and fifty. The six photo pranksters, now the Meal Magicians, needed just a hundred and ten.

Finally the shuffleboard team, who had settled on Naughty Nibblers — in honor of the points shuffleboard players tried to "nibble" from their opponents — came up to the microphone. Tracy recognized most of them from their hours of practice on the center's state-of-the-art courts. Two men and three women stepped forward. Tracy thought she was getting good at estimating the total pounds Kitty might suggest. She was guessing maybe at most a hundred for the five of them.

"Is somebody else coming?" Kitty asked the woman in the lead.

"We lost our sixth member," a woman, who needed to lose about forty pounds, told Kitty.

Mr. Moustache stepped up from the back to join his teammates. "If we have to have six, I guess I can do it."

Kitty glanced at Tracy, then back at Mr. M. "I don't think we can let you," Kitty said. "You don't need to lose weight. That throws off the calculations."

He didn't seem surprised. Instead he turned to Tracy. "You've played with us, right?"

She frowned. "I think Kitty's right. It's not personal. I hope you realize —"

"Don't go on and on, okay? My point is, you've played a game or two with us. We could say you're an unofficial shuffleboarder, right?"

She had a sudden suspicion where this might be going. "Just for fun. I'm not really —"

"And you're not on another team, are you?" he continued, as if she hadn't spoken. "You're not on the staff team? Gladys said you didn't join."

"No, but I don't really need to —"

"Then join ours. What can it hurt? We need six people, you're available. . . ." He gave the tiniest shrug.

She had no way out. She couldn't refuse, not in front of all these people, including fellow staff members who were about to weigh in and join the fun. This was *her* project. She couldn't act as if she found the idea distasteful.

"Okay," she said with a smile. "But remember, the rule is that each participant needs to lose a minimum of ten pounds. You know that, right?"

He smiled thinly.

Tracy went on. "I've gained a little weight in the last couple of months, but not that much. So I don't think I'll qualify."

Kitty saved Mr. M. from answering. "If

you're willing, we can see."

Tracy took a good look at Kitty's expression. She had a sudden premonition that this was not going to turn out well. She frowned at Mr. M. and lowered her voice to a whisper. "All this because of one little bird?"

"Of course not. It's about supporting the rec center." He paused for effect. "Although it *was* a very special little bird."

Kitty now looked totally at sea. Tracy grimaced, then she stepped up on the scale.

The audience, who had only been privy to parts of the exchange, began to applaud. For all they knew, this was a promotional stunt.

Kitty asked a couple of questions, then took out her calculator at the same moment Tracy finally glanced at the scale's display.

"Oh my God!" Tracy leaned over, wondering if she could be reading the number wrong. "There's something wrong. There has to be."

"Not very wrong," Kitty assured her. "By my calculations, only about ten pounds wrong. You should have most of those off by summer's end."

Mr. M. held out his hand. "Welcome to Naughty Nibblers, and since it looks like you could use a few more games of shuffleboard, we'll get you right on the schedule."

After lunch Tracy had thrown all the snacks in her desk into the rec center Dumpster, and now she was starving. "There's got to be something I missed."

She jerked open drawers. "Brutal!"

She kept searching. "Thanks for nothing, world," she said as she slammed the last one shut.

Now she was talking to herself, too. Maybe she was hallucinating from starvation.

She rested her head in her hands and wondered if last year, before Marsh and good old Wanda had started cooking for her, she had been this hungry. She'd been raised to see fat grams and calories in every bite, and virtue in nearly invisible portions. She had gone out to lunch with girlfriends and turned up her nose at the bread basket, asked for salad dressing on the side, eaten, at most, half of what was on her plate, and never taken leftovers.

Of course, she hadn't enjoyed eating, either. That was the difference. She and CJ had dined in some of the world's most famous restaurants, and she had nibbled. Nibbled in Paris and Florence and New Orleans. Nibbled at Spago and Urasawa and Lawry's. Now she was ready to nibble the paper on her desk. Creative Cooks' steamed vegetables and slivers of chicken breast had already been a memory less than ten minutes after she'd consumed them.

She got up and went to the glass door, looking outside. The place was teeming with parents on their way to watch softball, and all the shuffleboard courts were in use. She wondered if she just offered herself as a sacrifice, would the shuffleboarders beat her over the head with their cues instead of asking her to slowly starve herself to death?

"Maybe I've been substituting food for sex," she muttered. "Maybe if I just hop into bed with somebody, the pounds will melt away."

"I'd be happy to test the theory."

She whirled and found a jeans-clad Marsh standing several yards behind her, a navy blue Rays cap under one arm. She put her hand against her heart. "You snuck up on me!"

"I did no such thing. I made enough noise to wake a giant. And what was that about hopping into bed?"

She narrowed her eyes. "I was not talking *to* you or *about* you. I had no idea you were standing there."

He didn't smile exactly, but he came close. "You're sure? I think you knew, at least subliminally. I think you wanted me to hear that."

"I think I want you to go watch your son's softball game and leave me alone."

"The other game's just finishing up."

"Where's Sylvia?"

His almost smile disappeared. "Why does it matter?"

She didn't like his tone. "It doesn't to me,

but it matters to Bay. He's been looking forward to her watching him play."

"Why are you talking to my son about Sylvia?"

Maybe she was irritable from hunger. Maybe she was exhausted. She opened her mouth to answer, then closed it again and waited until she had breathed deeply. Twice. It didn't help much, but the pause said plenty.

"What are you asking, Marsh? Do you think I'm pumping Bay for news about you and his mother? Maybe I've been asking him where his mother sleeps at night?"

"It sounded that way."

"I'm in charge of the youth camp. I talk to the kids. They talk to me. They tell me all sorts of things without my asking questions. Today one girl told me her grandmother died yesterday. It's not the kind of thing I'd ever think to ask, is it?"

"I doubt you were having a relationship with the little girl's grandmother."

Anger shot through her. It shot through tingling fingers that yearned to slap him and vibrated through her knees. Most of all, it resonated in her voice. "You've overstayed your welcome."

His shoulders drooped just a fraction. "Yeah, maybe."

"For the record, Bay told me he was going to practice extra hard this morning so he would get another home run. Then he said, without a bit of prompting, that Sylvia promised him pizza if he did."

"Damn." He brushed a lock of hair off his forehead, which was good, because until he had attacked her, she'd been itching to do it herself.

"If it's important to you, Marsh, I'll distance myself from your son the same way I've distanced myself from you. But I'm not going to push him away if he comes to me. I have a job, and being available to the kids is part of it."

"I'm sorry. I know that. The two of you are fond of each other. He talks about you a lot."

She imagined that infuriated Sylvia. Or maybe Bay was smart enough to know when it was best not to mention Tracy. Because the last thing the kid wanted was to make his mother angry.

"You and I don't seem capable of having a pleasant conversation anymore." She looked beyond him to the doorway, but nobody was there. She hoped Sylvia was outside with her son, but judging by Marsh's response, that was not the case.

"I wanted to see how you're doing." He paused. "I miss you."

"It doesn't show."

"I'll never look back on these weeks as among the finest in my life."

"Then send Sylvia packing."

"You know I can't."

"You know what? I *don't* know. You say you're putting up with her so she'll get to know Bay and maybe become a better mother. Well, where are the signs it's working? She's not here to see his game. Even if he makes a home run, how will she know? How will she measure whether he's finally good enough at *something* to rate pizza for dinner?"

The sound of her voice hadn't even died before she realized she had blown it. She was talking about Sylvia, not about *them.* By doing so, she had given Sylvia the upper hand, and now Marsh would have to defend both himself and his ex, because that's what people under attack always did. And in defending Sylvia, he would be drawing closer to her. It was a foolish strategy, no matter how good it had felt to utter the words.

"Stop!" She held up her hand. "Don't say a thing. It's none of my business. Bay's not my kid. He's yours, and he's hers. And I don't want to be in the middle. Put her name on your deed. Give her a gold-plated key to your front door. It's up to you. I don't know why we're talking about it."

He didn't speak for a moment, but he clenched his jaw, and his gaze seemed to drill holes everywhere it landed.

"How's CJ?" he asked at last. "I hear he's still in town."

"He is. And I'll ask how he is when I see

him tonight."

"So while my little family's off having pizza, you and CJ will be hanging out together?"

"Henrietta Claiborne invited us on a dinner cruise. She and CJ are old friends."

"Edward Statler, Henrietta Claiborne . . . When's the governor flying in to pay homage?"

She knew better than to defend CJ, but she knew a lot of things, and how much impact was that having?

"He's the kind of man who makes friends easily," she said. "CJ's fun to be around."

"A friendly felon. It has a certain ring."

"His conviction was overturned, so he's not a felon, and he seems to be trying to put a life together for himself. In the meantime, he's been a big help to me."

"Oh, good. That's a relief."

She ignored the sarcasm. "He has a lot of skills, and I see no reason not to take advantage of them."

"Maybe CJ's the right one, then, to help melt those pounds you mentioned."

She couldn't believe he had said that. She exploded. "Shall we talk about sex, Marsh? About who's doing it with whom, and where, when and why? Because CJ's still living in the Statlers' pool house, but Sylvia's living with *you.*"

He was silent a long moment; then he shook his head. "I think this is it, Tracy."

She didn't pause to think. There had been enough of that. "I'll tell you what, breaking up's getting old. So let's agree whatever we had is over for real, okay? No need for another repeat. No need to test the waters. We're done. Finished. What do you say?"

"No need to say anything. You're surprisingly articulate."

"Let me add another verbal gem, then. Goodbye."

He looked as if he wanted to say more but knew there was no more to say. He finally turned without any hint of ceremony and left.

Tracy swallowed tears and wished she could call him back. There was only one good thing that had come out of Marsh's visit.

She had definitely lost her appetite.

CHAPTER SEVENTEEN

Tracy got home in time to try on five dresses before she settled on a beaded black sundress. She had never been particularly fond of it, since the modified A-line design hadn't done much to show off her assets. But now that her assets were larger than life, the dress was her new best friend.

Theoretically, she knew moving from a comfortable size three to a snug five was not the end of the world. After the weigh-in, Kitty had pulled her aside to caution against losing more then ten pounds. For her height and body type, ten was more than enough to shed, and there was no reason ever to be as thin as a rail again.

Except that once upon a time Tracy's entire identity and most of her conversational repertoire had revolved around staying painfully thin. So what was she now? Fat, unloved, unhappy . . . and had she mentioned fat?

She forced herself to find jewelry that would improve the dress. She forced herself to find shoes. And when her mind veered toward Marsh, she forced herself to think about dress sizes again, which were as much bad news as she could handle at the moment without breaking down. If she started by desensitizing herself to an expanding waistline, maybe eventually she could progress to Marsh, whose absence in her life could not be fixed by eating lettuce instead of French fries.

For Christmas Alice had crocheted her a black angora shawl flecked with gold that was as lacy as a spiderweb, and before she went to do her makeup, Tracy set it on the purse she was taking tonight. She was just doing her eye makeup when somebody knocked on the front door. She heard Wanda's familiar voice.

"You home, Ms. Deloche?"

"I'm in my bedroom."

Tracy heard footsteps, then the sound of the refrigerator opening and closing, before Wanda wandered through the bedroom doorway and made herself at home on Tracy's unmade bed.

"Brought you pie," Wanda said without introduction. "Had some leftovers, on account of Sunshine running a special on éclairs, and I know you love my piña colada."

Tracy wondered how many calories one slice of Wanda's amazing piña colada pie was worth, and how many days of exercise it would take to work it off.

"Yum, I'll eat every bite," she told her friend — and, sadly, she would. "It's the good news in a day filled with bad."

"Wanna tell Aunt Wanda?"

"Not while I'm lining my eyes."

"That bad, huh?"

"Bad enough that I need gossip to take my mind off it." What Tracy really needed was a slice of pie, but she wasn't going to let that happen right before dinner. She had learned *something* from Kitty. "How's the shop?"

Wanda shrugged. "Good days and bad, like today. Mrs. Statler was happy with my pies. Last Friday I got a nice order from one of her guests, so she's passing on my name. Hopefully word will keep spreading."

"I still can't imagine Janya falling in that pool. It's just not like her to be so clumsy." Tracy glanced at Wanda, who was frowning. "Wait a minute. Something's up," Tracy said. "I didn't hear the whole story, did I?"

"Well, see, here's the thing. Janya didn't really *fall* in. More like she went in on purpose."

"What? She was in the mood for a swim and couldn't resist?"

"More like she was protecting me."

Tracy's day had been difficult. She figured even following the text in a third grade primer might be hard this evening. But following Wanda was impossible.

She nearly jabbed the eyeliner brush into her pupil when she turned. "I don't get it. How could jumping in the pool protect you? Were you drowning? Had you gone in first?"

"Well, you know CJ lives in the Statlers' pool house, don't you?"

"Don't tell me Janya was trying to protect you from CJ?"

"In a manner of speaking, yes. See, here's the thing. . . ." And Wanda explained.

"You were in CJ's house? Going through CJ's things?"

"Not his things, exactly. Not his underwear or his prescriptions or his refrigerator. Just a big mess of papers lying all over the place. They more or less called to me and insisted."

Tracy squinted at her reflection. What had started out as artfully applied eyeliner now looked like Cleopatra's handiwork. She faced her friend. "You went into a man's house and rifled through his papers, Wanda. What do you have to say for yourself?"

"I found some good stuff."

"Well, darn, tell me more!"

Wanda nodded. "That's what I thought you'd say, only Janya wasn't so sure. She made me wait to tell you until I checked everything out."

"Janya's not made of the same stuff you and I are. She was born kinder." Tracy reached for the makeup remover pads and began to wipe her eyelid. "Talk fast. I have to leave for the yacht club in five minutes or I'll miss the cruise."

"Well, la-dee-da! We certainly can't have that."

"Wanda!"

Wanda went through the entire story, detailing what she'd seen and admitting that she had "borrowed" a few pages she was sure CJ would never miss.

"They were just bad copies," she said. "Not like they were originals. He can always get more."

Tracy had been listening carefully. "So what do you think it's all about?"

"I think I stumbled on two separate things. One was all the drawings of Happiness Key. Land, houses, po-ten-tial houses."

"You know CJ's been talking about renovations and putting up some new houses where the old ones stood." Tracy started the eyeliner again and this time she made sure to keep her hand steady. "It makes sense he'd have detailed maps, surveys, statistics, deeds, all that stuff, if we're talking about developing Happiness Key, although what's *never* made sense is his interest."

"Okay. I guess. So that leaves the second bunch of papers, and they're a lot more interesting."

"More than —" Tracy looked at her watch "— three minutes' worth?"

"I'm going to give it to you fast, seeing as

you're leaving. The other papers were on Creative Development and Investment letterhead, and I don't know why CJ had them, unless he's doing some work with Statler. Lists of houses that had been sold, the purchase price, long lists of whatever needed to be done to them, who bankrolled the mortgages — which were always for a hundred percent of the purchase price. Then a bunch of loan applications."

"Sounds like the kind of thing a development company would normally have on hand, Wanda. What's the big deal?"

"Big deal is I drove by the house I had the address and information for."

"That you *stole,* you mean."

"That would depend on your definition. See, I think maybe CJ stole it first, because he sure didn't want anybody to see he had it. Looked to me like he'd shoved it back behind a sofa pillow when somebody came to his door."

"That's pretty far-fetched."

"Maybe, but here's the thing. Something *is* going on there. I know for sure. Like I said, I drove by the house. That paper I took claimed the new owner planned to do all kinds of work on the place, so he got a loan from a local bank for a hundred percent of the appraisal — which was more than the purchase price — so he could renovate. I could tell that much from what I have. And I can tell you what I saw. Not a thing was *ever* done to that house. Those repairs? Not a one of them was started, much less finished. The house is an abandoned dump. Probably in worse shape than when they bought it and spent the bank's money not fixing it up. And it's been foreclosed on, so now it's just sitting there."

Tracy was confused. None of this made sense to her. "I don't see how this works."

"I'll explain, 'cause now I understand it better. Somebody buys a house, okay? And they get the house appraised, as part of the loan process, but the appraisal's a fraud. The house is appraised for more than the asking price. A lot more. So then they go to the bank with that figure, and they tell them they need all that money because they have to make a long list of repairs. The bank's got the appraisal and figures everything's okay. They'll have a renovated house worth more than the appraisal, even if the new owner defaults."

Tracy's head was swimming, but she nodded as if she understood every detail.

"So then the new owner's got a big new mortgage that's worth a whole lot more than the house. He pays the original purchase price, then he takes all the extra, and pays off whatever appraiser helped him get that far, and he walks away. He doesn't make a single mortgage payment, and the bank is left with an abandoned house that's only worth a fraction of what they loaned. And we won't even talk about what that does to the price of all the other houses on the block."

Tracy started on mascara, and when she'd finished that, she moved on to her lips and finished them before she spoke. "Maybe you misunderstood. We're not financial geniuses. What do we know about the housing market or bank loans?"

"That's what I thought. So I showed everything to Kenny, and I told him I'd gone by that house and something was mighty fishy." She came over to the mirror. "And you know what he told me? He told me to stay out of it. He told me to stay way, *way* out of it. Not to tell anybody what I'd seen or done, and put some miles between me and the Statlers and that husband of yours, Tracy. And he told me he wasn't supposed to say even that much."

Tracy felt her stomach drop a good inch. "CJ?"

"I'm not even supposed to talk to you about that no-good ex of yours, only I know you haven't really shucked him off like you ought to. And what would I think of myself if you got caught smack in the middle of this?"

"Did you tell Ken where you got the information? Did you tell him you stole it?"

Wanda looked past Tracy's shoulder, although there really wasn't anything to see. "Not the whole version."

Tracy could just imagine what Wanda *had*

told her husband. "Does Janya know?"

"She's not exactly dying to be in my company these days."

"Nobody else knows?"

Wanda shook her head, but not in agreement. "I told Dana. She's right there in the shop with me every day, and she went with me when I drove by that house. She got out and peeked through windows, too. She was a real support until . . ."

"Until what? You stole somebody else's papers?"

Wanda lifted her chin defiantly. "Until I asked her to come along and tell Kenny what we'd seen — or rather, didn't see — at the house. Then she acted like I was a rattlesnake shaking my tail right at her."

"Why do you think she reacted that way?" Tracy asked, although she suspected this was a different subject entirely.

"I don't know. She's the best manager I could ask for. She's good at everything. But I notice she's a lot better with women than she is with men. Kenny's noticed it, too. He's good at noticing things like that. Comes with the territory. He says she's so short with him when he sees her at the shop, she's almost rude, like a woman trying to hide something."

Tracy was on information overload. "I don't know what to say about any of this. I'm about to go on a dinner cruise with CJ, and I can't get out of it. Henrietta Claiborne's the hostess, so my job's on the line."

"You'll be careful? You'll watch out? And you won't end up at his place tonight?"

"Wanda!"

Wanda held up her hands. "I'm a mother. I can't help myself."

"Not my mother, you're not. *My* mother pushed me into CJ's arms."

Wanda put a sympathetic hand on Tracy's shoulder. "Being a mother is a lot more than giving birth, although that's one heck of a wake-up call. But some of us are fit for it and some aren't, and the Good Lord can't always tell the difference, I guess."

Tracy managed a smile, although she thought right now she really had very little to smile about.

If she'd thought the day couldn't get any worse, on her way to the Sun County Yacht Club, Tracy glimpsed Marsh and Sylvia outside Gonzalo's. As she roared by, she saw Bay between them, one hand firmly tucked into each of his parents'. She couldn't see his expression, nor did she want to. She'd witnessed Bay's biggest grins and knew this one would be a double wide.

At least maybe Marsh had heard *something* she'd said. Or maybe poor Bay had just gotten that pizza party home run after all.

At the yacht club, she gave her keys to the valet and walked along the promenade beside the water. The clubhouse looked like something a freaked-out Scarlett O'Hara would have designed after that nasty old War of Northern Aggression, but Tracy knew from one lone evening there that the food and service were both first class.

In addition to a pool and golf course, there were four piers with a total of seventy floating slips — she'd asked the valet, who had pointed her in the right direction and given her a rundown. Each slip was equipped with a storage locker, running water, sewer pump and all the luxuries, like electricity, cable television and telephone service. Henrietta's slip was along the pier farthest from the clubhouse, where the largest yachts were berthed.

As she drew nearer, Tracy saw CJ. He was standing at the end of the pier, chatting with several people beside a yacht roughly the size of New Mexico. Henrietta wasn't going to be giving up many of the pleasures of home this summer. Tracy wondered if the yacht came with a masseuse and a cook. Henrietta had room to house a small circus if she needed entertainment.

CJ stopped talking and smiled at her as she approached, then excused himself and walked down the pier to meet her. He wore an elegant gray sport coat and a shirt several shades darker. CJ always carried himself like royalty, a stance easy enough for someone with his wide shoulders. For a moment she felt like the same young woman who had, at their first meeting, immediately set out to make him hers.

It lasted only seconds before her internal alarms began to sound, but she was painfully aware that she had, at least temporarily, succumbed.

"I remember that dress." He sounded as if the memory was a good one.

She kept her voice cool. "You probably remember everything in my closet, CJ. I haven't exactly been haunting Rodeo Drive since they stuck you away."

"I gave this one to you."

When they were married, CJ had been highly opinionated about what she wore, but he'd rarely selected any of it. Now she remembered that he had picked this dress out on a rare shopping spree together. Suddenly she was sorry she'd worn it, afraid she'd sent the wrong message.

He leaned over and kissed her cheek before she could turn her head. "Black was always your color."

"A good one to get used to. Mourning, and all that."

"Sounds like you had some day. Whatever put you in this mood, it wasn't my fault, okay?"

She let herself sigh. A long, deep and hopefully cleansing sigh. "Yeah."

"Here's my suggestion. Leave whatever happened right here, and when you step on board Henrietta's yacht, forget what it was. You need some fun, TK, and you need to relax and let somebody take care of you for a change. You're a big, independent girl, but even Wonder Woman probably needed a stiff drink and a neck rub every once in a while."

Big resounded in Tracy's head.

The advice, though, was stellar. She did need some fun, and after years of being taken care of, a few more hours of being pampered wouldn't hurt her. So what if CJ was involved in this Statler disaster, whatever it was? He wasn't going to play pirate tonight and hijack the yacht to Cuba, and she doubted anybody would arrest him for anything until they were safely back on land. Meantime, the night was theirs.

She put on a smile, and, surprisingly, it helped. "Let's enjoy everything about tonight."

"I'll enjoy being with you."

Despite herself, she was afraid she would enjoy being with him, too.

And what did that say about her?

CHAPTER EIGHTEEN

The night had few visible stars, and clouds drifted across the moon. Fortunately Alice's porch light fell softly on the flower bed beside her door, so Dana could see to dig. She was concentrating so hard that a shadow creeping toward her was the first clue she was not alone. She swiveled in horror and found Pete Knight standing just at the edge of the light.

"I announced myself," he said. "I was sure you heard me."

Dana's heart was pounding so fast she thought it might sprout wings and fly away. "I didn't hear a thing."

"I parked over at your place, and Lizzie told me you were out for a walk. I called to you when I got to Alice's mailbox." He paused. "I didn't expect to find you working in her garden this time of night."

Dana looked down. There might have been a garden here at one time, but now the sandy soil was blanketed with mulch and a collection of whimsical concrete statues. They were

Alice's practical solution to dealing with weeds and heat.

"Are you trying to surprise Alice with petunias between the elf and the toadstool?"

Since there were no flats of petunias in sight, she knew he was fishing for an explanation.

She got shakily to her feet and dusted her hands. "I don't think she'd welcome that surprise. She has enough to do without tending a garden."

"Lizzie says Olivia and Alice are away?"

"Alice took Olivia to see her father yesterday. They'll be home late tonight."

"I heard he's in prison."

Dana rummaged in her pocket, then stretched out her hand, balancing an earring on her palm. "I dropped the mate somewhere. I was standing here when I said goodbye to them, and I thought maybe this is where I lost it."

Pete took the simple braided gold hoop from her hand. "Wouldn't you have better luck tomorrow, when the sun's out?"

"It's supposed to rain tonight. I thought it might wash into the ground and disappear."

He handed back the earring. "Want me to help you dig?"

"I didn't find it, so I was just scraping back the mulch a little. They aren't expensive earrings, but a friend gave them to me. I always think of her when I wear them. I just hate to lose one."

"From what I can tell, that happens a lot. Women should start a new fashion. Wear different earrings in each ear all the time."

"I think it would take somebody higher up the fashion chain to get that going."

She pocketed the earring again, then stuck the hand trowel in the gardener's tool belt Lizzie had given her for her birthday and regretfully stepped away from the bed.

She started toward her house, but he stopped her with a hand on her shoulder. "Didn't you forget something? This." He reached into the shadows and retrieved Lizzie's metal detector. "I'm assuming you brought this to help you search?"

"Oh, thanks. Lizzie wouldn't have been one bit happy if I forgot that."

He stowed it under his arm to carry it for her. "Did you get a signal?"

"Lots of signals. I was so close to the house it was picking up all sorts of stuff. Wiring, you name it."

He fell in step beside her. She was a tall athletic woman, but Pete always made her feel petite, and despite herself, she had to admit she liked it.

"So why'd you drop by?" she asked.

"First, let me say you've trained your daughter well."

"Is that so?"

"As well as she knows me, she wasn't about

to let me into your house."

"Score one for Lizzie."

"Right. She can't be too careful."

This conversational thread disturbed her. "You sound like you know what you're talking about."

"I was an MP. Mostly I knocked heads together when I was dragging soldiers out of bars, but we also had cases involving families on the base. One of them involved a girl not much older than Lizzie who let a so-called friend in when her parents were gone, and lived to regret it."

Dana felt a cold chill, despite an evening temperature still in the eighties.

"We intervened in time," he added. "But that was a long time ago, and I imagine wherever she's living now, she's still double-bolting every door."

"No good mother lets that happen."

"You can't be everywhere, and you can't control everything when you're not. She was fifteen, and by virtue of her hormones she was sure she knew more than her parents, who were nice, careful people. It happens."

She tried not to think about what would happen when Lizzie was fifteen. Adolescence was already rearing its determined head. There would be fights, lines drawn in the sand, and there would be questions. So many, many questions. Adolescence was a time of discovery, and Dana had far too few answers to give.

"I suspect you came for some reason other than to test our security?" she asked, when they neared her house.

"I brought Lizzie a penny for her collection."

"And even with that, she didn't let you in?"

"I didn't tell her. I didn't want to tempt her to do what she knew she shouldn't."

"What is it?"

"A 1936-S. She told me she's been looking and looking."

"Please don't give it to her if it's worth a lot. She's still a kid. Next month she might be collecting postcards."

"How long's she been collecting coins?"

Dana glanced at him. Tonight Pete was wearing jeans cut off at the knees and a striped shirt unbuttoned to his breastbone. Casual clothing suited him, and he was beginning to look as if he belonged in Florida. "A couple of years, I guess."

"That sounds like more than a whim. And no, if she tries to sell it to a dealer, it might be worth a nickel. But I'm sure it's worth a lot more to her."

"How did you find it?"

"Luck of the Irish."

"You don't look Irish."

"I'm lucky enough to be." He nudged her shoulder companionably. "These days Lizzie's got me checking every handful of change, but I used to collect coins way back when. So I know the excitement of finding something you've been searching for."

They stood at her door, and Dana debated. Since their surprisingly fun night at the Little League game, she and Lizzie had enjoyed Pete's company more than once. He was laid-back and unassuming, and little by little, she was dropping her guard. But she had never invited him into her house — not unless he was making some repair — and now she knew if she did, everything would change. Because even if he *had* just come because he'd found the penny to give her daughter — and she wondered what the chances of that really were — she suspected Pete was not here only to see Lizzie. She'd felt ripples of sexual attraction between them, and had from the beginning. Now was the moment to put a stop to them.

Except that instead, as she unbuckled her tool belt and left it on the porch, she heard herself inviting him inside for a drink.

"You're sure?" he asked, as if he had witnessed the battle in her eyes.

A long-term relationship was out of the question. She wasn't going to stay in Florida, but more important, she wasn't in the market for any attachment, except to her daughter. Still, she had been without a man in her life or bed for so long that she felt parched and greedy, like someone lost in the desert, crawling toward the next mirage. And Pete *was* a mirage; she knew this. He would disappear, *had* to disappear, from her life.

But not tonight.

"Yes," she said. "Cold beer or cheap wine, take your pick."

"Beer, hands down."

She opened the door, and he followed. Lizzie was watching television, and she jumped up when she saw them.

"You found her!"

"She was easy to spot."

"Pete has something for you, Liz. I'm getting him a beer. Do you want anything?"

"Can I have one, too?" Lizzie asked, eyes shining.

"In about a decade."

"I'll count the days."

"Lemonade do?"

"I'm okay." Lizzie got to her feet. "You have a present for me?" she asked Pete.

Dana left them alone, although not very, since the house was small and didn't offer much privacy. When she returned, Lizzie was examining the penny as if it had come from a sunken treasure chest.

"Did you see this?" she asked Dana.

"I heard about it. Cool, huh?"

"I'm going to put it in my folder. I don't want to lose it." She looked up and grinned. "Then I'm going to bed. Olivia's coming over practically at dawn tomorrow to tell me about her trip. You know, before we go to youth camp."

Lizzie had never volunteered to go to bed this early. Yes, Olivia would probably arrive at the crack of dawn, but the two girls were together all the time, and Lizzie had never changed her sleeping habits to accommodate anyone. Then she realized Lizzie was trying to leave her alone with their visitor.

She wanted to laugh. She wanted to cry. "Sleep tight."

Lizzie rolled her eyes. "When do you stop saying that?"

"After I've drawn my final breath."

"Yuck." Lizzie belied the word with a big hug; then, on a whim, she hugged Pete, too. "Thanks again, Pete." She jumped back. "Night!" Then she headed for the bathroom.

"She's a great kid," Pete said, taking the beer and the glass Dana had provided, in case he wanted one.

"She is indeed."

"Where'd she get that hair? Yours curls a little, but hers is amazing."

Dana resisted the urge to touch her hair just because he had noticed it. "Her father's family, I guess. Certainly not mine."

"I gather you're divorced?"

She was glad that for once she could tell the truth. "I am, and Lizzie's father wanted no part of her."

"Sounds like a good guy to be rid of."

"Amen." She gestured to the sofa. "Make yourself at home."

"Are you joining me?"

"I'll be right back."

She returned with a glass of wine, turned off the television set and sat beside him. She held up her glass in toast. "To a nice man who likes kids."

"To a nice lady who likes kids."

They clinked.

"I get the feeling you know more about children than anyone would learn from simple observation," she said.

"Two sons. Educated, settled and happy. One teaching in Minneapolis. One in the air force, presently in Texas."

"And the wife that went with them?" She thought she had the right to ask.

"Ann died almost ten years ago. An emergency-room doctor brushed off the headache from a ruptured cerebral aneurysm and called it stress. She died two days later. With better medical care, she might have recovered."

"I'm so sorry."

"There was a lawsuit. It was settled, and suddenly the boys didn't have to take out college loans. We would have preferred having her and a mountain of debt."

"I'm sure."

He angled himself so he could see her better. "But that was a long time ago, and we're doing okay."

"And you retired from the military?"

He took a long swallow. "I'd had enough of knocking heads together. I figured I did my duty to flag and country, and between the settlement and consolidating some property, I knew I could quit."

"And now you're trying to figure out where to live. Even though it's probably beautiful in Alaska about now, and it's hot and growing hotter here."

"My cabin's rented out until the end of summer. That gives me plenty of time to figure out if I want to buy a warmer winter place or just travel around when I start going stir-crazy. How about you?"

She also took a sip before she spoke. "What about me?"

"From what I can tell, you and Lizzie are vagabonds."

"That sounds like a fun thing to be. In reality, our life is pretty hand to mouth, but we do okay."

"Why so much moving? Just Lizzie's allergies?"

"The economy's partly at fault, too. We settle in, I get a promising job, then the next thing I know they're laying off the last hired, or closing entirely. I've been working toward an education degree for more years than I want to admit, but credits don't always

371

transfer. If Lizzie and I can just settle in long enough so I can finish whatever courses I have to and do my student teaching, things might improve. Although, like everything else, teaching jobs are hard to come by right now." She was a little embarrassed. That was the longest speech she had given in his presence.

"Elementary school?" he asked.

"While they're still young and malleable."

"You'll be a good teacher. Any school system will be lucky to have you."

"How do you know?"

"I've seen you with Lizzie and Olivia."

"That's not much proof, but I think I will be, too."

He stretched out a hand but waited for her to acknowledge it, as if to say she could meet him halfway but it was up to her.

She knew better, but she inclined her head so that his fingertips brushed her hair, then her cheek. He stroked her skin for a moment, then lightly cupped her face.

She sighed softly. Nothing was supposed to feel this good. And only his fingers and palm were touching her. What would it be like to have more? To feel his whole body against hers?

"You're a loner," he said quietly. "So am I. Having that in common probably isn't much of a jumping-off place for us, is it?"

She wasn't surprised at the change of subject, or the assumption that came with it.

She knew she hadn't imagined the way the air sometimes crackled with sexual attraction when he was near. Pete wasn't a man who wasted time, and he *was* a man who picked up cues. She had probably given a number of them.

"It all depends on where you're planning to land," she said, leaning into his hand just a little more.

"I don't know how long I'll be around. I don't think you do, either."

"And your point?"

He dropped his hand, but only to her shoulder, where it rested lightly. His fingers began a slow, gentle massage, and waves of pleasure radiated through her.

"We could look at this two ways," he said. "Knowing time's short, we could forgo a lot of preliminaries. Or, knowing there's no future in the cards, I can finish my beer, and say good-night and goodbye."

The second made more sense. She'd been going with that choice for years, turning her back on possibilities, walking away before relationships could progress even this far. But she was tired of being alone, and Pete Knight just wasn't that easy to walk away from. He'd made it clear he wasn't expecting or probably even open to anything long-term. She had to stay around Happiness Key until her business here was completed. Maybe having Pete in her life would make everything harder. She didn't know. But weren't some obstacles worth working around?

She leaned closer, then, before she could change her mind, she brushed his lips with hers. "One has always been my lucky number. I'll go with door number one."

This time he cupped the back of her head and pulled her close. The kiss went quickly from casual and tentative to something that was neither. She inhaled the warm fragrance of his skin, part soap or shaving cream, part man. His lips were hard, but not bruising. He tasted like Budweiser, desire and tomorrow.

By the end, she knew she had decided to take a chance on Pete Knight.

"Lizzie is a constant in your life," he said, after he pulled away.

"She's spending the night with Olivia on Thursday."

His smile was slow. "Have I told you about my camper?"

She felt heat warming her cheeks. "I should have known you had a camper. It suits you."

"I'm renting month to month. It's on a little lake just north of here. Nothing fancy."

"Do you have a place to cook out?"

"A perfect place."

"I'll bring pie and steaks."

"No, I'll buy the steaks."

She touched his lips with a fingertip, then pulled away.

"Shall I pick you up?" he asked.

"No." She said it too quickly, but she wanted control. She wanted to have her own car, just in case she changed her mind. She would always need an escape.

"Then I'll draw you a map. Just call before you leave so I can start the charcoal." He took his bottle and unused glass into the kitchen, a clear sign, she thought, that he really had been somebody's husband.

When he returned, she walked him to the door, although she wished he didn't have to go. Waiting until Thursday to be alone with him seemed like waiting a lifetime. He stopped on the threshold and pulled something from his shirt pocket.

"I found this in the kitchen." He held out a gold hoop.

Dana stared at his outstretched palm; then she took the earring. "Where on earth was it?" But she knew the answer.

"Beside the microwave."

"In plain sight?"

"There's a clamshell on the same shelf filled with odds and ends. It was buried, but the overhead light caught the glint of gold."

"I can't believe it," she lied. "I guess Lizzie found it somewhere and put it there. She must have forgotten." She looked up at him. "Thanks, Pete. This is a nice surprise."

He searched her eyes, then he inched closer. And by the end of that kiss, she knew Thursday night, she would be driving north, map in hand, toward something she shouldn't risk. The earring was a reminder of how easy it was to make a mistake.

But she would go anyway.

Tracy wasn't much of a drinker. A glass of wine before or with dinner was a treat. Mixed drinks were calorie fests and, except for the occasional splurge, best avoided. Wanda's margaritas were an exception, of course, but then Wanda's exceptions had plunked fifteen pounds on Tracy's slender frame.

Unfortunately, Tracy, like anyone, was most prone to temptation when life was offering nothing but lemons. Even more unfortunately, tonight she had taken those lemons and imbibed them in the form of lemon drop martinis. Three, mixed by Henrietta's able bartender, which was a lot more liquor and calories than she had needed. And now she was paying the price.

"You're driving too fast." She gazed out the window through slitted eyelids. It was dark, but the lights flashing along the bridge were giving her a headache and a queasy stomach.

"I'm going ten miles under the speed limit," CJ said, a smile in his voice. Tracy hated it when he smiled at her and it didn't even show on his face.

She closed her eyes and leaned her head against the back of the seat. "Why does Edward Statler —" she tried to focus "— let you drive his car?"

"He and Sally keep the Vantage so their children will have their own ride when they visit. It was no hardship to offer it to me."

"I have a friend who'll give me a slice of pie anytime I ask."

"Same thing." The audible smile had widened to a grin.

"Better. You haven't had Wanda's pie."

"You win, TK. Maybe you'll share a piece someday."

"How obvious was it that I'd had too much to drink?" She could hear the liquor in her words — not slurred, exactly, but a shade too precise.

"Only to me, I think."

Tracy hadn't been sure herself until post-cruise, when her legs had wobbled as she stepped onto the dock. CJ had smoothly taken her arm, as if he was planning an intimate stroll toward the valet stand. Halfway there, he'd explained that the only car the valet would be getting tonight was his, and she would have to come back tomorrow for hers. By then she'd known better than to argue.

"Well, you set Henrietta's heart fluttering when you grabbed me on the dock. She wants us to get back together. She pulled me aside . . ." She swallowed hard. Why, after all that liquid, did she feel as if she hadn't had anything to drink in days?

"She pulled me aside," she tried again, "and told me that you made a lot of money for her friends over the years, and she is absolutely convinced . . . you'll beat those bogus charges against you."

"It feels good to have somebody stand up for me."

Tracy waited for the shame to wash over her because she herself had not stood up for him. She waited in vain. "Stand By Your Man" was not her theme song, at least not for this particular man. Maybe not any man, now that she thought about it, because hadn't she dumped Marsh today, simply because his ex-wife was living with him?

No, *dump* didn't quite cover what had happened between them. Unfortunately, she was too tired and dizzy to find another name for it.

"Henrietta isn't just somebody," she managed to point out. "Tonight . . . somebody said — I don't know who — that she's the richest woman in Florida."

"Edward's been trying to get her to invest with him for years."

"She seems pretty smart. She never invested with you."

"Here I'm driving you home, out of the goodness of my black heart, and you're insulting me."

"I am dredging up facts. I am dredging up *truth*. My parents . . . my parents have stopped speaking to me, for the most part, because . . . because they blame me for . . ."

"Yes, I know what your parents think. Your mother wrote me frequently while I was in prison."

"My mother?"

"I got almost weekly lists of the ways I ruined your life."

Tracy hooted. "She hasn't given that two minutes of thought, CJ."

"Granted, it was a minor theme in her body of work. The letters were entertaining, but so was watching the roach who crawled out from under my bed at night to search for crumbs. Prison's like that."

"Henrietta wants us back together."

"Yes, she's told me so, too. I'm supposed to woo you with promises of a new start."

Now was the time to tell CJ he had ruined her life. Only even in this state, she realized that particular line was her mother's, not hers. Because CJ hadn't ruined anything. Somehow he'd had the presence of mind to make sure that if everything fell apart, she got Happiness Key. And because of that, she'd begun a new and different life.

Of course tonight, sitting in the lap of luxury again, she had really, really missed the old one.

"I loved being waited on tonight." She opened her eyes and saw they had crossed the bridge and weren't far from home. "I loved . . . Chateaubriand from real Kobe beef. I loved the truffle paté. I loved the Krug 1990. . . ."

She realized she had forgotten to factor those two glasses of champagne into her liquor intake. And she had never done well with champagne. No surprise she felt dizzy. Mental note: Never again.

"You certainly seemed to."

She turned to gaze at him, eyelids still slitted. "And so did you, CJ. In fact, I'd say you enjoyed yourself *way* too much. Maybe that's why I had so much to drink."

"Because I was having fun?"

"You were working the room."

"We were on a yacht."

"Then you were working the yacht!" She lowered her voice, because raising it made her head throb. "I was married to you. I know what it looks like. You were making connections so you could use them down the line. I've never seen that much . . . *showmanship* displayed outside the Venice Beach boardwalk. I'm surprised nobody pulled out a checkbook and signed a blank check for you."

"Well, if I'm as notorious as they say, they wouldn't have to sign it. I could take care of that, too."

"What are you getting me into here, CJ?"

He didn't answer until miles later, when he slowed. They had just crossed the border to

Happiness Key, and they were nearly at her house.

"Right now I'm just trying to get you home in one piece," he said.

"I have a life . . . here. I have a rep-u-ta-tion. Don't ruin this. I'll run out of places where I can start over."

He turned into her driveway and pulled to a stop. "I'm not trying to ruin anything, TK. I came to Florida for a lot of reasons, and none of them involved exacting some kind of retribution on you for deserting me."

"I did not desert you. I divorced you, because . . ." She stopped squinting, opened her eyes and made sure their gazes connected.

She focused carefully on what she was about to say. "Because I believed everything that was said about you. And I still do. I was there, CJ. The signs were all around me, only I was too young and stupid to pay attention. But some of those friends of yours . . . weren't as presentable as your cockroach buddy, and not nearly as safe to be with."

"A good businessman doesn't turn his back on contacts who can help him. And yes, some were questionable, but nothing that *I* did was. Except trust the wrong people a few times too many, and not move quickly enough to shore up everything when I got the first whiff I was going to be investigated."

"There was more to it." She nodded forcefully and quickly wished she hadn't. "And that's the man I divorced. That CJ. The one who used people. The one who used me because I was so obli— oblivious to what he was doing."

"I think you need a good night's sleep." CJ opened his door, but she grabbed his arm.

"Don't get out!"

"I'm just going to help you to the door."

"Don't . . . bother." She gathered her purse and shawl, and managed to get herself out of the car with only a smidgen of difficulty. "I'm fine. Thanks for the ride."

He looked skeptical. "I'm going to sit here until you get to the door. Just to be sure you *can.*"

She didn't even look back — afraid that turning her head might bring on a wave of dizziness. She walked toward her door in something approximating a straight line. When she finally got there, she heard the engine turn over, then the sound of gravel crunching under his tires, and finally the sound of the Aston Martin disappearing down the road.

She sighed and opened her purse. And that was when she realized that the yacht club valet not only had her car, he had her *keys,* including her house key.

Janya's house smelled like Rishi's favorite *paneer jalfrazi.* It was too bad he had not bothered to come home to eat it. It was also too bad that he had not thought to call her and tell her he would not be home. After turning down her request to go away together for the weekend, as Wanda had suggested, he had promised a whole evening together. That was to be his compromise.

A compromise that was never enacted.

She had cleaned up the kitchen long ago, and Rishi's portion of dinner had gone out to the garbage, where she would not have to look at it and be reminded of her abandonment.

She was just getting into her nightgown when she heard a scuffling noise at the front door. She suspected Rishi had finally made his way home, but when no key turned in the lock, she went to the door and flipped on the light, peeking through the side window to see who was there.

Tracy stared back at her.

Janya unlocked and opened the door. "Is anything wrong?"

Tracy had one hand pressed against the wall beside the door, as if to prop herself up. "Alice . . . has my extra key. She's . . . not home."

"She and Olivia took the bus up north to see Lee."

Tracy nodded just a fraction. "That's right."

"You don't have yours?"

Tracy shook her head — again, just a fraction.

"Come in. Why are we talking on the porch?"

"I had . . . no place else to go. I couldn't go to Wanda's. She would never let me forget this."

"You are always welcome here." Janya opened the door wider and put her hand on Tracy's arm.

"I . . . had a bit too much to drink. I left my car at the yacht club."

"I suspected. About the drinking, I mean. Can you make it inside?"

"Yes. I didn't have . . . *that* much."

Janya still didn't let go of her friend's arm. "You must need a place to sleep tonight."

"If it's not too much trouble. Alice will be home by morning. Right?"

"Their bus gets in very late tonight."

"I can sleep on your sofa."

"No." Janya had already figured out the solution to both their problems. "There is a second bedroom."

"That's right. This is one of the *big* houses. Yours and Alice's." Tracy giggled.

"But that mattress is hard. You will sleep with me."

"With you?" Tracy looked around, moving her head very slowly. "Where is Rishi?"

"I do not know, and furthermore, I do not care."

"Janya . . ."

"Do not concern yourself. If my husband comes home tonight, he can sleep in the guest bedroom. His home computer and many of his files are there. He will feel more at home with them than he does with me."

"I'm too tired to figure this out."

"There is nothing to figure. I have extra nightgowns, and you will find a new toothbrush in the bathroom drawer. I sleep on the side beside the door."

"You're sure?" Tracy looked as if she was about to fall asleep on her feet.

"Go right into the bathroom. Wash your face and brush your teeth. I will bring you a nightgown."

Tracy looked pleased to be given an order. "I can do that."

Janya guided her in the right direction, just to be sure. When she was confident Tracy was following directions, she went into her room and rummaged for an extra gown. Then she took it into the bathroom, along with a fresh towel, and set both on the counter.

A few minutes later Tracy came out looking ready for bed. Janya took her into the bedroom and pulled down the sheets. As she watched, Tracy sat, pulled her feet around and rolled over to the side of the bed by the wall.

"You need an elephant in here," Tracy said, closing her eyes. "And a pomegranate. So you

385

can get . . . pregnant."

Janya was glad Tracy was lying down, since she was now making even less sense than before. Janya didn't need an elephant, and she didn't need a pomegranate. She just needed a husband in her bed. And of the three, she was afraid Rishi was the one who was completely beyond her reach.

CHAPTER NINETEEN

Somehow Tracy made it through Tuesday morning. Janya woke her early and drove her to the yacht club, with a terse explanation that Rishi had come home sometime after midnight. Luckily Tracy was able to convince an employee to get her keys, since the valets weren't yet on duty. Then, head pounding, she drove home, showered and changed for work. She had time for one cup of coffee, but even that was too much on an unsettled stomach. If nothing else, she was jump-starting her weight loss. She would have to mention hangovers as a possible solution to the other Naughty Nibblers.

By midafternoon she was feeling a little better. She had lunched on half a turkey sandwich, no chips, and iced tea with artificial sweetener. Gladys brought her an apple to eat as a snack. She would do a little grocery shopping on the way home, and fill her fridge and cabinets with low-calorie food. By summer's end she would fit back into all her clothes.

For what? And for whom?

That sent her rummaging through the supply closet. At Christmastime the swim team coach had given all her kids PEZ dispensers filled with assorted candies, and Tracy thought an extra Daisy Duck had ended up here. What could one little piece of candy hurt?

When she heard footsteps she guiltily slammed the closet door, realizing "footsteps" was a misnomer. These feet were running toward her. Bay appeared in the doorway, followed by one of his counselors, a young man named Gary, who was definitely earning his pay.

"Our group's got the pool now, but Bay wants to talk to you. You have a minute?"

Tracy remembered her "discussion" with Marsh yesterday. She doubted she and Bay were supposed to be having any talks. But as she'd told Marsh, making sure the kids were okay was part of her job. And she sure wasn't going to pump Bay for information she didn't want to know.

"I'll bring him outside in a few minutes," she promised Gary.

Gary looked relieved. She wasn't sure if the relief was because he'd gotten rid of Bay temporarily, or because Tracy, who'd been annoyed at everyone since she walked in the door, wasn't annoyed at the interruption.

She motioned to the sofa. Bay joined her.

"So, what's up?" she asked.

He bit his lip, as if he wasn't sure where to start.

"I saw you at Gonzalo's last night," she said. "You got your pizza trip."

"I didn't see you."

"I was just driving by. I saw you in the parking lot."

He bit the other side of his lip. "They put mushrooms on the pizza."

Bay wasn't a picky boy. After all, Marsh was a fabulous cook and inclined to use whatever fresh ingredients he had on hand. She'd eaten everything from gator to conch at his table, and Bay had eaten them right along with her. But mushrooms were taboo. She knew that. Everybody who had ever eaten at the same table with Bay knew that.

"Somebody in the kitchen wasn't paying attention," she said.

"My mom ordered when Dad and I were in the bathroom, and she forgot to tell them."

Tracy just nodded, keeping her thoughts to herself.

"I don't like mushrooms."

"Yes, I know." She nodded again. "So you scraped them off and ate everything else."

"Not 'zactly."

"Uh-huh." More nodding.

"I kinda made a fuss, and Mom got real

mad. But the mushrooms had touched everything!"

"So they ordered you something else?"

"Mom said I had to eat what she ordered
or just go hungry."

Tracy wondered how she had gotten herself
into this position. Here she was, hearing Sylvia stories straight from Bay's mouth, and all
she really wanted was a date with a Daisy
Duck PEZ dispenser.

"So you made yourself eat it anyway,
right?" she asked, hoping for a happy ending.

He shook his head.

She knew if Marsh had been handling the
situation, he would have ordered something
else for his son, then talked to him later about
not making a fuss in public. Marsh spoiled
Bay, it was true. Tracy had been forced to
call him on it more than once. But Marsh
was trying to make up for the absence of a
mother in Bay's life. And in the year since
she'd met him, Marsh had become better at
setting limits.

Sylvia, it seemed, was about nothing else.

She patted Bay's knee. "I'm sorry, kiddo. I
used to feel the same way about onions. I
know it's hard to make yourself eat something
you hate."

"I spoiled the evening."

That sounded like something he'd heard
and was repeating. "I know you're disappointed," she said.

"So I have to learn how not to do that anymore. 'Cause I don't want my mom to leave 'cause I'm a brat."

For a moment she didn't know what to say, but that was fine, since she wasn't sure she could speak anyway. That was the thing about kids, something she was learning every day. Who they were and what they thought was right there, out in the open, waiting to be trampled on. By the time they were teenagers, they learned to hide their secrets. But unless a child had been abused or threatened, his secrets were right there for the world to see.

"Bay, you're not a brat," she said at last. "But you do have a temper. The good news is you're learning to control it."

"Not fast enough."

He sounded so grown-up suddenly. She wanted to hug him in commiseration, but that wasn't going to help.

"You're trying hard this summer, in every way," she said. "You're going to make a few mistakes." And Sylvia was going to make a million more, she added silently. "But don't get too worried, okay? Nobody's perfect, and a boy your age isn't supposed to be. I know your dad . . . and mom understand that."

"I think I'm the reason they got a divorce."

This launched a quick reply. "Of course you weren't! Grown-ups do what they do for a million reasons, but not because a kid doesn't like mushrooms on his pizza."

"I was prob'ly a bad baby, too."

"Bay." She put her hands on his shoulders and shook him a little. "Get that idea right straight out of your head. Your mom and dad got divorced because they realized they didn't want to live together anymore. And you were not a factor."

"I want them to be married again."

And there it was. Simple, unadorned and so terribly sad.

She sat back. "That's totally up to them, Bay. Nothing you do can make a difference. My parents are divorced, too, only I was old enough when it happened to see the divorce was all about them and not about me. You're a little too young to understand, but take my word for it, okay?"

"Mom said if I behave — really, really behave — she's gonna give me a super birthday party."

He hadn't heard her. Tracy wasn't surprised. Because when did logic have anything to do with the heart?

"I might need some help," he continued. "Can you help?"

"What do you want me to do?"

"Gimme some behavior lessons."

"You want the party *that* badly?"

"If I behave, maybe she'll see how nice it is to be together, you know? We could be a real family again."

Tracy's heart hurt. It was a physical pain,

and not, she was afraid, because she had abused her body last night. She knew for a fact that Sylvia would not stay in Palmetto Grove. Miami, maybe, where there was plenty of need for a criminal lawyer of her caliber, but if they became a family again, then Marsh and Bay would have to uproot and move with her. Maybe that had been her plan all along. Marsh wouldn't leave Florida, Tracy was certain of that, but he might be persuaded to move to a part of it where Sylvia could be happy, just so Bay would have his mother full-time again.

Or maybe Sylvia was simply leading this little boy on, a child so blinded by hope and love he was incapable of seeing the truth. Maybe she was offering him this possibility so he would try harder and make her life easier, the way parents bribed cranky toddlers with ice-cream cones.

"Well, the first thing you need to do," Tracy said carefully, "is forget about little mistakes you've already made. So forget about the pizza, okay? Just be kind whenever you can. That's the most important thing you can do. And if you get mad, try to work it out and don't yell."

"Will you help?"

"Tell you what, if I see you getting mad, I'll pull you aside until you have a chance to recover. Okay?"

He nodded gravely and got up. Tracy rose,

too, and took him out the sliding glass door, around the girls playing shuffleboard and over to the pool, where Bay's group was batting a beach ball back and forth in the shallow end.

"You won't tell my dad, will you?" he said. "You know, about the stuff I told you?"

She caught the eye of his counselor and nodded, then dredged up a smile and patted Bay on the shoulder. "I won't." She didn't add that Marsh no longer wanted to hear anything she said anyway.

On her way back she was circling the shuffleboard court when Olivia — who she hadn't realized was one of the players — stopped her.

"Can I talk to you, Tracy?" Olivia asked.

Tracy's eyes flicked to the colorful mural over the rec room door. She expected to see a new hand lettered addition: "The doctor is in," but apparently that message was only in the eye of the beholder.

"Tell your counselor you'll be with me," Tracy said, nodding. "I'll meet you in the rec room."

She settled herself on the sofa again, and Olivia, hair plastered to her neck and legs growing longer by the moment, came over and flopped down beside her.

"Rough weekend?" Tracy guessed. She had known it wouldn't be easy for Olivia to see her father in prison. In the last months Olivia had stopped talking about the things that had happened to her family last year, though she probably still talked to her grandmother. All in all she seemed to be recovering, but it was clearly difficult.

"It's a long way there and back," Olivia said.

Tracy nodded, feeling like a bobblehead doll.

"I don't want to talk about that," Olivia added.

"No problem."

"I want to talk about Lizzie."

That surprised Tracy. "Did you two have a fight?" At Olivia's age, girlfriend fights were the worst. Tracy remembered a few and inwardly cringed.

"No." Olivia scrunched up her face. "It's just that she's tired of moving around. She says she and her mom have moved dozens of times, and she's sick of changing schools and losing friends."

Tracy considered. She wasn't sure why Olivia was telling her this, because obviously Tracy couldn't make Dana stay at Happiness Key. She wondered if Olivia wanted to fix her friend's life as a way of making up for the problems in her own. Maybe seeing her father had set Olivia thinking.

"Being a single parent is hard," Tracy said, feeling her way. "I imagine Dana has to go wherever she can find a job."

"I don't think that's it."

"Really?" Tracy said in a noncommittal tone. She was getting pretty good at the counseling stuff, and she wasn't even sure how it had happened.

Olivia lowered her voice. "That's why I came. To tell you what Lizzie said. She said her mom is afraid."

"She told you that?"

"They've been moving forever. That's what Lizzie said. And her mom won't answer questions. When Lizzie asks about her dad, her mom says she's too young to understand everything. But then she acts even more afraid. So Lizzie stopped asking, but she still really wants to know."

"I see." Tracy didn't understand why Olivia was telling *her* this.

"Last year . . . when my dad . . ." Olivia rubbed her eyes.

Tracy knew the girl didn't want to go into everything her father had done. Lee Symington was in prison for abusing his mother-in-law, and there was a possibility he might be on trial down the road for murder. Tracy wasn't even sure how much Olivia knew or was ready to know.

"That was a hard time for you," Tracy said sympathetically.

"Back then, before everything, you know, happened, I was afraid things were wrong at home."

"But Lee's your father, and you were listening to him, the way you'd been taught. You can't blame yourself, Olivia. You're not a grown-up." The advice sounded familiar. She'd just told Bay the same thing.

"But I don't want that to happen again. Not ever. From now on I'm going to speak up, no matter what. So that's why I'm telling you about Lizzie and her mother. Because maybe something is really wrong at their house, too, and what if I didn't say anything? The way I didn't say anything last year."

"Okay." Tracy took the girl's hands. "Now you've told me, and I'll see if I can figure out if we need to help Dana and Lizzie, okay? If you hear anything else that really worries you, let me know. But you don't have to spy or dig for information. You've done your part now. You can get on with being best friends and enjoying your summer."

"I'm not going back to see my father."

The change of subject didn't surprise Tracy, since the subject had never *really* changed in the first place. "That's your decision." She hoped it really was and nobody would inter-fere.

"He's a bad person."

Tracy didn't respond, although she heartily agreed.

"Yesterday he got angry and told me I was no better than my mother."

"That's a compliment, Olivia. From what I hear, being as good as your mother would be

397

an extraordinary achievement. I know I would have liked her a lot. All of us would have."

"I told him it was a good thing I wasn't like *him*. That I'm never going to be like him, no matter what." Olivia stood.

Tracy rose and hugged her, and Olivia cuddled close. Then Tracy set her away, keeping her hands on the girl's shoulders. "You'll do fine without him, sweetie. You have a lot of people who love you for the wonderful person you are."

Olivia's eyes glittered with tears, but she managed a little smile.

Wanda had seen wrung-out sponge mops that looked better than Tracy Deloche. The woman badly needed a piece of pie, but she wasn't having any. She was sucking up coffee, though, like she hoped it would bring blood back to her brain.

"I could pour some whiskey in that," Wanda said. "You know, hair of the dog . . ."

"Don't even say it. Please." Tracy put her head in her hands.

"You ought to go home and get some sleep."

"I need to talk to everybody." Tracy looked up. "Except Dana."

"Well, the others ought to be here in a minute." When Tracy had called to announce a meeting, Wanda had suggested they do it at her house. Ken was in Georgia, and truth be told, her place felt lonely. Besides, having company gave her a good reason to clean the place up, something she didn't do as thoroughly now that she was working so many hours at the shop. Ken was coming home tomorrow, and she wanted him to be able to find his way through the door.

"How are things at Wanda's Wonderful Pies?" Tracy asked.

"They'd be a lot better if the Sunshine Bakery would just quit running specials. Today it was two big old chocolate chip cookies for a dollar. They got to be bringing them in from somewhere else. Nobody in that place could bake a decent cookie if her life depended on it."

"I bet nobody buys pie there."

"Their pie still doesn't look good as mine, and that's a fact. Dana stops in now and then to check."

There was a tapping on the door, and Janya stepped in before Wanda had to answer. "I brought spiced nuts."

"You are all trying to knock me off my diet." Tracy reached for the coffeepot and poured more in her cup. "I finally admit I've gained weight, and you're trying to make me gain more."

Wanda sniffed. "The world spins around and around, and guess what, Ms. Deloche? It doesn't spin around you."

"It feels like it does. Maybe that's just my head."

"You can leave early, and we'll eat after you go."

"I've got to get used to saying no when there's food sitting in front of me. I'll just sit here and look sad."

"Won't bother me none."

Alice knocked and let herself in, as Janya had done. She looked tired. The long bus trip and the emotional turmoil had taken their toll. She looked as if she needed a night of fun, not a night of problem solving.

"Alice, you sit," Tracy said. "We'll wait on you, or rather, Wanda will."

The women questioned Alice, sympathizing as Wanda poured coffee and set out a frosty glass of iced tea for Alice. She also brought out blackberry pie, and Tracy admitted her mouth was watering, but she didn't change her mind.

Alice waited until the sympathy had dwindled. "I don't think . . . we'll do it again."

Nobody asked why. Wanda figured that had been Olivia's decision, and she knew the other women figured the same thing.

"Olivia's the reason I asked everybody to come," Tracy said.

Wanda listened as Tracy recounted the conversation on the rec room sofa.

"I think that's everything. She's worried," Tracy finished. "And honestly, so am I. Either something's going on with Dana, or Lizzie has an imagination she can't control."

"How is Lizzie doing in youth camp?" Wanda asked.

"No problems at all. She seems to be a well-adjusted girl. She makes friends easily. She's a fabulous volleyball player and an all-around good athlete. She and Olivia are best friends, but they don't exclude other kids. I haven't heard one complaint."

"So whatever Dana's been doing seems to be working out," Wanda said.

"That's true."

Janya took a small bite of pie. She looked tired and preoccupied, a lot like Tracy. "This could be nothing. Olivia often talks to me, and this is the first I have heard of it."

"I know, but I think seeing her father yesterday . . ." Tracy glanced at Alice. "Well, I think it convinced her she needs to make sure she's open about things right when they happen."

"You have any ideas?" Wanda asked. "Because this is all new to us."

"I've been thinking about it all afternoon. Let's say the asthma is just a cover story. Olivia claims Lizzie's allergic to cats, but apparently not very. If Lizzie's telling the truth, then asthma's not the reason they move so frequently, because there are cats everywhere. So that's the first thing we know. They move a lot, and Dana lies about the reason."

"Wait a minute." Wanda retreated, then came back with a yellow legal pad from Ken's desk. "We'll make ourselves a list."

She wrote down what Tracy had said.

"This is much the way it was when we were trying to find Herb's family," Janya said. "We are detectives again." Herb, who had lived in the house Dana occupied, had been a man of secrets, and the women had been forced together after his death to discover them.

"Never let it be said we slacked off." Wanda poised the pen over the pad. "Okay, what else do we know?"

"Know for sure?" Tracy asked. "Well, we know Lizzie thinks her mother is afraid. We don't know if it's true, but we know Lizzie thinks it is."

"Then that's what I'll put down." Wanda did.

"And did you not say that when Lizzie asks about her father, Dana seems even more afraid?" Janya asked.

"That'll be number three." Wanda made sure it was, then she looked up.

"I've got something to add. I think Dana's afraid of the police, you want the truth. Whenever a cop comes into the shop, and you better believe they do since I give 'em free coffee, she always comes back into the kitchen to tell me, so I'll go out and say hi. Only she doesn't come back out."

"That's kind of flimsy evidence," Tracy said.

"She might want to give you . . . privacy," Alice pointed out.

"No, it's different. And Kenny's noticed how standoffish she is with him. He told me she acts like a woman with something to hide."

Everybody was quiet as Wanda wrote that down.

"There is something else. . . ." Tracy looked at the others. "Dana pays me in cash. Never by check."

Wanda added her piece. "She told me she doesn't want to pay bank fees. She asked me to pay her right out of the till, said it was easier. Although now that you mention it, I've never seen her use a credit card, either. She does have a social security number."

"What else do we know?" Tracy asked. "For sure."

Nobody said anything until Alice spoke at last. "We know she is a good mother. Dana is . . . devoted."

Everybody nodded, and Wanda added that to the list.

"And put down that Lizzie's well-adjusted," Tracy said.

Wanda wrote some more, then held up her list. "So here's what we have. The devoted, frugal but restless mother of a well-adjusted girl lies about why she moves so much, is uncomfortable around cops and reported to be afraid when the daughter questions her about her father." She looked at her friends. "That's not very much to go on."

"She's divorced," Alice said. "She told me. She is divorced from Lizzie's father."

"That's right." Wanda wrote that, too. "So now she's the divorced, devoted, frugal but restless mother."

"I have a theory," Tracy said. "If you want to hear it. I've had all afternoon to think about this."

"I'm all ears," Wanda said. "Everybody else?"

Janya and Alice nodded.

"If Dana's on the run, then she has to be running from *somebody*."

"Do we know she is on the run?" Janya asked.

"No, but it's an educated guess. She's lying about the moves. Alice takes care of Lizzie when Dana works, and she's never had an asthma attack, has she?"

Alice shook her head. "She seems healthy."

"So why else would she move so often and lie about the reason? Why else would she avoid checks and credit cards unless she's afraid somebody's trying to find her?"

"If she is running," Janya said, "who is she running from?"

Tracy poured herself yet another cup of coffee. "Lizzie doesn't know anything about her father. Doesn't that jump out at you? She's old enough to know something. So maybe this is more than just a mother and father who didn't get along, or a father with no interest in being one."

"Or a father who refuses to admit a child is his," Janya added.

Tracy fiddled with her spoon but didn't take another sip. "Maybe Dana is trying to stay one step ahead of an abusive ex. Maybe she's afraid he's going to grab Lizzie and make off with her, so that's why she moves so often and why she's so protective."

"Then why is she afraid of cops?" Wanda asked. "If I'm right and she is. Because if her husband is trying to kidnap Lizzie, the cops would be her new best friends."

"Not if she doesn't have legal custody."

The women all fell silent.

"That's a stretch," Wanda said at last.

"Maybe, but maybe not." Tracy put down the spoon, as if she realized she was fidgeting — and no wonder, with all the caffeine in her system. "We've all heard stories. The powerful father gets custody because he has unlimited resources and can hire fabulous lawyers. The mother knows he's abusive and dangerous to her child and tries to tell people, but somehow it's all turned around, and she becomes the target."

"That is sad," Alice said.

Tracy patted her hand and went on. "Dana could be protecting Lizzie with all these moves. Maybe they've even changed their names. It seems possible, doesn't it?"

"It's a pack of assumptions." Wanda put down her pen. "But darned if they don't fit."

Tracy continued. "She was very leery of Pete when he first started doing work here. We all noticed how rude she was, and how fast she pulled Lizzie out of sight. Could be she thought he'd been hired by her ex to find her."

"She's not leery now," Wanda said. "He came into the shop this afternoon, and I could swear they were making eyes at each other."

"Dana and Pete Knight? A Happiness Key romance. Weird," Tracy said.

"You got your own romance on the key."

"Not anymore." Tracy looked down at her cup. "Marsh and I officially called things off yesterday."

"That explains . . ." Janya fell silent.

"What does it explain?" Wanda demanded.

"It explains why I showed up at Janya's door last night tipsy and keyless," Tracy said.

"I missed a lot, it seems." Wanda sniffed.

"I'm sorry, dear." Now Alice patted Tracy's hand.

"It's hard to be in love with a man when another woman has all his attention and a room in his house."

Wanda knew she had to do something or tears were going to flow. "We are all truly sorry, but we'll leave that conversation for sometime when it's not like pouring salt in the wound, okay? Let's get back to Dana."

Tracy looked grateful.

"We could just ask her," Wanda said. "Tell Dana what we've figured out and offer to help any way we can."

"Wouldn't that send her running off again?" Alice asked.

"I think we need a bit of proof before we go off half-cocked," Tracy said. "Shall we try to look into things first?"

"Ken could look into it in a jiffy, but if we're right, she's avoiding the police. So I can't ask him to help us. If he found out she was really breaking the law, he'd have to report it."

"Then don't tell him." Tracy picked up the spoon, put it down, then picked it up again and kept it clenched in her fist.

"So where do we start?" Wanda asked. "We know her name and that's about all."

"And that might not be her real one," Janya reminded them. "Herb's wasn't. We know it is easier than people think to live under an assumed one."

"Do you remember when we first tried to find out about Herb?" Tracy gestured, and the spoon fell out of her hand. "Sorry about that."

"A little bit wired, aren't we?" Once and for all, Wanda moved the spoon out of Tracy's reach. "So where did we start with Herb?

I don't remember."

"We started with his references. I phoned the pastor of a church he'd attended years before, and that was the first step."

"You have Dana's references?"

"I have, but I never bothered to call anybody once I knew we all liked her. I'll do that tomorrow. If they're real we'll be able to figure out some places she's lived. Maybe we can go from there."

"Does the youth camp require a birth certificate?" Janya asked.

"Yes, at the time the kids are registered."

"Does someone make notes on what is on it?"

"I don't know, but you better believe I'll check. If that's the case, we'll know where Lizzie was born."

"Smart thinking, Janya," Wanda said. "You're a good friend to have in a pickle."

"Not if a swimming pool is involved."

"I think that's only one to a customer. You're safe for the rest of your life."

Janya smiled a little. "That is a very good thing."

CHAPTER TWENTY

On Wednesday Tracy spent the evening searching the Internet, using what little information she knew about Dana to see if she could find more. Although it was a long shot, she started with Facebook and My-Space, hoping to find that Dana had set up her own chatty profile. When that proved useless, she tried Google, but for once the search engine was surprisingly unhelpful.

Almost everybody Dana's age showed up someplace. A family member in an obituary. A list of attendees at a meeting or a party. Signers of petitions. Employee rosters. But the only Dana Turners that Tracy came across were too young or too old or too male. They played professional soccer or the violin in their small-town community orchestra. Those Danas had large families, or no children, or wrote blogs about last week's sunset at Waikiki.

She had discovered little more from Dana's references. Tracy had spoken to Dana's most recent landlord in an Atlanta suburb, but the woman had contributed nothing significant. Dana was a good tenant. Lizzie was charming, wasn't she? The woman, who sounded just a bit ditzy, thought Dana had worked as a receptionist at a car wash, but she wasn't certain.

She *had* said Dana always paid her rent on time and, oddly enough, in cash. That part, at least, was memorable. As was the length of Dana's stay there. Short. Three months, or possibly only two.

Tracy had left voice mail messages at the other two numbers on Dana's list, but she didn't expect to learn anything more.

By eleven o'clock she gave up. She had ended her session by narrowing the search to Atlanta and the surrounding area, using Dana's and Lizzie's names as search terms. She'd checked out car washes, coin collecting, gardening, but she really knew so little about her tenant that no other terms had come to mind. In the end, she had a big nothing to show for an evening's work.

She fell asleep with computerized images flashing behind her closed eyelids, complete with tinny sound tracks. She worked a loud ringing into her dreams, too, until it became too insistent. She opened her eyes to find herself in the dark, computer asleep for the night but phone bleating merrily.

With one uncoordinated sweep of her hand

she knocked the phone off the bed table, but she managed to grab it just before it hit the floor. With no daylight barriers to self-pity, she wondered who cared enough to call at this time of night.

"H'lo?" she managed.

"Is CJ there with you?"

Tracy might be having trouble waking up, but that moved her up the ladder a rung. She sat upright and combed her hair back from her face. "What gives you the right to ask?"

"Don't get on your high horse, Ms. Deloche, just answer the question!"

"Wanda, it's past midnight."

"Is he there or not?"

"No! He's not here. He's not sleeping with me, so now you can go back to bed with life's biggest question answered."

"Well, it's a good thing. Because he's probably going to get arrested in a little while."

Tracy held the cordless phone in front of her and squinted at it, as if she might see an instant replay. She put it back to her ear. "That's seriously bogus."

"It is not bogus. And I'm not supposed to know, and you're certainly not supposed to. But I got all worked up about you, considering what a mess you've been lately and all."

Now Tracy was fully awake. "I have not been a mess." She realized that her messiness was not the larger issue. "What exactly is going on?"

"I still think this recent bitchy mood could be early menopause, but we can tackle that later. Here's the scoop."

Tracy listened, her eyes growing wider until she wasn't sure there was room for them in her face.

"We're going over there," she said, when Wanda finished.

"No way, girlfriend. Kenny will skin me alive."

"You can move in with me if he tries. Wanda! We have to go now and see what's up."

Wanda sighed. "I'm already dressed. Get your butt out of bed and throw some clothes on it. I'll drive."

"Well, I can kiss all future orders from Sally Statler goodbye, that's for sure," Wanda said as she swung left to the bridge. "That is unless she wants to take an Elvis Surprise to old Ed, with a file baked in the middle."

Tracy couldn't summon up a sense of humor. "You know that dinner cruise?"

"I wouldn't say I know it firsthand. We don't exactly hang out in the same social circles, you and me."

"Be glad. CJ was everybody's new best friend. He practically salivated over the other passengers. I wondered what he was up to. It was nauseating."

"I kinda don't think CJ was the reason your

stomach was upset. It had to do with all that liquor you drank."

"Wanda!" Tracy stared out the window. Unlike Southern California, this part of Florida rolled up the sidewalks at night. There was never much activity in Palmetto Grove after Early Bird Specials ended. Ahead of them the city was dark and quiet, and not at all the kind of place one expected to encounter a police raid.

"Go over it again," Tracy demanded. "I'm fully awake now."

"Kenny and a bunch of folks — and not all from the local office, either — are going to arrest Edward Statler for all kinds of things. The list goes on and on and on. . . ."

In California Tracy had seen a list like that with CJ's name at the top. It was amazing how many charges law enforcement agencies could drum up when they wanted somebody in custody badly enough.

"Ken told you all this?"

Wanda didn't answer right away. "Well, not exactly, if you want the truth. See, Kenny's good about not giving stuff away, and I needed more than what he was telling me. So I more or less made friends with one of the dispatchers who drops by for pie, and, well, I've been listening closely when the cops are gabbing at my counter. Molly, the dispatcher, knows I baked for the Statlers' reception, so when Kenny called to say he'd be real late

413

coming home, I called Molly to see what was up. And she told me."

Tracy was all admiration. "You're something else. You were born to pry and then to gossip about it."

"I don't want to make it sound like too much fun. I know you're not all that sure how you feel about your ex."

Tracy would have denied that, had it not been true. She wasn't sure how she felt, and she wasn't sure why.

"You think he's involved?" she asked.

"I found those papers in the pool house, where he's living, remember? How can he not be?"

"I don't even know what to hope for."

"This is one of those gated communities," Wanda said, as if she knew changing the subject was a good idea. "How come we don't have a gate out at Happiness Key?"

"If we had a gate, it would be the kind you get out and loop to a post."

"I'm not getting in and out of my car to open and close some gate."

"Well, there's your answer."

Wanda slowed a little and began to search the side of the road. "We're going to have to park somewhere and find our way in."

Tracy had a bad feeling about that. "Isn't the development fenced?"

"Not the beach side. We'll find a way." Wanda made a left, then another left, and parked on the side of the road. "It's just ahead. We'll go down to the water and walk along the shore."

"It's that easy?"

"Not all that much room to walk. Better take off your shoes."

Tracy considered. Maybe she'd been crazy wanting to see the action up close. Maybe she'd been even crazier entrusting her safety to the woman at the wheel, but it was too late now to turn back.

"You mean we're wading," she said, sensing the truth.

"More or less."

It turned out to be a lot "more" than "less." Tracy rolled her capris way above her knees. About half a block from the gatehouse they sat on a seawall and slipped off their shoes, then lowered themselves to the narrow strip of sand below. Luckily the tide was out, although the occasional big wave still washed against the wall. The pungent salt water was tainted with something that smelled like refrigerator leftovers, abandoned over summer vacation.

"So much for all the security money can buy," Tracy said, grimacing as the sand oozed like muck between her toes.

"Anybody asks, we're beachcombers."

"What are we looking for?"

"Stuff to sell at our flea market booth."

"Get real. Do I look like somebody who

415

has a booth at the flea market?"

"I'd advise you not to make a point of that, case we're caught."

"We don't even have flashlights."

"Don't need 'em. We find stuff with our toes."

Tracy snorted. Wanda started along the seawall, and Tracy followed behind her, squinting to see the seaweed-clotted sand at her feet in the moonlight. "Will you recognize the house from here?"

Now Wanda snorted. "It'll be the one with the cop cars surrounding it."

They fell silent. Tracy tried to focus on where to step. Barnacle-encrusted driftwood littered the "beach," and once she nearly stepped on a horseshoe crab lying on its back. There were no shells to speak of, but there was far too much trash for her taste. She hoped she and Wanda didn't encounter broken glass or rusted hooks, although she knew that was the definition of optimism.

The gatehouse was way off to their right, but Tracy knew when they'd passed it because the scenery changed. Now they were slipping past houses set back from the seawall by patios or mondo swimming pools glowing like sapphires in illuminated display cases.

The first dock was a nasty surprise. She nearly collided with Wanda, who had stopped just in front of it.

"I didn't think about this," Wanda admitted.

Tracy could hardly criticize, since neither had she.

"Don't get near the boat," she whispered, inclining her head to the end where a behemoth cabin cruiser was moored. "It's probably got a security guard cuddled up to an Uzi."

"Over or under, name your poison."

Tracy rolled up her pants legs one more turn. "Under, but yuck."

"Yuck is right."

They waded out into the water until they were deep enough to fit under the dock if they bent almost double. Tracy didn't look above her for any number of reasons, primarily because she didn't want to know what was dangling over her hair.

They got past that dock safely, and the next one, too, although Tracy felt something gouge her foot when she cleared the second.

"Ouch!"

Wanda stopped and held up her hand. Tracy stopped, too. Wanda pointed. The seawall was lower on the other side of the second dock, and Wanda crossed to it and hiked herself up, stooping once she was up on the wall.

She motioned, and Tracy joined her. She saw a line of flowering trees along what looked like a white gravel path around the side of the yard, ending at the road. Wanda pointed again. Both women rolled their pants legs down and put their shoes on. Then they quietly started walking along the path.

A dog came out of nowhere. One minute they were alone, their destination just ahead. The next a yapping ball of white fur was barreling toward them. Tracy liked dogs in their place, which was, in her opinion, in somebody else's house. Chase, Wanda's greyhound, was perfectly fine, because he belonged to Wanda, and besides, he looked fabulous in the black studded collar Janya had found at a garage sale. But the snarling little dog streaking toward her was not fine. Not fine at all.

Before she could shriek, Wanda stepped between her and the dog, and grabbed what turned out to be an unkempt poodle by the scruff of the neck, shaking him gently.

"You will not bark one more time," Wanda said, holding the dog up to her face. "Do you understand?"

The dog quieted immediately.

"Now, I'm going to put you down, and you are going home the moment I do, and no mistake about it."

The poodle moaned.

"Okay then, we're set." Wanda placed the dog on the ground and it took off running in the opposite direction.

Tracy had seen Wanda in poodle-bossing mode before. She had the same reaction now

418

that she'd had the first time. "You ought to consider Special Forces instead of a pie shop," she whispered.

"A woman learns what she needs to know."

They finished their trip in silence and with no more complications. Wanda turned left, and Tracy caught up with her.

"Are we close?" she asked in a slightly louder tone, now that they were out of the yard.

"Another couple of blocks. You okay?"

"I think I cut my foot in the water."

"You had a tetanus shot?"

"I'm up-to-date."

"You can walk?"

"I can hobble."

"Then hobble this way."

Two blocks later Tracy was sure she'd cut her foot, because her sandal felt sticky with blood, and she was limping. Luckily the cut seemed to be in the instep and not where she put the heaviest pressure on it, but she was glad when Wanda pointed ahead.

"Lights, camera, action." There were three police cars in a semicircle in front of what looked like the largest house on the water.

"How are you going to explain our presence to Ken?" Tracy asked. It wasn't the first time the question had occurred to her, but she hadn't wanted to set Wanda thinking too hard about the answer.

"I'll tell him you heard what was happening to CJ and wanted to come see what was up."

"True, as far as it goes."

"Let's just not let it go any further, okay? If Kenny asks, I'll do the talking."

Ken Gray *would* ask, too. But Ken had lived with Wanda a long time, and he probably knew protest was futile.

They approached the scene warily, but they weren't the only onlookers. Even in a prestigious gated community, a little evening drama was appreciated. And watching the mighty — in this case the residents of the community's largest home — go down in flames was a real-life crowd-pleaser.

Tracy sidled up to an older couple, she in a royal blue cashmere robe that probably added ten degrees to an already hot evening, he in Bermuda shorts and a saffron-colored golf shirt that was turned inside out.

Tracy smiled, as if she knew them. "Who'd have thought?" she said. "The Statlers."

"Yes, who?" the woman said. "And to think they were vetted by the home owner's association before they bought that house."

"Of course," Tracy said, as if she had been on the committee herself. "But so many things can be hidden."

"I hear this is all about drugs," the man said, lowering his voice.

Tracy tsk-tsked, then she smiled again and wove her way closer in. By the time she made it to the front, she'd heard theories about slave labor, gunrunning and Cuban cigars.

Wanda looked distinctly out of place with her lacquered semi-beehive, her cat's eye glasses, her sparkly spandex pants. But Tracy had to hand it to her friend. She looked out of place enough to be right *in* place. Wanda could carry off almost anything.

"They already took Edward Statler away," Wanda said softly. "We got here too late for that."

"What about CJ?"

"I heard they're questioning Mrs. Statler inside. That's all."

If anybody in the crowd could understand what Mrs. Statler was going through, it was Tracy. She felt a familiar ache, the way she had the night CJ was taken off to jail, and her house and life were legally ransacked. She hoped Mrs. Statler was as guilt-free as she had been. She hoped the woman would land on her feet somewhere and make a fresh new start.

Although Tracy's own fresh start was beginning to smell like the beach along the seawall.

Tracy didn't know what to do next. She didn't want to ask anyone in authority about CJ. She really didn't want to align herself with him, having spent too many years in that position. But she didn't want to leave until she knew what had happened to him, either. For some reason she felt she owed him that.

"I'll find Kenny," Wanda said, noticing Tracy's expression. "I'll ask him about that no-good ex of yours."

"Wait." Tracy grabbed her friend's sleeve. She pointed with her other hand. CJ was just coming out the front door, a cop on either side of him. Her heart did a cannonball to her toes.

So he had been questioned, too, and now it looked as if he was on his way to the police station.

Take two.

"You buck up now," Wanda said. "You're divorced from the man. You knew what he was before this. There's nothing new here."

Tracy didn't reply. Maybe there was nothing new, but a replay was painful enough.

The three men stopped just outside the door. Tracy was straining to see if CJ was handcuffed. Then, as she watched, one of the cops clapped his hand on CJ's shoulder and laughed at something CJ said. As her jaw fell to her chest, the other officer offered his hand, and CJ shook it. She blinked once, twice, three times, because surely something was wrong with her vision. When she'd finished blinking, she saw CJ picking up a suitcase. Then he started down the walkway.

"CJ!" Without thinking, she stepped forward, even though several officers were keeping the crowd at bay, but CJ didn't see her. She saw Ken Gray come from around the

422

side of the house, and she waved frantically to get his attention. He was obviously surprised to find her there, but she pointed at CJ, then at herself. He seemed to understand. In a minute he had called to CJ and pointed Tracy out in the crowd.

CJ saw her and smiled, a big radiant smile that seemed to chase away the darkness. Then he started in her direction.

"Stop being such a baby." CJ took Tracy's ankle firmly in his hand and stretched it over his knee again.

"I'm not being a baby. I have glass in my foot. And you're making it worse."

"I am not making it worse. I am removing it piece by piece, and unless I knock you over the head first, I don't know how to do it without a little discomfort."

"A little?" She barked a humorless laugh. "You're poking those tweezers all the way up to my navel."

"You caught me. This is really all about me getting my hands on your trim little ankle."

Trim little did the trick. While she was thinking about how nice it was that at least one part of her was still trim and little, he retrieved another sliver of glass."

"Ouch!"

"I think that's it." CJ shone the desk lamp he'd commandeered at her foot and bent close. "Looks good. Now I'll wash it out and put some antibiotic ointment on it, and a bandage, and you'll be all set."

"I'll wash it out!"

"And how, pray tell, are you going to do that? You're not double-jointed."

"I can get to it well enough."

"But I can get to it better. You don't want an infection, do you?"

"Since when did you become Dr. CJ?"

"I'm thinking medicine will be my next career. There are so many new and better ways to fleece the public." He got up. "Stay right there and don't move a muscle, or I'll chase you down, and it won't be pretty."

She didn't remember a time in their marriage when CJ had been this solicitous. Of course, in those days they'd had plenty of people around to take care of anything that came along. CJ had prided himself on having the largest staff he could manage. And she had to admit, he had been good to them. Generous and soft-spoken. For a man with an overblown ego, he still knew how to make people feel he cared.

Witness this performance.

He returned with a soapy washcloth and a bowl of water, and sat down at her feet again. "You've always been squeamish. I think that's why you never wanted children."

"Come on, you were the one who didn't want children."

"TK, you were always criticizing the young

424

mothers at the club who were preoccupied with their babies and toddlers. You couldn't imagine anybody getting such a charge out of dirty diapers and breast-feeding."

"I never gave the whole thing much thought, but that was because you told me you were too old and busy to be a father. The first time we went out," she added. "Before we even went to bed together."

"That's because I wasn't in the market for some sweet young thing who wanted to chain herself to me with a love child. That was before I realized I wanted to marry you."

"Well, aren't you a little late getting around to telling me?"

He was silent, and surprisingly gentle. Even though her foot stung, his hands on it felt delicious.

He dipped a clean washcloth in the water and began to wipe the soap off with slow, circular motions. "I guess I really was too old and too busy."

Hollywood trivia came with her upbringing. "A lot of men older than you start second families. Tony Randall was in his seventies."

"They had wives who made a point of wanting children. But maybe staying childless was best in the long run. My future's still uncertain. What kind of father could I be from prison?"

"CJ, exactly what went on tonight?" Tracy and a skeptical Wanda had removed CJ to

Wanda's car — walking along the road this time, since nobody at the gatehouse cared who departed. Now that Edward Statler was in jail, CJ no longer had a place to live. Especially since, apparently, CJ had helped put him there. Tracy, grateful that he, too, hadn't been hauled away in a cop car, had volunteered to let him sleep on her couch tonight.

After all, a similar arrangement was working so well for Marsh and Sylvia.

"I admire your self-control," he said. "I've been here nearly half an hour."

Tracy had showered as soon as they walked in, hot and sweaty, and feet and legs slimy from the walk along the seawall. That was when she'd realized the cut on her foot really needed attention. All of that had delayed their conversation, but there was more to it.

"I figured you must feel pretty beat-up by everything that happened," she said.

He looked up from her foot. "You're a nicer person than you believe."

"So?"

He gently patted her foot with a towel until it was dry. "Edward invited me to Florida for a reason. He needed somebody to do work that he thought I'd be uniquely qualified for. Plus he figured I had nowhere else to go and would be so grateful, I'd bury any ethics I had left."

"Let me guess. The work wasn't legal."

"Edward's been running major scams all over Florida for years, and a lot of people are involved."

"Maribel?"

He smiled. "Why? Do you have a personal interest in seeing her put away?"

She wondered if CJ had picked who to turn in, based on some code known only to him. She would probably never know, and besides, Maribel didn't matter. "Go on."

"Edward was pretty good, so it wasn't apparent, not with the mess all the banks are already in."

"Let me guess again." She pretended to think. "He bought houses, using shills and crooked appraisers, then he got banks to loan him — or rather, the shill — the entire price of the house plus the additional that the appraiser claimed it was worth. Then when the papers were all signed and sealed, and the money was delivered, the shill disappeared, Edward and the appraiser pocketed the extra money, and Edward was that much richer."

CJ looked genuinely surprised. "How did you figure that out?"

She winked. "My secret."

"Well, you got part of it. What's the other part?"

She thought about the papers Wanda had seen. "Fake loan applications?"

"Not fake, but close. Doctored. They were applications from real people filled out as a 'service' by Edward's employees. The applicants didn't make nearly as much money as the applications claimed. Based on the falsified figures, they were then given adjustable mortgages. Of course they defaulted when they couldn't make the rising payments, and lost their homes. After foreclosure, Edward snapped the houses back up at a percentage of what they were worth, then moved to the next and final phase, which you've so wisely recounted to me."

"What a scumbag."

"Not my choice of terms, but close enough."

"But what was your part in all of this?"

"Not very complicated. Right away I realized what was going on, and I knew I couldn't have anything to do with it. First, it wasn't good karma. Second, it wasn't even vaguely legal. Third, I'm already in enough trouble. So even though Edward was generous, I went to the authorities with evidence about what he'd been doing. He was already under investigation, and what you know is the tip of the iceberg. They asked me to get more information, and I did."

Tracy was still trying to convince herself she had heard the word *karma* come out of CJ's mouth. Plus her foot was still in his lap, and for some reason she was reluctant to ask him to hurry so she could resume ownership.

"And earned some brownie points while

you were at it," she said.

"And earned some brownie points, yes. But really, I don't know if that will matter in the long run. I helped here, but nobody's going to call this a wash with what's going on in California."

"But you did it anyway."

"I'd like to leave Florida under my own power, not escorted by marshals."

She had expected something so different. A repeat performance of their Southern California drama. A fresh chance to despise him. Instead, CJ was now something of a hero.

CJ as bad guy she was used to. That she could deal with. But CJ as hero?

"So what do you think?" He had put ointment on her foot as he talked, then covered it with fresh gauze. Now he fastened tape in place and snipped the ends with her kitchen scissors.

"About my foot or your story?"

"Your ex-husband helping the cops and the Feds?"

"I think I need to sleep on it."

"Thanks for offering me the sofa."

For a moment — less than a moment, really, a zeptosecond — she considered telling CJ he could just sleep with *her*. He was the one who had pointed out that divorced couples often got it on after the decree. Familiarity might breed contempt, but it also bred, well, familiarity. And the idea of having familiar, attractive CJ next to her on the mattress again was enticing.

He leaned forward, and she didn't move away. Instead she put her foot on the floor so he could get closer. His smell was familiar, something earthy enhanced by a touch of expensive cologne. She remembered the first time he had kissed her, how thrilled she had been that he had chosen her. How practiced his lips and hands.

They were still practiced. They grazed hers, just touching her with enough finesse that she felt the tickle all the way to her navel. And, okay, beyond. She couldn't deny it.

Loneliness could do that.

That was when she realized where her thoughts had led: straight back to the man she was really lonely for. She pulled away.

A sofa was not an invitation into her life. A sofa was not an invitation into her bed. She really didn't know who this man was anymore, and that was a good enough reason to back away, even without Marsh in the picture.

"The linen closet's in the hallway," she said, getting to her feet with a wince. "Towels, sheets, a light blanket. The bathroom and the living room are yours. I'm going to bed."

"I'll look for another place tomorrow, I promise."

"You're going to stay in Florida?"

"I could go back to California and let them lynch me."

"Thanks for fixing my foot."

"Thanks for coming to check on me tonight."

She didn't know what to say to that, because in the long run, that was exactly what she had done. Now she had the rest of the night to figure out exactly why.

CHAPTER
TWENTY-ONE

Dana had a surprise for Pete, and not one she thought he was going to greet with enthusiasm. As much as he liked Lizzie, he, like Dana, had been counting on an evening alone.

In fact, since Monday, Dana had given far too much thought to the subject.

"Why does Pete live so far from us?" Lizzie didn't sound glad to be traveling north with her mother. Her evening plans, too, had been altered, and not to her liking.

"I think it's a great place for fishing," Dana said. "And Pete loves to fish."

"He could fish near us."

"He does sometimes. After work. But there are different kinds of fishing. Saltwater, freshwater. He can catch freshwater fish in the lake." Up ahead, Dana saw her exit and changed lanes to prepare.

Lizzie wasn't exactly whining, but the sound was similar. "I wish Olivia hadn't gotten sick."

As she left the interstate, Dana wished the same thing. Olivia had a full-fledged summer cold, probably picked up on the trip to visit her father, and both Dana and Alice had thought it best not to expose Lizzie to Olivia's germs. Neither of the girls had been happy about the decision.

"Alice says if Olivia's better by Saturday, you can spend the night then," Dana reminded her.

"Is Pete glad I'm coming?" Lizzie still sounded peevish.

Dana didn't know, because she hadn't been able to warn him. When she called, as instructed, to tell him they were on the way, she'd gotten his voice mail. Since Lizzie had been nearby, she'd only said she was about to hit the road. As she tried to figure out how to break the news that Lizzie was going to be with her, the window of opportunity ended with a click and a dial tone.

"Pete likes you," she said, not answering the exact question.

"Was this supposed to be a date?"

Dana could feel her cheeks heating. "Something like that, I guess."

"You don't go on dates."

"Not often."

"Men look at you like they'd like to date you. I watch them."

"We need to find better things for you to watch."

"I'd like to have a father. Course, Olivia has a father, so I guess it's not always a good thing."

Dana was silent. She knew her daughter was digging for information. Lizzie was getting better and better at it every day.

"I told her at least *she* knows who her father is," Lizzie said.

"I doubt Olivia finds that much consolation. And for the record, a date is not the same thing as saying 'I do.' Pete and I are friends. But we have separate lives and separate plans. Don't expect more, okay?"

"Do we have plans? Are we going to move again? Don't you like your job?"

Dana wondered just how long she could get away with the lifestyle they led. At what point would Lizzie rebel and demand to know why, exactly why and no lies please, they had to move yet again?

"I like my job just fine," she said, "and I'm not in any hurry to leave. But managing Wanda's shop isn't a career, Lizzie. I need to finish my degree and do my student teaching, and there's no university close enough to make that feasible. Once I can teach, we can really settle down." She hoped it was true. They would relocate to some isolated community that needed a teacher and finally stay put.

Of course, finding the money to make that dream come true was a nearly insurmountable hurdle.

"Nobody else moves the way we do." Lizzie shifted in her seat, as if she couldn't wait to get out of the car.

"If we were a military family, we'd move all the time. And what if I was a trapeze artist in a circus? Did you ever think of that?"

Lizzie didn't laugh. "Then our friends would travel with us. We don't have friends, or at least we don't keep them. I want to be Olivia's friend forever."

"Let's not borrow trouble, okay? Can we just enjoy tonight and not make a complicated life plan before we even get to Pete's?"

"Why aren't we there yet?"

Dana slowed at the road sign up ahead, and made a right turn onto a scrub pine and palm-studded country lane. "We almost are."

A few minutes later they entered a campground. She stopped and went into a combination general store and office, and explained why she was there. The man behind the counter gave her directions to Pete's campsite and a red parking tag to hang on her rearview mirror. The speed limit on the grounds was ten miles an hour, but even that was too fast. Children played on the side of the dirt road, and campers walked back and forth between live oak and pine-shaded campsites, talking and laughing. The sites were set a comfortable distance from each other, not like some Dana had seen that were as cramped as old-fashioned drive-in theaters.

"Where's the lake?" Lizzie asked.

"I think we're driving toward it." She was paying attention to numbers on metal stakes in front of each site, but she saw they weren't close yet.

"It would be fun to live here. There are a lot of kids."

"Maybe you can meet some of them."

"Maybe . . ."

The road wound left past more campsites, rows of oleanders and crepe myrtle, several spacious bathhouses, and a campfire circle that looked big enough for half the residents to gather and toast marshmallows. There was a small zoo, with exotic birds in a large mesh aviary, and what looked like a collection of reptiles. Lizzie was getting interested.

"Why haven't we camped?"

Dana glanced at her daughter. The only kind of camping she would consider wouldn't involve a campground like this one, not with so many people, so many strangers. How could she know who these campers were or where they'd come from? How could she trust that one of them might not be someone she had met before, someone who would ask questions?

Someone who might feel compelled to report seeing her to the wrong people.

"Let's file that away as something fun to try," Dana said.

"That's what you say when you have no intention of doing something."

"Tell you what, we'll start looking for camping gear at the flea market. We'll make a list and see what we can find."

"I wonder what it's like to just go to a store and pick what you want and not worry about money." Lizzie sounded genuinely curious but not as if she felt sorry for herself. The same way she might ask what it would be like to live in a grass hut or an igloo.

"I see the lake." Dana pointed.

Lizzie leaned forward too fast, and her seat belt snapped her against the seat before she caught a glimpse. "Is it big?"

"Big enough for waterskiing, I bet."

"I'd like to water-ski."

"Maybe we'll have time for you to learn." Dana remembered her own attempts when she'd visited Happiness Haven as a girl. "I had a couple of lessons once. I let go of the rope the moment the boat started to move."

"That's silly. I wouldn't."

Dana drove a little farther. Pete's campsite was number four, as close to the lake, apparently, as the campsites went. Here all the campers were larger and looked permanent, as if they were part of the landscape.

"There it is," she said after a moment. Pete's camper looked surprisingly roomy, unmistakably an Airstream, with a screen enclosure attached to the entrance to make a mosquito-free porch. She spotted several folding chairs under the mesh. Outside, a grill was heating. Real charcoal, with smoke rising in wisps.

She pulled to a stop, wishing she could explain Lizzie's presence without her daughter standing right there, but just then Pete stepped outside, and his expression didn't reflect a moment's disappointment when he saw he had two guests.

"Hey," he said, smiling at both of them. "Two for the price of one."

"Olivia's sick," Lizzie said, taking the explanation out of her mother's hands. "And Mom won't leave me at home by myself."

"Your mom. A real pain in the neck, huh?"

Lizzie went to him for a quick hug. And when that was over, he stepped to Dana and kissed her cheek. "It's good to see you both."

She heard the message. He understood. He wasn't upset with her, and he wasn't going to act as if his entire evening had been spoiled. She'd known a lot of petulant men who acted out in a variety of ways if they didn't get what they wanted. She'd been married to one.

Any doubts she'd had about Pete Knight vanished in that instant.

"Why don't you and your mom satisfy your curiosity and take a look inside?" he told Lizzie. "Then, if you want, I'll introduce you to my neighbor's daughter. She's about your age, and I bet she'll show you around the campground."

Lizzie peeked at her mother, and Dana nodded. "I'm sure you want to check it out."

"And tell that mom of yours there's a salad in my refrigerator, and dressing, if she's willing to toss it for me," he finished.

For a moment Dana felt as if she were living the all-American dream. Everything about being with Pete felt so comfortable and right. Dana prayed that in the days ahead, everything would continue to be both.

Rishi had apologized for missing the special evening he and Janya were supposed to spend together. He'd claimed that late in the afternoon, he had fallen asleep on the couch in his office and slept until well after midnight, when he'd awakened in horror to find the building dark and everyone gone.

Rishi was not a good liar. His eyes had not quite met hers, and he stumbled twice as he spoke, as if his agile brain could not keep up as he manufactured details. Had she felt secure in her husband's affections, Janya might have attributed both to his shame at disappointing her. But since this rejection was one of many she had lately suffered from him, she knew it for what it was. He was not ashamed; he was hiding something.

Janya had not made her suspicions known. The next morning, after she returned from taking Tracy to retrieve her car, she listened to Rishi's explanation, nodding. She did not bother to tell him that late in the afternoon, when she had called to remind him they were spending the evening together — and wasn't it sad that she had needed to do so? — his assistant had reported that Rishi was already gone for the day. She had even complained because he had given her a pile of work, since he would not be back.

When a surprised Janya asked her to check, just to be certain, the woman had further reported that Rishi's car was no longer in its parking slot, and in fact, someone had seen him drive away.

Foolishly Janya had believed a repentant Rishi was on his way home to spend the afternoon with her, as well. The fact that he never arrived had been that much more disappointing, until anger seeped into its place.

When Rishi's apology and excuses had finally ended that morning, Janya had nodded one more time, then gone into the kitchen to make coffee. By the time the pot filled, Rishi had already gone to work.

Since then, he had come home each night just in time for supper, but afterward he had excused himself to work in the second bedroom. Later he'd only come to bed when Janya was sure to be sleeping. Although she wasn't asleep, she'd made certain to let him think he had gauged correctly.

Tonight he arrived home on time once again. He looked tired when he walked in, and tired when they said their prayers. She dredged up enough courtesy to ask him about his day, although she didn't follow with more questions. She served a simple supper, having talked herself out of telling him to feed himself, and she refused his help afterward when he offered to assist with cleaning the kitchen.

"I assume you will be working again?" she asked, as she picked up their plates.

"I thought, perhaps, you might like to go for a walk."

For a moment she thought she had grown so used to English that her command of her native tongue — which Rishi used whenever they were home alone — had declined. Surely there must be an explanation for what she thought she had heard.

"Did you say a walk?" she asked, when she realized he was waiting for her answer.

"It seems cooler tonight. And the humidity is lower."

She thought about all the things that could be accomplished on walks and settled on the one that seemed most likely. Rishi had something to tell her, and he wanted to do it where she would be forced to listen.

"I must clean up," she said, turning away.

"Leave it for later, Janya. I told you I would help. But let's do it after we come back. The sun is setting. I rarely get to see it."

She nearly suggested he cut a new window in the west wall of his office, since that was where he spent most evenings. Except that was apparently no longer true, and she was afraid tonight he wanted to tell her why.

And didn't she need to know, so she could make plans for her future?

"I will soak the dishes." There was only resignation in her voice.

"Good. We can walk along the beach."

"Give me a few minutes."

"I'll meet you on the patio."

She changed into pants and a long-sleeved shirt, both of the lightest cotton. She fastened her hair back from her face with barrettes but didn't bother with jewelry or refreshing her makeup. Nothing she did seemed to entice Rishi. She was tired of trying.

"You look lovely," he said when she joined him.

His response sounded perfunctory, the kind of thing husbands learn to say early in a marriage to keep their homes and lives peaceful. She nodded, but she didn't smile.

"Shall we walk?"

They strolled down the road, then took the closest path to the beach. The public beach at the other end of the key was sugar sand perfection. This end, some of which Tracy owned, had never been improved and was still the way nature had created it. The beach itself was uneven here. There were places where they could walk abreast and places where single file worked better. They skirted obstacles, the skeletons of boats that had washed up on shore, tree trunks, piles of shells, tangled lines and old tackle boxes abandoned by fishermen. Fiddler crabs darted along the waterline, and seagulls and terns flew low, searching for their last morsels until morning.

The sun was sinking rapidly now on a coral-streaked horizon. Janya was always surprised that the sun took so many hours to sweep across the sky, then rushed through its dramatic exit like a Shakespearean novice, racing through his final monologue as he launched himself toward the wings and his dressing room.

"The sand looks clean and soft here," Rishi said, after they had walked a distance in silence. "Shall we sit?"

Janya lowered herself to the ground and pulled her knees toward her chest, wrapping her arms around them. Rishi sat beside her.

"Have you heard from Yash?" he asked.

Yash was Janya's younger brother, the one member of her family who had stood beside her at a time of great difficulty in her life.

"He called several nights ago," Janya said. "He is definitely going to start classes at the University of South Florida in the fall. He was very excited."

"You didn't tell me." He sounded perplexed.

"You weren't home."

"You should have called me at work."

She glanced at him. "Should I have? I will remember that. From now on, when I have important news, I won't wait to share it with you in person, since that time might never come. I will call you at work and ask your assistant to relay the message."

"Janya . . ."

She turned her gaze back to the water. "Let's watch the sunset, please."

"I . . . I'm sorry I haven't been . . . more available."

"Are you? That's good. Being sorry can at times be helpful. I rather doubt it will be this time, though, since you have been sorry many times lately, but nothing has changed."

"It's just that this is a crucial —" He stopped abruptly. "It's just that . . ."

She waited a long moment. As explanations went, this was not a good one.

She changed the subject, or thought she did. "It always surprises me that photographers can take such perfect pictures of a sunset but not even begin to convey the real experience."

She glanced at him again and realized she hadn't changed the subject at all. "Sunsets are like marriages, aren't they? Someone could take a photograph of ours, and it might look happy and solid to anyone viewing it. But the photograph would not convey the truth. I am not quite certain how long the photographer could continue, under these circumstances, to get acceptable images, either."

For a moment he looked angry. "Do you think it helps to be critical?"

"Did it help when I was not?"

"This is just a difficult time for me, that's all. Many things happening, and I'm caught up in all of them."

"Things I should know about?"

He shook his head. "Nothing to worry about. Just things that are keeping me too busy."

"Too busy . . ." She wanted to add "to make love to your wife," but the words wouldn't come. They had begun their marriage as strangers trying to find a life together. They had overcome difficulties, begun to grow closer. But intimacy? The kind that grows between two people who can say whatever they must without recrimination? They hadn't reached that point, and now she was fairly certain they never would.

She sat silently and watched as the sun was devoured by the hungry gulf. Darkness would come quickly now, but from here they could easily pick their way back to the road. She started to stand, but Rishi held her back.

"I am sorry," he said softly. "This is a stressful time. I *am* sorry."

She thought about telling him she knew he had lied to her. She thought about demanding an explanation. But something in his tone stopped her. Rishi sounded genuinely sad, perhaps even more than sad.

Desolate.

She put her hand on his cheek and gazed into his eyes. "Show me you are."

He looked startled. Hope, and something that might be desire, blazed suddenly in his eyes. "Here?"

"There is no one here to see us."

"On the sand?"

"Have I married a prissy old woman? To worry about such things? If you are sorry for ignoring me so thoroughly in the past weeks, then ignore me no more. Beginning right now."

For a moment she thought he would comply. His eyes were filled with longing. He reached around to cup the back of her head and bring her close. Then he froze.

"I . . . I think there's someone on the path. I saw a shadow."

She turned in the direction Rishi's gaze had traveled. The path, which they would take back to the road, was empty.

"There's no one there," she said.

He moved away and got to his feet. "I saw a shadow. This is no place to . . ." He let the words trail off.

Sighing, she got to her feet, too. She could finish the sentence for him, but there were so many possible endings, there was no time to voice them all.

No place to make love.

No place to be honest.

No place to set their marriage to rights.

No place to tell her that he no longer wanted to be married to a woman who could not bear his children.

She brushed the sand off her pants and straightened her shirt.

"You're right. As they say in this country, what was I thinking? Let's go home."

She started across the sand to the still-vacant path.

Dana sat next to Pete in his screen room, a glass of merlot on the fold-up table beside her. The Airstream was air-conditioned, but even with the sultry temperatures outside, it was nice to be where the air smelled like pine and wood smoke, and the sounds of children laughing and playing were punctuated by the bellows of frogs and the hum of radios.

"I'm assuming Lizzie will find her way back," Dana said, not really worried.

"She's having a ball. You may not be able to wrestle her back into your car."

"You've been so nice about this."

"Lizzie's always welcome."

"Well, when you saw us, I'm hoping you

447

felt at least a trace of disappointment that you and I weren't going to be alone tonight."

"More than a trace."

She leaned over and kissed his cheek, then his lips, when he turned them to her. "Thanks for hiding it."

He laced his fingers through hers. "My boys were born when I was practically a kid myself. Two was plenty, since we were all growing up together. But I did miss having a daughter. You must have been thrilled when you learned you'd had a girl."

These were choppy waters, and Dana trod carefully. Despite years on the run, she could still sort lies from truth, and as long as she could, she didn't want to lie to Pete. At least not any more than she had to lie to everyone.

"I've always loved kids," she said.

"You didn't want a daughter more than a son?"

Dana thought back to her pregnancy. "I wanted a healthy baby."

"Did you get one?"

Dana thought back to the infant who had fought for every breath in a preemie's incubator. "Lizzie looks pretty healthy, wouldn't you say?"

"I would say."

"Love makes all the difference." The moment she said it, Dana wondered why she had. That sentiment didn't fit the conversation they were supposed to be having, although it certainly fit Lizzie's life.

Pete interpreted. "In other words, you took good care of her, despite the asthma, despite all the childhood problems that cropped up, and you have a healthy girl to show for it."

She was relieved he had somehow made sense of it. "That's what mothers do."

"That's what they're supposed to do. Not all of them comply."

For a moment fear streaked through her, as it so often did. Had she given something away? Would Pete grow suspicious? With all the moves and the accompanying fishy excuses, her peculiar lack of attachment to anyone but her daughter, their lives looked suspicious enough.

"Most of them try," she said. "It's a tough job, and some mothers just don't know where to begin. Nobody ever showed them how."

"Who showed you?"

They were going too deep. She was sorry the conversation had taken this turn. "I had an ordinary childhood, where my needs were taken into consideration, and I was expected to behave." Deftly, she turned the spotlight to him. "Sometimes it's just that simple, don't you think? Was yours the same?"

"My father was career navy. You'd better believe we were expected to behave."

She laughed softly. "Somebody took good care of you, though. You understand how it's done."

"My mother doted on all her children, and my father doted on her. He didn't dare cross any lines. If she thought he was demanding too much, she pulled him to one side and things changed. He was a good man who was better when he was around her. We all were."

"A testimony to motherly love." Dana saw her daughter coming back with a couple of the campground girls. "And speaking of mothering . . ."

She got to her feet and unzipped her way out of the screen room to greet Lizzie, who waved goodbye as the two other girls started back down the road.

Lizzie was sweating and flushed, and she looked tired. Dana thought the girls had probably made the entire circuit, some of it at a run.

"You look beat, kiddo. Come on in and have a seat. I'll get you some water."

Lizzie didn't respond. She hung her head and shook it from side to side. Dana decided to let her catch her breath, but Pete got to his feet and joined them.

"Are you okay, Lizzie?"

She shook her head again. Dana was instantly alarmed. Maybe Lizzie had already caught Olivia's cold, or maybe she was just overheated and dehydrated.

She moved closer, and then the cause of Lizzie's distress was obvious.

She stooped, so she could see Lizzie's face.

"Were you petting a cat?"

Lizzie croaked a "yes."

"The neighbor a couple of campers over has two," Pete said.

"Is that where you were?" Dana asked her daughter.

Lizzie nodded. "Ear . . . lier."

"Let's get your rescue inhaler. Did you leave it in the car?"

Lizzie looked up, stricken. "I didn't . . ."

Dana felt panic begin to gnaw at her. The last doctor to see Lizzie had convinced Dana that at eleven, Lizzie was old enough to prepare for an asthma attack on her own. She was the right age, he had cautioned, to learn how to handle one herself, so that by the time she became a teenager, carrying and using her inhaler would be second nature and nothing to be embarrassed about around her peers. Dana was allowed to check with her daughter when she left the house to be sure Lizzie had what she needed, but Lizzie had to learn to handle her asthma on her own.

Tonight Dana had forgotten to check. She'd been in a hurry to see Pete, and she had been lulled by all the months of Lizzie's good health. Apparently Lizzie had been, too. They'd even cut down the daily meds she was supposed to take, with no repercussions.

"I should have reminded you," Dana said, guilt warring with panic. "It's not your fault. I should have —"

"Dana." Pete put a hand on her arm. "Let's make her comfortable."

"But she doesn't have —"

He gave a sharp shake of his head to silence her. "She's going to be fine. Lizzie, take my seat." He led the girl into the screen room and over to his chair where he helped her sit.

Then he stooped in front of her. "Okay, now the most important thing you can do is relax your shoulders and neck, okay? I know it's hard, but you have to do it. Just feel the muscles let go, a little at a time. Don't fight with them. Let everything drop." He waited. Dana saw Lizzie's shoulder droop a fraction.

"Terrific!" Pete put his hand on her arm. "Now watch me and breathe with me, okay?"

Lizzie's eyes were wide with alarm, and Dana could hear her wheezing loudly.

"Purse your lips. Like this." Pete showed her, as if he was about to play a round of Taps.

Dana went to her daughter and put her hand on her shoulder to comfort her, but Pete had control now, and he was calm and useful, while inside, she was falling apart.

He spoke slowly, as if they had all the time in the world. "We're going to breathe in through our noses. Then we're going to breathe out through our mouths. But we're going to do both as slowly as we can. Try not to gasp for air, okay?"

Pete began to breathe, keeping eye contact

452

with Lizzie. Lizzie tried to follow his example, but with limited success. Pete kept encouraging her softly, as Dana felt more and more panicked.

"I can't . . ." Lizzie wailed.

"Sure you can," Pete said. "You're going to be fine in a few minutes. But breathe with me. Again now."

Dana closed her eyes and tried to think where the nearest emergency room might be. There was a hospital in Palmetto Grove, of course, but they were a good twenty-five minutes north of the city. If they left now, would that be better for Lizzie? Should she get her daughter into the car right this minute, wheezing and all?

"Hey, that's good." Pete sounded pleased. "Let's see if we can do that even slower."

Dana looked down and saw that Lizzie was concentrating and trying to follow instructions. Dana prayed it was working.

Four long breaths later, she realized it was beginning to. She could feel her daughter's shoulder relaxing bit by bit. And the strained, shallow sound of her breathing had lessened.

Ten minutes passed before Pete stood.

"Rest if you need to," he told Lizzie, "but keep up the breathing a little bit longer."

"I feel a lot better."

"I know you do, but let's make sure the worst is really over, okay? Then your mom will drive you home, and you can use that missing inhaler of yours."

Lizzie nodded.

Dana realized all too well that she was the one who should have been guiding Lizzie through the slow breathing. But she had completely lost her cool. Had she tried to, her own anxiety would have communicated itself and made things worse.

"Where did you learn that?" Dana knew she still sounded frightened. Her voice was high and breathy.

"My youngest son had asthma as a boy."

She felt Pete looking at her, as if trying to understand why she had fallen apart. If Lizzie's asthma was serious enough that they had been repeatedly forced to move because of it, shouldn't she be as used to this as a parent could ever be?

Dana had no answers. None she could give him, anyway. She couldn't explain that Lizzie's attacks were so rare that the only time they came to anybody's attention was when Dana used them as an excuse for moving. She had panicked because she had been completely surprised.

"I'm sorry," Dana said, not sure which part of the evening she was apologizing for. The attack. Her reaction. The lies that probably made him wonder what kind of mother she was.

"No need to apologize."

"It was a lovely evening. The best. I'm sorry

it ended . . ." She didn't want to say more, since Lizzie was sitting right there.

"You ought to get her home."

She nodded. "We'll head out now."

"I'll drop by this weekend to see how you're doing."

Time to say no. Tonight was just another example of how *any* kind of relationship complicated her already-complicated existence.

But this was Pete, who had helped her daughter breathe again. Pete, who took her at face value and didn't ask for anything she didn't want to give.

Pete, the man she was falling in love with and couldn't seem to push away.

Not yet.

She managed a smile. "We'd like that."

"Lizzie," he warned, "I'm going to kiss your mother. She needs it. She was worried about you."

"Go ahead," Lizzie said.

"Pete —" But Pete stopped Dana's words with a sweet kiss she couldn't seem to break away from.

"Now let's get Miss Lizzie out to the car," he said when it had ended.

Twenty-five minutes later, as Dana turned off the bridge onto the road to Happiness Key with Lizzie sleeping beside her, she realized it was time to move again. Perhaps past time. Unfortunately, for once she couldn't do what all her instincts screamed she must. For better or worse, she was trapped at Happiness Key. With Pete. With the women who offered unqualified friendship. With memories of past summers in this place and the legacy that had come with them.

"It's your fault, Fargo," she whispered. But even as she said it, she knew it wasn't true.

How could she blame a dead man?

CHAPTER
TWENTY-TWO

Wanda was sprawled on Tracy's sofa as if she belonged there, Tracy's cordless phone nearly welded to her ear by now.

"That's right, Dana. No, not Diana. Dayna. Right. All I can remember is that she lived in Fresno, and she asked me to stop by and see her if I ever came through town, and I —" Wanda stopped, shaking her head in disgust. "Well, thank you for your time. You have a good weekend now, you hear?"

Tracy put a can of diet cola on the coffee table for her friend. "Another bust." It wasn't a question.

"The man never heard of a Dana Turner. Nice enough about it, though."

"So how many people have you called?"

Wanda glanced at the list of phone numbers belonging to Fresno Turners that Tracy had printed from the Internet. Some of them had come with interesting addendums. Professions, ages, the names of others in the household. Even Tracy was a little shocked at how much people could find out by consulting the online White Pages.

"Thirty," Wanda said, looking up. "With a lot more to go."

"Does the word *futile* mean anything to you?"

Wanda set down the telephone and stretched. "It will the minute you come up with a better plan."

"When we were trying to find out about Herb's life, at least we had papers to go through. We don't have squat about Dana, just the info on Lizzie's birth certificate. Knowing she was born in Fresno, and her full name is Elizabeth Anne Turner just isn't enough. *E.A.T.,* by the way. How's that for an acronym?"

"Works for me. You're the one that's obsessed with food."

Tracy had to admit it was true. Not only was she on a diet, she had to phone at least one of her teammates every day to offer support — that was one of Kitty's ironclad rules. So what else did she have to think about?

Dangerously close to rummaging through the fridge, she went back to the subject of Dana Turner's past. Getting a copy of Lizzie's birth certificate from the center had been good luck, but so far that was all the luck they'd had.

"I don't know what you're going to find out even if you get a hit. Who's going to tell a stranger something important on the phone? And there's nothing else of interest on Lizzie's birth certificate except her mother's name, which we knew. Not even Dana's middle name."

"Well, now we know the father's listed as unknown."

"So what would be the reasons for that?"

Wanda listed possibilities. "Maybe she really didn't know? It happens. Or maybe she just didn't want Lizzie to trace him once she's older. Or maybe he asked her not to, because he was married and didn't want his wife finding out. Or maybe she thought he'd try to take Lizzie away if she made it official."

"Maybe none of that matters, Wanda. If they're running away from something or somebody, wouldn't they just change their names?"

Wanda and Tracy had already gone through this. Wanda's theory was to start with what they knew and work from there. But she'd also admitted that Tracy had a point. There just wasn't any good reason to go through the motions if the birth certificate was a fake and they didn't even have the right names. If Dana Turner was really Heidi Schirmer or Zelda Young, then they were wasting their time.

Wanda glanced up at the clock. "I gotta get home. Besides, I'm sitting where CJ sleeps. I don't like lolling around on the man's bed."

"He's not here enough to call it that. I'm not sure what he does all day, but he doesn't do it here."

"At least he got himself a rental car. Now when's he going to get himself another place to live?"

It was a reasonable question. CJ had slept on Tracy's sofa for three nights. As a thank-you for the past two, he'd come back each evening with dinner, and he'd even cleaned up afterward. He brought bottles of good wine, flowers and his own charming company. He was attentive, helpful and easy to talk to. He hadn't tried to get into her bed.

And he was overdue to leave.

"I think he's working on it," she told Wanda, because she hated to tell the truth. CJ hadn't mentioned moving out, and, worse, she hadn't asked him to.

Wanda looked skeptical. "You need some reminders about what the man did to you?"

Tracy wondered. Since her arrival in Florida she'd gotten used to living alone, even decided she liked it, but these days, since CJ had shown up bearing gifts and companionship, she had realized that deep inside, she craved more than just an acceptable place to lay her head. She wanted a home with somebody who loved her. And as bonded as she was to her neighbors, she needed a man in her life.

"Nobody knows better than I do what he

put me through," she said.

"Lordy, woman, there's a 'but' in your voice."

"I wonder, Wanda, if maybe I just dredged up all the things that weren't right in our relationship and buried the things that were, you know?" She held up her hand when Wanda started to interrupt. "From what I could tell when the whole mess in California was going down, CJ really was at fault. He was responsible for everything that happened to us — to me. I was so furious —"

"You had a tiny right to be."

"Maybe I did, and maybe I didn't. Look how much help he was to the authorities here. What if he was telling the truth about California all along? What if he just screwed up a little, then things started snowballing before he could fix them? What if the authorities dug him a hole, herded him in that direction, and he just stumbled into it because there was no place else to go?"

"You don't believe that."

Tracy didn't. Not yet. But she was steadily growing less sure where she stood on the guilt of one CJ Craimer.

"I'll tidy up the rest of these calls at home tonight," Wanda said, getting to her feet. "Kenny's gone again."

Tracy was relieved to be finished with the subject of her ex. She walked Wanda to the door. "I wish Ken could run Dana's name.

461

The Internet's fine as far as it goes, but that's not far enough for us."

"If we could, I'd ask him to look into missing children from the Fresno area."

Tracy, who admittedly had been thinking about many other things, hadn't thought about approaching the problem that way. "Wanda, that's brilliant. Why didn't you suggest it before?"

"Because I don't want Kenny involved."

"He wouldn't have to be. There are all kinds of missing children Web sites, complete with photographs. That's something I can check out tonight."

Wanda looked pleased, but she quickly sobered. "It's probably going to be a big waste of time. Even if Dana and Lizzie are running, kidnapping might not be involved."

"Or it might be, at least technically. I just can't shake the feeling she's running from Lizzie's father, afraid he's going to snatch their daughter."

"That sounds like a lot of time online."

It might or might not be. Tracy could get lucky right off the bat or find nothing of interest after hours of searching. She was just glad to have something to do. Now she would be less likely to fill her evening with snacks. She would also be less likely to wonder what was happening at the other end of the key. Bay had told her that Sylvia was visiting an old friend in Sarasota for a few days. All weekend she'd had to fight the temptation to drop by his comfortable old Cracker house with some flimsy excuse, and see if she and Marsh could find common ground for one more heart-to-heart talk.

"You make those phone calls anyway," she told Wanda. "I'll do my research. And we'll see if anything turns up."

"You know, we could just ask Dana and swear ourselves to secrecy."

"Could you really do that? What if she admits she committed a crime? Could you keep that a secret, too? Even from Kenny?"

"What are the chances she'd be dumb enough to confess? No, I think asking would be safe, except maybe she'd hightail it out of here."

"I'd rather know what we're dealing with. Then we can tell her we want to help. If we wait and do it that way, she'll know we aren't going to turn her in, because we would have done it already. If she's on the run, she must wish somebody would help."

Wanda stepped out to the porch. "Well, I, for one, have to be careful here. I can't get Kenny into the middle of some dustup or other. If she's done something really bad . . ."

Tracy's own moral compass was spinning round and round with CJ, and she wasn't sure where it was going to settle. "I'm not sure I'd be the best person to judge, and I'm not sure I'm up to making logical choices about Dana."

"Then let's leave that to our neighbors. We'll do a little more work on this, then we'll get together and have us a chat."

Tracy watched her go. The sun was still high enough in the sky that she probably had hours before CJ returned. For a moment she imagined just getting in her Bimmer and heading down the road to Marsh's house. Did she need an excuse to see him other than an apology? One of them had to make the first move or there was never going to be a reconciliation.

Assuming she wanted one.

In the end, she went back inside and turned on her computer, typing in *Fresno* and *missing children*. Then, with a Diet Coke, a rice cake and a grimace, she began to dig into Dana's life once more.

Pete arrived just as Lizzie was leaving. The girl opened the door, saw him on the doorstep and beamed a welcome.

"I'm going to Olivia's for our sleepover! Mrs. Brooks is taking us to see a movie, then we're going to Gonzalo's."

"Makes me wish I was eleven again."

"No boys allowed."

"Not until next year," Dana said, after she'd kissed her daughter goodbye and watched her scamper off to Olivia's house. "Next year boys will be invited, even enjoyed."

"Is twelve the magic number?"

"It was when I was a girl. So far, neither Lizzie nor Olivia seems all that interested, but that won't last."

"I imagine the boys are going to be interested in both of them. Maybe I ought to teach a little Happiness Key self-defense class."

Dana was so glad to see him, she suddenly felt tongue-tied. She just smiled, probably foolishly.

"So Olivia's okay?" he asked.

She forced her tongue to form words. "A lot better, and probably not contagious. I think the movie is Alice's attempt to keep them quiet while Olivia finishes recovering."

"And how's Lizzie?"

She realized they were standing on the porch, and she hadn't even invited him inside. "Oh, come in. Where are my manners?"

"I've got a better idea. You come outside. Let's go for a walk."

"Now?"

"You know a better time? Premosquito, pre-sunset, post-thunderstorm."

They'd had one of their frequent storms earlier in the day, and while it had raised the humidity, it had also lowered the temperature. Their world smelled fresh and new, and even here, a breeze whispered lightly against her bare skin.

"By the time we get back, Lizzie will be at

the movies," she added.

"That did cross my mind. I'll have you all to myself."

That sent a shiver racing through her. "Walking as foreplay," she said. "Unique, but it works for me."

He looked surprised. "Is that why you think I'm here?"

"One of the possibilities." She lifted her chin. "Of course, it doesn't have to factor in. We could play checkers. I'm pretty good, even if Lizzie's better."

"You strike me as a woman who's good at many things. My hope is to see how many."

Shivers again. Delicious and rare in her life. She savored them while she could.

"Come on." He held out his hand and glanced down at her feet. "I'm going to show you my favorite fishing spots, and you've got the shoes for it."

She was still wearing sneakers with socks, after her trip to buy food for an easy supper. "Aren't you afraid I'll blab?" she asked, taking his hand.

"You know, Dana, I've never been less afraid about anything. I've never met anybody less inclined to share information."

How could she refute that? Although she was disappointed the subject had come up. "I've never been a big fan of chatter for chatter's sake."

"Me, either. And like you, I don't trust

everybody." He stopped and waited until she looked up at him. "But I hope you know by now, you can trust *me*."

She trusted nobody, but she smiled anyway. "I guess if you don't see all your favorite fishing holes in the local paper next week, you'll realize you can trust me, too?"

"You mean I have to worry those shiners I'm so good at catching are going to end up in somebody else's bait bucket?"

"The next time you catch something worthwhile, bring it over and we'll have it for dinner. You clean, I'll cook."

Still hand in hand, they walked toward the point. Pete really *was* a man who didn't chatter for the sake of it. He repeated his question about Lizzie, and Dana told him she was now vigilant about taking her inhaler along when she left the house.

They walked in comfortable silence. She was glad he had dropped the "trust me" and "secrecy" topics. She imagined he *was* frustrated at how little she told him. She was always torn between making up an elaborate past she could expound on at length or keeping her answers to a bare minimum. Both were suspicious. The elaborate past could easily be unveiled as a lie, and refusing to talk was a sign she was hiding something. In the end, not talking was simply easier than trying to remember all the facts of a manufactured life.

"First spot," Pete said, pulling her to the right, not far beyond her house. "Have you been here?"

Years ago, "here" had been a playground for the children who visited Happiness Haven. A rickety swing set had resided just beyond where they stood now, along with a seesaw that had launched more than one child toward a concussion. The real draw had been a pirate ship the owner, who was the husband of Dana's mother's favorite cousin, had built from a beached dinghy, pilings and leftover timber. She imagined that now such a contraption would be the target of endless lawsuits, but she missed it. She had spent many wonderful hours walking the plank.

"Lizzie's been all over the place," she said. "I think maybe we've walked through here to the water. It's one of the places where the mangroves haven't taken over again after the last hurricane destroyed so many."

"I'm convinced this is a prize place to fish, only I haven't caught anything except somebody else's fishing pole. I think the fish are gearing up for one mad rush in my direction."

"What is it about fishing that attracts you? Apparently not the idea of man defeating nature."

They had almost reached the water before he spoke. "Being quiet in a quiet place. We're fast using them up, you know, the quiet

468

places. They're harder to find. Most people talk just to hear their own voices. I don't mind that, but I need the break, too."

He tugged her toward the shore. "This is where I like to stand. Of course, I can only fish when the tide's high enough. Evening's best. Just before dark."

"Pete, how would you know it's best if you haven't caught anything?"

"Sometimes I don't even bring my rod."

She was touched that he'd revealed so much. "You just come here and . . . what?"

"I stand here and watch night fall."

"The sunset's better on the other side of the key."

"It's not sunset. I like that, too, but here, you can feel the world growing still. Then, if you listen, the night sounds begin. A little at a time."

She listened to the waves gently lapping against the shoreline and the calls of water-birds.

He pulled her close and kissed her. "I knew this place was missing something. Now I know what."

His lips were warm and salty. He perched a hand on each hip, his fingers settling at her waist. She smoothed her palms up his T-shirt. They took their time exploring, tongue teasing tongue, her breasts flattening against his chest.

"You said spots," she said at last. "Fishing

spots. Are there more?"

"One more. Do you really want to see it?"

"Is it sufficiently different that I'll get my money's worth?"

"Come on."

They followed the sandy path back to the road and ambled in the direction of the point again. The air was growing even cooler as evening fell. She couldn't remember just strolling this way with a man. Her husband had possessed a driving, restless energy that propelled him at warp speed through life. He'd been happy on crowded sidewalks, at parties where he could circle the room and talk to every stranger, in stadiums surrounded by thousands of people he would never meet. But strolling? No, that had been beyond him. He had needed a destination and a fast car to get there.

Only when Pete began to veer into the brush did she realize where he was going. For a moment she held back.

He stopped. "You want to go home? Maybe we've done enough for one day?"

She had easy excuses. Heat. Fatigue. The desire to get him into her bed, which was the only excuse that was real. She almost used one of them, any one would do, but something stopped her. She wondered what it would be like to walk this way with Pete. There were so many memories. She wondered if walking down to the water with him would send some of them scurrying back into dark corners, a better place to reside.

"Your call," he said. "I don't want to wear you out."

She liked the way he said that. Just a hint of promise. She wondered if he would be restrained in bed. Somehow she doubted it.

"I've been here." She wasn't sure how that slipped out. Worse, she wasn't sorry it did.

"Exploring?"

"Yes. But you can show me where you like to stand and tell me about all the fish you've caught."

"How did you find it? I think there used to be a genuine path back this way, but when I found it, there wasn't anything but some broken branches and trampled weeds."

There was so much she could say, and nothing she could really tell him. Except one thing. She wouldn't tell him how she knew this story, of course. But the little lie that would preface it was nothing. Sharing the story? That seemed right.

"When I worked at The Dancing Shrimp, an old man told me about this place, and the story that goes with it," she said. "Do you want to hear it?"

"I'm all ears."

"He told me how to find it. He was too old to come and show me himself, but his directions were good."

"Sounds lucky for you."

They walked single file, and she let Pete take the lead. Clearly he, and maybe others, had walked this way since the night she had come bearing ashes. The brush had been trimmed back, and the path was smoother. She followed him, thinking of other times.

After a few minutes they came to the clearing. It, too, seemed larger now, although probably only a few branches had been removed.

"It's some view of Palmetto Grove, isn't it?" she asked.

"That's probably why I come. I do catch fish, but not many. It's like being in another world. Green everywhere you look, and the sand extends out at low tide, so I can wade into the bay."

"I hope you watch for alligators. They aren't as rare as some people think."

"I haven't seen any here, but I always watch out."

She had seen one. A small one sunning itself right beside the water. She and the other children had run screaming back to Happiness Haven, their day a complete success. Of course, because of that, she'd warned Lizzie so many times about the possibility that Lizzie knew exactly how careful to be.

"So there's a story?" Pete asked.

"I don't know if it's made up or if it's really true."

"Does it matter?"

"Years ago all the locals called this place Fortunate Harbor." She gestured to include a much wider area. "It wasn't always the way we're seeing it. Hurricanes and changing tides and probably even climate change have affected the shorelines. Lots of what used to be beach is now underwater. I'm told," she added. "People who used to come to this area on vacation probably can't find a lot of their old haunts because they've changed, or they just don't exist anymore."

"That's true in a lot of places." Pete had been looking at the water, but now he looked at her. "Why did they call it Fortunate Harbor?"

"It's a love story." She smiled. "Sure you want to hear it? You don't strike me as a man who goes for that sort of thing."

"Try me."

"Well, once there was a lot more land out that way, toward the point." She gestured. "Palmetto Grove Key wasn't shaped the way it is now. Even just twenty years ago there was quite a bit more. But it dipped in right here, so this was more or less a protected cove, sheltered by land on three sides, because it broadened out again on the other."

"That's not hard to imagine. It's still something of an inlet, and the land fans out on both sides, at least a little. You can see it from the water."

"You've been out this way in a boat?"

"A couple of times."

"Then imagine being on a ship trying to sail to the harbor in Palmetto Grove. There used to be a real one there, you know, before it silted up and was no longer commercially viable."

"What kind of ship?"

"That I don't know. Maybe only a fishing boat, but a terrible gale whipped up while they were far out in the gulf, so they tried to make for land. First they lost their sails, then they lost their main mast, and finally, the ship began to break up out there somewhere." She pointed. "Much too far from Palmetto Grove Harbor to make it. Some of the ship's crew jumped overboard and tried to swim to shore in the high winds, which wasn't easy, because the waves were fierce and the key was wild, with no bridge to the mainland, and few people lived out this way to rescue them."

"I can imagine this."

"There was a woman on board, maybe the captain's daughter, I'm not sure. The captain was swept overboard trying to save the mast, but the first mate took over and tried to see his daughter to safety. He was young and handsome, and I think she'd had her eye on him."

"Are you making this part up?"

"Are you going to let me finish?"

He put his arm around her. "Go on, then."

"By the time they got around the end of

the point and into the bay, most of the crew had abandoned ship, and they were listing badly, swept wherever the waves wanted the ship to go, and taking on water quickly. The first mate tried to get the woman to swim with him, but she had never learned, and he knew she would drown immediately. The lifeboat was useless. One of the masts had fallen on it. And he knew he couldn't tow her all the way. They would both drown.

The first mate wasn't willing to leave her to die alone. So he told her he would stay with her, no matter what. And they clung together expecting to die. Except that before the ship could break up entirely, the waves swept what remained of it here, into this very cove, which was protected a little. And by the time what was left began to sink, they were close enough to shore that, by clinging to some of the wreckage, they were able to ride out the worst of the waves until he could help her to land."

"And so this was actually a very fortunate harbor for two young people who might have died," Pete finished.

"Fortunate in many ways, the old man told me. Because the couple went on to marry, then settle here on the key and raise their family. And every year, on the date of the shipwreck, they came to this cove and spread flowers in the water. In fact he told me, when he was a boy, their descendants still came and continued the tradition. But I guess

475

there's no one left to do it anymore."

"I never guessed you would be such a romantic."

"Did you like my story?"

"I liked it a lot. Two people clinging together in the face of disaster. Then fortune gives them a chance at a new life."

"It's as bad as a fairy tale, I guess. Life's not like that."

"Don't give up on it, Dana."

She turned, her breasts pressing against the side of his chest, her hip and thigh resting between his legs. "Do you believe we can be a harbor for each other in times of storm? People, I mean? All people, if we care enough?"

He pushed her hair back from her cheek, as if he wanted to make sure she could see his face. "I'd like to be your harbor. At least while I can."

"I would be fortunate to have you."

He pulled her into his arms, but he didn't kiss her. He just held her close, her head resting against his shoulder, her body full against his. She could feel the inevitable changes in him and feel her own body responding. The passion would come later. She could feel it tightly leashed inside him. But first came the healing.

She didn't want to guess how Peter Knight knew she needed healing. Nor did she want to think about how, in one of the sacred and secret places of her childhood, and now the grave of a man she had loved, she could feel the ragged pieces of her life slowly coming together in his arms.

She just leaned against him and let time stand still.

CHAPTER
TWENTY-THREE

The number of missing children sites was staggering. Children who had been snatched from one parent by the other, even taken illegally to foreign countries, made up the bulk of the cases. Stranger abductions, though far more newsworthy, accounted for only a fraction.

Tracy had no idea what she was looking for. She was fairly certain that if Dana and Lizzie were running from Lizzie's father, Dana had taken the girl some time ago. Lizzie seemed too well-adjusted to have recently gone through something that traumatic. She also seemed not to know her father's identity.

Which certainly matched the information on her birth certificate.

If Dana hadn't acknowledged Lizzie's father, the chances that he had legal custody and wanted her back seemed small. Perhaps, since that time, he'd used DNA testing or other evidence to establish his claim. It was even possible Lizzie's father wanted to find her so he *could* prove parentage. So many things were possible, and the more she delved into the matter, the less she was sure which direction to go.

Lizzie was ten, nearly eleven. What would she remember? She herself was three times Lizzie's age, which meant she'd had a lot more time to forget, but looking back, she thought she could remember details from her first year of preschool.

If Lizzie's memory was similar, then it seemed probable she and her mother had run away by the time Lizzie was three, not much later, or Lizzie would remember troubling things about her past. And as far as Tracy could tell, Lizzie wasn't troubled by anything except the frequency of their moves.

Although she knew her reasoning probably had Swiss-cheese-style holes, she decided to concentrate on Lizzie's earliest years. She plugged each one into a search with keywords like missing child, kidnapping, California girl missing. On the theory that the birth certificate could be a fake, she looked at cases nationwide and couldn't believe how many turned up. Luckily — for her, not the children's parents — a huge proportion had been runaways and could be discounted immediately.

She had planned to go through the cases year by year, one by one, but midnight — along with three rice crackers, a small handful of almonds, an orange and two cups of hot tea — came and went before she finished the first year. She stood and stretched, wondering, as she had since early in the evening, where CJ was. While she'd been out for a quick jog, he had left a message telling her not to expect him until late. But now it was more than late, and he still wasn't home.

"Make that *my* home," she corrected out loud.

She was reminded of all the times CJ had disappeared and never mentioned his reason or whereabouts when he returned. She showered and got ready for bed, but by one o'clock, when she finally turned out her light, CJ still wasn't cozied up on the sofa. She hoped that wherever he was, the bed was even harder and narrower.

By noon on Sunday she was at the end of her search. She had three leads. One, a two-year-old girl in Modesto, California, had disappeared with her mother just as the court was about to make a custody ruling. Details were sketchy, but there was one photo of a blond cherub with a flat baby nose and plump cheeks. She didn't really look like Lizzie, but Tracy remembered her own baby pictures and the progression of school photos that had followed. No one would have been able to match her photo at two with the one of her at eleven.

The only photo of the runaway mother was

blurry and unrevealing. Her face seemed rounder than Dana's, but the poor quality of the photograph made that a judgment call. And perhaps, if this was Dana, she had lost weight in the intervening years, which could account for the differences.

The second lead was even more of a long shot. Infant twins, a boy and a girl, had disappeared from a farmhouse in central Oregon where they'd lived with foster parents. Their mother, who had been given permission to visit for the afternoon, had vanished with them. There were snapshots of the babies, and a few years later some age-progressed photos that showed a dark-haired boy with a crooked smile and a little girl with curly blond hair. But Tracy hadn't been able to find anything recent.

Of course, if the girl was Lizzie, where was the boy? And except for the hair — which was a computer-generated guess — the girl really didn't resemble the preteen Tracy knew. The photograph of the mother was no help. Taken at a distance, it showed a woman holding two babies. She could have been almost anybody, even Tracy herself.

The third lead was the most interesting, and Tracy's excitement mounted as she read. Ten years ago authorities in Missouri had investigated the kidnapping of a toddler by her maternal aunt. According to the authorities, the child's mother had been at home

481

with the baby on the night she'd tripped and taken a fatal tumble down the steep basement stairs. The aunt insisted the police investigate the sister's husband for murder, but the death was ruled an accident.

Shortly afterward, the child disappeared from the home she shared with her newly widowed father, and Auntie disappeared from her job and life in St. Louis. The photo of the aunt set this possibility apart from the others. The woman had a long face, like Dana, and hair that was neither curly nor straight, blond nor brown. In the photo she had her arm around her sister, the baby's mother, and *her* hair was lighter and curlier. Something like Lizzie's might be when she was a young woman.

Okay, nothing to jump around the house about, but a lead of sorts. Now she just had to figure out how to get more information than the Internet was providing.

She got up and stretched, tired from too many hours of computing. She wondered if somebody had abducted her ex, who hadn't bothered to call this morning, either. She took her emotional temperature and realized she didn't know how she would feel if CJ disappeared from her life again. Right now she was too annoyed to gauge.

She was making lunch when he finally walked in. She met him in the living room, half a tomato sandwich in her hands and eyes narrowed. "Well, this is a new definition of *late*. Or did you say late morning *tomorrow* and I missed it?"

"TK, I can explain. Really." He smiled disarmingly, a smile she remembered oh-so-well. "And you'll probably find it funny."

She glared at him. "I'm laughing on the inside."

"I was on Nanette's yacht. Sort of an impromptu party. We went for a sail. I, well, I haven't been sleeping soundly, so I was tired. I had a couple of drinks and started feeling woozy. I asked her if I could lie down, and went down to the guest cabin and fell sound asleep. When we docked she tried to wake me, but I guess I was really out of it. So she left me there for the night."

She remembered the occasional morning when she hadn't been able to wake him, no matter how hard she tried. Most of the time CJ had boundless energy, but it sometimes led to exhaustion.

"And this morning?" she asked.

"I remember how much you like to sleep on weekends. I didn't want to wake you."

"Look around. I used to do a lot of things I don't do anymore. I got up with the sun this morning."

He turned up his hands as if to say, "How was I to know?"

"Just don't assume *anything* is the way it used to be," she said.

483

"So you've pointed out more times than I can count."

"If you're going to stay here, do me the courtesy of letting me know you've decided to sleep around."

"Got it."

"And why aren't you living somewhere else, anyway? I bet Maribel Sessions would melt into a warm puddle of goo if you asked to crash with her."

"As a matter of fact, *she* asked *me*."

Despite a healthy survival instinct, a jolt of jealousy shot through her. Annoyance followed quickly. Why did she care?

"So why aren't you there?"

"I'm beyond needing women who hang on every word I say like it was a Mikimoto pearl."

"I'm so sure . . ." she said sarcastically.

He sent her the same smile he'd started with. "Which is why I like sleeping on your sofa."

"Where apparently you are, in addition to getting little attention, getting little sleep."

"I think I've solved that."

She sent him a thumbs-down signal. "You are *not* going to share my bed."

"No, I'm going to be Nanette's guest for a while."

This surprised her. She knew Henrietta liked CJ. But to invite him to live on board her yacht? She felt instantly protective of the older woman.

484

"CJ, what are you doing?"

"Finding a more comfortable place to close my eyes."

"Henrietta is the patroness of the rec center, where I happen to work. I *so* don't want you screwing up my job."

"How could my sleeping in her guest cabin interfere with your job? I thought you'd be happy to have me out of here."

"Isn't it time to go back to California and see what's going on with your case?"

"I have a cell phone. When they need me, I can fly out the same day. And who knows, one day maybe the Feds will come to escort me."

She studied him. "There's something here I'm just not seeing."

"Who taught you to be so cynical?"

Her gaze didn't flicker.

He held up his hands again. "Okay, okay. But if you don't trust me, look up all the legal gobbledygook on one of those legal databases, and you can read everything about the case you ever needed to know."

"Fix yourself a sandwich if you like." She gestured to the kitchen.

"May I still come by and see you?"

She considered. He looked like a little boy trying to get back into Mommy's good graces after tracking in mud. "Is there anything I can do to stop you?"

"Do you want to?"

That, of course, was the question she couldn't seem to answer. In fact, there was another one, too. Why was she even the tiniest bit sorry he was trading her sofa for a berth on Henrietta's yacht? These were questions too complex for simple answers. Unfortunately, she couldn't deny she was going to miss having him here, miss having him bring her dinner and entertain her when she was down.

"I want to be something more to you than a boarder and a burden," he said, his voice low, almost a caress.

"What's the next step up? Pain in the ass?"

"You know what I mean. I want you to trust me. I want you to know you can count on me. I want you to smile when you see me coming."

She knew he wanted more — and hated that she knew it. She'd lived with him too long not to understand his bottom line. CJ wanted back into her life and bed. He was inching his way forward, and she was letting him.

It was a darned good thing he was clearing out.

"I'm leaving in a little while," she said. "A good time for you to pack."

"I don't have much."

Why did she think *that* wouldn't last long? Despite traces of nostalgia, she couldn't shake the feeling CJ was after something besides her. Or maybe she was just part of a larger scheme. And therein, of course, lay all their problems. She wondered what it would take to make her really trust him.

"A miracle," she said out loud.

He cocked his head. "Excuse me?"

She realized she'd answered her own question. "Miracle Whip," she improvised. "Fat free. It was on sale this week. And tomato and bread. All on the counter. Help yourself."

She was pulling into Marsh's driveway before she let herself think about her destination. In her heart, she'd been heading toward this end of the key all weekend. All she'd needed was an excuse. Strangely enough, CJ had given it to her when he mentioned legal databases. Now she just had to find the courage to use it, even though Marsh might well reject her.

The tin roof of the Cracker house shimmered in the afternoon sun, and she could hear the whir of an air conditioner from the back. Marsh only used air-conditioning in the worst weather, and today qualified. As she turned off the engine and slid out of her seat, her blouse stuck to her back. Her hair felt as flat and lifeless as a day-old soft drink.

At moments like this she missed California. Had she still been married to an unindicted CJ, she would have spent the morning at the country club, on the golf course or tennis court. About now she would be lunching with a friend, eating a beautifully presented salad and sipping sparkling water with a twist of lime. They would be gossiping about, well, *somebody*, and the service staff would be standing by, in case they needed a crumb brushed off the table or a napkin straightened.

And she would be bored. Not that her life had needed to be boring. There'd been plenty of women in her circle who made each day interesting and relevant. She just hadn't been one of them. Apparently she had needed to fall flat on her face before she picked herself up and took a good look at the world around her. Even she could see that was pathetic.

She had parked next to Marsh's car, and thankfully, the rental Sylvia drove was gone. She had hoped to catch Marsh or Bay outside, but the yard and porches were empty. For a moment she almost used that as an excuse to leave. Then she steeled herself. Now she was a woman who made things happen. She could do this. If Marsh didn't want to help her, see her, have anything to do with her, that would be his loss.

That sentiment got her to the door. She was trying to dig up another that would move her hand to the doorbell when the door opened and Marsh appeared on the threshold.

"Last person I expected to see," he said.

"Obviously you're the first I expected, since

I'm standing on your doorstep."

"It's cooler inside."

"A bonfire is cooler."

She was careful not to touch him as she moved past him into the house, although some part of her thought throwing herself into his arms might be just the thing.

"Just in the neighborhood?" he asked.

She stalled. "Where's Bay?"

"Spending the day with Adam."

Last summer Bay and Adam had been archenemies, but now they were inseparable. She wasn't surprised. Childhood was like that. Adulthood? Unfortunately, a different story.

"I'm guessing you know Sylvia's not here," he added.

"Bay told me she was gone for the weekend."

"Else why would you appear?"

"You have to admit, she's more fun to be with when she's not around."

He smiled. "Since you had to walk from the car to my door, you'll need to rehydrate. What would you like?" He went through a long list. She waited, aware that her palms were sweaty and her hands were not as steady as she might have liked.

"Water," she said, when he'd finished.

"With ice? Without ice? With lime? Without? Sparkling. Plain. Imported or domestic. From the refrigerator or the tap?"

"If I ever start missing you again, I'll remember this moment."

"That sounds promising. Have you missed me?"

"From the tap. With ice. No fruit."

He started toward the kitchen, and she followed. The house looked exactly the same. She wasn't sure why that seemed significant, but it did. Yes, a woman's flip-flops were parked near the door, but out of the way, as if they weren't supposed to be there. There were no other signs Sylvia was in residence.

And that was when she realized why it was important.

Nothing in the house had changed. Sylvia wasn't adding her own little touches. No new pillows on the sofa, no pictures on the wall. Even the straw place mats were the same ones Tracy remembered from any number of fabulous meals.

Sylvia was staying here, but this was not her home, or at least not yet.

She almost smiled. By then, though, Marsh was handing her a glass.

"So?" he asked, after she'd taken a long drink.

"I have a problem, and you're the only person I could think of who might be able to help me."

"That's me. Helpful R Us."

"It'll take a while to explain."

"I'm not charging by the hour today." He

490

gestured to the next room, where a comfortable couch flanked a fireplace. She remembered doing some extraordinarily delightful things on that couch. If Bay hadn't been sleeping upstairs at the time, their life might be on an entirely different track right now. Scruples didn't always pay off.

She settled on the sofa with her water. He settled beside her, one arm stretched along the back, his hand not quite in reach of her shoulder, as if he had carefully gauged.

Marsh was wearing khaki shorts, and of course he was barefoot. His shirt had more pockets than a billiard table, and the fabric was a shade of cocoa that enhanced the brown of his eyes. He had trimmed his hair since she'd last seen it, but it was still just long enough to pull back in a ponytail.

"I like the way you're looking at me," he said.

"I'm just checking to see what, if anything, has changed."

"Conclusion?"

"Not on the outside."

His smile didn't quite make it to his eyes. "You look healthy and happy."

And fat. She was wearing shorts with an elastic waistband, the only shorts from her California wardrobe that still fit. The blouse was stylishly pleated at the front, a great look for a pregnant woman, not so much for anyone else. Healthy and happy were definitely not what she was after.

She nodded, simply to acknowledge his words. "Let me tell you a story."

"I'm all ears."

She was careful not to name names or explain her association with the "woman in question," but Tracy told him as much about Dana and the neighbors' concerns as she could without pointing fingers. Then she explained what she had discovered on the Internet.

"So I found these three cases. They're all long shots, but I won't know how long until I get more information. And I've looked up the names on Google, you wouldn't believe how many times. I need a database system with more oomph."

"Why doesn't Wanda just go to her husband and ask him to check?"

"Wanda doesn't want Ken involved."

"More like Wanda doesn't want Ken to know what she's doing."

She smiled a little, because Marsh knew Wanda too well. "That, too."

"Because if he did, he might have to do something, then Wanda would lose her assistant."

She wasn't surprised Marsh had guessed Dana's identity. He was, of course, a lawyer, and talented at putting facts together. "Marsh, I need information and no action here. If you look into this, can you promise you won't tell anybody if you dig up something suspicious?"

"No."

She put her water down and scooted forward to stand. But Marsh put his hand on her shoulder to hold her back.

"I'm assuming I won't find anything so suspicious I'll have to do anything," he said. "Because I'm only going to delve into the first layer. The rest of you can take it further, if there's any need to."

"So, in other words, if you see Dana staring back at you from a Wanted poster, you have to act. If you just get us some information that doesn't necessarily lead anywhere, you're okay with that?"

"It's up to you, Tracy. I'll be glad to run the information through LexisNexis, but you'll have to accept the consequences."

She took out the sheets of notes she'd made and handed them to him. "Like I said, all long shots. We have no idea what we're looking for, or even if there's anything *to* look for."

He didn't even glance at the notes as he set them on the table. He still hadn't removed his hand from her shoulder.

"Was I your only solution? Or do you have any other reason for coming today?"

"You'd really like me to get down on my knees and beg for forgiveness, wouldn't you?"

"All kind of lascivious thoughts come to

mind with that image."

They smiled at the same time. "Not going to happen," she said.

"A man can hope."

"I've missed you." That much she could honestly say. "I haven't missed the fights."

"I did come up with a solution."

"Did you?"

"We should introduce Sylvia to CJ and see where it goes."

"With all the problems waiting in California, they'd never run out of things to talk about."

"He could be her new full-time job. Match made in heaven."

Their gazes were locked, and neither seemed inclined to look away. "He's been sleeping on my couch," she said, "but he's moving out today."

"Why don't I come take his place? I'll leave Sylvia here with our son. That should dislodge her even faster than a job at a top tier law firm."

"You could start out on the couch. . . ."

They were leaning toward each other, and Tracy's heart was pounding in her ears.

Outside, a car door slammed. Tracy ignored it, but Marsh pulled back and got up.

"Were you expecting somebody?" she asked, thinking perhaps he was worried Bay had been returned early for some infraction. But Marsh didn't answer. He went to the window and looked out, then he turned, and his expression said it all.

"Sylvia." It was not a question.

"Isn't there some expression about the bad penny turning up and turning up and turning up —"

"She's home early."

She heard the "home," and, worse, she saw that the promise of a moment that might have led to the return of something wonderful was gone.

"I should go," she said.

The front door slammed so quickly Tracy knew Sylvia must have identified her car and run full tilt up the stairs. "Marsh, are you home?" she called. "I couldn't stay away. I missed you and Bay too much."

Sylvia had not only seen Tracy's car, she had sensed danger and was planning an all-out assault.

Tracy got to her feet. This was Marsh's game now. He could tell Sylvia that he and Tracy were on their way out, and the house was all hers. Then he could take Tracy's arm and guide her to his pickup. So what if Tracy's tires were in shreds when she returned and the paint job keyed? She could cope.

But before Marsh could do a thing, Sylvia entered the room, followed by Bay. "Look what I found," she said. "Bay called *me* on my cell to see if it was all right if Adam spent the night. Isn't that sweet? He knew I'd be driving home, and I'd probably be tired tonight, so he checked first to be sure. Of course I said yes. So here they are. I picked them up myself."

As if for emphasis, Adam appeared, carrying a backpack.

Sylvia was chalking up points. She might be tired, but she was going to prove she was too good a mother not to let Bay have a friend over. In fact, she had even gotten the boys herself. What a gal. Of course now Marsh couldn't leave with Tracy, not with Sylvia in charge. Not with two boys to be responsible for. Not with her lack of parenting skills.

Sylvia's gaze flicked over Tracy. "Nice to see you again," she said. "It's been a while. Would you like to stay for supper? The boys and I are going to make spaghetti."

Earthworms with arsenic sauce. Tracy knew better. "I was just leaving." She smiled at Bay and Adam; then the smile, which had been perfunctory, broadened. "Hey, guys, something tells me it's video game night. Guitar Hero?"

Bay's eyes flicked to his mother for permission. What could Sylvia say but yes? She gave a short nod.

Tracy laughed affectionately. "I bet you'll be up half the night. You might need another friend or two to share the fun."

"Jeremy," Adam said, poking Bay in the

496

side. "And Frankie. I bet they could come, too."

"I'm on my way," Tracy said. "I'll just let myself out. Marsh? Sylvia?" She smiled her brightest smile. "Have an awesome evening."

She hedged one quick glance at Marsh. His expression was veiled. She wondered if he was imagining the night to come or wishing his family hadn't come "home" when they did. After all, for a moment there, he'd almost had the best of all possible worlds. Tracy on his couch, Sylvia in his guest room.

She closed the front door quietly and saw that Sylvia had nearly penned in her car, but Tracy hadn't been raised in L.A. for nothing. She backed out without scratching the paint. She couldn't say the same about her heart. But she was fast getting used to that.

CHAPTER
TWENTY-FOUR

Tracy liked the Naughty Nibblers. Today she was cheering on her comrades while simultaneously trying to invent an emergency that would keep her from stepping on the scale. Kitty had scheduled the weigh-ins for Mondays, right before lunch. Last week Tracy had dropped a pound, which was not, in the scheme of things, anything to crow about.

She knew why she hadn't lost more. After struggling with calories the entire week, she had left the encounter with Marsh and Sylvia and taken a detour straight past the drive-through window at The Captain's Catch for their ultimate deep-fried seafood basket, which contained a sampling of every creature to be found in the gulf — and some from the swamp, as well.

She had eaten every single bite.

Okay, so last week hadn't been stellar, but she'd only had that one — albeit gargantuan — lapse. This week she had lapsed consistently. Never with quite the same flair, but she wasn't sure long runs on the beach at dawn were going to make up for slices of Wanda's raspberry cream pie, or Janya's eggplant, with its thick buttery tomato sauce and homemade chapatis to sop up every drop.

"Lillian, you've lost four pounds altogether. Congratulations." Kitty's green eyes were shining. Nothing made Kitty as happy as somebody else losing weight.

Everybody clapped, and Lillian, a blond woman in her late sixties who needed to lose about twenty-five more, beamed.

Sid had lost five altogether. Like Lillian, Bart had lost four. Betty had only lost three. Yolanda, in her forties and formerly a heavy smoker, had lost only two, because she was also trying to cut down on cigarettes.

"Okay, Tracy," Kitty said, with a huge smile.

Tracy didn't like that smile, and right now she didn't like Kitty. Was the woman a sadist? Didn't she know how humiliating this was? Then she remembered that Losing to Win had been Gladys's idea, spurred on by Henrietta. Tracy was never going to forgive any of them — or Mr. Moustache, either, who had gotten her into this fix because of a stupid bird.

"It's been a tough week," she prefaced.

"The hardest time to lose weight," Kitty said agreeably. "But it's also a good time to learn what our triggers are and how we relieve stress. I'm sure it's taught you something, right?"

"Right. How much I love to eat."

The women giggled. Mr. Moustache, who had come to lend support, along with half a dozen other shuffleboarders, gave a snort that could have meant almost anything.

Tracy didn't have a prayer of getting out of this. Gladys was on the sidelines watching, along with Woody and several other staff members. She stepped up to the scale, refusing to look down.

"Three pounds altogether," Kitty said. "Good for you, Tracy. Now think how well you'll do when you don't have a tough week."

Tracy looked down, and indeed, she had lost three pounds in the two weeks of the contest. She put on a smile and stepped down. Everybody was applauding.

Lillian took Tracy's hand. "It's easiest to lose weight when you have as much to lose as I do. But you're doing great."

Now Tracy's smile was more genuine. "Don't tell Kitty, but I think I sweat off every pound running in this heat. It's all water."

"Whatever you're doing, keep it up. I want that morning at the spa."

After all the weigh-ins were finished and the staff team — which had taken the name Staff Affection — had been declared the week's winner with a total loss of twenty-six pounds, Gladys grabbed Tracy.

"I almost forgot. Marsh Egan left something

for you at the front desk when he dropped off Bay."

Tracy was surprised at the things Marsh's name could still do to her body, the subtle ripples of pleasure in parts she'd almost forgotten she had.

"Did he?" She sounded normal. That was encouraging.

"He was in a hurry, or I'm sure he'd have brought it down to the rec room."

Maybe she *hadn't* sounded normal. Gladys looked sympathetic.

Since Gladys obviously knew something, Tracy realized she had to address the subject. "From the day Sylvia arrived, our relationship hasn't exactly been progressing."

"Men can be such idiots, can't they?"

"You think?"

"He overcompensates with Bay. He always has." She looked as if she was debating before she spoke again. "This isn't my business."

"Make it yours. I don't mind."

She pulled Tracy a little farther into the hallway and away from exiting traffic. "Sylvia was perfectly clear about not wanting a baby. Marsh convinced her to see the pregnancy through."

Tracy wondered why Marsh had never mentioned this.

When Tracy didn't reply Gladys went on. "I think — I *know* Marsh feels responsible for Sylvia's lack of interest in the boy. He feels like he pushed her into having Bay, and though I know he wouldn't, *couldn't,* change anything if he could do it again, he's still suffered a lot of guilt. I believe . . ." She got closer. "Do you want to hear my opinion?"

Tracy gave a short nod.

"I believe he thinks the only way he's going to move past his guilt is to make Sylvia see she can be a good mother if she tries."

Tracy's head was swimming. So this decision to let Sylvia have the run of the house wasn't just about helping Bay have a relationship with his mom. At least some of it was about Marsh himself, and the responsibility he felt for placing the burden of a child on a woman who didn't want one.

Only didn't it take two, as her mother had always said, to tango? Wasn't Sylvia *there* when Bay was conceived? How could the boy's existence be Marsh's fault entirely? Tracy knew Marsh, and she was afraid she knew Sylvia. Marsh would never have married a woman who was adamantly opposed to having children. Sylvia had either changed her mind after marriage or lied before it.

She was betting on the latter.

"I just thought you might want to know," Gladys said.

"I wish it helped, but I still don't hear Sylvia packing her suitcase."

"She will, just as soon as something better comes along." Gladys was not a judgmental

502

woman, but her opinion of Sylvia was clear.

They were no longer alone, and by the time Tracy had chatted with a few more Losers, Gladys had left and returned with a large manila envelope. She handed it to Tracy.

"Patience," Gladys said, "is a virtue."

"Patience is not in my repertoire."

"Then it's a good thing to acquire, dear." Gladys left the way she'd come, and Tracy impatiently headed downstairs.

The rec room was more than the rec program's office. At times, like now, it was a rec staff gathering place, because Tracy welcomed company. Two staffers who weren't on duty had brought lunches. Two more had dropped by to finish paperwork. Tracy had to wait until the place cleared out before she could open and examine the information Marsh had sent along. That, of course, was only after she'd accepted half a pastrami sandwich, three cookies and a slice of chocolate cake.

She took care of a few things that couldn't wait, then she got up and closed the door. Finally she opened the envelope.

Inside were about a dozen photocopied pages, and a booklet entitled *Identity Theft: What You Must Know to Stay Safe.* She flipped through, looking for a note in Marsh's bold handwriting, but there was nothing. Marsh had done the favor she had asked for, but not one thing more. No apology, no expression of affection, no reason for Tracy to think he wanted her to exercise the patience Gladys had touted in the hallway.

Disappointment erased any sympathy Gladys had generated. If Marsh was so emotionally involved with his ex-wife that he was *still* trying to reconcile her to the birth of their son, then Tracy was blessed to be rid of him.

"Whatever," she said out loud, and tried to believe it.

She forced herself to concentrate on what she *did* have: possible answers to the mystery of Dana Turner. Since she had no intention of stealing anybody's identity, she slipped the booklet back in the envelope. Then she sat down, told herself she had thrown Marsh on the back burner of her life and began to read.

Thursday nights the neighbors usually got together for supper, and this Thursday was the chosen night to discuss what Tracy had discovered. It was perfect because Dana had sent regrets. Pete was taking the Turners and Olivia fishing for the afternoon, and Dana doubted they would be back in time for dinner.

This week was Tracy's turn to host, an obligation she usually fulfilled with deli food, and tonight was no exception. On the way home she stopped by the supermarket and bought half a dozen containers of salads, and she had displayed them on a lettuce-lined platter, next to a basket of rolls fresh from the freezer case via her oven. Wanda had volunteered to bring pie, and Tracy had not tried to dissuade her.

Wanda showed up first, with what amounted to two pies, although both pans were filled with assorted leftovers from the day's selection. Tracy carefully stored them in the refrigerator, although she wanted to dive right in.

"You ever get serious about that diet, I'm in trouble," Wanda said.

"Like you don't have the entire police force hoping you have a pie or two left every night." Tracy poured iced tea into a pitcher and handed it to Wanda to place on the table. "And I claim that slice of orange blossom special."

"So what's so all-fired important you made this a command performance?" Wanda demanded.

Tracy had hoped to get her friends together for this discussion earlier, but summer was taking its toll on people's schedules. And meeting without Dana or Lizzie was tricky, particularly since she didn't want Olivia to overhear the conversation, either.

"I want to wait until Janya and Alice are here," she told Wanda. "So I don't have to go through it more than once."

"There's that much, you can't repeat it?"

"It's complicated."

"Must be, if you're not willing to just spill it soon as you got the chance."

Janya arrived next, followed closely by Alice. Tracy finished putting the food and serving utensils on the table, then poured wine for everyone but Janya, who took a small glass of juice.

They elected to stay inside, rather than walk down the road to their favorite beach, as they sometimes did. The thermometer had leaped to ninety-four in the afternoon, and even though it was a little cooler now, a passing storm had bequeathed humidity as thick as fog. Tracy's air conditioner was rattling away, and even at that, barely keeping up.

They sat in the living room, but even the pale, fresh colors and the cool tile floor Tracy had installed herself didn't provide much of an oasis.

"How's business?" Janya asked Wanda.

"Good on days the Sunshine Bakery doesn't have a sale. It's like that woman knows when things are getting under way for us, and she does something to overtake me. A customer goes in and buys a cookie on sale and maybe a loaf of bread, he's not coming all the way to Wanda's for a pie, too. He just buys what she's got."

"You think she's outsourcing all her baked goods?" Tracy asked.

"They . . . have changed," Alice said. "I go in. I check to see. The bread was always good.

But the rest looks different and better."

"I think she's bringing them in," Wanda agreed, "but I don't know how she can afford to do it and still charge the same old prices. She's going to run out of money soon enough. Or I am."

Everybody protested, but Wanda shook her head. "There's no call for her to lose money on pies. Ought to be room for both of us in this town. She could leave the pies to me, and I could leave everything else to her. But she's not thinking like that."

"She can't afford to have your very good products next to her very bad ones," Janya said. "Why would I choose a cake that is not well made when I could choose a pie that is?"

Wanda smiled a little. "You said it, I didn't."

Janya and Alice told the others about their week, but neither one in great detail. Janya hadn't been her serene self for weeks now, but Tracy knew this was not the time to bring that up. They could only handle one crisis at a time.

"You know I have news," she said, when the conversation turned to her. She explained about the Internet research and how little she had turned up.

"So I went to Marsh and asked him to run some names at his office. They have an awesome database. Marsh showed it to me once. As a matter of fact, CJ was the one who reminded me about it."

Wanda's head snapped up, and her eyes narrowed. "CJ knows what you're doing? He knows you're suspicious of Dana?"

"No, he mentioned the database in regards to his case back in California. Point is, I realized that might be a good way to see if there was more than I could find. So I went to Marsh and asked for his help."

Janya leaned forward. "You and Marsh are back together?"

"No." Tracy gave a sharp shake of her head. "Let's not go into that, okay?"

Janya sat back and folded her hands.

Tracy tried to explain. "It's just I'll be completely sidetracked if I start talking about how that witch of an ex-wife is still living with him and doing everything she can to come —" She stopped and swallowed. "See?"

Janya nodded.

"Anyway, I know Marsh did the search, because he dropped some papers off at the rec center. And he found things. That's what I need to talk about."

Tracy pulled out copies of everything Marsh had given her. She'd made a packet for each woman, and she handed them around. But she didn't wait for everyone to read what they had, because that would take too long.

"You can read those later. The first thing you'll see? The people we know as Dana and

Lizzie Turner aren't." Everyone was looking at her now, the papers forgotten. "Lizzie, or Elizabeth, the real Elizabeth Turner, died almost ten years ago. You've got the obituary. She was born to a woman named Dana Turner. The real Dana was, is — I don't know that part for sure — a member of a doomsday religious sect that lives on a communal farm outside Fresno, California. They have some seriously different ideas, like they don't believe in marriage, or certain kinds of medical intervention, or being on the grid. They don't have social security numbers —"

"That's illegal, isn't it?" Alice asked.

"Apparently not, because they don't. There's some kind of religious exemption. Anyway, it doesn't matter. Because this Dana person gave birth to a daughter who was born with a heart defect and died a year later. There's no father on the birth certificate because women on the farm say that God is the father of all of us, and it's an affront to list anyone else. All this was in a newspaper article. The people at the farm refused surgery for the child at first, and the girl's pediatrician had to go to court to get permission. That's why it made the papers for a day or two. The child died anyway. It wasn't a big story, which is probably why it either wasn't on the Internet or I missed it. And it's ten years old."

"It's a sad story." Janya's expression

matched her words.

"It is, but that's not really why we're here. Because, for our purposes, it's just the background. The fact that the woman we know as Dana Turner stole those identities is *our* story."

Wanda, cop's wife that she was, had clearly grasped the important facts. "And they'd be good identities, too. A child with no social security number and a woman who refused one. All Dana had to do was get copies of the birth certificates, apply for a social security number for herself and maybe for Lizzie, and she'd look as legitimate as anybody in the world."

"Exactly," Tracy said. "Marsh even included a booklet on identity theft, I guess so we could see how easy it is. Apparently he forgot we're already pretty expert on the subject because of Herb."

"But why?" Alice's question was the obvious one, but she was the first to form it.

"That's where the rest of the papers come in. I did research before I gave Marsh some names to look up. I found three cases that might have something to do with Dana, all long shots. Turns out none of them are relevant. He found updates I hadn't been able to on the Internet. One woman had gone back home to finish her custody fight. Another was apprehended by the police and her children were returned to their father. The third fled to Indonesia with her sister's daughter, and she's never been extradited."

"So where did that leave you?"

"After Marsh found Dana's and Lizzie's names and figured out our Dana had stolen them, he must have gone back to see if he could find anything that would lead a woman to steal someone else's identities, some reason a woman who lived in that area and knew about the Turner situation might need one. At least, I imagine that's how his thinking went, since he just dropped off the papers and left me to guess."

Nobody spoke. They were all too smart.

"I don't have any way to prove that this case has anything to do with Dana or Lizzie," Tracy went on. "But everything fits."

"Well, what is it?" Wanda demanded.

"The whole thing took place in Stockton, California, not that far from Fresno, just about the time the real Elizabeth Turner died. Carol Kelly, a single mother of a baby girl, was being stalked by her ex-boyfriend, a guy named Ray Strickland, who was the father of her baby. He was an ex-con, an unsavory guy with a couple of brothers just like him at home, and plenty of money. Apparently she had both custody and a restraining order, but whenever she told the police this guy was peeking in the baby's window or standing on their doorstep, Strickland had a brother or friend alibi him. The cops believed her, but they couldn't do anything about it. Whenever they drove by, nobody was there. The guy was mean *and* smart."

"And you think she changed her identity and got out of Stockton?" Wanda asked.

"It's worse than that. Thing is, she and the baby both disappeared one day. They just vanished, and there was no sign of a struggle. The only things missing were her purse and car. And the next week they found the car in a shopping mall about fifty miles away. Without the baby's car seat."

"Did they pursue this?" Janya was frowning, as if she couldn't believe such things happened. "Did they arrest the boyfriend?"

"No, that's the hardest part to explain. Because he disappeared, too."

Everybody fell silent.

Wanda was the first to speak. "Well, how hard is that to figure out? He killed her, then he took off with the kid. It wouldn't be the first time something like that happened. He knew he would be the prime suspect, and maybe his brothers wouldn't alibi a murderer."

"It's possible," Tracy said. "Or . . ." She looked around the room. "It's possible that she killed *him,* and now she's running because she's afraid *she'll* be caught."

"Oh . . ." Alice put her hand to her lips. "That's not possible. Dana is not . . . a violent person."

"Well, we don't know Dana is Carol Kelly, but let's say she is. Couldn't we all do whatever we had to, if our child was threatened?"

"No." Janya shook her head. "No, she would run away, yes, but she would not kill the man before she did. Not Dana."

Tracy was surprised the two women were so certain. She could imagine herself cornered, the way Carol Kelly might have been, imagine herself doing what the other women believed Dana could not.

"I think she could do it," Wanda said, agreeing with Tracy. "Dana would do anything to protect Lizzie. Still, that doesn't mean she did. And from what you've said about the baby's father, even if he didn't kill her and she just took off, he would know to stay out of sight, because he wouldn't want to go to jail for murder."

"Wait, why would he worry about jail? Whether he killed her or not, there was no body," Tracy said. "And no sign of a struggle. She just vanished."

"Doesn't matter. The cops had plenty of evidence this Ray guy was stalking her. Some smart-aleck prosecutor might try to pin a murder on him, just on circumstantial evidence. Besides, and this could explain a lot, with him and her gone, too, it sure looks like *somebody* got murdered. One or the other of them. Murder stays on the books until it's solved, right? That means the cops might still be looking for Carol Kelly, alive or dead, and could be Ray Strickland thinks they might find her someday, even if *he* can't. If they do, he can pop up out of nowhere and come after her."

"We have a lot of ifs and buts," Janya said. "Many more than we should."

"Well, I guess it's time to show you the clincher." Tracy had kept a packet of information for herself, and now she pulled out a photo.

"This was in the packet, only it was small and hard to make out. So I took it into a print shop and had it blown up, and the computer guy there did some work on it." She held it up, and everybody leaned forward to see.

The photo showed a pregnant woman in her late twenties or early thirties, standing under a flowering tree. Her chin-length hair was pulled back from her face with barrettes, and she was smiling. Tracy wondered how many times the woman had smiled since.

They passed the photo around, and each woman took a good look. Wanda was the first to speak, although she sounded doubtful. "That *could* be her. Eleven years ago. Same long face. Same type body."

"Darker hair," Janya said, "but that is easily explained."

"If Dana showed me this photo and said it was her . . . I would not question," Alice said.

514

"But I wouldn't . . . think of it otherwise."

Tracy had been even more impressed with the enhanced photo, and more certain. In her opinion the resemblance was strong. But now, at the others' lukewarm response, she wasn't so sure. The nose might be different, the forehead higher. It was so hard to tell from a photo that old and doctored besides.

She finished trying to make her case. "This Carol Kelly wasn't living far from Fresno, where Elizabeth Turner was born. She might have seen the newspaper article about the Turners and realized she could steal their names, get their birth certificates and make a break for it. Maybe she was so afraid of Ray Strickland that she left everything but her baby daughter and ran right then. Or maybe by the time she took off she already had the birth certificates, another car parked at that shopping mall, even money in a different account that nobody knew about."

Tracy's front door opened, and as they all turned to see who was there, Dana walked in. She looked flushed and happy, more like one of the gang than she ever had before.

"Hi, everybody," she said. "It was too hot to fish, so Pete dropped us off. The girls want to eat frozen pizza and watch *Wheel of Fortune,* but I don't. Is it too late for me to join you for dinner?"

515

CHAPTER
TWENTY-FIVE

While everybody except Dana remained absolutely frozen, Tracy did a quick calculation. Each woman was holding a stack of papers, and no matter how hard or creatively she tried to hide them, Dana was going to notice. Plus, the horror on everybody's faces was unmistakable. Tracy hadn't seen so many guilty expressions since, at age ten, she had caught her parents about to do the old switcheroo with another married couple in the shadows of the faux boulders beside their free-form swimming pool.

"We were just . . ." She was thinking fast, but Dana's mind was faster. Her smile died.

"My timing's bad, huh? I'm sorry. I should have called." She turned to leave, but Wanda jumped to her feet.

"Dana, don't you go now. We got serious business going on here, yes, but you need to help us figure it out."

Dana didn't move. For a moment Tracy thought she might bolt. Dana's body was tensed, a sprinter at the starting line. Then her shoulders drooped and she turned.

She didn't even try to smile.

Tracy knew better than to pretend nothing was wrong, because it was a lie she wouldn't be able to maintain. "You're our friend," she said instead. "And we want that to continue. Please . . ." She gestured to a place beside Wanda on the sofa.

Dana was clearly debating, but at last she sat gingerly on the edge.

"So what's this about?" she asked.

Tracy expected Wanda to jump right in and explain, but when the other woman didn't, she tried to figure out how to begin. At last she just plunged in.

"Everybody here likes you, and everybody was worried. It seemed to us that you were hiding something, that you were afraid. And we thought maybe, if we knew what you were afraid of, we could help."

"Did it occur to you that you could make matters a lot worse?"

Tracy wondered. Hadn't they all believed they could make things better if they just knew the truth? Or had this just been another detective game, something they'd gotten good at when they tried to find Herb Krause's family?

There was no tiptoeing around it. She started with what they were sure of. "We know you're not really Dana Turner, and that the real Elizabeth Ann Turner was a child who died of a heart defect when she was a year old."

"Aren't you the clever sleuths?"

"It was never like that," Wanda said. "Not about us just being clever. You need to believe that. Olivia came to us. She was worried about Lizzie. And, Dana, you do act like a woman who's running. We needed to know why."

Dana didn't answer.

"Can you talk to us?" Tracy asked. "Tell us what's going on? Because nobody here is going to turn you in. As far as we're concerned, your name really is Dana Turner."

Dana's gaze fell to the papers on Wanda's lap. "You seem to have a pretty thick dossier. Why don't you tell me what you know?"

Tracy hesitated. This was not the best way to approach the situation. Dana should tell *them,* so they could check her facts. Yet here they all sat, the papers on their laps. They couldn't pretend they didn't know more than what she'd already said.

Tracy watched Dana's face. "We think you might be a woman named Carol Kelly from Stockton, California, who disappeared with her baby daughter, Sarah, almost eleven years ago. The baby's father was stalking you, and you vanished in the night. So did he. Either you left because you were afraid he would harm you and your daughter, or . . ."

518

Dana's eyes didn't flicker. Whoever she was, whatever she had done, along the way she had learned to protect her thoughts and feelings like a professional. "Or?"

Tracy shook her head.

"Because I killed him?" Dana suggested.

"A man threatening a child. A mother afraid for the child's safety." Wanda started to pat Dana's knee, then seemed to think better of it. "Women have killed for a lot worse reasons."

"We are talking about a life," Dana said, anger flaring in her eyes. "I am not a murderer."

Tracy wondered if she had also learned how to act. The anger seemed genuine, but anger always seemed genuine in movies, too, when the actor was talented enough.

"Who are you?" Tracy asked.

"My name is Dana Turner. My driver's license says so. I have the birth certificate to prove it."

"What are you afraid of?" Alice asked. Maybe if any of the rest of them had spoken, Dana would have stood and walked away, but Alice, who understood fear, had so much compassion in her voice, it seemed to melt Dana's resistance. "We want to help. We are your friends," Alice said gently.

Dana closed her eyes. A long moment passed. Then Dana spoke softly. "I am afraid . . . I could lose my daughter. I am afraid . . . I will not be given the years I need to raise her."

Tracy felt the words tear through her. "Are you Carol Kelly?"

Dana didn't move; she didn't speak. Then she gave the slightest nod. "And now, will you report me? Because I fled with my daughter? It's not a crime, is it? Taking my child to safety? Running from danger so I can raise her unharmed?" She opened her eyes. "Would you jeopardize Lizzie's future now that you know?"

Wanda looked almost ill. "You've been running since she was a *baby*?"

"From state to state. From town to town. Trying to get an education so I can support her. Trying to earn a living. I had family and friends at home, but I can't contact anybody. Surely you can understand that? I can't tell anybody I'm safe or alive. The moment I do, he'll come after me."

"Ray Strickland?"

Dana hesitated; then, as if she was taking a chance, she nodded again.

"But he disappeared, too," Wanda said. "If you didn't kill him, where is he?"

"He's the reason I have to look over my shoulder. He's good at what he does, but he's never been quite good enough." Tears filled her eyes. "Not yet, anyway."

"You poor thing." Wanda patted her hand. "But have you seen him? Do you really know he's still after you and Lizzie? I mean, from what we can tell, the man disappeared off the face of the earth. Maybe he's dead. Maybe you're running for no good reason."

"I didn't kill him. You have to believe that. But if he's dead? The world is a better place."

"You have reason to think he's still after you?" Tracy asked.

"Enough." Dana looked into the distance. "People asking questions that shouldn't need answers. Cars driving slowly past our apartments at night, shining lights in our windows. Lizzie talking about a man who hangs around her school playground and watches. . . ." She gave a bitter laugh. "All the things *you* would never notice because they don't seem to matter, but they're painfully clear to me. Not because they're true, but because they might be."

"You have not seen him?" Janya asked.

Dana hesitated. "I think maybe I have. Twice last year. Once from the back at a park near our house, watching children playing soccer. Once in a shopping mall when I went to buy Lizzie shoes. He was sitting by a fountain, close enough to get wet, but he was so intent on watching people passing by, he didn't even notice. I wasn't completely sure it was him. Time's passed. But that was why we moved *here.* We left in the dead of night. I drove as far as I could without falling asleep at the wheel. This is where we stopped."

Tracy tried to imagine what that was like. Trusting nobody. Always looking over her shoulder.

"You can't go home and let the police . . ." Alice hesitated, to find the right words ". . . sort this out?"

Dana shook her head. "No one understands. It's not possible to protect us if he knows where we are."

"And here?" Tracy asked. "Are you safe here?"

Dana looked stricken. "I thought I was until tonight."

"No one on this key is going to harm you," Wanda said.

"Your husband is a cop!"

Wanda looked hurt. "Do you think Kenny knows about this? I haven't said a word to him. Not one word, and I don't plan to. Because at the least, he'd have to do something about the identity theft. There has to be a law against getting documents under somebody else's name."

"Then how did you discover all this?" Dana demanded.

Tracy felt guilty. "It's my fault. I asked a friend to run some names through a database. He's the one who put this together."

"And now who will *he* tell?"

"Not a soul. He has no interest in telling anybody, I promise. He did it as a favor to me. I'm sure he's already forgotten the whole thing."

Dana put her head in her hands. "How can I know that for sure?"

Tracy couldn't answer that. Wanda, too, looked unsure. But Janya rose to the occasion.

"Dana," she said in her musical voice, "you can run again. This is true. Tonight. But here, you're not alone. There are many eyes to watch over you. We can be certain no questions are asked that should not be. We can watch for men who are too interested in the things that happen at Happiness Key. We can spot cars driving slowly past your house. You will not be alone here. We are careful. We are . . . observant. We will help you keep Lizzie safe."

Wanda put her arm around Dana. "She's right. Not only won't we report you, we'll watch out for you. You've got a good place to live here. A job where you're valued. Friends for you and Lizzie. If you take off again, you'll end up in another cheap motel. No job, nothing for Lizzie to do. And she's so happy here. We're so happy to have her. Don't do that to her."

Dana sat back at last. "I am so tired of running."

"I can only imagine," Alice said.

"Maybe you'll have to run again," Tracy said. "But not, I promise you, from us. We'll just try to make sure you're safe. Stay. At least until you think he's found you again."

"He could be watching right now."

"He'd better not be," Wanda said. "Kenny's got a gun, and I'm not afraid to use it."

"Oh, great," Tracy said. "There's something that'll make us all sleep better. Leave the guns to Ken, okay? Just keep your eyes open. We're all agreed?"

"You'll promise?" Dana said. "That you won't tell anybody about the . . . irregularities in our papers?"

"Who's interested in irregularities?" Wanda said. "Whole world's falling apart around us. We got plenty to think about besides you. But you try to leave, I'll find you. The heck with old Ray Strickland. I'll find you and drag you back by the hair on your head. I can't lose you now. You're the best manager a pie shop could hope for."

"We all promise." Tracy looked around. "Right?"

"Right," they said in unison.

"Okay, it's time to eat," Tracy said. "And we've got pie in the refrigerator when the salads are gone. And the rolls were hot once upon a time, so just pretend, okay?"

Dana rose. Tracy wondered if she would make an excuse to leave, and if tomorrow morning Herb's house would be empty again. But instead she moved toward the table with the others.

"I haven't had friends in a long time," she said.

Wanda put a hand on her shoulder. "Well, you got some now. Take advantage of us as long as you can, okay?"

"I might need some help remembering how."

Alice slipped her arm around Dana's waist. "These women? They saved my life."

For the first time Dana looked close to tears. "I hope it doesn't come to that."

Tracy did, too. She hoped that the stranger named Ray Strickland stayed far, far away. Because despite all their brave words, if he didn't, she wasn't sure what five women and two preteen girls would be able to do about it.

Wanda was the last to leave. She fussed over the pie pans, scrubbing both until even the most advanced laboratory couldn't have proved pie had ever resided there. Then, when everyone but Tracy had left, Wanda went to the living room window and watched the women disappearing toward their respective houses.

"So, what do you think?"

Tracy was storing leftover salads in her refrigerator. She spoke from the depths, so her voice sounded hollow.

"I think if she's still here in the morning, she'll stay. But after what she's been through, it's going to be hard to trust us completely."

Wanda was having problems putting the whole scenario together. Being a cop's wife, she knew about stalkers. How hard they were to escape from. How volatile their emotions. How unlikely they were to think about consequences. All a stalker wanted was his prey. And even celebrities, with all the money in the world for security, sometimes died at their hands.

But something was bothering her. Something was gnawing a hole in all the explanations and promises. She just wasn't sure what it was.

The refrigerator door slammed. Then Tracy came into the living room. "What do you think?" she asked Wanda.

"I don't know. I just have this itchy feeling in my head, like something's scratching to get out and I can't get in there to set it free."

"That's colorful." Tracy flopped down on the sofa. "You know Dana better than anybody else. Maybe something she said before? Something you know about her that's not matching up?"

"Nothing like that."

"Do you think she killed Ray Strickland?"

Wanda wondered. Dana had been adamant. Her denial had been emotional, although she'd been careful to hide her emotions the rest of the night. But Wanda didn't think that was what was itching at her.

"Not my job to find her guilty of murder," Wanda said. "That would be up to a jury."

"Maybe if she'd told us the story, I'd be worried about her spin, but the newspaper spelled out the facts. Ray Strickland was bad through and through."

"And if she did kill him, why would she run? Nobody's found a body. She could have gone about her business, knowing she was free."

"Works for me," Tracy said. "So let's just say she didn't kill him, and the guy really is out there trying to find her . . ."

Wanda slapped the window ledge. "That's what's bothering me."

"Glad to be of help. What did I say?"

"A guy trying to find her. What if Ray Strickland's not working alone? What if he's hired people to look for her?"

"And how would he pay for that?"

"You said he had plenty of money."

"Well, that's what the paper said, but she's been running a long time. And he hasn't exactly been earning more, at least not so anyone knows."

Wanda gave a snort of disbelief. "A guy like that could change his identity in a heartbeat. He probably already had a closetful of aliases. He could be living out in the open under another name in another state, still pulling off jobs with his brothers, and spending his free time searching for her."

"You're being kind of creative with the facts, Wanda."

"Maybe so . . . But what if Pete was hired to find her?"

"Pete?" Tracy almost shrieked the name.

"You said he was an army MP? Do you know how many private investigators are former cops or military? They learn what they need, then they leave the force or whatever, and they've got skills they got to do something with. So they hang out their shingle."

"And you think maybe that's what Pete did?"

"Of course, maybe Ray himself didn't hire somebody. What if he's dead after all? He's got those brothers, right? What it they're trying to find Carol Kelly, too, on account of them wanting to know what happened to Ray?"

"Hmm . . ."

Wanda could see all the possibilities, too, many to ignore. "Pete just showed up one day looking for a job. Kind of convenient, wasn't it?"

"No, I found him at Randall's, remember? I put a note up on the bulletin board about needing a handyman."

"And he was right there, watching you."

"How would he know I was going to be there posting a notice? I'm not even sure if I knew myself when I went inside."

"He could have been following you, to see

if he could find an opening to talk to you and feel you out. Who knows? He could have been following all of us, hoping he could find some excuse to hang out around here and watch Dana."

"And why would he be watching her? Why doesn't he just tell whoever?"

"Maybe he's trying to find out if she really *is* Carol Kelly. Maybe he's trying to find proof. This is a cop's wife talking. Kenny's a detective, remember? He's done a lot of stranger things than that to find out what he needs to know."

"Dana and Pete have a thing going, remember? His car is outside her house until very late on the nights Lizzie's staying at Alice's."

"All night?" Wanda was shocked. She didn't know things had progressed that far.

"They've got Lizzie to think about, even if she's not in the house, so no."

"Why didn't I know!"

"Because you come home from Wanda's Wonderful Pies and fall into bed ten minutes after you eat dinner."

"Well, how do you like that?" Wanda was stunned. Dana hadn't said anything to her about things getting that serious, and they worked together every single day.

Tracy was watching her. "So I'm sure if Pete was working for Ray or his brothers, by now he'd have everything he needed and they'd be sitting on Dana's doorstep."

"I still don't like it." Wanda made a decision and nodded hard, to seal it. "I'm going to ask Kenny to check out Pete."

"No! We can't do anything that'll make him suspicious about Dana."

"I won't even mention her name. I'll just tell him you're worried about the new handyman, that something he told you about his past sounded fishy, and you wanted to know more."

"Me? Don't you dare."

"Then I'll invent another reason, you being so prim and proper about this."

"Wanda, please don't involve Ken. I just have a bad feeling that one way or the other that's going to lead back to Dana. Okay? Take it from me, Pete's just a regular guy. I called some of his references. Nobody had a bad thing to say about him, and none of them live in California."

Wanda still felt uneasy. "Okay, but I'm going to keep a good eye on him. You should, too."

"After everything we've figured out today, it's easy to feel a little paranoid. Let's just not take it to extremes. I'll watch, you watch, and we'll talk if anything seems odd. Okay?"

Wanda got her pie tins off the table where she'd set them. "I never figured when I moved out here there'd be so darned much intrigue. Next thing you know, James Bond will come blasting down the road in one of

530

those cars with all the fancy gadgets, and we won't pay him any mind. He'll just be business as usual."

"The intrigue's all over. I bet tonight was the big excitement. Now we can all settle down and get back to our normal lives."

Wanda hoped Tracy was right. But on the off chance she wasn't, Wanda planned to keep her mouth shut, her next idea to herself, and her options open.

CHAPTER
TWENTY-SIX

Janya kept herself busy after her aborted beach encounter with Rishi. She had always been careful not to take more jobs painting murals than she could fit in and still be a good wife. Now she scheduled work that kept her away from home as many hours as possible.

She painted scenes of Italy on the walls at Gonzalo's, working late at night when the restaurant was closed. She traveled to Fort Myers and painted sumptuous tropical gardens on the patio wall of a twenty-room mansion, making more money than she had ever expected to from a single job and coming home too late each night to converse with her husband.

She wasn't sure which of those pleased her more.

Now it was July 4 and a weekend, but she was too tired to work, anyway. It was no surprise that despite the holiday, Rishi was at the office. She planned to catch up on shopping and cleaning, since she had to live in the house, too. But by 10:00 a.m. she still hadn't summoned energy to do much of anything.

She was sitting with her feet propped up, staring at the ceiling, when someone knocked. Before she could answer, Wanda opened the door and thrust her head over the threshold.

"You there, Janya?"

"I suppose I am."

Wanda came in. "It's a national holiday today. I closed the shop in honor. You're supposed to be all peppy and animated."

"I have nothing to celebrate."

Wanda flopped down beside her. She was wearing lavender shorts and a tube top of shocking pink. With her coppery hair, she looked as if she were trying to monopolize an entire section of the color wheel.

"Me, neither." Wanda folded her arms. "Ken was supposed to be back by now, but he got held up until tomorrow. Ain't that a kick in the head?"

"At least he will be coming home."

"Things still aren't any better between you and Rishi?"

"The name sounds familiar, but I can't remember why."

"There's my answer."

"My mother called this morning. She wanted to know if there had been progress giving her a grandchild."

"At least she's calling again."

"And I am disappointing her again."

"It doesn't happen overnight, Janya. She must know that."

"It will not happen at all until I have a husband who remembers how to find me in his bed."

"Ouch."

"Shall we talk of something different?"

Wanda clapped her hands together, as if to liven up the conversation. "Let's have a picnic. Just you and me. The others are all out and about. Tracy's at the rec center for some tournament. Alice and Dana took the girls to see the Palmetto Grove parade, but they'll be back this evening to watch the fireworks."

"It is good Dana is still here."

"I know. I didn't totally expect her to be, but it's sure better for her than running again."

"You will watch the fireworks tonight, too?"

"There's a good place to see them over the water. Remember? We found it last year."

"Last year Rishi and I watched with you. This year he will be at the office."

"More reason for you to have a good day anyway. Won't do to let him think you're pining away."

Janya knew that nothing would be gained by staring at the ceiling. There was a brown spot the size of a walnut where the roof had once leaked, and if she gazed at it long enough, she knew she would decide she had to repaint it.

"Shall we go to our beach?" she asked.

"I have cheese —"

"And pie?"

"I have pie."

"I will see what I have to go with it."

They agreed to meet at Wanda's house, which was closer to the beach. Janya washed and sliced fresh vegetables, and added yogurt raita. She put chapatis and canned fruit juices in a wicker basket, changed into her bathing suit and cover-up, then went to find Wanda.

She was almost there when she glanced up and saw Pete Knight getting out of his SUV, which was parked in Dana's driveway. Oddly enough, he was heading straight toward her mailbox. He glanced around, but he didn't notice Janya. Opening the mailbox, which stood beside the road, he took out a stack of mail, leafed through it, then shoved it in the pocket of his shorts. He turned, as if he was planning to get back in the driver's seat, and realized Janya was watching him.

"Janya." He waved.

She started walking again, bypassed Wanda's house and continued toward him. She waited until she was almost there before she spoke.

"I thought there was no mail delivery today." She didn't mention that she also thought the mail in this box belonged to Dana.

"I'm about to meet Dana in town. She called on her cell and asked me to get it on my way in. She and Lizzie got home so late last night, she forgot to check, so I told her I'd bring it with me."

"She must be expecting something important." She said it with a smile.

"She ordered something for Lizzie, and she wants it to be a surprise. She was worried Lizzie might get the mail this afternoon before she could. She knew I was over at Tracy's installing an electrical outlet on the front of her house."

The explanation was casual; the man was casual. Janya still sensed something else in the air.

"Well then, enjoy the parade," she said.

"I'll probably miss it, but we're going out to lunch."

She nodded a goodbye and turned back toward Wanda's. Halfway there, Pete passed her and honked his own goodbye.

Wanda was waiting at the door. "What was that man doing over at Dana's when she's in town?"

Janya told her what she had seen and Pete's explanation. Wanda stood perfectly still for a moment. Then she exploded.

"I told Tracy I wouldn't do it, but I'm going to!"

"What are you going to do?" Janya asked.

"I'm going to have Kenny check out Pete Knight. I won't tell Kenny a thing about Dana. I would never go back on my word about that. But I never actually promised not to have Pete checked out."

"He didn't act like a man who was doing anything wrong."

"We told Dana we would watch out for her, and that's what I'll be doing. Do you trust him?"

Janya liked Pete. But did she trust him? That was a different question. In the past she had made enough mistakes in judgment that these days, she was slower to form opinions. Unfortunately, now — with everything they knew about Dana and Lizzie — she saw shadows everywhere. It was a burden.

"It did seem as if he explained too much to me," she said. "Of course, perhaps he realized it did not look good, going through someone else's mail."

"Well, we'll know soon enough," Wanda said. "Or we'll know soon as Kenny can get back to the station and find out for me. I don't know when that will be, him doing all that traveling and those classes. But just as soon as he's able." She nodded decisively. "Meantime, keep those gorgeous brown eyes of yours open, you hear?"

"It will give me something to do."

Wanda turned, and got a quilted bag and

pie plate from the table behind her. "Well, we got something to do right now, you and me. Let's go have ourselves a Fourth of July picnic."

Janya so rarely called anyone that in the late afternoon when she picked up the telephone to call her brother and heard the stuttering signal that announced a voice mail message, she wondered how long ago it had been left. Perhaps Rishi had called while she was on the beach to tell her that, yet again, he would not be home before midnight. If so, he had wasted words, since that was only what she expected. Perhaps her mother had left a message before her call that morning. Or perhaps Janya had won a free weekend at a Miami time-share resort, an opportunity to lower the interest rate on her credit card, or a free inspection by a pest control company.

She punched in a number to retrieve the message and waited until a recording came on the line.

"This message is for Mr. Rishi Kapur," the disembodied voice droned. "This is Hazel, at Dr. Peterson's office, and we just want to remind you that your follow-up appointment is tomorrow at 9:00 a.m. Please call back to confirm you will be here." Then she left a number.

Hazel — whoever she was — hung up. The automated operator came on the line and reminded Janya of all her options. She could play the message again. She could delete, save, play other messages. . . .

Janya hung up without punching another button.

Dr. Peterson?

Who was the mysterious Dr. Peterson? And why did Rishi have an appointment with him? Unless Dr. Peterson saw patients on the Sunday of a holiday weekend, Rishi had probably already been and gone to this follow-up.

And *what* was he following up?

She supposed she could ask him, if she ever saw him long enough for a conversation. That would be the expected thing to do, the behavior of a dutiful wife. Perhaps Dr. Peterson was a dentist who had found and filled a cavity. Or perhaps he was an internist, and Rishi's blood pressure had been high. This last would not surprise her, considering his recent behavior.

Or maybe something was wrong with her husband that he was reluctant to share. Something seriously wrong.

She shoved the thought away, but it sprang back. Could *that* account for the way Rishi had been acting? Was he so worried about his health that there was no room for her in his life just now? Perhaps he was dying, and he wanted her to adjust slowly to losing him.

She tried to remember if she had noticed anything different, other than his disinterest in her. Had he lost weight? Was his skin sallow? Was he wincing or moving frequently, like someone in pain?

The truth was, she had been so hurt, she hadn't noticed much of anything about her husband. When he entered a room, she left. And the need to leave was rare, because for the past weeks she had made a real attempt not to even be in the same house with him.

She went to discover what she could about Dr. Peterson. According to the White Pages, there were three in the wider metropolitan area. With a sigh she punched in the number for her voice mailbox again and listened to the message, gazing at the doctors' phone numbers as she did. The message was from Dr. *George* Peterson, which was really no help, since there was no other information listed.

She was on her way to the computer to see what she could find when she realized she should simply dial the office to see if there was a recording. She did, and waited until the phone rang four times. Then Hazel began to speak.

Janya listened carefully, pressed the hang-up button, redialed and listened again, before she put the telephone back in its cradle.

Andrology Associates?

She completed her trip to the computer and turned it on. An hour later she was still clicking links when she heard the front door open.

Perhaps Rishi had come home to see the fireworks with her. That was good, because he was about to see all the fireworks he had ever bargained for, right here and now.

He came into the second bedroom, where she sat at the desk. She made no attempt to hide what was on the screen. She swiveled and examined him.

"I came home early," he said. "I thought perhaps you wanted to go out to the beach . . . ?"

"This is not early, Rishi. It is Saturday, the Fourth of July, and you should not have been at work at all."

"I —"

She made a slashing motion with her hand. "I do not want to hear any more of your lies. There is no project so important you could not take this day off. To pretend otherwise is to say out loud that I am a fool."

"I don't —"

"Please be quiet!"

He looked astonished. She had never spoken to him this way. She had never spoken to *anyone* this way.

"Tell me where you were yesterday morning at nine o'clock," she demanded.

He was startled. She could see it by the way his eyes widened. He hesitated. She knew he was trying to calculate what she might know.

"I will tell you, since you find it so difficult," she said. "You were at the office of

Dr. George Peterson, an andrologist. And shall I tell you what his specialty is?"

"Janya . . ."

"Male infertility." She gestured to the screen behind her. "He has written articles for medical journals. The abstracts are online. And I am educated enough to know what all those long, difficult words mean, Rishi. He seems particularly adept at varicocele repair."

He swallowed. Then he turned and walked out of the room. She was after him like a stone released from a slingshot.

She grabbed his arm. "Is that why you saw him, perhaps? This specialist so famous that his articles are on the Internet?"

"I can see you aren't in the mood for my company tonight. I will go back to work."

"If you do, I will be gone when you return. And I will not be back at all."

He turned, and he looked horrified. "You would leave that way?"

"I will not live with a man who lies to me."

"I have not lied."

"And have you told the truth?"

Rishi looked the way he might if someone close to him dropped dead at his feet. He passed a hand over his face, but he didn't reply.

"Rishi, have you told the truth?" she repeated a little softer.

"Would you tell the truth, if you knew it

meant the end of everything you ever wanted?"

The anger that had been building for weeks disappeared. Just like that. Gone, but, as the English saying proclaimed, not forgotten.

"We will sit and work this out," she said. "We must."

"I don't think we can."

"You will sit, then, and *I* will work it out."

He didn't smile, but he went into the living room and chose a seat on the sofa. She joined him.

She was the first to speak. "We must start with the truth. All of it."

"What do you know?"

She hesitated, and the night she and the other women had confronted Dana flashed through her mind. They had told Dana everything they'd discovered, but since then, Janya had wondered if they shouldn't have let Dana tell *them* instead. What additional details would they know now, if they had?

She had learned from that experience, and now she shook her head. "No, I'm sorry, but you must tell me."

He looked cornered and thoroughly miserable. For a moment she didn't think he would speak. Then he cleared his throat.

"When I inquired about securing a loan to develop a new project, I was asked to take a physical. It was simply a precaution. They wanted to be certain I would be around for many years to see the project to conclusion."

Janya nodded, trying not to look either patient or impatient.

"It was a very thorough physical. The doctor asked about children. I told him we had not yet conceived. He suggested the fault . . ." Rishi cleared his throat again ". . . the fault might be mine."

Janya had suspected this after her research, so she only nodded again and tried hard not to show emotion.

"He did a test. And it showed that my . . ." Now he looked humiliated and lowered his voice. "My sperm count is low."

"That can happen," Janya said carefully. "I have heard of that."

"You know what a variocele is?"

She had mentioned the word. She relieved him of some of the burden. "I do now. It is a group of enlarged veins in a man's testicles."

He spoke mechanically, as if he had distanced himself from emotion. "They are not completely certain why this impacts fertility, but it's clear that sometimes it does. And while surgery is not always helpful, sometimes it is. So I had surgery."

"When did you have it?"

"Months ago. Three months."

"And you have hidden this?"

He didn't respond to that question. "Do you remember the night I told you we would spend together, but I came home late? I had a small complication, an infection. I went to the doctor for antibiotics after leaving work, but he sent me through the emergency room for tests, to be sure nothing worse was wrong. I was supposed to be home in time, but they did not finish until late in the evening."

"Weeks ago," she said. It was not a question.

"Yes."

"You have known about this for months, then?"

"Yes. The physical was in March."

She didn't remember Rishi telling her he was going to a doctor, but it was possible he had, and the news had seemed so ordinary, she hadn't wondered or worried. Rishi was in excellent health and most likely afterward he had reassured her all was well. He was young and strong.

And possibly unable to father a child.

"And now what does Dr. Peterson say?" she asked.

He glanced at her, but she saw the guilt.

"You didn't go in yesterday, did you?" she asked.

He gave a slight shake of his head.

"Because you are afraid to find out?"

"I was very busy yesterday."

"You are lying again."

"No, I *was* very busy. But, also, I did not want to find out what he would say."

"You would know something this soon?"

"They will take samples every three months to compare with those from before surgery."

Janya sat back and considered everything he'd said. Finally she spoke, her voice rising against her will with every question. "And there is a reason you haven't told me any of this? A reason I had to discover it accidentally? A reason you have let me suffer, believing you no longer wanted me because you thought I was the one who could not have a baby?"

"How could you ever believe that? That I wouldn't want you!"

She turned, and without thinking, she shoved him hard. He was so surprised, he yelped.

"Do you ever listen to yourself?" She pushed against his chest with her palms again. "Do you?"

"Stop that."

"I would like to shake you, Rishi Kapur. You would not leave me if I was unable to have babies? You cannot imagine *how* I could think such a thing? And yet you believe I would leave you? You have not made love to me for weeks because . . ." She narrowed her eyes. "Why not?"

"Because it was a lie! At first I told myself things would be fine, that the surgery would fix everything. But as time passed, the truth was clearer. Even with surgery, the odds aren't good, Janya. To make love to you, to have you hoping for a baby, and to know that I could not give you one and might never be able to! I just . . . couldn't."

She was still angry, but she knew what she said now would matter for a lifetime. She tried to choose her words carefully.

"What must you think of me? You believe that having a baby is all our marriage is about?"

"You married me expecting a traditional life together. We married to have a family. You didn't know me. You certainly didn't love me."

"I —"

He held up his hand. "Yes, I know you married me to leave an unpleasant situation, but you also expected to make a new home here. With me. With children. And what if I can never give you that?"

She took a deep breath. "Marriage is not an equation. Love plus children does not always equal a happy marriage. But respect plus love? That is an equation that always ends in happiness, no matter the circumstances. And we have both."

She grabbed his hand and held it against her cheek. "I love you, Rishi. It's a love that took time to grow, and it's growing still. But it is not a love based on whether you can give me a child. The world is filled with children. If we cannot create our own, perhaps we will raise someone else's. And will we be less happy because of it? Will we love them less? Will we love each other less?"

He began to weep, this man who almost never showed his feelings. It was a measure of how deep his emotions ran, the fear he had experienced every day since finding that he might never father a child. The horror he felt at the prospect that he would lose his wife.

Janya put her arms around him and drew his head to her chest. "Rishi, Rishi, I love you," she crooned in her native language. "And I will love you more each day. How could you not know?"

He put his arms around her waist, and they held each other until holding was no longer enough. She lay back on the sofa, and he undressed her before he undressed himself.

"Nandi the bull is watching," she whispered as he took her in his arms. "We should close the door to the puja room."

He made a sound low in his throat. "Don't move. Unlike the bull, I'm not made of stone."

He wasn't. He was made of warm, willing, human flesh and need. Even better, so was she. She opened to him and moved with pleasure in his embrace.

CHAPTER TWENTY-SEVEN

When Wanda noticed Rishi's car in the Kapur driveway, she figured she could skip the fireworks. Rishi would probably keep Janya company, and she sure didn't want to interrupt that.

With nothing better to do, she decided to use the evening to catch up on work she'd been putting off at the shop. She needed to do an honest-to-goodness inventory of supplies, followed by placing orders for whatever she was missing. She needed to look at her own hastily scribbled notes and figure out which pies were selling best, so she could move them to the top of the weekly lineup. She'd been itching to give the refrigerator a good scrubbing, and what better time than now, when nobody else needed to get into it?

With that last in mind, after a quick sandwich she pulled on an old pair of capris and a faded *Miami Vice* T-shirt that was practically an heirloom and drove into town, fuming at the ramped-up holiday traffic on the bridge.

Since the park where the fireworks would be launched was miles away, she found a parking spot right in front of her shop. The only sign of business as usual came from a bar one block down, where loyal patrons were probably watching some distant city's festivities on television and didn't know the difference.

She was heading toward the door, key in hand, when she heard a muffled crash. She took another step before she completely processed the sound. Her first assumption was that the noise came from a neighboring shop, but one quick glance in either direction showed no lights shining in either.

She considered her options. Nobody in town could summon a cop faster than she could. On the other hand, nobody had more to lose if she simply imagined an intruder. She could just hear the razzing she would get every time one of Kenny's buddies stopped by for pie. She could picture a couple of the biggest jokers on their hands and knees, looking under counters every single visit, just to be sure Wanda's so-called intruder wasn't hiding again.

Instead of whipping out her cell phone, she edged closer so she could take a quick peek. The drawn café curtains hid her body from view, but she was tall enough that she knew she could just see over the top of them. If somebody was there, they would most likely be in the front of the shop, where the safe resided, but of course the safe was as empty as a preacher's pockets. If somebody had broken in, they weren't about to come away with anything for their trouble, not unless they were itching for pie pans or a sack of pastry flour.

She took a deep breath, and thrust her head forward for a quick look. The streetlamps cast just enough light for her to see that the room was dark and, better yet, empty. Nothing seemed different from the way she'd left it. Nobody was fiddling with the safe. The doors to the kitchen were closed. She debated whether to go inside. Sure, she'd heard a noise, but who could say from where? Maybe a cat had knocked over a garbage can in the narrow delivery alley behind the shop. Maybe a car had backfired, or a door had slammed and echoed along the empty street.

Or . . . maybe not.

The walkway that ran between her shop and the shop to the right was lit by the glow of streetlamps on State and intersected at the back with the delivery alley. Neither was used much, but Wanda made sure the alleys stayed free of trash. She could slip behind the shop and peek into the kitchen by way of the lone window beside the back entrance. Then, if nothing looked amiss, she could let herself in that way. If all was not well, she could sprint back to her car, lock herself in and call the station. All in less than a minute.

She sidled up to the rear door and put her ear against it, just the way she had when her son and daughter were teenagers with more secrets than she liked. At that moment, the fireworks began, and even though the display was miles away, the sky lit up, and the noise drowned out any possibility of eavesdropping.

She waited until the first flash was extinguished, then slipped past the door and peeked in the window.

She didn't expect to find anybody inside. But there, right there in her kitchen, somebody was squatting on the floor! Somebody dressed in dark clothing, like a roly-poly ninja, shining a flashlight into the corners. Worse, Wanda recognized her intruder.

She didn't think twice. She stabbed her key into the lock, and in a moment she had leaped inside, switching on the light in one fluid motion as the door slammed behind her.

"What in the heck are *you* doing in my shop?"

Startled, the woman gasped and toppled backward, landing on her broad bottom. She held up her hands as if to ward off an attacker, then she tried to cover her face, but it was too late.

Wanda strode over and grabbed Frieda Mertz by the shoulder and shook her. "I said, what are you doing here! You broke into my kitchen!"

Before she could shake the woman again, something scurried over Wanda's foot. She looked down and saw a mouse heading under her stove.

A mouse. Under her stove. In her kitchen.

"What have you done?" Wanda screeched.

By now Frieda Mertz had her arms over her head, as if to ward off blows.

"I . . . I was just walking by, and I . . . I thought I saw you in here. So I . . . I came around back to see if I could . . . talk to you . . . and the door was unlocked and . . ."

"Liar!" Wanda was furious. "You broke into my shop, and you let that mouse loose!"

She felt something on her leg and looked down. A palmetto bug, one of Florida's infamous giant flying roaches, this one longer than her thumb, was making its way up her shin.

She screeched, did a little jig and brushed it off. The bug took wing and flew to the closest wall, where it landed with a whir and a thud.

"What . . . . Have. You. Done . . . !"

Frieda Mertz took advantage of Wanda's impromptu dance and scrambled to her feet. Wanda saw where the woman was heading and blocked the door. She made a grab for Frieda, who dodged her, but not skillfully. Frieda banged into the island Wanda used for rolling out dough and yelped in pain.

Another palmetto bug flew past Wanda's

head and landed beside the first one.

"You brought those varmints in here and let them loose, didn't you?" Wanda demanded, as a third bug launched itself from the floor at Frieda's feet and headed for the stove.

Frieda looked as if she was going to make another dive for the door, but Wanda was quicker. She locked it with a twist of the double bolt.

"You try to go out the front way," Wanda said, when Frieda turned to run, "and I'll have every cop in Palmetto Grove on your tail."

"I didn't do it . . . I didn't —"

A mouse streaked across the floor and behind the refrigerator.

Frieda fell silent.

Wanda assessed the situation. She had caught the woman in her shop, setting vermin loose. She was sure that on Monday, the health department would get an anonymous tip that the kitchen at Wanda's Wonderful Pies was infested. Wanda would have to close down until she convinced them an exterminator had done his job. By then, the word would be out, and nobody would ever set foot in the shop again.

And what would happen now, if she called the cops and reported what the woman had done? Would they have to report the incident to the health department? And even if they didn't, were they capable of keeping this fiasco to themselves? Or would the word leak out, until nobody ever bought another piece of pie she had baked?

"Why?" Wanda asked at last. "Why would you do such a thing?"

Frieda sniffed. Then, as Wanda watched, tears began to roll down her cheeks. Wanda raised an eyebrow and waited.

"You . . . ruined me!"

"What are you talking about? All those sales you've been running, your place is brimming over with customers."

"I'm . . . in debt up to my eyeballs. All those sales cost me big."

"So you thought you'd come over here, drop off a few souvenirs from your own kitchen —"

"There's nothing like this in my kitchen! I got them —" She had the good sense not to finish the sentence.

Wanda nodded. She was balling her hands into fists, relaxing them, then balling them again. She wanted nothing more than to leap on the woman and pound her to the floor. But she was too good for that. Or at least she wanted to be.

Somehow she managed to keep her voice even. "So you decided to pick up a few bugs here and there, buy a couple of mice at the pet shop . . . Somebody's pet boa constrictor's going hungry tonight, on account of you. You already called the health department?"

Frieda shook her head.

"All I ever wanted was to bake my pies," Wanda said. "Just pies. Nothing else. All you ever had to do was let me. We could have coexisted."

"You ever fail at something?" Frieda asked.

The question surprised Wanda. "Stay there," she said, then she turned and opened the utility closet beside the door and took out a broom. She leaned it against the counter. "How many bugs you let out?"

Frieda calculated. "Six," she said. "That's the truth."

Wanda envisioned a sea of little German roaches, the kind that were too small to eradicate easily. The kind that bred and bred and bred. "Any little ones?"

Frieda cleared her throat. "Not yet."

"Where are they?"

Frieda grimaced, then she reached in the pocket of her voluminous pants and pulled out a jar.

Wanda could see that the contents were brown and writhing. She wrinkled her nose and held out her hand. "You give me that."

Frieda held it out, and Wanda took it. Stiff armed, she held the jar in front of her and took it to the back door, unlocked it, and set the jar outside in the alley, watching Frieda all the while. Then she shut the door and locked it again.

"Anything else?"

Frieda turned her pockets inside out to show they were empty.

"How many mice?"

Frieda paused, as if she wanted to find a way to avoid answering, then she sighed. "Three."

"How'd you get the rest of your little friends inside?"

Frieda, tears still streaming down her face, pointed to her feet. Just behind the woman, Wanda glimpsed a larger jar and several small cardboard travel carriers, like the ones she remembered from the days when Junior had kept gerbils.

"I've failed at a few things," Wanda said. "I never took it out on anybody else, though."

"My husband left me." Frieda sniffed loudly. "Two years ago. For a woman half my age. You ever fail at that?"

Wanda waited.

The rest of Frieda's monologue just gushed out. "I sold our house and took all the money I got in the settlement. I . . . I figured I'd show him I could make it just fine, maybe even better, without him. I always baked bread. It was the one thing people always said about me. That I baked the best bread. So I bought the bakery. Only bread just didn't seem to be enough, so I started making desserts, too. Then you came along."

"And you tried to cheat me."

"I couldn't afford you! I was barely hanging on. And those pies? I knew they'd make all the difference. I never ate anything like one of those pies."

Despite herself, and against every intelligent inclination, Wanda felt a shiver of pride.

"I wasn't good at much in my life." Frieda was no longer crying. Wanda thought maybe this confession was too sad for tears. "I wasn't pretty. I got through high school but never went to college. My kids caused more trouble than a bus full of rattlesnakes. They got through school okay, but not 'cause of me."

"You don't know that," Wanda said, before she realized she was trying to soothe the woman's feelings. "Of course, maybe you do," she added, with a glare.

"Then Amos just left. And the woman he left me for? She's a floozy, and she doesn't have a brain in her head."

"What's all this got to do with me and these critters you're about to remove from my kitchen?" As if to illustrate Wanda's words, one of the palmetto bugs buzzed across the room and started crawling toward the ceiling.

"I've got loans for my loans. The bank refuses to give me more credit. I can't compete with you. I can't keep running those sales. Pretty soon nobody's going to darken my door. I've been buying those cookies and pies, and selling them below what they cost me. I don't have your knack with pies, and now somebody's opening one of those cookie chain stores at the mall. Did you know?"

Wanda hadn't, but it didn't really matter to her. She sold pies. They sold cookies. Some woman in the next town made wedding cakes.

"The answer to all that's simple. You can stop competing," Wanda said. "I mean it. Stop baking pies. Send the people who want them over here. You liked making bread, so make bread. Sell take-out sandwiches and use the bread you baked yourself. Make dinner rolls. You ever taste those rolls that come from the grocery store?" She made a face. "You could corner that market if you're any good. Change the name from Bakery to Bread Store or Bread Bakery. Reinvent yourself."

"I couldn't even do *this* right." Frieda gestured to the room. "I fail at everything. I figured you were closed today. How should I know you'd be over here this evening? It's the Fourth of July."

Wanda knew exactly what she had to say next. "You did something else wrong. You know what? I've got a security camera. It recorded every little thing you did tonight. So it's all on film, and so is this conversation."

Frieda clapped a hand over her mouth. "Where?"

"You think I'd tell you, so you can damage

the evidence?"

"I don't believe you."

"Did you forget my husband's a cop? And what kind of cop's wife doesn't have the best security?"

Frieda let out a wail, and despite herself, Wanda felt some pity for the woman, especially since she had no security camera — nor, apparently, any kind of decent lock on her back door.

"I get real tired of folks who blame other folks for all their troubles," Wanda said. "That's like an epidemic these days. You did this to yourself, or at least everything that happened here tonight. But you can fix it. It's not too late to do something right, Ms. Mertz. So here's what you're going to do. You're going to get every single bug you let loose in here. I'm going to stand in the corner and count. Once you get six, then you can get the mice."

"What if I can't find them?"

"That would be your loss. Again. Because if you don't, and if when you're all done you don't scrub this floor and these walls and any place those varmints have been, then I'm going to get that tape I mentioned, and I'm going to march it right over to the police station. If you do manage to clean up your own mess, and I'm satisfied, I'll just file that tape somewhere you'll never find it. And if you ever, ever do *anything* that looks like another act of sabotage? I'll pull the tape right out and find the best way to use it against you. Maybe I'll start by seeing if the local TV station would like to have first dibs."

"You're not going right to the police?"

"You think I should?"

"No!"

"You gonna keep trying to undercut me?"

Frieda took longer on that one. She finally shook her head.

"You gonna consider going into the bread-baking business and leaving the pies to those who know how to make them?"

"I don't know if I've got what it takes anymore. All the joy went out of baking bread when the worry came in."

Wanda felt another stab of sympathy, and this time she couldn't overcome it. She couldn't imagine what it would be like to lose the joy of baking pies. Her entire world would feel darker and more threatening.

"Just give baking nothing but bread a try again," she said. "You make up some circulars. I'll even keep them on my counter and send folks that want some your way."

"You would do that?"

"Call me an idiot."

Frieda sniffed. "Frieda's Fabulous Bread."

Wanda almost smiled. "How're you gonna trap those mice?"

"Any way I can."

"I suggest you get to it."

"You never answered my question."

"Which question was that?"

"You ever fail at anything?"

Wanda considered. "A couple of times I nearly failed at giving somebody a second chance."

"When?"

"Tonight, for starters."

"It's . . . nice of you, I guess. Not to turn me in."

Wanda waited.

"You think maybe we're going to be friends?"

Wanda didn't have to think twice. "Not a chance in the world."

Frieda sniffed again. "Well, at least I won't try and fail again."

Wanda settled herself, leaning back against the door, to supervise the vermin eviction. "You ain't no slow leak, Frieda. You do catch on eventually."

CHAPTER
TWENTY-EIGHT

During the summer, Tracy's job expanded to weekends. Theoretically she didn't have to be at every match, meet and tournament, but it wasn't unusual in July and August to have two or three important events running simultaneously over the weekend. When that happened, she was happier in residence, making certain everyone stayed out of everyone else's way.

Truthfully, hanging out at the rec center was something to do now that her social life was as fascinating as an amoeba's. In fact, if her distant memory of college biology was correct, the asexual amoeba could divide itself for company, something Tracy had yet to perfect. CJ had dropped by a few times, once to tell her he would be spending a week in California holed up with his attorneys. Marsh, of course, had as good as disappeared forever.

She spent this Saturday out on the ball field and beside the pool. When she finally headed toward her aging Bimmer and opened her cell phone to check the time, she wasn't surprised to find she had never turned the thing on. What would be the point? Who would call that mattered?

Now she saw she had two messages, both from CJ. She didn't check, figuring she could do that once she put her feet up. Too exhausted to even stop and pick up fast food for dinner, she headed back to her house, sure she had something there she could munch on, even if Kitty wouldn't approve.

She was almost home when she noticed the cars. Three of them parked along the roadside by her house, with a glistening late-model panel van bringing up the rear. Before she'd even parked, she heard music from the direction of her yard. Only one person came to mind.

"CJ!"

Thunderous, she pulled into her driveway and cut the Bimmer's engine. When she opened the car door, the song blaring from a radio was something she recognized from a decade before. She heard laughter, men's laughter. And over both, the familiar rumble of her ex-husband's voice.

She was circling the house toward the back when the smell hit her. Wood smoke. Roasting pork. Barbecue sauce. At the back corner, she stopped and stared. Men, half a dozen or so, were standing around an unfamiliar grill in what passed for her backyard, sucking on beer bottles and laughing uproariously. Two unfamiliar picnic tables draped with blue tablecloths stood off to one side. A man and a woman wearing white aprons were bringing bowls to adorn them.

CJ, standing at the grill, noticed her first, although one of the other men turned and gave her a smile that could have toasted a cheese sandwich. CJ handed his spatula to the man closest to him and strode toward her.

"What —"

He sliced his hand through the air to stop her. Then he grabbed her arm and led her back the way she'd come, far enough that they wouldn't be heard.

"I called you twice," he said.

"I'm no longer required to keep my cell phone by my side so I can be at your beck and call." She shook off his hand. "What's going on here?"

He lowered his voice even more. "I had to make a judgment call, TK. I'm sorry, but when you didn't answer, I decided to go ahead with this."

"That part I can see. Who are they? And where did all the stuff come from?"

He actually looked proud. "It's amazing what you can accomplish if you're in the know. Nanette's favorite caterers took care of everything. They brought in the grill, the tables, the food. You use the best, you get the best."

"Who-are-all-those-men?"

"Shh . . ." He took her arm, even though she tried to shake him off again, and pulled her farther away. "Listen, don't spoil things, okay?"

"If I punch you in the stomach, will that spoil anything?"

He released her again. Quickly. "They're contractors. The best in the area. I've been talking to them about the houses I designed. They're all so busy trying to drum up clients with easy money, I haven't had much luck getting any of them out here. This morning I ran into Leroy — he's the guy with the toupee — and I realized if I invited them for a cookout, I'd get at least some of them out here. So that's what I did. A cookout and a look around the property. Serve barbecue and they will come."

CJ wore his little boy smile, the smile she had once found so endearing. She still wanted to punch him.

"What were you thinking?" She slapped her hands on her hips. "Have I ever said I wanted you to go ahead with this so-called plan of yours?"

"I'm not going ahead with anything. They're here to look the place over. One of them may or may not be interested in building a spec house for you. We're in the early stages, and you can axe the whole thing if you're not happy. But I'm just trying to help you."

"Help?"

"Look, ever since I first heard about this property, I knew it was rich with promise. One of my associates knew the place backward and forward. He used to come here as a kid, and when he described it to me, I couldn't believe nobody'd ever cashed in. Happiness Key has never lived up to its potential, and now you've made that harder by cutting yourself off from millions. But you can still make a good income here. That's all I want for you. I owe you that, TK. Don't make it impossible, okay?"

Her head was swimming. First, she was exhausted and dehydrated. Second, she was just exhausted. She had looked forward to raiding her cupboards and watching reality shows on television. She was in no mood for a party or another perplexing conversation with her ex.

"Change into something pretty, and come out and meet them," CJ said, his gaze flicking over her rec center T-shirt and shorts. "The food's to die for. You'll be relaxed and happy in ten minutes or less, I guarantee it."

CJ leaned over and kissed her on the cheek, then disappeared back the way he had come. To his credit, he did not pat her on the butt to get her moving, as he would have in their mutual past.

A few minutes later Tracy was staring into her closet when she realized why she was feeling so bugged. She was doing what he told her to without question. Changing into something pretty and doing her duty as CJ's hostess had once been her entire life. And now, when she'd had a chance to stand up to him and refuse, she had simply taken the more familiar path. Because now, like then, she was under the influence. Not of alcohol or drugs, but of a man who was absolutely certain he knew what was best for everyone.

The problem? In this case, she wasn't certain he didn't. And that part was familiar, too.

The guys were all friendly, and they all had names straight from Central Casting, like Buck and Skip and Leroy — who had a toupee that looked like seaweed. To a man, they admonished Tracy for signing the conservation agreement. They pored over CJ's plans and made suggestions on better sites, shaking their heads in dismay when he explained that under the agreement, the houses had to be built on the footprints of the old cottages. They walked by her neighbors' homes and made jokes about the shoe box designs and the condition they were in. They drank more beer than Randall's could have fit in its refrigerator case, and consumed their weight in ribs and smoked sausage.

By the time they began to depart, Tracy had developed a splitting headache.

Inside, during her pursuit of ibuprofen, she found the caterers — a couple who called themselves Jack and Jill — rinsing dishes in her sink before piling them into plastic crates for the trip home. Jack was tall and blond, with what, in California, would be considered a surfer tan. Jill was dark-haired and petite, and every bit as capable as Jack at hauling mega pounds of supplies.

"We're just about done, Mrs. Craimer," Jack told her.

"Deloche," she corrected automatically. "Tracy Deloche. CJ and I are not married." Anymore . . .

"Oh, that's right. Sorry. I did know that."

"Everything was great." Tracy manufactured a smile.

"We've packed up the leftovers and put them in your refrigerator. You and Mr. Craimer will have plenty to eat."

This time she didn't bother to correct him. "Great." She thought about Kitty, who would be panic-stricken with all that rich food so close to Tracy's mouth. This time her smile was more genuine.

"Well, I'll leave you to it," she said. "Thanks for everything."

"While you're here," Jack said, "I've got the bill. Would you mind looking it over?"

CJ was outside saying goodbye to the men, and she didn't want to switch places. "Sure, let me see."

Jack rummaged through a notebook with slips of paper hanging out the sides and produced a bill with a copy in yellow attached. "Sorry, it's not our neatest work, but this was really sudden. Luckily this picnic was stuff we could pull together quickly, and it was easy to figure out the costs."

Tracy took the bill and scanned it. Despite the scrawl and a few notes along the side, she could see it was carefully itemized. The total surprised her, but if these were Henrietta's favorite caterers, of course they hadn't come cheaply, plus they'd been asked to pull off something of a miracle in the time allotted. She just wondered where CJ had come up with the money for everything. The amount was comparable to six months of her grocery budget.

"Looks good," she said, handing it back.

"Great. I'll give you a copy. Here's the slip for you to sign."

Tracy frowned. "I'm sorry?"

"Mr. Craimer gave me your credit card. I already swiped it. I'll just enter the amount since you've okayed everything, and we'll be all set."

"I'm sorry?"

He frowned, as if he wasn't sure what to say next. He spoke slowly, as if that would make all the difference. "Mr. Craimer said you would be taking care of the bill? We have to have a card on file before we even buy a napkin. Our standard policy."

"I think there's been a mistake. Let me check with CJ."

Jack held out the slip. "The card he gave me did say Tracy Deloche. Mr. Craimer said you would be taking care of this. Was he mistaken?"

Tracy stared at the slip, read the familiar number from the credit card she kept for emergencies in her desk, then stretched out her arm to take it. Her hand was shaking with fury, but she managed a credible signature. These were Henrietta's caterers, and she couldn't take a chance that they would complain to the rec center benefactress. CJ had out-maneuvered her once again.

CJ!

Jack looked relieved. "We'll just finish packing up," he said.

"Not a moment too soon."

He looked as if he could hardly wait to escape.

Tracy found ibuprofen and doubled the dose. Jack and Jill dismantled the tables and grill, packed them in record time, then roared away in their van, and the contractors peeled off one by one until only CJ and Tracy were left.

She had managed to be polite. She supposed the fact that she *could* be was a sign that she really had matured since her days as the pampered princess of Bel-Air.

CJ followed her inside, and she resisted the desire to lock the door behind him. In the kitchen he opened the refrigerator and gazed at the multitude of containers.

"You've got quite an assortment of leftovers. You won't go hungry this week, that's for certain."

"Oh, they'll have to last longer than a week, I think. Because that's my entire grocery budget until Christmas."

"Yeah, Jack and Jill are a little pricey, I know, but they're the best. Who else could have pulled this off? I'm sure it'll be worth it."

"To whom?"

He closed the refrigerator. "To you. I'm sure not getting anything out of this."

"Good thing, since apparently this was my investment. Totally."

He looked perplexed. "Well, sure. I mean, if I had the money, TK, I'd have treated you, but I don't have two nickels to rub together right now. Maybe if my case is dismissed, I can go after the government for some of what they took from me — us, but until then, I'm as good as penniless."

"So you, the penniless pauper, planned and executed a party on my credit card which you just happened to find in my desk?"

He ignored the part about the desk. "Not a party. A business meeting. And it went well. It went *great.* Buck and Leroy are both interested in building the houses. They've got great ideas for financing —"

"I don't care!"

He fell silent.

CJ towered over her, but Tracy put her hands on her hips, went up on her toes and stood nose to nose. "How dare you throw a party, dig up my credit card and use it to pay for this! These contractors are *your* friends, not mine! And I don't have the money, no matter how fancy their financing is, to build anything here on the key. Not now, probably not ever."

The warmth in his eyes faded. "You never did have a head for business."

"And you never had a thought for anybody but yourself."

"Oh, is that right? You think I did this for myself? Just what am I getting out of it?"

"I'll tell you. You got to play the big man again, CJ. You entertained those guys with my money, and you looked like the CJ everybody used to know. Only you're not that guy anymore, remember? You've been to prison. You've lost everything. You've made everyone who cared about you miserable. There are people all over Southern California who wish you were still rotting in Victorville!"

"And you're one of them? Only you're in

Southern Florida now, living on property I made sure you would keep if anything happened to me."

"Scant comfort when the Feds were carting away my life, piece by piece."

"What life was that? The one I'd made for you? The one I'd given you without a string attached? The only thing I asked for was loyalty and love. And clearly, TK, you had neither to offer. Because when the chips were down, you abandoned me so fast I thought I was watching one of those old Road Runner cartoons. And you left me alone to handle everything on my own."

"Don't you dare try to make me feel guilty!" She was shouting now, but she didn't care. "You only told me the truth when you knew you were finally finished! I was one more detail you had to take care of before they took you away. And sure, you left me this place, but I'm still trying to figure out why, because you could have left me something I could sell or really use to start over. But no, you left me Happiness Key, with conservationists crawling all over it to keep me from doing a thing."

"I don't have to put up with this."

"No, you don't. But apparently I have to put up with a credit card bill I'll be paying for the next year. And I have to put up with reminders of our life together, which I'd rather forget."

"You know what I'm reminded of? That

after everything I've done to show you I've changed, that prison changed me, you're not able to see anything but a stupid credit card bill. You can't see that this party was for you, for *your* future, not mine. I chose Happiness Key for you *because* it had problems, enough that I hoped the Feds wouldn't bother trying to find a way to steal it, too. And I chose it because I had faith in your ability to handle things here. More faith than you've ever, apparently, had in me."

He was making inroads. Even as she was still boiling over with outrage, CJ was beginning to make her question herself. She saw it, felt it and somehow couldn't stop it.

"You are slick," she said, her voice lower. "You always have been, and I have no way of knowing what's real, and what's smoke and mirrors. How can I tell if prison did anything for you? You've never even admitted there was anything that needed to be changed."

He ran a hand through his hair, clearly distracted. "I told you before, I wasn't as careful as I should have been. I let power go to my head. It's a common affliction. But don't tell me you didn't enjoy the rewards."

She heard a jackhammer inside her skull, but somehow she kept talking. "I don't know anything, except that you made a big mistake by throwing this party today. Don't ever do anything like this again, because next time, I'll tell them to bill it to you, even if Henrietta has me fired. I won't rescue you, and I won't play nice. If you're really trying to get into my good graces and prove yourself, this wasn't the way."

"Is there any way to do that, TK? Short of sprouting a halo and angel's wings?"

He didn't wait for a reply. He moved around her, careful not to touch her. In a moment her door slammed, and she was left alone to wonder how one man could raise so many conflicting emotions in one woman.

Tracy thought of herself as relatively uncomplicated. She slept easily and well, rarely gave in to stress, and rarely worried about the things other people obsessed about, except maybe her weight. Apparently those days were behind her.

By five the next morning she gave up pretending to sleep and went for a long run before the sun blazed a path to another miserable day. Afterward she took a glass of ice water out to her patio and watched the world grow lighter.

Why did a relatively uncomplicated woman choose hideously complicated men? Before CJ's reappearance, she'd had a lock on her love life. She and Marsh had been within a hairbreadth of taking their relationship to the next level, and her opinion of CJ had been fixed in stone. She had done all the psychological work an uncomplicated woman ever did and relegated CJ to that slot in her life reserved for *very* big mistakes.

Now Marsh was gone and CJ was back, taking up a lot more space than she had reserved and spreading guilt like dandelion down. And just like dandelions, guilt was turning Tracy's easy-care psyche into a weed patch.

Two men. Two unbearable complications. She was unsuited and unprepared for this much angst, and unsure what to do next.

As Tracy sat staring morosely at the street, "next" arrived in a late-model Jaguar. She recognized the car and its driver just as Henrietta Claiborne stepped out from behind the wheel. Tracy got to her feet, all too aware that she was still dripping sweat.

"I thought you might be an early riser," Henrietta said, coming up the walkway. "Gladys gave me your address."

Tracy held up her hands. "I've been jogging. You might not want to get too close until I shower."

"Have you had breakfast?"

"Not yet."

"Good. I brought it with me. You go take your shower, and I'll have everything ready by the time you get out."

Tracy didn't know what to say. Surely Henrietta, with all her millions, Jaguar and yacht, had better things to do on a Sunday morning than fix Tracy breakfast. On the other hand, who was she to look a gift horse in the mouth?

She ushered Henrietta into the house and kitchen, then retreated to the bathroom, where she followed orders, taking an extra few minutes to wash her hair. She scrunchied it back from her face, and put on clean shorts and a T-shirt, then she went to join the rec center's benefactor.

"I'm out here," Henrietta called from the patio. "It's still in the shade. Want to brave it?"

Tracy discovered Henrietta had set out a platter of cut melons and berries, bagels and cream cheese, and a pitcher of orange juice.

"This looks fabulous. I can make coffee," Tracy offered.

"No need. I brought lattes, if that's okay?"

"Better than okay, but how did you know I'd just be sitting outside waiting for you?"

"That's the thing about being filthy rich. I can take chances."

Tracy remembered never having to think about money. Never worrying about what she spent or what happened to the things she bought. Never clipping coupons, or balancing the joys of a perfect artichoke against a whole bag of carrots and a head of lettuce.

"Have a seat. I'll be right back," Henrietta said.

A moment later Tracy accepted the pricey Starbucks ventisized latte with pleasure. She remembered Starbucks, too.

"So . . ." Henrietta took a seat across from Tracy. "You and CJ have had a falling-out."

There were many things Tracy could say about her ex, but it was not like CJ to run crying to anybody. In fact, the CJ Tracy married had never been outwardly upset with her. Instead, he had simply canceled a social engagement she was looking forward to, or occasionally he had just "forgotten" to come home at night, a stern reminder that she was already wife number three, and he might be scouting for candidate number four.

For some reason, she had put up with it.

"Did he tell you that?" Tracy asked after a careful sip.

"No. Or rather, not until I pulled it out of him. CJ's one of those men who simply hates to appear weak. Most self-made men are that way. They claw their way to the top, and they can never pause, never look down, never hint they've lost their way. They're afraid that if they do, they'll topple all the way to the bottom again."

"CJ's already toppled. Been there, done that."

"He told me about the barbecue."

Tracy tried to smile. "I have enough leftovers for an army. When we're done with breakfast, we can start on lunch."

"I think he feels badly. Does that help?"

"Not that much." Tracy accepted the platter of melon from Henrietta and put some slices of honeydew on her plate. "Tell me, aren't you feeling a little put upon yourself, having him camping out on your yacht for so long? It's been what, a month now?"

"He's very engaging company. A woman my age doesn't have much to offer a man except a listening ear and whatever resources she can spare. I happen to be able to spare a great deal."

"This is a personal question, and I know it borders on rude, but are you being careful? Because with the charm come the requests."

"In other words, is CJ trying to milk me for all I'm worth?"

"Maybe just some of what you're worth."

Henrietta considered. "Can we just say that I may have come into my fortune through the hard work of my second husband, but I've tripled it in the years since his death."

"I know you're nobody's fool."

"I certainly am not. Do I trust your ex completely?" Henrietta shook her head. "Do I leave myself open to manipulation or fraud?" She shook her head again. "Do I think CJ's a better man now than the one you married?" She smiled. "In that last instance, what *I* think is relatively unimportant."

"I'd still love an answer."

"Then I would have to say the jury's still out."

Tracy felt a little better. "I've been sitting

580

here reassessing my worth as a human being. And you know what I've been thinking? When I realized that CJ was going to jail, and we were going to lose everything, I took off so fast I probably whipped up a forest fire."

"You were young — *are* young. The whole situation must have been a terrible shock."

"But did I desert him when he needed me? Should I have done more?"

"Nobody can answer that but you. I will say this. CJ's not a man who accepts help. He makes bargains, but he would never want to be in anybody's debt. I imagine he presented everything to you with that in mind."

Tracy could hear Henrietta's admiration for CJ, but she also heard caution. She felt better, but she was still confused. She wasn't sure either of them saw the real CJ — if there even *was* a real CJ. "Are you here to ask me to give him a second chance?"

Henrietta smiled, and Tracy glimpsed the much younger woman, who had clearly been a beauty.

"I would never presume such a thing," Henrietta said. "I may be an old woman in love with love, but I'm not one who would ever insert myself into a situation. I only wanted you to know that CJ realizes he made an error yesterday. I think adjusting to this different world he finds himself in is something of a stretch. Perhaps I've done him a disservice by giving him such a luxurious place to stay. But I've known him for years, and I believe that before any of us realize it, CJ will be on top of the heap again. I'm sure he has a plan, and he's executing it even now."

"I hope it's not one he'll get executed *for.*"

"I had one other reason to visit you," Henrietta said. "I'm having a house party in Palm Beach the last week in August. Youth camp will be finished, and I'd like you to be my guest. CJ has already accepted. Please come and keep an eye on him? I promise you'll have a wonderful time."

Tracy remembered house parties. She remembered invitations to estates with names instead of addresses. She remembered yachts and private jets and days of never having to lift a finger to care for herself. A wave of nostalgia swept over her. "I'd love to see your house. I'd love to spend that time with you."

"Excellent. I'll count that as a yes." Henrietta glanced at her watch. "And now I really must go." She swept her hand to encompass the table still brimming with food. "Now you have breakfast leftovers to go with your others. You'll be okay, despite CJ's lapse?"

Tracy was embarrassed. "Absolutely okay."

"I like your little house. I would be comfortable here. You've made a good life for yourself. Remember that in the days to come."

Tracy was still wondering exactly what Henrietta had meant an hour after the older woman had left.

CHAPTER
TWENTY-NINE

Wanda hadn't expected Dana and Lizzie to stay on the key. After the way the women had mishandled their piss-poor attempt to figure out who and what Dana was running from, she'd expected Dana to pack in the dead of night and run. Instead, four weeks had passed since that night at Tracy's house, and Dana and Lizzie were still in residence.

Something was up, though. Now Dana always looked tired. In fact most of the time she looked like a horse that had been rode hard and put away wet. Wanda didn't know if her manager was staying up nights worrying her neighbors might turn her in, or just worrying Lizzie's father might catch up with her as easily as Wanda and the others had caught on to her.

During quiet times at the shop, Wanda had tried to get Dana to open up, but quiet times weren't as common as they'd been. In the two weeks since Frieda Mertz had gotten out of the pie business to concentrate on bread

— which was, apparently, decent enough bread at that — Wanda's Wonderful Pies was more or less holding its own. She figured that in addition to the Sunshine Bakery's pie customers, the "eat local" trend was helping, since folks seemed willing to pay more for pies that were made from fresh ingredients. Plus, since it was the season for family reunions and pool parties, several more caterers had begun to order in bulk.

The new rush didn't leave much time to talk to Dana, though, and Dana seemed to prefer it that way, since she always had something important to do whenever Wanda tried. The only thing Wanda knew for sure was that Dana and Pete were still spending a lot of time in each other's company. He stopped by the shop on some pretext a couple of times a week, and they left together to go out to dinner or a movie. For better or worse, Wanda suspected there was more going on than dinner and entertainment. In fact when Lizzie was staying overnight with Olivia, Wanda suspected Dana and Pete were entertaining each other up a storm. But whether they were or weren't, something still wasn't right in Dana's life.

On Thursday, Wanda flipped the Closed sign about half an hour earlier than usual. Dana came in from the back, where she had been scrubbing the sink. She always did a good job, but the kitchen would never look as clean as it had the night Frieda scrubbed the room from top to bottom after catching all the critters she'd set loose. During the process, Wanda had taken a secret photo or two with her cell phone. She figured someday she would need something to smile about.

Dana handed Wanda her time sheet for the week. "Everything's clean and put away. And you've got ten crusts in the refrigerator for the morning. Were you able to get the lemons?"

Juicy Florida lemons had been surprisingly hard to come by this year, but too many people thought summer and lemons went together and needed their lemon meringue pies like they needed a tan or brand-new flip-flops.

"I got a big old bag coming tomorrow. If they're any good that should help."

Dana untied the strings of her apron. "I called Alice and told her I'd pick up the girls at youth camp. So I'd better scoot. Want me to check back afterward?"

"I won't be here. What with Kenny home for a change, I plan to make a real dinner tonight. And I got plans for the rest of the evening, too."

"He goes back to Georgia next week?"

To Wanda, Dana didn't sound casual. She sounded like a woman who hoped the neighborhood cop would stay as far away as possible. Yet, if Dana needed protection from a stalker, why wasn't she happy to have Ken close by? Unless she had, as she had so vehemently denied, taken the law into her own hands and ended Ray Strickland's stalking once and for all.

"Wanda?" Dana sounded perplexed.

"Sorry." Wanda realized she hadn't answered. "He goes back on Monday. For another week. Then he'll be home awhile until September rolls around. I'll sure be glad to have him here." She met Dana's eyes. "You should be, too."

Dana didn't pretend to misunderstand. "I can't involve the police in my situation. You have no idea how far Roy's reach extends and how many people he's paid off to look the other way."

Wanda was offended and knew it showed. "Kenny wouldn't sell you out to anybody."

"I'm sorry, I know that. I'm not questioning Ken's honesty. But one cop gets involved, others down the line have to, especially with Roy going underground."

"I haven't told Kenny, and I don't intend to." Wanda didn't add that she *had* asked Ken to check on Pete, and now that he was back at the station today and tomorrow, she hoped he would have time to.

"I appreciate it, Wanda. You know I do. I'm sure you don't like keeping secrets from your husband."

"You go on now. I'm ready to go myself.

I'll lock up."

After Dana left, she did just that. The back door had a sturdier lock now, one Frieda Mertz would never be able to thwart with a credit card. Wanda was ashamed she hadn't replaced it first thing before she moved in, her being a cop's wife and all. She figured if Ken had been around more, he would have insisted.

But Ken *was* going to be home tonight. She smiled, and even though nobody was there to see it, she wiggled her penciled eyebrows coquettishly.

An hour later she wasn't wiggling anything. She was looking at the report an exhausted Ken had handed her just before his cell phone rang. She'd read it while he had one of his normal grunting, one-word-answer conversations with somebody at the station. The facts about one Peter Knight were scribbled in Ken's slanty handwriting, since checking out Pete wasn't exactly aboveboard.

"Nothing wrong with him I could find," Ken said, slipping his phone back in his pocket. "A stand-up guy."

"But it says here Pete was a cop."

"I thought you already knew that."

"He told Tracy he was military."

Ken took the notes and pointed. "That, too. Army National Guard in North Dakota. Weekend warrior. Military police. He put in twenty years before he retired."

"Why didn't he tell Tracy he was a police detective, too?"

"Maybe he thought it didn't matter. What's worrying you?"

Wanda couldn't tell Ken the truth. Not without using Dana's name. "I just don't like that he didn't mention it, that's all. I mean, guys who don't come clean about simple things are capable of hiding others."

"He doesn't have a blemish on his record. Not anywhere. Started young and worked his way up. Now he's just here enjoying the rewards." Ken grinned boyishly. "Which I'm hoping to do after I get back this evening."

"Back?"

"Sorry, but they've got a guy in custody who might be the one who broke into that jewelry store over on Tanner. Remember? I was working on the follow-up before the Georgia opportunity. But I'll just be gone a couple of hours, and it's still early. When I get back, if you don't feel like making dinner, I'll take you out. Anywhere you want to go."

She was too busy considering what she'd learned about Pete to be offended. Besides, she knew better than to protest. Ken was so much happier at his job than he'd been last year that she sure wasn't going to interfere.

"I'll see you when you get back," she said. "We'll figure out what to do then."

He kissed her goodbye. She waited until she heard his car drive away, then she headed out the door to find the other women and discuss what they should do next.

Dana's uneasiness was growing. She had come to Happiness Key for two reasons. She'd fulfilled the first before she and Lizzie moved in, but fulfilling the second seemed increasingly impossible. She was superstitious enough that speaking ill of the dead was forbidden, but as always, she wished that the man whose ashes were now eternally a part of the bay and gulf he had loved, had never tantalized her with the promise of a better life for Lizzie.

Had he not, she wouldn't be in this place with women she was, against her better judgment, beginning to regard as friends. She wouldn't be in this place with Pete Knight, who she was, against her better judgment, falling in love with. She wouldn't be in this place where her real identity and reason for being here might be discovered.

"Then I can go?" Lizzie asked. "You're going to let me?"

Dana pulled herself back to the conversation at hand. It was five o'clock and only growing later. "Okay. Just get your pajamas and things together while I check with Alice. And don't forget your inhaler."

"I already told you, Mrs. Brooks said she would drive us to Jody's house."

Jody was another youth camper, and she

had invited Olivia and Lizzie to her house for a sleepover. Sleepovers, like so many things, had been rare in Lizzie's life. There were no cats on the premises — Lizzie had made sure to check — and Jody lived just over the bridge in a development Dana was familiar with. She could reach her daughter in minutes if she had to, and while Lizzie was away and the light was still good, she could use the metal detector and search just one more time.

"I'm going to check anyway, because that's what mothers do," she told her daughter.

Lizzie rolled her eyes, but not for long. She was off like a Thoroughbred at the starting gate to stuff her backpack.

Dana called Alice and was reassured that yes, Alice would drive the girls to Jody's house. She was going out for dinner anyway, so it wasn't an imposition.

Dana hung up and calculated. Pete was due that evening, but if Lizzie left now, Dana might have as many as two hours to search.

Lizzie was back in minutes with her pack weighting her narrow shoulders, and her eyes dancing. She promised she had everything she needed, including the inhaler. Dana thought of all the things she'd been forced to deny her daughter and was glad this had not been one of them. At least when Lizzie looked back on their months here, she would have happy memories.

Dana gave the protesting preteen a hug and

sent her on her way. Ten minutes later, after she witnessed Alice's car backing out of the driveway, she went to the utility shed at the back of the house to get the metal detector. She was hauling it around the side to her car when she saw her neighbors approaching. Tracy, Wanda and Janya were walking together, and they looked oddly serious. For a moment Dana considered ducking back the way she had come. She could go inside and pretend she wasn't home. But when Tracy raised a hand in greeting, Dana knew she'd been spotted.

She leaned the detector up against the cinder block wall and told herself to behave naturally. Maybe this was just another invitation to an impromptu sunset party. Maybe the women had seen Lizzie leaving with Alice and Olivia, and thought she might be lonely.

At closer range, the women's grim expressions put that fantasy to rest.

"What's up?" Dana asked, willing herself to sound calm.

"You have a minute?" Wanda asked.

"I was just heading out for a walk."

"We've got something we have to talk to you about."

Not "like to" talk to you about. "Have to," as if Dana's own opinion in the matter was of no consequence. She wondered if, in pursuit of a happy ending, Wanda had broken her word and told her husband all the things

591

the women *thought* they knew about her. She wondered if he was even now digging into a past that had nothing to do with hers.

"Would you like to come inside?" she asked, with no genuine invitation in her voice.

"We don't need to trouble you. Let's sit out here." Wanda gestured to some folding chairs in the shadiest spot in the yard.

"Why don't I get some cold drinks for —"

"No need," Wanda said. "But there's something you got to know."

Dana gave up trying to delay the conversation. She gave a slight nod and led the way. Wanda pulled one of the chairs closer so that the women formed a circle.

"So what's this about?" Dana struggled to sound calm.

"I promised I wouldn't tell Kenny anything about you, and I didn't," Wanda said, without preamble. "But I didn't promise anybody I wouldn't have him check out somebody else. Janya here came across Pete looking through your mail a couple of weeks ago —"

"On the Fourth of July," Janya said. "He claimed you had asked him to pick it up and bring it into town when he joined you there for the parade."

Dana tried to remember if she had ever asked such a thing. Her relationship with Pete was filled with little intimacies now. It had become difficult to keep up her guard and

592

not involve him in the minutiae of her daily life.

"I can't say I did, but I can't say I didn't, either," she said, fear like a spider scurrying up her spine.

"I didn't like it," Wanda said. "What did we know about him except what he told Tracy?"

"He gave me references, and I called them," Tracy said. "I didn't have any reason to be worried. Everyone said he was great."

"But nobody told her the whole truth," Wanda said. "And the truth is that Pete retired in the spring from the Grand Forks, North Dakota, police department. He was well-respected, a detective with a lot of years on the force, but why didn't he tell Tracy here, or you, for that matter, what he really did for a living?"

For the first time Dana understood, *really* understood, how her daughter felt when she could not suck air into her lungs. Dana was so stunned, so frozen, that for a moment she was afraid she might never be able to breathe again.

Janya, who was sitting closest, put her hand on Dana's knee, reassuringly. "Perhaps he did tell you?"

Dana willed herself to breathe, willed herself to act as if this was not a surprise. But she was sure she had already given herself away. She scrambled for something to say, something to make them leave so she could make sense of it.

But there was no sense to be made. Pete Knight must have tracked her here to Florida where, because of her family's connection to this place, she should never have come. Now he was probably making certain he had the right woman before he destroyed her life and her daughter's.

"I thought Pete was in the military," she said carefully, keeping her voice as light as she could. "But maybe I just misunderstood."

"He was," Wanda said. "National Guard. So he wasn't lying. He just wasn't telling everything."

Tracy leaned forward. "Dana, like Wanda told Janya and me, a lot of ex-cops become private investigators after they retire or leave the job behind. Is it possible Pete was hired by somebody in Stockton to find you?"

"I don't think so," Dana said. This, at least, wasn't a lie. "It's a stretch to think any of the Stricklands would go as far afield as North Dakota to find an investigator, isn't it?"

"But we don't know he stayed in North Dakota after he retired. Maybe he always wanted to live in California, so afterward he went there."

"I guess it's possible, though unlikely," Dana said, trying to sound skeptical. "But he's been here in Florida since May, and it's nearly August. If he believed I was Carol Kelly, then he would have found all the proof

594

he needed by now and gone on to another job."

"How? By looking through your mail?" Wanda asked.

"I may have asked him to get it that day. I just don't remember." Dana steeled herself to lie. "I'd trust Pete with my life. He's not trying to hurt me or Lizzie. He's a good guy, and I'm sure I would have picked up something, some vibe, some clue, by now if he was investigating me. I know you're all worried, but I think Pete just suspected I'm not that fond of cops, so he didn't make a point that he'd been one. That's all."

Wanda didn't look convinced. "I'm going to ask Ken to find out if Pete did go to California after he retired. Maybe he got a P.I. license and Ken can find out. The laws are different in different places, but we could check."

"Please don't," Dana said. "Really. Please don't. Ken's going to wonder what this is all about, if he doesn't wonder already. Then he'll be asking questions about *me.* You're going to chase me away, Wanda. And I know you don't want to do that. I'll be careful. I'll pay attention and watch Pete closer for a while. I will, I promise. You're all good friends."

Tears sprang to her eyes because they *were* good friends, and after today she would never see them again.

"You're sure?" Wanda asked.

"Please, just leave this alone now. I've been warned. I'll handle it from here."

The women glanced at each other. Dana saw Wanda give the slightest shrug. Dana hoped that meant she had a little time. She needed just enough to pack up the few indispensable things she and Lizzie owned, and drive across the bridge to drag her protesting daughter away from her new friends. All before Pete arrived for the evening.

Pete, who had probably been on her trail for years.

Dana got to her feet in dismissal. "Thank you for caring. Lizzie and I are lucky."

"You'll be careful?" Tracy looked concerned.

"I'm the most careful person you've ever met." Except, of course, this once, when caution had failed her completely.

The others stood, and Dana walked them down the driveway. All dreams of a better life for Lizzie had evaporated. If she and her daughter were lucky enough to get away, they would continue their hand-to-mouth existence. Before his death, Fargo had tried to set her life and Lizzie's on a better path. Dana hoped it gained him points in whatever afterlife had awaited him.

Then again, her brother had never believed in an afterlife. From earliest childhood he had lived exclusively for the moment. Only at the end, in prison, when he knew his moments were numbered, had he thought to contact her and tell her to go back to Happiness Haven and search for her own happy ending.

"You will be okay?" Janya asked.

"I make a habit of it," Dana said.

"You let me know if you change your mind," Wanda said. "I still think Ken could do a little research and put your mind to rest . . . or not."

Dana managed the trace of a smile. "I'll do that. You have a good evening."

She watched them walk down the road. Time was passing. Pete hadn't been clear about when he would arrive this evening, so she didn't know how much time she had. She just knew that she had to time her departure carefully. She didn't want the women to see her leave, but she couldn't wait until it was dark or Pete might show up.

She thought of other times here, times when she and Fargo had still been young enough to believe that life was easy and happiness was guaranteed. His life had ended in a prison hospital.

She hoped that hers didn't end in prison, too.

CHAPTER THIRTY

"So, did you believe her?" Wanda asked, as the three women started back toward their houses.

While they were still in earshot of Dana's place, Tracy had asked herself the same question and been unable to answer. Now that they weren't, she still didn't have a clue.

She tried to put thoughts into words. "Like I said when you first told us about Pete, he and Dana have had more than a few opportunities for serious pillow talk. And if you watched her expression when you told her Pete used to be a cop, you know she was stunned. She looked like somebody who just found out her best friend was murdered."

"But would it not be bad enough news just to learn the man you were intimate with hadn't told you something so important?" Janya asked. "That could explain the reaction."

"No, it was more like she thought she was in danger."

"I need a drink and a chance to mull this over," Wanda said. "You two have time?"

As usual, Tracy had no plans for the evening. Every night since her breakfast with Henrietta, she had considered calling CJ to apologize. Every evening she had stopped short of picking up the telephone.

Maybe she was simply not a person who forgave easily, although she'd never thought of herself that way. But she couldn't seem to overcome her suspicions. She was unconvinced that CJ's arrival in Florida had been motivated by a desire for a reunion with his ex, yet she couldn't find any other reason for his presence here or his interest in making Happiness Key a going concern. He had gone over the property with a fine-tooth comb, just to help her.

Maybe prison had changed him after all.

"I've got a great bottle of Zinfandel," she told Wanda, thinking of the one Marsh had arrived with on the night she'd ruined their plan for mutual seduction. "I've been saving it, but I don't know for what."

"You keep saving it," Wanda said. "I'm making margaritas."

They followed Wanda to her house. Janya rarely drank, but she made an exception for Wanda's margaritas. The women didn't have much to say as Wanda assembled ingredients and the blender whirred. They took the finished product into her eye-popping living room, with its neon colors and tropical prints. George, a lime-green stuffed monkey puppet, peered down from a shelf adorned with photos of Elvis at his sexiest, and Wanda's kids and grandkids.

"So help me, I'm losing my mind, but I'm beginning to see why you painted these walls orchid," Tracy said. "It's a lift just to walk in here."

"You need a lift?"

"I need to understand why my life has fallen apart again."

"Take more than some paint on my walls to do that."

Tracy wanted to get back to the reason they were here. "What are the chances Pete Knight was hired to look for Carol Kelly?"

Wanda looked annoyed. "I can't believe she doesn't want me to check with Kenny."

"What do we know for sure about Dana?" Tracy asked, to circumvent the oncoming diatribe.

Janya was the first to speak. "We know we like her. We know she is an exemplary mother."

"She's a good worker," Wanda said. "She pitches in no matter how dirty or hard a job is. She's creative. She doesn't sit around and wish business was better. She makes it better."

"She is . . ." Janya looked as if she was searching for the right word, as Alice often had to do. "Wary," she said. "Careful with what she says. Perhaps suspicious is not too strong a word."

"That could be explained by that Roy Strickland and his brothers," Wanda said. "It only makes sense."

"Ray," Tracy corrected automatically. "Ray Strickland."

"No, it's not," Wanda said. "Roy."

"I'm the one who got Marsh to look this up, remember? I'm the one who got the printouts. I can guarantee you, it's Ray Strickland. *Ray.*"

Wanda didn't respond, and Tracy thought she was just preparing an argument.

Then Wanda's eyes widened. "*She* said Roy."

"She who?"

"Dana! This afternoon at the shop. That's where I got it from. I was trying to get her to open up, which is like trying to pry open an oyster shell with your fingernails. I told her Kenny would be staying home for a while, and she looked unhappy. So I said she ought to be happy he was around, too, just in case. Then she said she didn't trust the police and . . ." Wanda stopped.

"What did she say?" Tracy demanded.

"She said *Roy* had paid off a lot of cops, or something like that."

"I think you just heard it wrong," Tracy said. "Ray, Roy, easy mistake."

"No, I didn't! You can bet your ever-loving tushy I was concentrating on that insult to cops in general, but I heard the name right. Dana said *Roy*. The only reason it didn't hit me then was because I was so busy trying to defend Kenny."

Janya interceded. "If this man is stalking her, why did she use the wrong name? Is that not something she would remember only too well?"

The women looked at each other.

"Not if she'd never heard it until the night we confronted her," Tracy said, brain in overdrive. "Not if Dana *isn't* Carol Kelly, and she'd never heard of anybody named Kelly or Strickland until that night. We hit her with a lot at the same time, remember? *We* told *her* who she was. We didn't ask her to tell us. Could she have mixed up the names? Because neither Roy nor Ray meant a thing to her?"

"Then who is she?" Wanda looked angry now. "If she's not Carol Kelly, *who is she?*"

Tracy continued thinking out loud. "And if she's not Carol Kelly, and she's not from Stockton, California, she could be from any-where."

"She could be from North Dakota," Janya said. "Perhaps she and Pete knew each other before this, and she was unhappy we learned more about him."

Tracy continued guessing. "Or maybe Pete really is on her trail for something else, something we don't know yet. It's pretty clear she's running. And it's just as clear she wanted to throw us off the scent, so she played along with our bad amateur detective work."

"I'm confused," Wanda said. "And I'm angry. Here we've all been so worried about her, trying to watch out for those Strickland goons, giving her all the sympathy we can, and she's been lying to us."

"If she is lying," Janya said, "I think the reason must be a good one. I would not assume she is just trying to, what is it you say, pull the cotton over our heads?"

"Pull the wool over our eyes," Tracy said. "And we did that ourselves. Dana never came to us, *we* went to *her*. But don't forget, we discovered for real that she borrowed another woman's and child's names and birth certificates. That's indisputable. What would you do in her situation if somebody confronted you with that, then supplied a perfectly sympathetic, logical reason before you had time to invent one yourself? Would you say, no, wait a minute, let me think of a better explanation?"

"She could have told us the truth!" Wanda said.

"Not if it's a truth we're better off not knowing."

"I think she will leave now," Janya said softly. "I think Pete must be part of this in

603

some way, and now that she knows he was a police officer from North Dakota, that will scare her into her car and over the bridge forever."

"Maybe that'll be better," Wanda said, clearly upset at the lies.

Tracy could understand. Of all of them, Wanda was closest to Dana. She was the one who had told Dana about the house, the one who had offered the woman a job. She was the one who had introduced Dana to the other women and vouched for her.

"Think of Lizzie," Tracy said quietly. "If we can help, we should."

"We don't know who we're helping do we?" Janya asked. "If Pete came here to find her, we must ask why."

"We need to go back and talk to her," Tracy said. "We need to see if there's anything we can do."

"You're not exactly the best judge of character," Wanda said. "Seeing as you married CJ and went juking with Lee Symington whenever you could. You're a psychopath magnet."

Tracy noticed Wanda didn't mention Marsh. "Are you coming or not?"

"Don't go and think you can leave me out of this." Wanda put down her margarita and strode to the door. "*You* coming?"

Dana had already packed her own suitcase

and started on Lizzie's. She hated choosing what mattered most to her daughter, but there was no time for a consultation. Her hands were trembling, and she was trying to think ahead as she threw in underwear and jeans and pajamas. She had cash hidden in her closet, not much, and tomorrow was payday, but she would have to say goodbye to her paycheck. She couldn't wait another day to leave, and after she moved on, she couldn't send for it.

She didn't know how far the cash would take her. She had an emergency fund in a bank account in Texas, money left from the sale of her parents' farm fifteen years ago, but not much. The account was the only cushion she'd ever had, and it had dwindled from five figures to four. Now it was on the downward slide to three. But she would have to take what was left and close it. This was the emergency that had always haunted her.

"Damn it, Fargo. Why did you send us here on a wild-goose chase?"

She threw in the stuffed seal Lizzie always dragged with her from town to town. She threw in books and CDs and, of course, the beloved coin collection. The suitcase was bulging, but she managed to zip it. She was wheeling it toward the back door when someone knocked on the front.

She stood, terrified, and hoped whoever it was would go away.

That was not to be. She heard the sound of a key in the lock and the door swung open. Her neighbors were inside before she could protest.

"You're not Carol Kelly," Tracy said without a greeting. "We've figured that much out. Help us figure out the rest of it."

"I'd like you to leave," Dana said, drawing herself up to her full height. "This is my house, and you're intruding."

"It doesn't look like it's going to be your house long," Wanda said with a sniff. "Seems to me you're heading somewhere, and I'll bet you don't intend to come back."

With the evidence right there, Dana couldn't object. "There's no law against moving on."

"There might be if you *broke* the law."

She slumped a little. "Please. You've been my friends. Just let this go. Let *me* go. I can't stay —"

"Because of Pete, right?" Tracy said. "Because of what we told you about him?"

"It doesn't matter."

Wanda moved closer. "Sure it does. If he's a threat, we can help. Kenny can —"

"No! Please, don't tell your husband!"

Wanda fell silent. Finally she shook her head. "I'm going to have to tell him, Dana. It was one thing to stay quiet about somebody stalking you. But what if you're the guilty party? You've already involved us in your lies.

How can we let that go on?"

Dana began to cry. She had been running so long, and she never got far enough away, no matter where she went.

Janya moved closer, then put her arm around Dana's shoulders. "Please, nobody wants to hurt you."

Dana couldn't seem to stop the tears. "This is about Lizzie," she said through them. "That's all you need to know. Whatever you do, whoever you tell, she'll be the one who suffers."

"Why?" Tracy asked, moving to Dana's other side. "Is this a custody issue? Are you running from Lizzie's father?"

Dana knew she couldn't lie again. The women wouldn't rest until they knew, and now they would track her. They would involve the police. She was sure of it. She put her face in her hands. "No, Lizzie's father is dead."

"Did you kill him?" Tracy asked softly.

Dana's head shot up. "No! I haven't killed anybody! I never even knew him."

"How can that be?"

"Lizzie is not my child!"

The room went still. Even the clock on the wall seemed to stop ticking.

"You kidnapped her?" Wanda asked. "My God."

"It's not what you think. It's not what it sounds like. Please. Just let it go."

"What are the chances?" Tracy asked.

Dana knew that was just an expression, but in this case, a sensible one. What *were* the chances? Dana realized the women would never rest until they knew everything now.

"I have to sit." Dana made her way to a chair. She lifted her T-shirt and wiped her eyes on the hem.

"You need to tell us what's going on," Wanda said. "The truth."

Dana hadn't told the truth in so long, she wasn't sure she remembered how. But despite the possible consequences, the truth was a glimmer of light. The truth, and nothing but. A gift taken from her. And now her gift to give.

"I don't want to talk to Kenny, but I will," Wanda said.

Dana didn't know what to do except trust them. "My real name is Isabel Carlsen. Eleven years ago I was a social worker in Grand Forks, North Dakota. I worked in Children's Services."

Janya had gone into the kitchen for a glass of water, and now she handed it to Dana, who took a grateful sip.

The story was long, but there was no time for the nuances. Dana outlined the facts. "My caseload was long, too long. I worked night and day trying to do my job. My husband left me. He wasn't a man with much patience. We'd . . ." She took another sip, because this part was hard. "We'd lost a baby at birth. I worked harder to forget both things, I guess."

She was a little calmer now, but her voice had lost all traces of animation. "I was careful not to let my clients work their way into my heart. If you've ever done that kind of work, you know how hard that is. But I did okay, except for one little girl. A baby, Ivy Greenwald. Greta, the mother, had never married. The father on record died in some accident, and his parents refused to believe the child was his. The government thought she was, and after his death made Social Security payments for the baby. Greta was a chronic liar and a drug addict, and Ivy was tiny and had problems from birth. We didn't want her to go home with Greta once she was well enough to leave the hospital, but the judge assigned to the case thought she'd be fine, and of course, Greta wanted the Social Security. That judge was a sticking point for all of us, a man who believed children are the property of their parents and the state must respect that. In my three years with the agency, he never agreed to terminate any parent's rights."

"That's awful," Tracy said.

"Over the course of Ivy's first year we went back to court twice. I spent so many hours working up the case. Making impromptu visits, gathering evidence. Ivy was wasting away, but Greta took a parenting class, and she made promises. The judge thought she was trying, and that was good enough for him."

She looked up, and the emotion returned. "Then, one night, after we had failed three times to take Ivy and put her into a responsible foster home, I made another surprise visit. By then Greta realized the judge was never going to remove Ivy, and she didn't even try to hide what was going on. I heard Ivy wailing. They lived in a hovel, and the lock on the front door was broken. Any money Greta got went straight for whatever drug she was using that month. I let myself in. Greta was passed out on the floor. And Ivy was in her crib, covered in filth. You have no idea. I can't describe it. Her diaper hadn't been changed, probably for days. On the floor beside the crib was a bottle. The milk was obviously spoiled. It was thick and clotted, but the baby . . . the baby was trying to reach it."

She swallowed, and the picture, which had never really left her mind, came back in detail. She realized the other women were seeing it, too. Janya's eyes were filling with tears.

"So I took her." Dana cleared her throat. "I knew even if I got her into temporary foster care again, the judge would just send her back to her mother after Greta sobered up. I knew without a shadow of a doubt that Ivy wasn't going to survive the system. I just walked over to the crib, and I lifted her out, and I stepped over Greta on the floor and I took her. And I have never let go of her in all these years."

Wanda looked stricken. Tracy, too, had tears in her eyes.

"How in heaven did you get away with it?" Wanda asked.

"Providence. Greta finally came to, and I guess she had no memory of anything that had happened for days. That's what the papers said months later. The baby was gone, and she didn't know where. She probably wondered if she'd left Ivy somewhere, or given her to somebody or done something worse. So she didn't report her missing. She just kept taking the Social Security payments and hoped nobody would notice Ivy was gone."

"Somebody must have," Wanda said.

"Eventually the neighbors reported they hadn't seen or heard the baby, and when somebody finally investigated, Greta couldn't tell them where she was. Because she hadn't reported it herself, Greta was arrested. They had no body, no evidence, but they held her awhile on charges of neglect and fraud."

"And where were you?"

"By then we were in California. I'd quit my job and pleaded burnout. That wasn't uncommon, and nobody really questioned my decision. It certainly wasn't the first time somebody had just refused to come back to work. Ivy improved so quickly in my care it was almost a miracle. After a start like that, some children lose the will to live and wither away. I've seen that, too. But not Ivy. She's a fighter and always was. I saw the newspaper accounts of the Turner mother and baby after we got to California, and knew taking their identities was my chance for a fresh start. So I secured copies of their birth certificates, and we became Dana and Elizabeth Turner."

"And what about Ivy's natural mother? What about Greta?"

"The local cops looked everywhere for the baby. They wanted Greta for murder, of course, but months had passed before Ivy's disappearance was discovered, and they knew they had little chance of finding a body. Greta told them she'd been so afraid she'd be accused of murder that she kept silent. It was one of the few times in her life she actually told the truth."

"You let her go to prison for a crime she didn't commit?" Wanda asked.

"No. Believe me, had it ever gotten to that point, I would have returned. I wouldn't have let the woman spend her life in prison, not even if she deserved it. But they finally had to release her, with the idea, I think, that they would arrest her again if a body was found. Two weeks later Greta overdosed and died.

No body, no evidence, the obvious suspect dead by her own hand. Most people thought poor little Ivy was just another casualty of a legal system that doesn't value children."

"Then why are you running?" Wanda asked.

"This was an emotional case for everybody. The cops who were working it wanted closure. Even after Greta died, they kept searching. Of course I couldn't ask anybody what was going on, couldn't contact any of my old friends or colleagues, because that would lead straight back to me, but I discovered whatever I could. And one day I saw my name mentioned in an interview with the police chief. The police were looking for me because they thought I might have some insight into the case as Ivy's social worker."

"They didn't connect your disappearance with the baby's?" Wanda sounded incredulous.

"They would have, if they had known exactly when Ivy disappeared. But, of course, Greta would never tell them, because I suppose she knew the longer Ivy's disappearance had gone on, the more guilty she'd look. Their best guess was off by a whole month."

"Well, luck fell your way on that," Wanda said.

Dana felt as if she couldn't stop until it was all out in the open. "More than you know. After I left Children's Services, my caseload was divided among the other workers while my replacement was trained. Apparently somebody made a scheduled visit to Greta, who must have passed off a friend's baby as Ivy. The worker was a stranger to the case and wouldn't have known one baby from another. Supposedly the house looked clean enough, and Greta was sober. That much was in the papers. More time passed before the real Ivy's absence was discovered. So the visit confused the timing, too."

"But still somebody is looking for you?" Tracy asked.

"Because the system had done so little to protect her, Ivy's loss was strongly felt. The judge was forced off the bench. Learning the truth about the baby's death became even more important to some of the detectives on the police force. The case is still mentioned in the local papers. Not often, but often enough. And I can't take the chance of anybody ever connecting Lizzie and me with Isabel Carlsen and Ivy Greenwald. Because that would destroy my daughter — and she *is* mine. Make no mistake about it, Lizzie is mine in every way that matters. If I hadn't taken her when I did, I am absolutely sure she would have died."

The other women didn't try to dispute that, each of them clearly affected by what she had heard.

"Does Lizzie know any of this?" Tracy asked at last.

"No."

"Are you going to tell her?"

This was a question Dana asked herself over and over, but she didn't have an answer. "If I can. If the time is ever right. But probably? No."

"How do you think Pete Knight tracked you here?"

Dana twisted her hands. The women knew so much now, but there was more. She debated what to tell them, but her lies were all used up.

"I had a brother. Fargo was a free spirit who lived by his own rules. My parents thought he was the family black sheep because he was always in trouble. We were a churchgoing family, but Fargo hated religion and any kind of rules, and that infuriated my parents. I was the only one at home who ever tried to understand him. The happiest times we ever spent together were here, at Happiness Haven."

Tracy looked the most surprised. "You mean the old resort? The one this house is part of?"

Dana nodded. "We always stayed in the cottage Alice lives in now. My mother's cousin and her husband owned the place. His family built it. Fargo, my mother and I came every July during school vacation. Mom helped in the office while we were here, and Fargo and I had our run of the place. I think Pete must have learned that somehow and decided to see if I'd been back to this area."

"I'll be," Wanda said. "You've been here before. And here I was, showing you around."

"After I took Lizzie and ran, Fargo was the only person who knew what I'd done. Our parents were gone by then, and I was sure he, of all people, wouldn't turn me in. By then Fargo wasn't just a black sheep, he'd been in and out of jail on half a dozen different charges. He was the last person who would ever go to the police. He even helped a little. Sent me money a few times, and did some checking in Grand Forks, so I'd know what was happening with the investigation. For a while he was my eyes and ears. That's how I knew the cops weren't letting go of the case the way they might have."

"Pete's name never came up?"

"Fargo couldn't get too close."

"What does your brother have to do with this now?" Janya asked.

"Fargo went to work for somebody in New Mexico. I don't know what he did. I probably don't want to know. I am sure he was making a lot of money, and from time to time he sent me some. Dana Turner has no college degree. Isabel Carlsen's master's in social work is useless, so I had to take low-paying jobs to support us, and sometimes it wasn't enough. But a few years later Fargo was arrested for a bank robbery that had taken place years before. He went to prison and died of kidney failure. But before he died, he sent me a letter."

She paused, wondering if she should share the words that were engraved in her memory. Then she shrugged, because she had given up hoping they would do her any good now. "I couldn't go to the prison to visit him, of course. I couldn't identify myself as his sister and chance someone finding me. So Fargo wrote me as if Dana Turner was a girlfriend from his past. And he asked that I be given his ashes after cremation. His final letter came with them."

She looked up. "I committed his ashes to the bay at a place just at the edge of your property, Tracy. It's a little inlet the locals call Fortunate Harbor. It was our favorite place as children. Ask a native about it someday. They'll tell you the story of how it got its name."

"What was in the letter that made you come here? Did he just ask you to scatter his ashes there?"

"It was strangely cryptic and flowery, nothing like his usual letters, which were riffs on prison life. He said he wished he had more to leave me, but the memories we shared were a haven of happiness."

"Happiness Haven," Tracy said, understanding right away.

"Yes. Then he went on to say he hoped I

would find those memories in my heart and examine them carefully, because memories are golden. He ended by saying I would be fortunate if I looked to the heavens, where he would be watching me, because then I would have the key to my own happiness."

"A strange message," Janya said. "What do you think he was trying to tell you?"

"Fargo and I rarely spoke. But in our last phone call before he was arrested, he told me he was working on something big, and if it panned out, he was going to share the results. He liked to brag, so I didn't pay much attention at the time. I told him I didn't want any ill-gotten gains, but he said he had earned this fair and square. He told me he was going to 'our old stomping grounds,' and when I asked him what he meant, he said he couldn't say more, but he sure didn't mean the family farm."

"So he came here?" Wanda asked.

"It's all there in the letter. Happiness Haven, the key to happiness — Happiness Key — my being 'fortunate' if I paid attention to what he was trying to tell me."

"Look to the heavens?"

"Yes, because he would be dead by the time I got here. And the only thing I would have to go on was his letter."

The women pondered Dana's words. Tracy was the first to speak. "What do you think it means?"

"I think Fargo buried something, and I can only imagine it's gold, since he says our memories were 'golden.' Coins or bullion, I don't know. It's on the key somewhere. I think he converted his assets and buried the result for safekeeping, so if he got into trouble, the gold would be waiting for him when he got out of prison. But years of hard living caught up with him."

Tracy didn't look convinced. "I can see why he didn't just stash whatever it was in a bank where it could be traced back to him and confiscated. But why here? The land didn't belong to him. Wasn't he afraid someone would develop it and find whatever he'd left in the process?"

"I've figured that out. At the time of our last phone call, the husband of my mother's cousin was in a nursing home, but he still owned the property. By then Happiness Haven had been abandoned for some time, and the only thing of value was the land. Fargo must have thought burying whatever he did was a temporary measure, and that even if the old man died, any sale would take long enough to complete that he'd have plenty of time to get back and dig up whatever it was. But things turned out differently. The old man died immediately afterward, and his heirs, our distant cousins, sold the property immediately. Your husband bought it, Tracy, to turn it into Happiness Key, and right afterward, before he could get back here, Fargo went to prison."

"And whatever he left behind is still here," Wanda said.

Dana rose. "I'll never know. I've got to leave tonight, before Pete gets here. And you've got to let me. Please. I have to protect Lizzie. If all this comes out, I'll go to jail and they'll slap her in foster care. Our life isn't perfect, but I'm the only mother she knows."

"What you did?" Wanda said. "It's what anybody who loves kids would have done in —"

"Look to the heavens," Janya said, interrupting. "I think perhaps you have made a mistake, Dana. Exactly where have you looked for this golden memory?"

Dana was perplexed by the question. "I've dug everywhere I could think of."

"So that's why you've been so hot to plant all those flowers," Wanda said.

Dana listed the places she'd looked. "I've dug all around Alice's cottage, where we used to stay. And in front of the office, where my mother used to make us wait while she finished work in the evenings after it got dark. Fargo used to wade into the pond there and get whatever coins people had tossed for good luck. I thought maybe that was the memory he wanted me to 'examine.' But there's nothing there. I've gone over and over every area I can think of with Lizzie's metal detector.

I've found nails and sheet metal and no treasure. I've gone over every inch of the area around Fortunate Harbor, because we used to play pirates there and buried treasure, boxes of bottle caps and shiny rocks. I've been going at night with a flashlight after Lizzie falls asleep. Nothing."

"But have you looked to the heavens?" Janya asked. "As he told you to? You said he hated religion. Did he believe in heaven?"

Dana considered. "No, he was very outspoken about that."

"Then perhaps he only wanted you to look up? A metal detector could find coins buried in the ground. He would know that, and he would protect himself from that possibility, wouldn't he? In case someone else knew what he was doing? Perhaps he put this treasure somewhere high. In a tree? Where no metal detector would locate it."

The answer was so simple, yet in all the months Dana had pondered Fargo's letter, in all the hours she had searched, wondering if she had forged an imaginary legacy from a dying man's final words, she had not thought of simply looking toward the heavens.

"I have a brother," Janya said. "I know that brothers like to climb trees. Yash always hid in the gulmohar tree in our courtyard so he could spy on me."

"Fargo was always in trouble for climbing. He would do it the moment my parents turned their backs."

"There aren't any trees around Alice's house. Besides, anything in a tree out in the open would be seen. Nothing where the old office used to stand, either," Wanda said.

A shiver crawled down Dana's spine. "There are trees lining the path to the water at Fortunate Harbor. Fargo used to climb them when he could. He was watching for pirate ships."

"I think we need to see what we can find in this Fortunate Harbor of yours."

"I can't. Pete may already be on his way here."

"Call him and tell him not to come tonight. Tell him you have a headache," Tracy said.

"I tried earlier. He didn't pick up. He doesn't always have his phone turned on."

Tracy came at it a different way. "Then leave a note on the door telling him something came up. We'll drive your car down the road and park where it can't be seen. If Pete comes, he'll leave again. Then, when you're ready, with or without whatever your brother left for you, you can leave, too."

"You'll let me?" Dana asked. "You'll let me leave, and you won't ever tell anybody what I've told you?"

"Let you?" Wanda clapped her hands in emphasis. "We'll stall Pete, if need be. I'm a cop's wife, but I know sometimes there's a difference between the law and what's right.

You took the hard road when you took that baby, but you tried everything the law allowed first. And now you got to protect her again."

Dana looked from woman to woman to be sure Wanda spoke for all of them. She saw that she had. "I haven't had the luxury of friends since I left Grand Forks." She choked out the next words. "Thank you."

Wanda cleared her throat. "We got to get going. We'll help you get your stuff in the car." She grabbed Lizzie's suitcase and rolled it toward the door.

"Mine's already there," Dana said.

"I'll pack up everything you didn't have time for and send it if you let me know a safe way to do that," Tracy said.

Dana knew she would never contact any of them again. She had already put them in jeopardy by telling her story, but she nodded. "Thank you."

"Let's get out of here." Wanda went to the window. "Nobody's out there. Let's boogie."

Dana took one last look around before she closed the door for the last time. This house had been the closest thing to a home she and Lizzie had ever shared. But she was no fool. Pete had found her once, and now he would pursue her again with a vengeance, sure at last that he'd found Isabel and Ivy.

Unless a miracle occurred, she and Lizzie would never have a home again.

CHAPTER
THIRTY-ONE

Tracy's head was spinning. Dana's situation was so precarious, and yet so strange. They were looking for modern-day pirate's gold with about as much chance of finding it as Florida's many treasure hunters, who were convinced fortunes lay just off the coast in sunken galleys. Instead of a map with X marking the spot, they had a letter that might or might not contain something other than a dying brother's good wishes.

Something was nagging at her, though. Something that had to do with this and yet didn't. Everything had progressed so quickly that none of them had been given the time to think carefully. Still, at the edge of her mind where she couldn't quite grasp it, there was something else. Something nagging and nagging.

"New Mexico," she said out loud. Dana had just parked in the scrub beside the road, well up from the houses. Tracy had walked this path before. She knew it led down to the bay, but it wasn't one of her favorite hikes. The path was narrow and overgrown, and to her mind, infested with creatures she preferred not to think about.

"What?" Dana asked.

"You said your brother worked for somebody in New Mexico."

"That's what he told me."

"Did he say anything else?"

"Why?"

"Just think. Please."

Dana got out of the car, and the others followed her. It was still visible from the road, but a casual passerby probably wouldn't notice. They could only hope Pete didn't drive out to the point after he saw Dana's note.

"He said he was working as a troubleshooter. I didn't ask him what kind of trouble. With Fargo, it was best not to know too much."

"He never gave a name? Never gave a description?"

"No. We avoided that kind of thing. I never told him anything about where I was or what I was doing, either. At the end I called him in prison on a disposable cell. He had an address for me, but it was a drop box and impossible for anyone to trace. We were careful."

"What's the problem?" Wanda asked. "You have some idea about this?"

"CJ had an office in New Mexico."

The women turned and looked at her. "We had a house there. He did a lot of business out of that office, even though he was based in California."

"A lot of people probably have offices in New Mexico," Wanda said.

"I know, but listen. Fargo came here and buried something. Dana, you say you think he was here right before the land changed hands. But what if CJ was already in the process of buying the property, and the deal just hadn't been finalized? What if Fargo was the one who told CJ about this property in the first place?"

The conversation that had been nagging at her suddenly crystallized. "The last time I saw him, CJ told me an associate or assistant, whatever, was the one who told him about this place. He said the guy knew this land backward and forward because he used to come here as a kid."

"My word." Wanda was waving her hand in the air like a kid trying to get the teacher's attention. "But even if that's true, what's it got to do with this?"

"Don't you get it? I've been trying to figure out why CJ came to Florida after prison. I've been suspicious all along, even though he's been behaving above reproach. I've even been feeling guilty about my suspicions!"

Tracy was furious now. She'd been questioning herself, beating herself up for not being loyal, for turning on CJ when he'd needed her. And all this time, he'd probably been here because somehow he knew his associate, Fargo whatever his name was, had buried something of value on the property.

"It explains everything!" It was all coming clear to Tracy in a rush. "CJ knows about whatever Fargo hid, Dana. That's why he showed up here. He wants it. And all that prowling around and helping me figure out what to do with my property? He's just been using that as an excuse to search for whatever it is. Digging here, digging there, water table my eyebrow! None of it had a thing to do with improving the land so I'd be set financially. That's why he didn't show up at my front door right at the beginning. Instead he just drove me crazy whenever I thought I caught a glimpse of him. He was searching, hoping he'd find whatever it is right away so he could leave the area without alerting anybody."

"You're making sense," Wanda said.

Tracy could hardly speak, she was so angry now. "And get this!" She took a deep breath and exhaled the rest of her conclusions. "I've wondered from the beginning why he left me Happiness Key, right? Why not something more liquid that would really help? I'll tell you why! He knew I wouldn't be able to sell this place. The real estate market. The conser-

627

vationists. At that point he probably thought, at worst, he'd get a few years in prison, and I'd still be here trying to get rid of this place once he got out. He'd be able to get whatever it was and disappear, and I'd be none the wiser."

Everybody was silent for a moment.

"How would CJ know about Fargo's treasure?" Janya asked.

But Dana had the answer. "If Fargo worked for CJ, then maybe whatever Fargo hid here really belongs to CJ. Maybe Fargo even hid it for him."

"Then why didn't CJ find it?" Janya asked.

Tracy had the answer. "Maybe Fargo didn't hide it where CJ expected him to. Or maybe he moved it afterward."

"Then why did Fargo tell Dana he earned whatever it was fair and square?" Wanda asked.

It was a question only Dana could answer. "Because cheating somebody like CJ would seem like a normal day's work to my brother. Maybe they had a falling-out. Maybe he knew CJ was cheating everybody else, and he figured stealing from a crook wasn't stealing at all. That's how he thought. Morality was a sliding scale to Fargo."

"You don't think this had to do with that bank robbery he went to prison for?" Tracy asked.

"No, I never did. He was just the lookout.

He never even went into the bank, and the guys who did were captured while they were leaving. So Fargo got away, but he never got a thing. Somehow, though, the police caught up to him a few years later. He was pretty sure somebody tipped them off. Fargo had a loose tongue whenever he drank, which he did regularly."

"Maybe CJ tipped them off," Wanda said. "If he wanted whatever it was, what better way to keep Fargo from coming back and taking it?"

"If this is all correct and CJ is involved," Janya said, "then Dana needs to leave even more quickly than we thought. Perhaps he has been watching, too."

"Only if we find whatever it is," Wanda said. "Let's go. Time's a-wasting."

As they started toward the water, Tracy was fuming. Her theory about CJ's part in this was just that, a theory. But every single detail fit. And no matter how charming he had been, how insistent that prison had changed him, she knew her ex was capable of this and worse. She hadn't been disloyal, unforgiving, ungrateful. She had been suspicious and *smart.*

Her sociopath antenna was finally fully tuned and receiving signals.

"This is it," Dana said, when they neared the water. "Fortunate Harbor. There was an old rowboat and a dock when we were kids.

This was like heaven to us."

"Heaven," Janya said. "Look to the heavens."

As one, the women all looked above them to a leafy canopy of green. Nothing glinted in the dying light of day.

"Did your brother climb one of these trees?" Tracy asked, staring up.

She could see Dana trying to picture the little inlet as it had been in the past. "I'm sorry," she said after a moment. "It looks completely different than it did when we were children. That was such a long time ago. There *was* a tree with a branch hanging over the water that somebody tied a rope to. The most foolhardy kids used to swing out over the bay and drop into the water. Fargo was one of them, of course, but they didn't do it often. The swimming here wasn't as good as in the gulf, and the drop-off was shallow. One boy broke his ankle."

"There's nothing like that now," Tracy said.

"That's probably because the water's edge is farther out than it was. The shoreline's changed," Dana said.

Tracy felt her excitement growing. "Which tree do you think it was?"

"I just don't know." Dana's tone was plaintive. "It's been thirty years."

"Let's assume it's that tree you mentioned, the one with the rope." Tracy headed toward the water. The trees closest to the shore were scrubby and small. But just behind were larger ones. None had branches extending toward the bay, but a lot of years and a lot of storms had passed.

"I'm going up," Tracy said, pointing. "I think that's the best candidate."

"Do you need a boost?" Wanda asked.

"Just what I need, you bruising my butt."

"See if I ask again."

Tracy grabbed a limb and swung her feet toward the trunk, inching her way along the limb until she could swing a leg over it. The limb was sturdy but too narrow for comfort. She reached for another, which looked as if it offered more security. She concentrated on inching higher. Years had passed since college and the Outward Bound training course she'd had to complete for one of her classes, but the skills she had learned were serving her well. At last she was high enough in the tree to look down at her friends and wave.

"You see anything?" Wanda asked.

Tracy grabbed a limb above her and slowly stood so she had a better view. The limb holding her weight swayed, and for a moment she thought she was going to tumble to the ground. She gripped harder and slowly turned her head, searching for anything that looked out of place.

"No, nothing."

"Darn," Wanda said. "I hoped it would be that easy."

Tracy tried to figure out the best way down. She was high enough that she could see almost every branch in the tree, and there was nothing unusual here, nothing but bark and leaves and traces of Spanish moss. Climbing higher would be difficult if not impossible. She couldn't believe a man, much heavier than she was, would have attempted it.

Trying to figure out the best way to lower herself to the limb that bore her weight, she carefully moved closer to the trunk until her back was against it. She grasped a different limb and had begun to slide so she could sit again when something in the next tree caught her eye. She stopped and leaned forward, holding tightly as she did. The branch she was standing on swayed as her weight shifted.

"That's not looking safe," Wanda called. "That branch is bending like a twig. You come on down now. I don't want to have to catch you."

"There's something in that tree." Tracy held on with one hand and pointed with the other. "I can't tell what from here, but that's my next stop."

"You decide that after you get down. Come on now, Ms. Deloche. I don't like this one bit."

Tracy stared harder, trying to figure out what she was looking at. She supposed it might be a natural phenomenon, something

632

as distasteful as a hornet's nest, but she didn't think so. The shape seemed rectangular, more symmetrical than Mother Nature designed. The reddish-brown color looked like rust.

A metal lockbox.

She shimmied down to the branch, leaned forward and grabbed it, and swung down so her feet were dangling several yards from the ground. She let go and landed hard, but she didn't topple.

"Nicely done," Janya said.

"You looked just like a monkey," Wanda said.

"I don't have any more time." Dana glanced at her watch. "Pete could get here any minute. I have to leave if I'm going to have any chance of getting away. I've got to get Lizzie, and I've got to go. There's too much at stake to wait."

"I saw something. I mean it," Tracy said. "I think it might be a lockbox." The women were staring at her as she went on. "Dana, can you wait five more minutes?"

Dana looked torn, but she gave a quick nod.

"Wanda, I'm sorry, I *will* need that boost." Tracy strode to the tree in question and looked up. A good-sized branch had broken off and lay rotting beneath the tree. She suspected it had once been the first step in climbing higher. "Look, you can see the sky through these branches. You can see heaven."

"Someday we'll have a talk about your butt

getting bruised," Wanda said. "For now, Janya, get over here."

Janya joined her, and she and Wanda crossed their arms and held hands. "Do it," Wanda said.

Tracy put one foot in their hands and leaped toward the tree. The women lifted her and managed to raise her high enough that she could inch forward until she was lying across the closest branch. From that point she was able to hold on tight and shimmy up until she was sitting.

The vantage point was different, and it took her a moment to figure out where to go next. But she grasped the next-highest branch and pulled herself up, then one more level. And there it was.

"I was right!" She inched forward and grabbed the handle. But just before she tried to swing the box forward and toward her, Wanda shouted.

"Stop!"

Tracy stopped.

"If there's gold in that thing, it's going to be heavy as a sack of bricks and pull you right off balance."

Tracy realized she was right. She needed a better angle, but she wasn't sure how to get it. She settled herself against the trunk and swung her legs over the branch toward the lockbox. She was able to wedge herself in tightly enough that she thought she'd be okay.

"If I can dislodge it and lift it high enough, I'm going to drop it," she said. "No way I can climb down with that thing in my arms and live to tell about it. So everybody get out of the way."

The women scurried to each side of the tree. Tracy leaned forward, grasped the handle and pulled. At first nothing happened, but when she gave a harder jerk, it moved. Not far, and not fast. But an inch or two.

"It's large, and it's really heavy," she called. "It's not stuck, it just weighs a ton, and my angle's not that good."

"Try again," Wanda said. "Pretend that's CJ's head."

Tracy growled, and with all her strength, she tugged again. The lockbox gave way, and with one final effort, she managed to heave it toward the ground. When it hit, the crash was substantial.

She didn't wait to see if the box flew open. She straddled the branch, and then, when she couldn't climb any lower, she swung herself down and dropped to the ground with an even harder thud than last time.

Gold coins glistened at her feet.

"Look at that." Wanda was the first to speak. "Is that what a fortune looks like?"

"If only I'd figured this out weeks ago." Dana sounded on the verge of tears.

Tracy knew what she meant. If Dana had found her brother's treasure sooner, her relationship with Pete wouldn't have had time to blossom, and she wouldn't have opened herself up to betrayal.

"Scoop it up," Tracy said. "Let's put it back in what's left of the box."

"Krugerrands," Dana said, squatting beside the lockbox. "Each one an ounce of pure gold, and worth whatever gold's worth on the market on any given day."

"Give a good guess," Wanda said. "Some of us have no reason to know those kinds of things."

"Lizzie dreams about owning one of these someday." Dana's voice sounded choked. "Close to a thousand dollars each, I think."

Wanda whistled. "There must be hundreds of them here."

"Seven hundred and ninety, to be exact," said a man's voice from behind them. "Unless Fargo pocketed some before he put them there, which he probably did."

Tracy whirled around to see CJ blocking the path. CJ, as she had never seen him, dressed in dark clothing with a gun held casually in front of him.

"CJ!" She narrowed her eyes. "So you're exactly what everybody said you were."

"Just a businessman, and the coins you're so generously stacking belong to me."

"They belonged to Fargo Carlsen," Dana said, getting to her feet.

"Sorry, but they never did. When my life

started going south, I converted as many of *my* assets to Krugerrands as I could. Hard to do without raising any red flags, but I managed."

Tracy was furious. "How did you think you could get away with this?"

"Simple. It was Fargo's job to drive here with me and bury the coins. He was the one who told me about this property in the first place, and since the Feds already had their eye on me, we agreed he would bury the money under the foundation for the air conditioner at the last cottage — the one Miss Turner moved into, as a matter of fact. In the meantime, I made sure that even if I went to prison, you'd keep the property. I assumed you wouldn't find a way to sell it for a while, although I had no idea I'd get the kind of sentence I did."

"Too bad it didn't stick," Tracy said.

That seemed to pass right over CJ's head. "Of course I came here with him to make sure it got done right. Then I had Fargo watched to make sure he didn't come back a week or two later and steal the coins himself. Apparently the people watching him weren't worth what I paid them."

"That seems pretty risky," Tracy said. "He could have taken the money and run."

"But he didn't run. He kept working for me, and there were no sudden signs of wealth. Besides, I knew a lot about old Fargo, and he knew I did. I told him when I came back to find it, if the money wasn't waiting where it was supposed to be, I would turn him in to the cops for any number of things. I figured that would keep it safe awhile. Of course, as soon as I was sure I was really going down, I did turn him in. That prevented him from coming back once I went to prison. I knew he wasn't going to tell anybody what he'd done for me. Just one more illegal act he'd have to serve time for. I fell down, though. I didn't stop him from getting the word to his sister." He gestured toward Dana. "That's who you are, right? But I guess I lucked out on that score. You found it for me."

"Why didn't you just leave when you didn't find it where he buried it?" Tracy demanded.

"I figured he'd moved it. There were no signs it was in his possession, like I said. I figured he'd moved it right after we buried it, and he was just waiting for the right moment to grab it and run. So I was pretty sure it was here somewhere."

"You really are something. Coming here. Lying your way onto my sofa. Turning in Edward Statler, who's probably a saint compared to you. Sponging off Henrietta."

"Quiet, TK." CJ smiled a little. "As a matter of fact, seeing you again was a nice bonus. You're all grown-up now. I kind of like you this way."

"What are you planning to do now?" Dana asked.

Tracy admired how calm Dana sounded, not at all as if her entire world was collapsing.

"I'm going to take the money, and I'm going to leave," CJ said, waving the gun as he spoke. "And none of you are going to say a word, because there's something going on with your friend here, right? I heard enough a little earlier to know that. You're running from something, and I'm betting it has to do with that little girl of yours, Dana. The one who doesn't seem to know who her father is. There's got to be a story there. And I'll be happy to tell everything I know if anybody tries to turn me in."

"It was never your money," Tracy said. "You ripped off your investors. I bet not one bit of this is honest money."

"Surprisingly, some of it is. But I was sure I wasn't going to be able to convince anybody of that. So I took care of myself, and now I have a nice little nest egg, so I can start over. Do you know how tricky it is to extradite somebody from some of our South American neighbors? And how cheaply I can live like royalty?"

"I wish you'd just gone there first," Tracy said.

"You could come with me." CJ smiled a little more. "You liked having everything you ever wanted. You were happy. We could start over."

Her expression must have been the answer he needed. He nodded. "Got it. Solo act, then." He motioned with the barrel of his gun. "Now, all of you work together like good friends and fill that box. Then I'll be on my way."

"Doubtful," said a man's voice.

Before CJ could whirl to face him, Pete stepped out of the shadows and hit CJ in the back of the neck with a thick branch. He slumped forward and didn't move.

Pete stepped around him and lifted CJ's gun from the ground. He examined it a moment, then moved past the women and over to the shoreline. He heaved the gun into the water, and it made ripples well into the bay beyond.

"Somebody see if he still has a pulse," Pete said.

Tracy was the first to reach CJ. She put trembling fingers against the side of his neck. CJ's pulse was strong and steady enough. "He does."

"That's what I hoped for." Pete looked around, and his gaze rested at last on Dana. "You okay?"

She just stared at him.

"You know who I am?"

She gave a curt nod.

"Obviously that works both ways."

640

That time she didn't nod. She just waited.

"Here's what we're going to do," Pete said. "Everybody listen carefully. I want this over with before he wakes up, because I don't want to hit him again. We're going to pick up every one of those coins, and then they're going into my SUV. Dana, I'll give you my keys. It's newer than your car, and in a lot better condition, plus CJ won't be looking for it. We'll throw your suitcases in, too, then you're going to get Lizzie, and you're going wherever you think you need to. I won't be following. If you want to leave my car somewhere and buy something nobody can trace, you have my cell number. I'll pick it up wherever you tell me to. In the meantime, if you'll give me your keys, I'm heading off in your car. If CJ comes looking, it's me he'll find."

"Why?" Dana moved closer so she could see his expression in the near darkness.

He met her eyes. "I was lead investigator on the Greenwald case, and it haunted me. I couldn't find peace until I had all the pieces. I have them now. I thought you were Isabel Carlsen, but I had to be sure. And while I grew more certain, I also realized the truth. The important one. Ivy Greenwald's been laid to rest, and Lizzie Turner deserves a mother who loves her. I don't know all the details, but I can make some good guesses about how you've managed all these years.

641

You could say I'm just going with the spirit of the law this time."

"We'll be running the rest of our lives."

"No reason. CJ isn't going to be looking for you. You know too much about him now. He won't want you talking to the cops. And how could he prove this money belongs to him? He's not supposed to have any money."

"What about your colleagues?"

"I'm the last one from Grand Forks who couldn't stop looking. Someday maybe I'll tell the right people that I finally tracked down Isabel Carlsen through her brother's mail from prison —"

"That's how you found me?"

"I had to do some fast talking, but yeah, that's how I found you. I'll let people know you had nothing to add to what we already knew, and I've laid the case to rest."

"Could it be that easy?"

He hesitated. Then he touched her hair, just for a moment. "Has it ever been easy?"

They shared a long look. Uncomfortable, Tracy glanced at the other women. Wanda knelt and began throwing coins in the lockbox. In a minute Tracy was helping, and so was Janya.

Tracy stood when all the coins had been returned to the box. "Are we just going to leave CJ like this?"

Pete stepped away from Dana, but reluctantly. "He'll be coming around any moment.

We'd better get moving."

Pete took the box and led the way. Tracy brought up the rear. She took one more look at CJ, who was beginning to moan softly, then she followed the others out to the road.

Pete handed Dana his keys, then he helped Wanda and Janya transfer the suitcases to his SUV. Dana took her own keys out of her purse and held them out without a word. He took them and nodded.

She looked at each of the women and ended with Tracy. "A case could be made that this money belongs to you," she said.

Tracy thought about the past two years, all the things she had lost and gained, and she smiled a little. "You know, there's only one treasure that matters here. Take care of Lizzie, and tell her we love her."

Eyes glittering with tears Dana nodded. She took one last look at Pete, then she stepped up into the driver's seat of his SUV. In a moment she was gone.

"Just like that," Wanda said. "Gone for good. Dana. Lizzie." She paused. "All that money."

Tracy put her arm around Wanda's shoulders.

"I'm taking off," Pete said.

Tracy had to ask. "Do you think you'll ever see her again?"

His expression was unreadable. "She knows my number."

"And if she calls you?"

"Maybe I'll let you know."

He got in Dana's car, and in a minute he was gone, too.

"We will have to walk home," Janya said.

Tracy started down the road.

"What about CJ?" Wanda asked.

"I'll drive back and check in a little while."

"You're sure?"

Tracy thought about it. "No."

"You will." Janya sounded certain. "And I will come, too, but I will ask Rishi to accompany us."

"And how will you explain that?"

"I will tell him you may have lost something on the path. And it will be true."

"He'll be gone," Wanda said. "I've seen it before. Men like CJ always pick themselves up. He lost this round, but he'll win another one down the road."

That reminded Tracy of her conversation with Henrietta. "I have to call Henrietta and tell her to have his suitcases waiting on the dock."

"Will she not want to know why?" Janya asked.

"Let's just say I think she'll trust me on this."

CHAPTER THIRTY-TWO

Tracy wasn't given to self-pity, but she wondered if the entire summer would pass before she finally caught a break. First Marsh. Then CJ, followed all too closely by Dana and Pete. And now, the final weigh-in for Losing to Win. So, of course, who was the very last loser to step on the scale? Not just the last from the Naughty Nibblers, but the last of the entire competition? The one who would vault the Nibblers to a successful first place or cement the deal for Staff Affection?

"Tracy?" Kitty repeated, with a big smile. "Everybody's waiting."

"I have really, really been trying," Tracy said. "No fast food, no chocolate. I work out every single day."

"So get on the scale," Mr. Moustache said from the sidelines. "Put those lost pounds where your mouth is."

Tracy had neglected to mention a few second helpings, and an extra spoonful of dressing here and there for the boring salads

645

she'd been consuming. And cheese. Cheese was too good to give up entirely, and who wanted the anemic, rubbery, low-fat version?

"Okay," she said, resigned, "but call off the lynch mob, okay? Because whatever this says, it's going to be bad news for somebody."

Kitty ignored her. "So, if Tracy has lost a grand total of ten pounds over the weeks of Losing to Win, then the Naughty Nibblers have a morning at the spa. Anybody taking bets?"

Tracy had to forestall that. She stepped up to the scale and refused, as usual, to look. Kitty waited until the digital display had finalized its verdict. Then she did her calculations.

"A total of eight pounds, folks. Tracy that's very, very good work, and you should be proud. But that does give the victory to Staff Affection, our proud winners!"

Everybody cheered, even the Nibblers.

Tracy stepped off the scale and wondered where she could go to quietly hang her head. In the past three weeks she had tried so hard. Her clothes fit comfortably again, zippers zipping with ease. She no longer resorted to loose-fitting tops, and she even liked the way she looked in a bikini.

The problem was, she had won the battle but lost the war.

Lillian came up and put her arm around Tracy's shoulders. "We're really proud of you.

You did so well overall, and it's nobody's fault we didn't win first prize."

"Do you suppose that's what they tell the silver medalists at the Olympics?"

"I mean it. Those weren't your two pounds to lose. Any one of us could have lost more and made the difference."

"I'm thinking of every mouthful I ate that I shouldn't have."

Mr. Moustache approached, and Tracy steeled herself.

"You look good," he said. "Do you feel good?"

"I'd feel better if we'd won."

"You always show up. That's half the battle. Take it from an old man. You just keep showing up, you'll be fine." He nodded before he walked away.

"That's a huge compliment, coming from Roger," Lillian said.

She went off to join some of the others, and Tracy gathered herself to congratulate the winners. That was when she saw Sylvia standing in the gym doorway. Looking right at her.

It really had been that kind of summer.

Tracy considered ignoring her, but in the end, she started in Sylvia's direction.

"Something up with Bay?" Tracy asked. She couldn't imagine any other reason the woman would be here.

"I want to talk to you."

647

Tracy considered a short lesson in manners, but she supposed that if Sylvia hadn't learned to ask politely for a favor by now, she never would.

She glanced at the clock. "I have some time right now."

"Not here. Why don't you walk me to my car?" Sylvia suggested.

Tracy liked that. *Car* meant Sylvia was leaving.

"Sure," she said. "If you don't mind waiting one minute."

She took off before Sylvia could answer and burrowed into the crowd around Gladys. "You did great! I'm proud of you."

Gladys gave her a quick hug. Tracy congratulated the others. When she turned, she half expected to see that the impatient Sylvia had left, but the other woman was still waiting.

They walked through the building in silence and out into heat shimmering in waves off the asphalt parking lot. Sylvia stopped on the sidewalk that ran in front of the center.

"I'm leaving town."

Tracy waited for a rush of joy that didn't come. And the reason was one boy, about to turn ten. "Not before this weekend, right? It's Bay's big birthday party tomorrow, isn't it?"

"I know when my son's party is."

Tracy figured anything she said now could

648

probably be used against her in a court of law.

"I'm leaving this afternoon," Sylvia continued. "I have a job interview in San Diego on Monday. I want this job. I need to go now, study the community, look more closely at the firm so I'll ask the right questions. I can't wait until the party's over."

Tracy was having no luck finding her tongue.

Sylvia glanced at her. "You disapprove. It makes no difference to me. But I know Bay's going to be disappointed, and no matter what you think, that does matter."

"Apparently not enough."

"I guess you're right, because I'm going anyway."

"So the point of this little conversation is . . . ?"

"I know you don't like me. You've had no reason to, so that's sensible. But I want you to know something. I've tried. I really have. But when it comes right down to it, I just don't have what it takes to be a mother. As a mother, I'm a great lawyer."

"You *are* a mother, though." Tracy thought about what Gladys had told her. "Even if you more or less got talked into it."

"Do I strike you as the kind of person who allows accidents to happen?"

"You wanted Bay?"

"I thought I could cope with a job *and* a

649

baby. Other people were doing it, and I'm more intelligent and hardworking than most of them. After I got pregnant I had second thoughts, and yes, Marsh did some fast talking to be sure it went forward. But I'd made a deal, so I saw it through. I'm just good at deals and bad at motherhood."

"Why are you telling me this?"

"You probably wonder why Marsh put up with me this summer. Very likely it's hard for you to see."

"You could say that."

"After my job ended, I figured this was as good a time as any to try to establish a relationship with Bay. I knew it would mean the world to him, and I owed him that. Marsh let me try, and that's a measure of what a good guy he is. He knew it was important for our son."

"Did it work?"

Sylvia assessed her. "Marsh let me try, yes, but I think he knew I wasn't going to be a success. He's a realistic man, and he knows me better than anyone in the world."

"So why did he let you?"

"Bay has a lot of fantasies about mothers. He's always believed if he could just get my attention, everything would be perfect. I'm sorry to say that now he knows that's not true. I'm not his fantasy mom, not even when I'm trying my best."

"Are you saying Marsh allowed you to stay

650

so Bay could watch you fail?"

"Nothing that direct. I'm sure Marsh hoped he was wrong. But he knew if he wasn't, Bay would end the summer with a more realistic view. And that's the way it turned out."

"Leaving before his party is a huge dose of realism, Sylvia. Maybe more than anybody needs."

"I talked to Bay, told him what was going on. He told me to go." She paused, and when she spoke again, there was just a trace of emotion in her voice. "He meant it."

Tracy couldn't find anything to say to that.

"Bay and I will be friends one day," Sylvia said. "When he's an adult and I know how to talk to him. When we have things in common. I can see he's a great boy. I just don't have anything to add to his life." She paused, and clearly she didn't want to admit the next part. "Not as much as you do."

"Me?"

"I know you and Marsh haven't seen each other in weeks. I know I'm the cause. I can't say I'm sorry. When I arrived, I had a different vision of my future, and you weren't in it." She held up her hand when Tracy tried to speak. "But you should understand one thing. Marsh only put up with my being here for Bay's sake. Our relationship ended years ago, and there's no resurrecting it. He was very clear about that, and having me around has been hard on him when he wanted to be

651

with you. I am sorry for that, because he deserves better."

Tracy wasn't sure what surprised her the most. That Sylvia was capable of being sorry about anything. That Sylvia was talking about Marsh as if their relationship really was over and had been for a long time. Or that Sylvia was talking to her about Marsh and Bay period.

Tracy tried to put what she'd heard into words, to be sure she understood. "You know, it sounds like you're trying to tell me it's open season on Marsh and Bay again, and you won't be standing in my way. But what makes you think it's that easy? You're finished with them, so now it's my turn?"

"There's just one thing you need to remember. This has never been about me or you. It's always been about Bay. Marsh tried to do what was right for our son. That's all. And somehow, I think you understand what that means. Better than I ever did."

Sylvia checked her watch. "I have to go if I'm going to catch my plane in time. As for Bay's having a big celebration tomorrow . . . It's going to be a lot for Marsh to handle alone."

Tracy heard the request loud and clear. "Sorry, I'm not invited, and I won't be in town. I'll be in Palm Beach."

"That's too bad. Bay would enjoy your company."

652

Sylvia looked Tracy straight in the eye. "I'm not proud of myself. In case it's not clear, I'm trying to do the best for my son." She paused, looking pained, but she continued. "And for Marsh. He loves you, you know, but he had to put a vulnerable nine-year-old first."

Sylvia had said *love,* a word lawyers didn't normally bounce around. Now the word was bouncing inside Tracy's head.

"I really do have to go," Sylvia said. "I think you and I are going to be seeing each other in years to come. Next time we do, let's start over, shall we?"

She left before Tracy could answer, which was a good thing. Because Tracy had no idea what to say to that.

By three on Saturday afternoon Tracy was finished with her packing. She was looking forward to getting out of town and trying to fit in with Henrietta's guests.

She and her neighbors had received an unexpected windfall. A closer search of the ground beneath what would forever after be called the "heaven tree" had turned up four Krugerrands that hadn't made it back into the lockbox. Tracy had given one to each of the women, including Alice, who put hers into Olivia's college fund.

She'd planned to buy a new wardrobe with her own. Her Florida purchases had come from discount stores and were not exactly what was expected at Henrietta's. In the end, though, she paid off the credit card bill that CJ had so unhelpfully bequeathed her and put the rest in the bank, in case Pete mailed her a time sheet for his final weeks of labor. She found enough in her closet that was relatively trendy and decided that anybody who looked down on her wardrobe would be somebody just like she herself had once been, before her world fell apart. That was somebody she really didn't care to know.

CJ wouldn't be at the party. She, Rishi and Janya had immediately driven back to Fortunate Harbor, but CJ was gone, and although Tracy later drove up and down the road looking for any sign of his car, she found nothing. She didn't know if he'd gone in search of Dana or not. If he had, he'd certainly gotten a huge surprise.

His suitcases were now in storage at the yacht club, courtesy of Henrietta. CJ had never come back for them, and Tracy figured he never would. He had no reason to show his face in Florida again. She hadn't checked with her California friends to see if he was in the news there, and she didn't plan to. She was finished with CJ Craimer forever.

As she wheeled her suitcase to the car, Bay's dilemma haunted her. Maybe the boy had told Sylvia she could leave, but she doubted that, deep inside, he'd been happy about it. Resigned, perhaps. More realistic after a difficult summer. Newly mature, even somewhat aware that the grown-ups in his life were far from perfect.

But Bay was turning ten today. A two-digit birthday. The first real prelude to becoming a teenager. And Bay would be some teenager. It was going to take two parents to keep the kid in line. Unfortunately for him, Sylvia was planning to wait for the finished product.

Tracy had bought Bay a present, two passes to his favorite movie theater and coupons for popcorn and soft drinks, but now she wasn't sure what to do with them. She hadn't given the envelope to him at the rec center, because that would have been a clear sign of favoritism. She'd considered mailing it, but since he was only five minutes away, that seemed silly. She'd considered dropping it off on the porch in the wee hours of morning, but that seemed cowardly.

Now she debated. Finally she went back into the house for the gift, as well as the envelope containing the booklet on identity theft that Marsh had left for her. Two excuses seemed best.

Back outside, she turned over the envelope to make sure the booklet was inside. The booklet slid out, and from its folds, so did something else. An envelope had lodged inside, only she'd never opened the booklet, so she hadn't realized it.

She tore it open and read the note. She left the booklet on the table, put the colorful envelope with the coupons on the front passenger seat of her Bimmer and decided she would drop it off on the way out of town. Maybe seeing Marsh would be awkward, but this was about Bay. And she wanted Bay to know she cared.

By the time she drove up to the old Cracker house, the party was just getting started. She figured that was good. With the ruckus, she could avoid Marsh, grab Bay, press the envelope into his hand and a kiss on top of his head, and leave. Surely something would turn out well this summer, and she hoped this would be it.

Parents in gas guzzlers and hybrids were disgorging a multitude of boys into the melee, and she had to wait until a parking spot was freed up in order to get out. She could smell charcoal heating and something smoking on the grill. She guessed hot dogs and hamburgers, and wondered how much luck Marsh would have getting the kids to eat anything green to go along with them.

She spotted Bay, but it took a moment for him to see her. She'd expected to grab him as he ran past, pursued or in pursuit, and she hadn't expected much of a welcome, considering the competition.

Instead he ran full tilt toward her, and when she held out her arms, he threw his compact body into them, hugged her hard and didn't let go.

She wrapped her arms around him and kissed his sweaty hair. "Well, buddy, happy, happy birthday. I brought you a present. I'll put it inside."

"You're going to stay?" He looked up, and his eyes shone like bright pennies. "You came to help my dad?"

She didn't know what to say. Everything the kid was feeling was right there in his eyes. Hope, despair, understanding, anger. And what could she do about any of it?

She lifted her gaze to the porch and realized Marsh was standing there — instincts honed, she supposed, to protect his son from yet another untrustworthy, marauding female with no maternal instinct. His expression was veiled, but he gave the briefest of nods.

"Do you want me to stay?" she asked Bay, turning her attention back to the birthday boy. "Because I know a couple of games you guys will love when everybody settles down."

"Will you? Please?"

She ruffled his hair, longer than it had been at the beginning of summer. For a moment she couldn't speak. Then she ruffled it again. "Darn right. That's exactly why I came, kiddo."

She took a minute to call Henrietta and give her regrets. Henrietta told her to come

657

tomorrow, but the older woman promised there would be other parties if Tracy couldn't make this one.

Tracy avoided Marsh, but definitely not Bay. She organized an impromptu egg toss and a pillowcase sack race. After they'd eaten and calmed down a little, she taught the boys to play Killer, and watched them die in helpless, hysterical agony whenever the secret "killer" caught their eye and winked at them. She took her turn at Guitar Hero and wowed everybody but Bay, who was better than just about anybody in the world.

As the afternoon wound to a close, she cleaned up, removing plates and glasses, starting the dishwasher at one point, because, of course, no party at the Egan house would include anything as heinous as paper products. She helped serve gargantuan slices of cake and dished up mounds of ice cream.

The boys left one by one, full, happy, still talking about their rides in the Egan canoe. They'd spotted a garter snake, climbed one of the live oaks, jumped on a rental trampoline. Tracy knew that future parties would include girls, and the entertainment would be substantially different. She was glad she'd been around for this one.

When just a few boys were left, Marsh came into the kitchen, where she was unloading the dishwasher.

He deposited an armful of dessert plates in

the sink. "You really don't have to do that."

"Really? I am *so* not going to, then." Despite her words, she kept going.

"What's this about anyway?"

"My best guess? A clean kitchen."

"We didn't expect you."

"Duh. You didn't invite me."

"Don't leave before we talk." He sounded serious.

She had every intention of leaving the moment Bay, who had already told her he was going to Adam's for the night, did.

She was alone in the kitchen again and had loaded the dishwasher again when Bay dashed into the room, his rubber-soled tennis shoes making horrifying screeching noises on the wood floor.

"I'm going!"

"You have a good birthday, buddy?" she asked.

He wrapped his arms around her for a quick hug. Then he was off again.

She sighed and took her impromptu apron — a terry cloth dish towel — out of the waistband of her capris. She'd just gotten her cue to head out.

"No you don't," Marsh said from behind her.

She didn't turn. "I'm supposed to be at a house party in Palm Beach."

"It's too late for a drive like that."

"I can do it."

"Please stay."

"You can't do the rest of the cleanup alone?"

He rested his hands on her shoulders. She jumped, not expecting it.

"*Please* stay," he repeated.

She sighed. "Maybe for a few minutes."

After he left the room again she finished cleaning up, and when she heard the final toot as Adam and Bay drove away, she went to find Marsh. He was standing on the steps watching Adam's parents' car turn onto the road. The old house seemed to sigh in relief.

"It was quite some party," she said.

"You made it better."

"I really didn't intend to stay." She paused. "He wanted me to."

"Of course he did. He adores you." He paused, then said, "What kind of party was waiting in Palm Beach?"

"Nothing that couldn't wait a little longer."

"I have a good bottle of Syrah, and I don't know about you, but I need a glass. Want to sit on the porch swing?" He gestured to the screened-in portion of the front porch.

She thought about other evenings in that swing, when they'd struggled to be mature and finish business before they gave in to temptation.

"Just one," she said.

She sat and waited while he went to get it, swinging and listening to the first murmurs

660

of evening. Marsh returned with a plate of cheese and fresh fruit, boiled shrimp and pâté.

"You mean the boys didn't eat this?"

"I figured if I survived this party, I'd deserve a little treat."

She waited to see where he would sit, but she wasn't surprised when he joined her in the swing.

"So I guess you know Sylvia's on her way to California."

"Will she get the job?"

"It looks good. If she does, Bay's old enough to fly out there by himself and visit her. She claims she'll take time off so he can."

"San Diego's a lovely city."

"You seem to know a lot."

"I am a fountain of information." She turned a little, reaching for a shrimp, as cover. "So, will you miss her?"

He lifted one brow. "What do you think?"

"I think you ought to answer a question before you ask one."

"Let's just say that I had to restrain myself from doing the happy dance when she told me she was finally heading out. Even though I feel badly for my son."

She'd needed to hear that. She pictured a clamp on her heart that had just been released. Everything seemed to be flowing again, just the way it was supposed to. "You weren't falling back in love with her?"

"Tracy . . ." He shook his head. "That's so far from the truth it's almost funny."

"It wasn't funny to me."

He removed the wineglass from her hand and linked his fingers with hers. "I know. I had no idea how to fix that. I wanted to. More than I can say. You don't know how many nights I sat right here and tried to figure it out."

"Is that why you sent me that note? The one that asked me not to give up on us. So it would fix things?"

He didn't answer.

"I just found it today, Marsh. I never opened the booklet you left me until this morning." But the note was home in her jewelry box now, a precious possession.

"Funny how things like that happen, isn't it? Almost makes you think we're in somebody's crosshairs."

"But there was Bay."

"There was. He's going to be all right, I think. He'll always love his mother, but now he realizes who she is. It's an important distinction."

"We're holding hands."

"We are. So while I'm holding you prisoner, tell me about CJ."

She did, leaving Dana and Pete out of the equation.

"And how did Dana fit in?" he asked when she'd finished, not one bit fooled.

"In a way I can never talk about."

"So CJ's gone for good. And you didn't have even the slightest desire to reclaim that fancy life you had with him?"

"I want a life with CJ the way I want an abscessed tooth, Marsh."

"I hear he's a smooth guy. Charming. Sophisticated. All the things I'm not."

She was surprised at the admission. He was a supremely confident man, but clearly he had his vulnerabilities. "You know, I've noticed that. I have this chart in my bedroom. You and CJ. Oh, and George Clooney. Check marks, the whole nine yards. You'll have to come and see it."

"In your bedroom?"

"Right above my bed."

"I've never gotten that far into the inner sanctum."

"You know who gets the biggest mark for charm?"

"Tell me."

"This redneck environmentalist who lives down the road. Here's what I find charming. He does what he has to, even when it's not fun. And sometimes he gives up what he really wants, so he can help this crazy little boy. He's not very good at explaining himself, which is a mark against him. But in the end, it's all pretty clear."

"Sounds like quite a guy."

"I think so."

"This house is going to seem awfully lonely tonight, what with Bay gone for the evening and Sylvia gone for good."

"Is it now?" She rested her free hand on his shoulder. "It's possible you might need company. You know, somebody to fill the gap."

"It's possible."

"And if I stay, just to help, can we draw all the shades and bar the doors? Just in case somebody from the past comes prowling around again?"

"We can, but speaking for myself, from now on, I plan to be way too busy to notice anybody but you."

She smiled, and she supposed that, against her better judgment, everything she felt was right there in her eyes. "You can speak for me, too."

"I'd rather just quit speaking altogether."

"You have the best ideas," she said, just before she kissed him.

EPILOGUE

"Three whole months I been open." Wanda looked around Wanda's Wonderful Pies, which was closed for the evening, and shook her head slowly, as though she couldn't believe it. "How many pies have gone through here, do you suppose?"

"You didn't keep track?" Tracy asked.

"Dana did that for me. It's here somewhere in the paperwork she left behind. Whoever takes her place can find it."

Janya was slicing an apple-cranberry pie with brown sugar topping. "Have you finished the interviews?"

"I've got a couple good possibilities. I'll have somebody helping me serve and bake by next week. I got to. You all can't keep coming in and pretending you're here to buy pie, when you're really just keeping the place going."

Tracy tried to look innocent and smile, but that was exactly what they had been doing in the weeks since Dana had driven away in

Pete's SUV. Stopping by on a regular rotation, washing dishes, pretending they had to practice making piecrusts, chopping apples and peaches, squeezing an endless number of limes and lemons, and tasting and critiquing Wanda's newest creations. Nobody had really expected to fool her.

"You're doing a lot of that smiling thing these days, Ms. Deloche," Wanda said. "The Cheshire cat has nothing on you."

"Something finally went right this summer." Tracy looked up from setting the tables they'd pulled side to side so they could all sit together. They had brought in pasta and salad from the Tuscan restaurant that had been CJ's only useful legacy, and would top it off with pie. They were having their own private anniversary party to celebrate Wanda's first successful quarter. Wanda's Wonderful Pies was holding its own, and in the present economy, that meant she was a winner.

"You and Marsh really going away this weekend?"

"Just the two of us. Bay's going to SeaWorld with Adam's family."

"Where are you going?" Janya asked.

"A romantic little hotel on the beach somewhere. Marsh said he'd surprise me. Which means a shack on stilts out in the water, with dolphins and sharks swimming right underneath us. Or alligators."

Wanda shook her head in disbelief. "You

and that tree hugger. I wasn't sure you'd ever get it on, you being so different and all."

Tracy really couldn't stop smiling. Life *was* filled with surprises, and some of them were good ones.

Somebody tapped on the door, and Wanda went over to let in Alice and Olivia. "Well, lookie who's here!"

Alice held up a bottle of champagne. "A celebration."

"We got pop in the back for you, Olivia," Wanda said, taking and admiring the bottle.

"I wish Lizzie was here," Olivia said, shrugging out of her backpack.

"Don't we all."

Tracy knew Olivia was saddest that Lizzie and Dana were gone. One minute she'd had a best friend, the next, Lizzie had disappeared without so much as a real goodbye. But Olivia had too many other friends to be lonely for long. At the end of youth camp she had been voted Most Congenial Camper. Olivia, like Lizzie, was a survivor.

"I'll just pop the cork," Wanda said, taking the champagne into the kitchen.

"Quick," Tracy said in a loud whisper to Olivia. "You have the present?"

Olivia's eyes were shining. She unzipped her backpack and pulled out a rectangular box wrapped in gold foil, with a copper-colored ribbon and bow.

"Ooh, pretty," Tracy whispered. "Did you

do this?"

Olivia nodded. "Janya helped."

"You two are an artistic team."

Olivia's gaze darted to Janya. "She wasn't feeling very good."

Tracy turned hopefully to her friend. "What's wrong with you?"

"Not what you are thinking."

"Oh, I'm sorry."

"There's no need. We are young, and the doctor is optimistic. In the meantime, I am enjoying my time alone with Rishi, who comes home early every night."

Wanda came out of the kitchen with the champagne and exclaimed at the gift. "Now, that's something special, I bet."

Alice held it out. "Go ahead and open it."

Wanda handed Tracy the champagne. "I don't have any fancy glasses here, but water tumblers will do."

Olivia scurried behind the counter to get some, and Tracy poured as Wanda picked endlessly at the ribbon.

"For Pete's sake, can't you just slide it off?" Tracy asked.

"I don't see any Pete in these parts. Not anymore."

"I think it's weird he left when Lizzie and Dana did," Olivia said.

"An odd coincidence," Tracy agreed.

Wanda finally managed to get the ribbon undone. She tore off the paper and lifted the top from the box. Inside was a pie server with an ornate Waterford crystal handle. *Wanda's Wonderful Pies* was engraved on the blade in flowing script.

Wanda clutched it to her chest. "It's fabulous. Like something out of Graceland."

"*Ire*land," Tracy said. "Close enough."

"It's too pretty to get chipped serving up pie all day."

"Maybe here, but not at home when we come for dinner."

"That's where it'll live, then." Wanda looked genuinely pleased. "Thank you."

Everybody hugged her in turn, and afterward Tracy passed around the champagne.

"Just one more thing," Wanda said, "before we toast. I got something in the mail today that we can toast, too."

She put her glass down, but Tracy noticed she didn't relinquish the pie server. She went behind the counter and came back waving a postcard in the air.

"Who is it from?" Janya asked.

"First, *where*. From Seattle. This funny-looking thing on the front? That's the Space Needle."

"And — it — says!" Tracy demanded.

"Not a lot, as a matter of fact," Wanda said. "But just enough. I'll read it to you." Wanda made a point of pulling her glasses lower on her nose and moving the postcard exactly the right distance away. Then she cleared her throat.

"*We're* having fun. Wish you were here."

Wanda looked up from the card. "Pete."

A moment of silence followed as everybody processed that. Then Tracy lifted her glass. "To Wanda," she said. "And many more pies in the future."

"And to Pete, Dana and Lizzie," Wanda added. "May they always be happy."

Tracy silently added, "And safe."

All the women lifted their glasses, even Olivia.

"So you think they left together? Do you think they'll come back?" the girl asked after everybody had taken a sip. "If Dana and Lizzie are with Pete, maybe they'll all come back and live here again."

Tracy knew honesty was best. "I don't think so, honey, but maybe someday Lizzie will write you."

Wanda finally relinquished her new gift and set it carefully back in the box. "You know, that does bring up a good point, Ms. Deloche."

"And that is?"

Wanda cocked a brow in question. "You got an empty house now. Just who are you going to rent to next?"

The employees of Thorndike Press hope you have enjoyed this Large Print book. All our Thorndike, Wheeler, and Kennebec Large Print titles are designed for easy reading, and all our books are made to last. Other Thorndike Press Large Print books are available at your library, through selected bookstores, or directly from us.

For information about titles, please call:
(800) 223-1244

or visit our Web site at:
http://gale.cengage.com/thorndike

To share your comments, please write:
Publisher
Thorndike Press
295 Kennedy Memorial Drive
Waterville, ME 04901